SORROWFISH

Anne C. Miles

Printed in the United States of America
First Printing, 2019

www.sorrowfish.com

ISBN 978-0-578-61219-5

Dedication

For Dad

Acknowledgements

I need to say thank you to a few people. Thank you, Rodney, for believing in me. You are my Peter, I love you. Thank you, Cheryl for all your hard work and patience. You are the best, and I love you. Thank you to the myriad of people who have commented, read, and cheered for me. The NBR group (you know who you are), Doug, and Jennifer. Your support and kindness has kept me going when I wanted to give up. Thank you Doug Perkins for your help catching typos and errors. Thank you Emily for your drawings and your heart. You are beautiful.

And thank you, my Storm King, for being You, and for teaching me that I'm never alone.

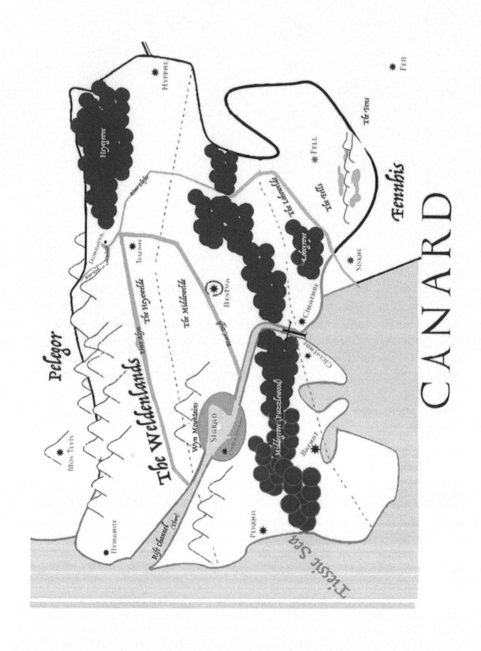

CANARD

Prelude

CANARD

Trystan's mouth watered as he approached the trestle table. It held the remains of the noon meal. He still wore a velvet surcoat, fancy dress for a bard, even one noble born. He stood out like a peacock among the other students in their dark-gray robes.

"Stars and stones, man. Where have you been?" Jerome waved across the table.

"I'm kept slaving morning till night, composing," Trystan said. He mimicked the baron's haughty nasal drawl and gestured to the heavens. "Pickell's ballad must be perfect!"

"What will be perfect is not being in the chorister rotation next week," Jerome said. "Master Standish has assigned three more manuscripts to copy, and he expects them by Tunesday." He plucked the heel of a loaf from the table, shoving it at Trystan. "Come on. We're late."

Trystan took his seat next to Jerome on a velvet-cushioned bench, out of breath. Narrow tapestries blanketed stone walls, punctuated by arched, stained-glass windows. These warmed the arena with a riot of gentle, colored light.

"We trade in melodies and myth. History, teaching, crafting, entertainment, and intrigue. These are the bard's calling." Master

Sondheim Terre's rich baritone rolled from downstage right. The gray-haired master crossed the stage, midnight-blue robes swishing. "However, another type of music can not only touch the heart, it can quite literally cause a storm. Today you will explore the difference between songs and *the Song*. This class is one of the most important you will ever attend.

"You've heard about *dewin*. Music mages. Dewin sounds like *divine* for a reason. Centuries past, these wizards held the power of gods. Life and death. Each descended into madness as the Wyrm fought the Storm King. A hundred ballads tell the tale, how instead of healing, the dewin killed. Since the War, only those who make lifelong vows to serve the Conclave learn to touch and use the broken Song. Magic."

Master Terre's blue eyes sparkled. He waved his hands, mock-casting a spell.

"Cantors keep themselves from madness through careful, strict adherence to ritual. Safeguards. Today we shall discuss the most sacred mystery: How to avoid using the Song, though you're a musician. How to sidestep madness. To do so, you must learn to touch the Song itself."

Excited murmuring broke out among the students. A hand shot up from the front row.

"Yes, Conor?"

"We aren't dewin. We can't use the Song with only our voices, so why would we go mad?"

"Excellent question. Dissonance in the Song itself causes the madness. Do you think your fellow musicians who take their vows of celibacy, truth, and baldness"—he tapped his thick head of hair—"are all dewin? Yet the Conclave acolytes and cantors wield the Song. They heal. They protect. And yes, they defend when necessary. All with the Song, while exposed to Dissonance. Without going mad, without dewin. How is it possible? Anyone?"

The hair on Trystan's arms stood on end. He'd both dreaded and anticipated this lesson. These lessons were taught to children in his home country, Pelegor. Trystan had discovered the Bindery teaching here in the Weldenlands sometimes conflicted with what he had learned there. Disclosing the differences often did not end well.

He decided to feign ignorance. His hand went up.

"They use special instruments?"

"Trystan proposes an interesting solution." Master Terre's deferential bow was only mildly ironic. "But no. The instruments you speak of *do* exist. But each is possibly as volatile as the dewin themselves. They are, therefore, forbidden. You may come across one such in the collection of a titled nobleman. Take care, and do not, under any circumstances, play the thing."

Master Terre's eyes rested on Trystan, pleading.

Trystan blinked. *Is Master Terre trying to warn me specifically?*

"Could a Crafter accidentally make one?"

The master arched a brow. He knelt to answer Trystan.

"No," he said in a voice pitched to reach only Trystan. "We don't know how to create them. The knowledge was lost with the majisters. When they disappeared, their secrets vanished too. For the best."

Terre straightened. "Now, how do you touch the Song without a forbidden instrument...or the voice of a dewin?"

Thornton Febwump, a third-year journeyman from Teredhe, answered. "Some ancient songs activate safely within range of certain plants."

"Why?" The master disappeared behind a curtain. He returned with a tray full of blooms.

Thornton's chest puffed out. "Those plants carry Virtue granted by the cyntae. Cantors use the blossoms as they go about their duties. Their Virtue guards us from Dissonance."

Master Terre nodded and held up a large blue flower. It chimed. "This is a tunebell," he said. "It's not the only flower with an aural nexus but is one of the most common. It will activate the Song. These flowers are restricted, forbidden for common use. Why?"

Jerome lifted his meaty arm with a grunt. "To grow such is a threat. Using the Song incorrectly might destroy you."

Master Terre said, "Indeed, Ser Niall. Lest anyone not fully grasp the point, allow me to demonstrate. I shall demonstrate only the broken Song's effects. Fear not. You will be perfectly safe."

Master Terre crushed the tunebell in his large hands. The Song oozed from his mouth like thick blood from a wound. The world melted with it.

Trystan just saw madness.

Fae, fickle spirits who haunted dewin, flashed on every side. Like flames, they appeared, vanished. People of all colors and ages screamed, gasped, cried, laughed. The world *shifted*. Emptiness yawned beneath Trystan's feet. Faces stretched into death masks with glowing eyes.

No wonder the dewin went mad.

Trystan focused on the words the master used. Unintelligible. Trystan tried to grasp even one. *Brenin.* A second later, it had slipped away. His mind would not hold the strange language.

Around him, students murmured with surprise and fear. Some fled the arena, hiding their eyes.

The singing stopped.

"Now you have seen the world as dewin must. The Song is dangerous. The Conclave guards its secrets for a reason. Over the next few weeks we will practice rudimentary exercises to protect your mind. We'll study blooms which can shield you and learn to recognize songs with potential to harm. You'll learn to take every precaution possible to play music which is only that...music.

"One slip **could** be your last."

Trystan jerked his thumb at a line of new apprentices being led up the stairs.

"Fresh victims. You can claim three and be finished with your manuscripts before Moonday."

Jerome surveyed the retreating figures. "I can't risk my scrolls on apprentices. Or bully near-masters into working on them." He glared at Trystan's silver ring. "Come on, I'll show you the lot."

Trystan gave a low whistle. "Standish let you take scrolls to your rooms?"

Jerome scratched the back of his neck. "*Let* is too strong a word. But if he wants these finished... Tell me what you make of them?"

Trystan fell into step next to the burly scriv. They passed the Composer's wing and turned into a narrow corridor. Jerome opened the door at the end of the hall, revealing comfortable rooms.

"I have something to tell you as well," Trystan said. He looked around while Jerome lit the lamps. The man was a curious sort, but Trystan trusted him. They had bonded over no small amount of ale and discovered a shared interest in dead languages. Trystan appreciated Jerome's insight and scholarship.

Jerome grunted and went to a sideboard for a decanter and two tumblers. "We'll have a glass first."

He poured generous portions and brought one to Trystan. "Let's have it then. Are you planning to hide from your fate or are you off to make your Journey?"

"I've been here less than a year. Would the masters allow it?"

"I think they'll call you soon, like it or not. You're noble-born, you have a keen grasp on composing. The cantors can't press you into the Arcanum. But as a proven master?" He raised his eyebrows, counting off on meaty fingers.

"You'll be married to a noblewoman, cementing power at court for the Bindery *and* your father, groomed to take a political position. You'll be coddled, favored, with no time for yourself and your studies. Or"— he leaned forward and lifted his glass—"you'll complete your Journey, be raised, and return to the ice halls from whence you hail. Where you face much the same prospects."

Jerome polished off his drink, settling back in his chair.

"Except the lady in question will be half goblin and bearded, which is why you left home in the first place. *I* have none of these problems. 'Tis pleasant to be a peasant."

"They're having me spend more time at court. And father wants me to marry the youngest daughter of Duke Finnegan upon my return. She has the voice of a gargoyle and a face to match. If I do make my Journey, it had best be a long one."

Jerome regarded his friend, eyes hooded by bushy brows. "Do you have a placement in mind?"

Trystan gulped, bracing himself. "Siarad."

Jerome sat up, spluttering. "Stars above! You're not planning to come back?"

"I'm not looking to be cursed. I'll leave, no worries. A placement in Siarad will give me time to learn but keep me away from court and the Conclave. I must leave and return at measured intervals to avoid the Dread's hold. It's perfect. The curse gives me a reason to travel, explore. I mean to find an enchanted instrument. So I will start my search in Siarad."

"Now, look here, Trystan. Every boy dreams of becoming the hero who sets the captive city free. Everyone wants to see the Caprices, hear them speak their oracles. You're a noble, a young rogue, and a damned curious jackdaw. All of that is bold enough. But a *forbidden instrument*?" Jerome's voice rose. "Are you mad? Do you realize what can *happen*? You could be ensorcelled. Trapped, unable to interact with the outside world. Caught, stripped from the Bindery, denied all music. You could be labeled dewin, put in chains. Your mind wiped of all you know. By the Wyrm's fat fang, you could finish destroying the

World Tree and end all things."

The scriv slumped, his eyes clouded with sickened fear. "Please. Tell me you jest."

"If I find what I seek, I won't use it. I want to *study*. Learn. There are safe methods. I could keep it in Siarad. The instruments are forbidden because they—"

Jerome interrupted. "Because they are dangerous. Playing such puts you in a frenzy." His voice flattened, brooking no arguments. "Those instruments release the broken Song unfettered. You'll lose your wits. Were you asleep in class today?"

Trystan pursed his lips.

"I've already played one."

"What?" Jerome's eyebrows shot up.

"The lute Pickell has me composing on, it's ancient. The tones coming from it are pure. It's..."—Trystan shook his head—"You cannot imagine. I'm not ensorcelled, I'm myself. The Conclave inspected his instrument long ago. They let it stay in his possession."

"Are you certain? It's truly one of those instruments?"

"I'm certain. According to the baron, a cantor inspected it. Pickell's ancestor saved a high-ranking majister before the Breaking, before the Conclave existed. It was a gift.

"House Pickell has had it for centuries without mishap. The baron wants a ditty for his wedding on this particular lute. It's a diamond in his coal bin to have something no one else can dream of. I suppose he has permission."

"The lute might be the only one still in existence. Perhaps it's just a clever copy or too old to function. Inert, no longer dangerous," said Jerome.

"It's active. The music is special. It's not plain melody. I feel a stirring, but with... I've never felt such before. The tones are palpable. *Something*...it defies description. But no ill effects. I've been playing it for weeks. Don't you think if madness had affected me, you'd know?"

Trystan sat down. "Jerome, it's nothing like the demonstration. There have been no strange warts on my fingers, no festering sores. I haven't been losing my temper. No fae have appeared to steal my soul. The music is haunting, but it's not causing madness."

Jerome was silent. Finally, he nodded. "I believe you. If what you say is true, the masters and cantors are lying. The lute should be confiscated. But the Conclave cannot lie, can they?" He frowned. "There must be something we don't know."

"That's why I want to go to Siarad," said Trystan.

Jerome's frown deepened. "We are musicians, Trystan, not cantors. 'We craft in melodies and myth.'" He quoted Terre in perfect mimicry. "The Conclave and its Arcanum deal in the Song. Leave it to them. Unless you're planning on joining the order?"

"No," Trystan said. "I'd rather marry the duke's daughter than spend the rest of my life in chastity and devotion to the cyntae. I'm not fit to serve.

"I've been reading any old text I can find. Whether I come across another instrument or not, I will understand how it works. Is it possible to use the Song without madness?"

He stood and plucked a piece of vellum from a stack on the scriv's table. "This is the symbol on the lute," he said, sketching the insignia he'd seen. Three stars within a circle.

"Help me. See if you can find any reference to this. But be discreet."

Jerome accepted the drawing, studied it, and cast it into the fire. "I will. But I fear any answers will only lead to more questions."

Trystan's mouth tightened. "I know. And Matins will come too early. It is late. I must go." He made the sign of the arc, a half circle scribed from shoulder to shoulder over his head. "Did you still need me to inspect your scrolls?"

Jerome waved him away. "No, I'll get an apprentice or three to help me tomorrow." His lips twisted in a wry grin. "Off with you, damned jackdaw."

Morning dawned cold over Bestua, mists covering its spires. Even in the dawn light, the Weldenland capitol bustled. Vendors hurried to shops and stalls. Carters loaded and unloaded wares from flatboats traveling the River Dyfi. The sound of Matins wafted from the Grand Arcade, blending with the dawn gray.

Deep in the Bindery archives, Trystan pored over a scroll. He traced a finger along the lines of cramped script, reading. "Those below shall be as above..."

The scroll was ancient. Trystan puzzled out the words and checked Jerome's note. It held only numbers, shorthand they used when sharing oddments to study. *Four. Three. Two.* Fourth chamber, third shelf, second scroll. It was the right manuscript.

Footsteps. He hastily pretended to be dusting, arranging scrolls as he worked. "Good morn, Trystan," a voice whispered.

"Good morn, Brother Bren," Trystan said. He bowed from the waist.

"The night has passed. Let us rejoice in the new day. You're summoned to the masters' circle."

Trystan followed, wondering why Brother Bren had fetched him, instead of an acolyte.

The master's chambers opened inward to a center cloister on the roof. They waited in full ceremonial robes. Bren took his place behind them.

Trystan faced the masters.

"Trystan dan Tenkor, we are gathered here today in the sight of cyntae and man. We call upon you to begin your Journey, to follow the call wherever it might lead and to become a master true," said Master Standish, stepping forward.

"We call you to walk this path, to shape your destiny," Master Hamish said, eyes twinkling beneath the hood of his robe.

"Journey to find the answers you seek. Find your melody and return in joy, my son." Master Terre's booming voice rolled across the courtyard. The Master Player was ever a showman. He stepped forward with a small flourish.

The last line of the call was spoken by the Master Crafter, the only master to hold the rank of cantor, also. The crafter not only served the Bindery, he wielded the Song. Master Aric Miller regarded Trystan, the supplicant.

Trystan bowed his head under the intensity of those eyes, the depth of the aged gaze from the young master. His mind raced.

The crafter alone has leave to use the Song as a cantor. Why? Trystan fought a frown as he realized *why* a crafter might need the skill. *He needs to wield the Song to craft forbidden instruments, I'm sure of it. But does he know how?*

"Journey under the arc, master your inner fire," he said. "Do you accept the call?"

"Yes, Master Miller, I accept the call."

"Witnessed and approved," said Brother Bren.

"Witnessed and approved," repeated the masters.

The ceremony finished, each bowed and drifted away.

Trystan was expected to pack and leave at once. He gulped. Highly unusual to be called before Pickell's wedding. Trystan breathed, stilling his racing heart.

The morning sun warmed him. Here on the roof, the world's business seemed distant. Faint city sounds wafted up, but Trystan concentrated on birdsong in the distance. He opened his eyes and looked up, lifting his hands in supplication. He was full of questions. Perhaps the Storm King would grant him guidance.

A jackdaw perched on the roofline, its beady eyes intent, unmoving and silent.

Trystan froze. *Jackdaws are never silent. How does the proverb go? When jackdaws are silent, the cyntae will sing.*

Outer Siarad wreathed the lake with thatch-roof houses and half-timber shops. A stone tavern jutted from a jetty at the lake's edge. Cobblestone streets wound through the village. Thick fog marked the bounds of the Dread. It hung, wrapping every person, caressing.

The island of Anach glowed, spectral. Legendary home of the long-dead Majisterium, its tower flickered with cold lights through the mists. Sometimes lights flared, hovering above the remaining towers or moving along the shore. No sound issued forth. Not even birdsong trilled for those with the heart to listen. Where once the majisters wielded the Song, only the Dread remained.

Trystan must record local traditions and set them to new music. He'd perform these to earn his golden master's ring. The Dread hindered Trystan's work considerably. It was difficult to think, much less compose.

A master bard held an invitation to any court, to all guilds. Bindery bards were welcomed everywhere, as majisters once were. In a way, they were more trusted. Though learned, they could not use the Song to manipulate leaders. They also weren't under the thumb of the Conclave, yet equal to it. That was why Father was counting on him to secure his master's ring.

Trystan started with the townfolk, asking questions.

"Aye, they're immortal," said Ben, the earnest innkeeper, as he polished his bar to a dull shine. It was early. The inn on the jetty had not yet filled with its usual mix of townfolk and seekers.

"You never know when Caprices will appear. They look a bit like cantors, but no bodies, just empty robes...and the Dread. Some say they served the majisters in the Tower. Others say they're spectres of the majisters themselves. Dead, but lingering."

Ben made the sign of the arc.

"Caprices don't come on a schedule, regular. Sometimes there's only one, sometimes upward of twenty or more. 'Tis why they are called Caprices. They move on their own whims. One minute the bridge is empty and the next? The bell tolls, and there they are. But only one ever speaks." He held up a declaratory finger, his round face solemn. "Mind you wear holly when you go to the seeking. Sprigs there." He nodded to the pile on a table in the corner. "Will guard you from the Dread."

"Why holly?"

"My gram said majisters wore it. When the Song was broken, folk took to wearing it. Mayhap it's the berries? Blood of the Tree. Looks akin to it. All I know is, it helps. Talk to Old Shep when he wanders in. He might know more."

Trystan nodded, wondering how to approach his real questions. *Were instruments made here, outside the Conclave's approval and inspection? They must be. But how?*

When the Caprice finally appeared, it spoke with the hollow voice of a mountain echo. It stood upon the crest of an impossibly long, translucent bridge. A throng of seekers gathered behind him. The mist swirled in the chill.

"Small choices shall rule large kingdoms as the day draws ever near. Do not lose hope. The jackdaw shall linger, and the storms shall begin. Each shall flee to his place. Your work does matter. Do not give up. Do not falter. Those below shall be as above. Shadows will fall across fen and glade and forest. The game is not a game..."

The Caprice continued until Trystan's mind wandered. *Why am I doing this?* He concentrated on recording the warnings, but he wanted nothing more than to pop 'round to the tavern, have a biscuit, and return later.

Much later.

When the caprices vanished, preferably.

He fought the urge to run.

That's the Dread speaking.

Immediately, he felt an overwhelming fatigue. He stamped his feet, huddling into his cloak. The curse changed tactics; if he didn't run, it would drain him.

Half the crowd was here to receive oracles. The other half, to ask questions. Each hoped for answers to their hardships. Tradition held a Caprice could solve any problem, so supplicants waited while the hooded monk spoke.

He fell silent. The crowd began to shout, all of them at once. Instead of motioning for order or answering them at all, the Caprice stood, silent and perfectly still.

The air grew thick as the cacophony continued. It dragged on, interminable. Trystan pinched himself as his eyes grew heavy. He nodded off once and just caught himself before he fell.

Desperate, he finally asked his question, hardly daring to hope he would be heard.

"Where can I find a starbound lute?" He wasn't sure the Caprice would know his meaning. Pickell's lute was marked with stars. But what else could he call it? A-lute-that-made-everything-it-played-living-and-real-and-golden? An enchanted lute? Trystan stamped his feet again, shifting his weight and tugging at his surcoat.

The Caprice fixed him with its empty gaze. It cast a shiver down his spine, piercing his weariness. The Caprice weighed his soul. A whispered voice answered, so close to his ear its cold breath chilled him.

"Seek Mod. Ask for a mirror, sing 'The Spider's Regret.'"

His skin prickled. The figure had not moved from the bridge's parapet, despite the chill on his neck. He might have run had he not been paralyzed.

The Dread, an undercurrent to which he'd almost grown accustomed, surged in a flood. He clutched at his throat, choking. His fingers found holly, pinned with the clasp of his cloak. The spines pricked his fingers. He took a deep breath.

He exhaled and looked at his hands. Where the holly had bitten him, a small drop of blood beaded. He focused on the redness, the bright color filling his vision. He inhaled the scent of the crushed leaves. He breathed.

Mod. It was one name in a large land, but it was clearly all he would receive. Trystan bowed respectfully and backed away. He would leave the city before sundown.

For over a year, Trystan journeyed. He travelled to every city in the Middewelde, seeking Mod. All he had was the name, but the Caprice seemed to believe the name alone was enough direction. He found a fisherman in Ferriton who went by Mod. The man enjoyed his song and gave him a coin.

In Teredhe, he heard of a woman named Mod who lived in the wilds near the Heyegrove. Trystan knew he couldn't possibly be seeking a woman. He dismissed the rumor and moved south to the Lowewelde coast.

In the Sundered Cities, he found four who claimed the moniker, all tradesmen. Two cobblers, one shipwright, and a banker. Each rewarded his questions with a baffled expression.

Trystan found himself in Baehnt, dockside. An urchin had tried to pick his pocket. He'd hauled the little thief by the ear to the tavern and fed him instead of kicking him and calling for the city guard.

The best person to consult would be a young pickpurse. They would usually be truthful if you gave them food, provided you met the right one.

This boy looked hungry but without the hardness that haunted the faces of some street children. He might have something like a home or family. They sat together in the small tavern as the boy devoured a meat pie.

"What's your name, boy?"
Dark eyes evaluated him over chewing. "Gint, milord."

"Well, Gint. Would you like some pudding?"
The boy's eyes grew sharp, wondering. He didn't answer.

Trystan sighed. No one was kind to a street urchin, not like this. "I just need information, Gint. I need honesty and information. I'm looking for someone to help me with my music. That's all. In return, I'll pay you. Consider this meal part of your earnings."

The lad understood commerce. He paused a moment, calculating silently, and cleared his throat. "Yes, milord. I'd like pudding."

Trystan waited for the pudding to come, reflecting on the extraordinary politeness of the waif. He waited, amused, until the sweet disappeared before asking his question. "My name is Trystan dan Tenkor. I need to find someone named Mod. Do you know the name?"

The boy's eyes lighted up in recognition. "Spinner?" he asked. His eyes clouded. "I can't take yer to *Mod.*"

Spinner. Was it a surname? A title?

"Can you carry a message? I'll sing you a song."

"What song?"

"'The Spider's Regret.'"

The boy leaned back, relaxing into his chair. "Sing it, then."

Trystan picked up his lute, an ordinary but serviceable instrument. He fiddled with the tuning pegs and motioned to the tavern keep, asking permission to perform. The man nodded. He got up and stepped onto the small dais reserved for minstrels.

The spider spun a home
The spider did not roam
Silken lace
It made with grace
The spider spun a home
The spider did allow
A place upon its bough
To a wasp
That tried to cross
But became ensnared somehow
The spider did release
Its enemy in peace
The wasp returned
The spider learned
Some hatreds cannot cease
The spider, it did fight
The wasp in the moonlight
When it was done
The spider spun
Using its hindsight
The spider spun a home
The spider did not roam
Silken lace
It made with grace
The spider spun a home

Scattered applause arose as Trystan finished. Gint smiled as the bard reclaimed his seat.

"All right, milord, and what is it yer be wantin'?" Gint asked.

"I need a mirror," Trystan replied. "Can you tell Mod?"

The boy blinked. He opened his mouth as if to say something but shut it again instead. Eyes glittering, he nodded.

Then he was off, running.

Trystan ordered another ale and settled down to wait for his return.

Within the hour, the urchin reappeared in the doorway. He beckoned Trystan outside. The pair threaded their way through one of the narrow alleys that snaked through the city. This part of Baehnt was the oldest. Gray brickwork loomed over them, narrow and tall, houses and shops built in rows running together. They cast the streets and alleys into deep shadow. Despite the close quarters, the area was remarkably clean. No refuse lay in the gutters, and the smells of fish and seawater did not overwhelm.

Trystan looked up, spying the Takers and the Watchers. Their stone eyes surveyed the streets. Trystan would see their heads slowly turn if he looked long enough.

Gint followed his gaze and grunted. "They're all over the city. I never saw 'em afore I came here."

Trystan nodded, understanding. "The Takers and bilgeworks must be in good repair. The city is very clean."

Gint shrugged. "I've seen a few of the Takers and Watchers moving about but have na spoken to one." He spat. "T'ain't natural to have stone move like tha'."

Trystan grinned, remembering a similar feeling the first time he had seen a grotesque. It was a Taker, and it absorbed refuse. Takers didn't *eat* refuse, but rather, channeled it away. A scribe had tried to explain to him how it worked once, along with the process that the grotesques used to transform the rubbish.

After an hour of listening, Trystan had decided it was easier to think of them as eating it, even though they weren't really alive. Disgusting to think that way, considering all they must ingest.

"Where is the closest aerie?" Trystan asked.

Gint slowed and peered up, as if the Takers might be listening. He held up his hand and pointed to the web between his finger and thumb. "This is the harbor," he said, pointing to the crescent. "The city is here." He indicated the middle. "The closest aerie is here." He pointed above the city where the Lowegrove began. "The aerie is in the tallest trees and cliffs there." His tone implied they should be avoided. "The Conclave Chapterhouse is here." He pointed above the northwest edge of the city.

Trystan nodded his thanks.

Another turn and they arrived at a series of steps leading down to a wide cellar door. Gint opened it and ushered Trystan into a wine cellar. Rows of bottles lined the walls, glistening in the light of hanging lanterns. They must have been below another inn or tavern, though he didn't know the city well enough to name one. There were too many, this side of town.

A rakish man dressed as a sailor, all in black, separated himself from the shadows. He stopped a few feet from them and bowed, clicking his heels together. "A mirror, milord." He gestured to a water barrel on a round platform, directly under a sconce.

"Are you Mod?" Trystan eyed the barrel.

It's a barrel. Mirrors are made of glass or polished metal, not barrels and water.

"No, milord," the man said, "but Mod can see you in the mirror. 'Tis a Spinner's mirror, milord." He pointed to the barrel again, as if this were explanation enough. Trystan looked from the boy to the sailor. He sighed and approached it. The lantern's flame flared. He could see the shadow cast by his head in the water but little else. The sailor turned a crank Trystan had overlooked. It creaked in a steady rhythm. A strange scent filled his nostrils, and a soft tune began to play. The barrel rotated on its platform as if dancing.

The water swirled, then smoothed into a motionless dark surface. It transformed, becoming a night sky filled with stars. A glowing web sparkled in the perfect sky. Silence cocooned Trystan while he watched, the music fading. The sounds of crank and water muffled and were gone.

The scent intensified. Trystan recognized the Warrior and the Cup in the vision. The familiar constellations awakened a longing for home. As recognition dawned, they faded. His own face flashed in their stead. And then there was only a barrel full of swirling water. The silence ended. The creaking and sloshing startled him. Trystan felt nauseous and disoriented. He stepped back quickly.

"What did you see?" asked the sailor, straightening. The platform slowed to a stop.

"I saw stars. A web of light. There was a night sky from my home in Pelegor. Constellations, the Warrior, the Cup. I saw my own face."

The sailor flashed a grin. Now his smile reached his eyes. He stepped forward, offering Trystan his hand in welcome. His voice changed as well, no longer accented or subservient. He clicked his heels together with the affectation of a Bestuan noble as he gave Trystan the half bow of an equal.

"I am Baron Tabor Demitri. It is good indeed to meet you. You seek a blessed lute that plays the true Song. We can help."

1

Louisville, Kentucky
2001

When Sara got to her studio, she started the coffee maker. The dark scent of coffee filled the room like incense. She poured herself a cup and walked slowly around her sculpture, considering it. The tall form dominated the space, hidden under its plastic shroud. Three days a week, she went to classes. But as a senior, Sara had two full days to explore her art: sculpting.

Sara stood on tiptoe and unsealed the plastic, letting it fall. The writhing column swept up from a copper base. It morphed, at first craggy and jagged, before it rose like a tempest. It flowed, becoming a creature of grace and stern visage. A fire elemental? No. Maybe wind. Something with heat and light and passion. *I'm still discovering you.*

Sara frowned at the unfinished face and set her coffee down, retrieving her tool belt. She began carving detail. A violin piece, a Caprice, floated through her mind, unbidden. Paganini's music often haunted her, the complicated strains sounding in her skull as if she were microchipped with her own private radio.

Images unrolled in her mind. She saw herself smashing the piece and starting over fresh. The scene hit her full force. She stopped, made a fist. Breathed. The desire to destroy the sculpture was so strong. The impulse would pass.

This urge to destroy alternated with its opposite extreme, when she knew her piece was perfect. Those days were really scary. She might decide to quit before she truly finished. She would fire the clay, and the piece would remain frozen forever. She would have to live with it, like an accusation.

Dangerous.

What if I can't do this?

The doubt surfaced, again. She ignored it and pressed on. Once she got started, everything would be okay.

When one of her pieces fired, Sara just prayed it didn't explode. A sculpture might transform a hundred ways into something others couldn't read. The vision could die, unrealized, as the process destroyed it.

Sometimes it did.

Maybe that was why she loved working with clay. It had to pass through a fire and survive.

Sara chewed her lip. Dr. Carol said she shouldn't pin all her hopes on this one sculpt.

Yeah. Right. It only stood as her final, the capstone of her portfolio. It was the difference between working in Hollywood and teaching third graders how to make pinch pots. No pressure. Nope. None at all.

Sara really hadn't finished anything since the accident. Oh, she'd submitted work, but it was substandard, not finished. The head of the program, Polly, had been patient, but Sara knew she wouldn't even graduate if she didn't present something exceptional.

Marilla screaming. Her face contorted with rage and anguish.

Sara gasped. Her twin's image flashed before her eyes, obscuring everything else.

So vivid.

You don't deserve a life. It should have been you. Selfish.

Her chest tightened. It felt heavy.

She focused on her breath.

In and out. In and out. Stay calm.

I won't think about her.

Not now.

I can choose.

Dr. Carol's instructions floated up. *Listen to the music in your mind.*

She focused. Tuned everything else out. *If you can't finish a piece, you can't succeed as an artist. Would you like fries with that?*

I can do this. I can do this. I can do this. I can do this. Just…start. Don't think, Meat, just throw. You'll only hurt the ball club.

Sara opened her eyes and began again. She let her mind go blank.

Her breathing quieted.

She dragged a step ladder over, climbing to reach the upper portion of the towering figure.

She should focus on the face. The whirling cone was becoming a person. Its hair needed to float. She picked, prodded, and picked again. A small brush flicked away crumbs. Nothing ever really matched what was in her head. But she was just beginning. Should she add another media to get the right effect? Wire? Maybe spun glass. She'd come back. Try again. She'd get it right. She'd get it done.

Sara set her tools down and stared at the form.

He needed a name, a strong name. Something mystic. Powerful, like him.

Storm King.

What was that, Norse? And probably the name of every villain in those stupid movies Peter likes.

"Till I come up with something better, Storm King it is. You remind me of a tornado."

She covered him with the shroud. A little part of her rebelled, a voice that urged her to continue working, to stay.

No, she had enough done. Tomorrow would come. In the meantime, the Storm King rested. *Maybe I'll sleep tonight, too.*

"So you're still sleepwalking." Dr. Carol Sherman pushed her glasses up her nose and made a note. "Are you keeping the dream log? Are you focusing on music to calm yourself?"

"Yep," Sara said. She winced as she searched her satchel. Her finger was sore. With a flourish, she handed her notebook to the therapist. Dr. Carol flipped it open and scanned.

"What do you hope to accomplish in today's session? What's bothering you?"

"Okay, this sounds nuts, I know it." Sara took a deep breath, and her questions spilled out in a torrent. "Am I really just sleepwalking? Or is there any chance my dreams are real? Say on a quantum level? Is that a thing? It sounds nuts when I verbalize it, but it's what I'm afraid of. I gotta name it, right? I got a splinter last night in my dream. I brought it with me, physical evidence. How is that possible? The dreams aren't real, of course. I know they can't be..."

Silence dropped like a cloak. *Please fix me. I'm losing it for real.* She heard herself breathing. Her blood pounded in her ears.

I'm not crazy. A few irrational thoughts are normal.

The doctor waited for her to continue, her thin eyebrows raised.

Sara pulled a plastic baggie from her pack and handed it
. to Dr. Carol.

The doctor's eye flicked over the splinter. She laid it aside. Her lips twitched.

"You dreamed you got a splinter and woke with one? Remarkable. Sara, your mind created a story about the event. How did you hurt yourself in the dream?"

"I touched a table in the gnome's kitchen," said Sara. She put her forehead in her hands. "I can't even believe I just said that. I'm certifiable. Crazy artist? That's me. Who dreams about gnomes? They're not even cute. They're kinda creepy. Why can't my crazy manifest with dreams about hot firemen?"

Ice-blue eyes flashed in her mind, halting her tirade. Peter.

Sara ignored him.

"Am I nuts? Do I just have daddy issues? Can we skip to the catharsis bit of all this before I sleepwalk into traffic?"

Dr. Carol chuckled and said, "Sara, stop trying to analyze what's real and what isn't. You know you were only dreaming. You aren't crazy. You're firmly rooted in reality. That's why you're mocking yourself. You're not seeing gnomes in your waking hours.

"Dreaming is healthy. Normal. You're not going to sleepwalk into traffic. You got a splinter in your apartment. That's what happened. You processed it to become part of your dream.

"In dreams, we work through pain. Your mind knows the level of stress you have, even when you aren't aware of pressure. Yes. You might be processing emotional pain. More likely? The accident, your twin sister going into a coma, all of that is causing you enormous grief. Your mind can translate a feeling of powerlessness to the experience of being a ghost. But you're beginning to heal and find your power. So now you touch something. That's progress. If you're concerned about the sleepwalking, I can prescribe—"

Sara held up both hands, palms out. "No pills. We've been through this."

"I respect your decision. And to some extent, I agree with you, but a compromise might be in order. No sleeping pills or antidepressants. But there's a natural supplement called 5-HTP. It helps you sleep.

Would you consider taking it?"

"I guess so." *If it will get you off my back. Wow.*

"Also, I have something for you." The doctor held out a silver necklace. "Use this as an icon."

"I'm not religious, Dr. Carol." Sara held her hand up, dismissing the offer. No way was she getting into some crackpot hooey.

"It isn't that kind of icon. You're an artist, I'm sure you understand the power of symbol." She handed the necklace to Sara. Sara took it, turning it over slowly. The words covering the square pendant were in a strange script she couldn't read.

"Ancient Hebrews believed an inscribed prayer protected their children from demons as they slept. They hung these on the walls of a child's room. They said Lilit-Abi. That's the origin of the word lullaby. This amulet bears the same protective words. It was my grandmother's. I'll want it back, but you can borrow it for now. Use it as a reminder. When you see it, remember, you're safe. You're not alone.

"Myth speaks to deep places within us. Those places aren't rational, so symbols can be effective. I've seen the power of suggestion and myth, even of prayer. If this doesn't help, we can try something else. Hang Native American dream catchers, perhaps.

"Now, how is your new sculpture coming? Have you been able to work?"

Sara made a face. "A little. Usually I end up daydreaming and all my time is just...gone. I can't focus. I did better today. But the last three pieces I turned in weren't close to finished, and if I don't up my game, I'll fail the practicum. I won't graduate."

"That's a lot of pressure."

"Tell me about it. Mom is on my case. She's loving it. She thinks the entire art gig is beneath me. Impractical. The truth is, I just remind her of Dad, and she hates it."

"Why do you say that?"

"He's a professional cellist. He left her." Sara shrugged. "Oh, he still comes home every few weeks, but he isn't really there. He doesn't try. They're strangers. He bailed on us years ago. Well, he bailed on me and Mom. He loooved Marilla."

Sara fought down her resentment as memories, long buried, surfaced.

Once, they were on vacation. She had swum out as far as she could. Too far. Mommy and Daddy didn't see her. They were building a sandcastle with Rilla. Sarah yelled and waved, but they still didn't see her. She sank under the waves. She kicked as hard as she could, and a tall girl saw her choking. The girl pulled her to shore. Sara sat on the sand, shaking and crying. Daddy said, "That's what you get for not listening to me."

He started yelling. Mommy started yelling. Everyone stared at them. Vacation was ruined. She had ruined it.

Dr. Carol made a note. "How so?"

Sara couldn't breathe. The memories were choking her. She recalled them as her six-year-old self, unable to stop. She closed her eyes and focused.

Another time, Dad's bow was broken. She hadn't meant to do it. She'd snapped it in two, and Daddy yelled at her. She broke everything. Daddy's face got all twisty and purple.

"Sara?" Dr. Carol broke through her reverie.

Sara's eyes popped open. She gulped and shook her head. "Sorry. Thinking about Dad. Remembering." She chose her words carefully, otherwise he would find out what she said, somehow. Mom would pry it out of her. Or it would come up in the next family group session. Sara wasn't sure she cared. But he wouldn't speak to her for weeks. "What was the question?"

"Why do you think your father loved Marilla more than you?"

"They'd spend hours watching old movies together. Their thing. But if I tried...or if Mom tried...to spend time with him, he'd make excuses and say he had to go practice, work. He'd yell."

"And he was unfaithful to your mother."

"He went away for almost a year. He wanted a divorce."

"How did it make you feel?"

Sara was silent. She wanted to scream, but held it in. If she spoke, she'd end up crying. She struggled to keep herself under control.

"Sara?" Dr. Carol prompted.

"I don't know what I feel. I feel numb," Sara lied.

"Try this. When you don't know what you feel, say what you think is going on, out loud. Use your body to help you know if it's true. If you get a twisty feeling in your stomach when you say how you feel, you probably aren't being honest with yourself. No twisty feeling? You're telling the truth as you understand it. Go ahead. Give it a try."

Heh, well she could try that. Anything to keep from crying. Sara reached out, trying to name how she felt.

"It made me feel like I was too much," Sara said. No twisty feeling.

Okay. She took a deep breath and kept going. "Too much. I was the loud one, the one that followed Dad around. The one that laughed too loud, never knew when to shut up. The one who wouldn't leave him alone. Begged him not to leave."

He would be at the door with his suitcase. She would be hugging his legs, crying hysterically. Marilla would hide behind the door, watching. He'd pull her away, set her on the couch and leave, angry. Angry again. He would be late for work. It would be her fault. She'd cry herself out, alone. Every week for years.

Needy. She was so needy. *Selfish.* She couldn't bring herself to say it out loud.

He couldn't wait to get away.

Her eyes prickled and a few tears leaked out. Sara fell back on old movie quotes out of habit.

"Insanity runs in my family. It pretty much streaks."

"*Arsenic and Old Lace*? But you're misquoting the line." Dr. Carol arched a brow.

Sara grinned through her tears. She plucked a tissue from the box next to her. "It's an old habit, a game I play to see if people catch my references. I do it when I'm nervous."

"And if someone catches the reference...?"

Sara wiped her eyes. "I don't know... I guess I trust them more. Extra points if they correct me."

Dr. Carol made a note. "So, Marilla is more reserved?"

Sara rolled her eyes. "She's always been kinda perfect."

Dr. Carol frowned. "What do you mean?"

"She wanted to be a doctor like Mom. She never pushed. She was quiet. She always studied, got good grades, kept her room clean.

"Dated one guy her whole life. Marilla was ladylike. Not a klutz like me. She made everything look easy."

And everyone loved her.

"So you feel you're different from your sister."

"Everyone said we were opposites. She was sporty, I was artsy. She was neat. I was messy. She was quiet, I was loud..."

"Did you get along?"

"I love her. I haven't been the best at showing it."

"Our time is almost up. This week I want you to journal, but instead of logging your dreams, I want you to log thoughts. Remember not every thought is verbal, so verbalize any impressions or images."

"I don't hear voices," Sara said.

"No, but you think about yourself. We all do. It's called self-talk. Write down what you're thinking."

"Honestly? There's mostly just music in my head. Soundtrack to my life. I don't think a lot."

It hurt too much.

"All right, if there's music in your mind, listen, Write down the lyrics, not just titles. Do this throughout the day, and we'll look at it together next week."

Sara stood, gathering her things. "Magic necklace. Inner voice. Lyrics. Got it."

Dr. Carol smiled. "And Sara? For the record, you're not too much."

Sara stiffened. *You don't know me.*

"Thanks, Dr. Carol. I'll see you next week."

2

Dane pushed hair from his eyes and yanked up yet another weed. Neat rows of vegetables, flowers, and herbs stretched across the field. He inspected the leek in front of him. It wasn't as large as it should be, this late in the season. Tunebells chimed softly, swaying in the wind. Their precious flowers needed to be harvested for oils. He still hated taking the delicate cups and leaving the stalks naked.

Tunebell scent reminded him of his mother. Her eyes, her laughter. He moved to the next plant, pushing her image away. Weeding was tedious, but it gave him a chance to feel the wind on his face.

The ground beneath Dane's feet gave slightly, soft with late summer rain. Birds sang, a symphony rising and falling as kinglets asked and answered questions only they understood. Dane planned as he worked, measuring the number of blooms he would need to create oils and infusions for his varnish.

He moved to the next row. In the distance, a jackdaw cried. The forest behind his rambling hold stretched up a rising slope. His was an island of order on the edge of the Heyegrove, the fabled forest of giant trees.

Dane sensed darkness flowing through the stone wall surrounding the property and the hedges enclosing his garden plot, reaching into his home. He raised his head. The jackdaw had sounded a warning, a harbinger of battle. Slowly, Dane lifted his eyes. A dark bird, its gaze fixed on him, perched on the hedge, eerily silent.

Jackdaws are never silent. Dane's breath caught.

The bird waited, still and soundless.

Dane shook his head. His real work was waiting. He would not pay heed to superstitions.

He threaded his way back to the cottage. As he approached, Dane heard his gnomish guardian, Pezzik, rumbling in the kitchen. She clanged pots and stirred something over the hearth. Pezzik would be grumpy. She always was, this early. Dane grinned and pushed through the half door.

"Avoiding the new lute build, I see," Pezzik said. She pointed at the mud he was tracking in. "That garden is mine to tend, and you know it." She clucked and bustled over, poking him out of his overshoes and swooping them up. She herded him into a chair at the wide-planked table.

Pezzik clanked a metal plate before him, filled a mug with goat's milk from an earthen pitcher on the sideboard, and set it down with a thump, punctuating her disapproval. "Women's work," she muttered, with an angry sniff. Her bulk, swathed in homespun, rounded the table. She stepped on her stool and settled on her chair.

"I've cared for tha' plot since yer poor Mama and Pa passed, and I've cared for you. You need to work the shop. See to your business, lad. I will see to mine." Her spoon waved admonishingly. She stabbed at her eggs and shoveled the bite in. Her blue conical hat bent like a wagging finger, reproaching him.

Guilt is the domain of women. Especially gnomemothers.

"I expect you are ready for the inlay. I'll have the Essence finished this evening. I'm brewing the base." Pezzik nodded toward the hearth.

"Heard jackdaws this morning," Dane said, changing the subject. "Might want to get the goats in early and gather the hens."

"Aye, bears are about, and they will thieve my fowls." Pezzik's brogue thickened when she worried. "I'll see to it." The fire crackled in the large hearth, its cheerful warmth chasing away the morning chill.

"We're likely to have a visitor soon," Dane said. Gnomes were very superstitious, and he could not resist tweaking Pezzik after she'd been so bossy.

Her eyes widened. "You saw one on the roof?" She squeaked in consternation. "Was it on the chimney?"

"No, it was on the hedge," Dane said. He fished an acorn from his pocket and placed it on the table in front of her, tapping it. "Death will not visit us this day, deema."

Pezzik blinked at the endearment and the acorn, her lips softening. She picked up the acorn and turned it over in her hands, nodding.

"The Storm King is in control. I know. He lets the great big trees grow from something so small…" She blinked and put the acorn in her pocket, suddenly businesslike.

"Enough extra to do with the bears about, but I suppose I can air the quilts and," she tapped the table thoughtfully, "a pie. We'll need pie for a visitor. Who could it be?"

She squinted, suddenly suspicious. "Have you paid the tax yet? I don't fancy entertaining a cantor. You'll have to prepare, hide the lute."

Dane laughed and rose to scrape his plate into the scrap pail. "I have the gold from the last cabinets we sold. It's enough. I'll pay it today. I have to go to town and pick up supplies. Don't worry, deema."

The gnome nodded, shooing him from the dishes. "Enough of that, get along with you now. You'll be hard pressed to finish this order as it is. I don't know what you were thinking, promising this lute so quickly." She herded him toward the door. "You'd think you could just sing the lute into being, to make such promises."

Dane stopped and stiffened in the doorway. The Song was not a topic he took lightly, ever. He couldn't, and she knew it. He turned to look at Pezzik.

Sheepish, she met his gaze. "Get on with you. I'll take care of the steading until you return tomorrow." Her voice softened, less gruff.

As if drawn by his thoughts, a ghostly form blurred into focus near the hearth. A small woman with short blond hair blinked in the sunlight. Dane's eyes fastened on her, the first of many fae who would flicker forth as he crafted this new lute. He'd learned as a boy not to be surprised by them. Sometimes many appeared, especially when he and his father worked together. Other times, there were only a few. They never remained long.

"It's begun," he whispered softly. Pezzik whirled in response, her eyes lighting on the figure.

"That one's barely formed," she said. "Hardly good for a chat."

Dane laughed at the gnome's disappointment as the fae touched the table and dissipated. "I'm sure there will be more. This lute must be special." He headed toward his workshop, leaving Pezzik muttering to herself.

Cabinets, tables, and chairs usually filled Dane's workshop. Today, he was plying his clandestine trade. An order had been received. Dane would fill it out of sight of the Conclave. He was dewin. In hiding and untried, but dewin none the less.

We serve the Storm King first, Pa would say. The transformation of their workshop felt like ritual. Special tools, braces, holdfasts, molds, and frame saws emerged from hidden nooks under the floorboards or secret compartments in the cabinets. Essences brewed for mystic varnishes, glues, and dyes lined a small shelf.

Wood curls pillowed his work from the night before. Dane checked the form for imperfections and set it aside. He swept the shavings into a small pile and threw them into the fire. His eyes wandered to the narrow leather box above the hearth. He removed the scrolls within. One he unrolled—a map. Tunebells connected him to his mother. The contents of this box brought his father to mind.

Dane traced spidering lines of ink. The smell of pipe tobacco enveloped him. Pa's voice rumbled in Dane's mind, full of travel stories that even now seemed fantastic.

He rerolled the map and replaced it, touching the other scroll as little as possible. He drew out gold from a side compartment. The tax must be paid, or he would indeed become a target for the cantor.

Dohnavur thrummed. The brook that ran through the center of town gurgled in harmony with the sounds of wagons creaking and hoofbeats on cobbled streets. Shopkeepers nodded as Dane passed. If the gaze of some lingered, brows slightly furrowed and sad, he refused to consider why. Today he had important business.

The mercantile stood in the center of town across from the inn, flanking the village green. Dane nodded at Poll, the broad man behind the counter. Poll flashed his teeth and retrieved a bundle from one of the shelves. He placed it in front of Dane with a flourish.

"That," he said, "is frippery. Are you having something made for Bell, a gift to soothe her ire?"

Dane shrugged, smiling easily at the large man. "You think a gift would tame her?" He scooped up the package.

Poll shook his head with a wry smile. His eyes flicked to the door behind Dane. "Going to be in town long?"

"Till morning," Dane said. "I have to pay my due to the Conclave and run a few errands. I'll sleep at the inn tonight and set out for home at dawn."

Poll grimaced at the mention of the Conclave. "Aye, there's a visitor in town, saw him go into the tavern. Tall man. Seemed to be looking for someone. Might be trouble, might not. You should get a look."

Dane arched a brow and turned toward the door. Poll was his oldest friend and a former neighbor, one of the few who knew of his secret craft. If he worried for Dane, he had reason, but at times he was worse than Pezzik. "You know I don't go running to meet trouble, old friend, unless I'm coming to visit you. But thank you." A draft ruffled his hair as he pulled the door open.

Dane's smile faded as he approached the Chapterhouse, a large building with a steep-pitched roof and arc-shaped window. Best get it over with. He shouldered his satchel and composed his features into a semblance of respect, opening the arched entry. He made the sign of the arc, working the honorific carefully. A badly worked arc could raise your taxes, it was rumored.

Stone walls supported a steeply pitched roof held up by ancient beams. The arc-shaped window and candles cast the only light. Dim and smoky, the air hung thick with cloying incense. It filled the space with haze. The Quiet Hall held benches where the faithful knelt to contemplate the cyntae. At one end, three acolytes stood, hands joined as they chanted, monotone, invoking blessings for the day. Young men and women joined the Conclave to have regular meals, thinking the life easier than farming or a trade. Apprenticeships were hard won in lean times. Dane didn't fault the students. But the price exacted in return was costly.

An arched corridor to Dane's right led to a small office, where the high cantor of the Heyewelde, Nadir Crawe, hunched over a desk. The high counter, some called him, if they thought he couldn't hear.

The man muttered to himself. A tome in front of him held long rows of numbers. He tutted and clicked his teeth, running a bony finger along the rows. Finally, he looked up. His eyes narrowed ever so slightly before he straightened his shoulders. The cantor gestured to a carved chair before his desk. "Dane, my son."

Dane sat and placed his pouch of gold on the desk. "First fruits given." Formal. He wanted this done.

The cantor nodded, possibly mistaking Dane's formality for piety.

"First fruits accepted," he said, eyes gleaming with unconcealed avarice as Dane slid the pouch toward him. Dane knew better than to wait for him to count it. He rose, bowing slightly from the waist, and made the sign of arc again. "'Tis all there, every penny."

"Of course," Nadir murmured, tucking it into a drawer. "I would expect no less from you, my son."

Because I'd have to suffer more of your odious presence if I didn't bring it all. Dane pursed his lips. "I'd love to stay and chat, Cantor, but I have a project that needs finishing…" He trailed off, hoping for dismissal.

Nadir steepled his fingers and eyed Dane for a long moment. The silence stretched. Dane suddenly was reminded of a jackdaw. Nadir's eyes were deep pools, his lean face all angles and hooked nose. He fixed Dane with his gaze. Silent. Searching.

He nodded, his expression carefully beneficent. "Of course, my son. We must speak at length soon. There are matters of…education…to tend to." Nadir's eyes drifted to the ledgers. "You may show yourself out. Blessings of the arc to you."

The cantor would lecture on the Apokrypha and its Arcanum for hours if you did not object, and sometimes even if you did. Education. Whatever one called it, such a session meant attempting not to sleep upright in the carved wooden chair. The cantor spoke in a singsong monotone on purpose, Dane was sure of it. He muttered quiet thanks to the Storm King for his good fortune as he stepped into the early evening.

Dane turned toward the inn. He needed to get home early in the morn. That lute would not make itself, no matter what Pezzik thought, and now he truly needed the rest of the fee. He promised himself he would only drink enough to be sociable. After all, he had to get gossip to share with Poll.

High Cantor Siles glared at the jackdaws before him. They clustered thick in his private courtyard, covering the trees and hedges. Their beaks gaped, soundless. He played a chord on his harp. The silence ripped like a veil. A cacophony of shrieks and screeching sliced the midnight air, rending the hush. The volume swelled, the sounds ruffling the courtyard pool. Images formed in it, starlight whorling. The scenes resolved into story.

The cantor tracked the pictures playing across the water. The bard, the renegades in Baehnt, a rider sent north. The young man in a garden, a dock, an old woman. The birds that were not birds bore witness, their report rippling forth in astonishing detail. He stilled the harp strings. Silence closed in, absolute and unyielding.

The images vanished.

He had seen enough.

"Go," he said.

The jackdaws shimmered, dissolving into formless shadow, a black cloud blocking all light, all hope, all joy. High Cantor Siles shuddered, robbed of sight and sound, cut off from all but the dank stench. They smelled like a grave, wet earth and rotting flesh. He inhaled, tasting their corruption.

"Go!"

As one, they vanished.

Siles turned and slowly made his way back to his study, brow furrowed. The air still tasted like death.

3

Sara headed to the Tank. She wanted nothing more than to bury her anxiety in the dirt that filled the huge greenhouse complex. The Tank was part of a work-study cooperative between the university and the state. Dozens of students worked here, growing hydroponic plants and assisting bioengineers with rare hybrids.

Work provided Sara with a welcome respite from the pressures of art. She could slip in among the plants and just be. No thinking. Sara slipped on her lab coat and protective gloves and read the clipboard hanging under her name. She was tasked to harvest forty industrial hemp plants in the south sector and to observe the Solidago varietals, noting their color, height, and general health.

Sara scanned the wall, reading the other names and clipboards that marched across the pegboard. Brandon, Heather, Amy, Toby, and Scott. She stopped at Scott. Scott Black, who looked like he'd walked straight out of a magazine ad.

Scott's clipboard was missing. He must be working today.

Quickly, Sara ducked into the small bathroom and rearranged her tousled hair. She rummaged in her bag for lip gloss and applied it. Now if she ran into Scott, she wouldn't feel like a complete loser. She stuck her tongue out at her reflection and headed for her station.

Carefully, she worked the custom chopper designed for hand harvesting. She just had to cut and bundle the plants. She fell into a rhythm. Her anxiety melted among the greenery. By the time she had the last bundles stowed and wheeled into the drying room, it was nearly time to leave. She ran to the Solidago. She scanned the fact sheet, smiling as she read the information associated with the golden flowers. Such beautiful lore for such humble plants.

Kentucky state flower. The name Solidago means to make whole. For many, these bright blooms symbolize encouragement and growth. They may be given to show support after a loss or in a difficult time. It is often thought that these flowers can help reduce depression. Goldenrod gives us determination so we may endure to reach the goal. The Ojibwe described the formation of the roots as gripping the earth in preparation for the difficult times ahead. Yellow is thought to stand for creativity and inspiration in life. For this reason, the blooms are a good choice for an artistic path. Solidago arrangements may also include other creative yellow blooms. Erroneously thought to cause allergies

Sara studied them, noting size and health on her chart. "I wish you could heal me," she whispered. The flowers rustled in reply, nodding. It had been a long day. The gnome's face flashed into Sara's mind. One tall bloom stretched, bending to brush Sara's cheek and comfort her.

Sara shook her head to clear it, feeling the weight of the day. There was obviously a draft in here. She glanced at her watch. Almost quitting time. She finished her notes and headed to stow her gear. She was so intent on leaving, when she literally ran into Scott, she didn't have time for her normal terror-of-a-gorgeous-guy to set in.

Instead, she bounced off him. When he turned around, she fixed him with a level look. "You really need to watch where you're standing when I'm in a hurry."

Sara grinned at her own comment, a little embarrassed.

"I'll bear that in mind," said Scott. He laughed, backing up and gesturing to the hooks behind him. "Sara, right?"

Sara blinked. He knew her name. She'd often passed Scott and waved but had never really spoken to him. "That's me," she said. "I also answer to klutz."

Scott shook his head. "Starry-eyed? Dreamer?" He flashed his own grin. "But never klutz."

Sara swallowed, her face warming. "Thank you, kind sir," she drawled. "I do so rely on the kindness of strangers." Mentally she kicked herself as she pushed past him to hang up her clipboard. *How many dudes would get a Streetcar reference?*

"You must think I'm pretty rough." Scott didn't miss a beat.

Sara faced him, gaping. She recovered and grinned. "I've always been adaptable to circumstances."

Scott tipped an imaginary hat and walked away, whistling. Sara watched him go, surprised by the exchange. There was more to this guy than a pretty face. She grinned all the way home.

As she fell into bed, her last thoughts were of golden flowers, reaching to comfort her. She fell asleep as soon as her head hit the pillow.

Sara woke, burrowing under her duvet with a groan. She bolted upright, immediately regretting it. Her head was pounding.

"Rough night?" Jane said from the doorway. "You look like hell."

Sara glared. Her roommate was entirely too cheerful.

"I made coffee," Jane said, nonplussed. "On my way to spin class, but it's the first day of school again… econ!" She rolled her eyes but smiled. "Wish me luck? And get moving."

Really, she should get her own place. "What is it? Six a.m.? I hate you," she said to the empty doorway. "A lot."

Sara padded to the bathroom, peering into the mirror. Dry, cracked lips, circles under her eyes, a mop of curls framing her heart-shaped, freckled face. She did look like hell. Her eyes seemed more brown than green or gold today. She winced. A new cut on her hand was bleeding.

She tried to remember last night's dream, but all she came up with was…an enormous broken tree? Blood seeping from it?

That was it. She was definitely signing up for a sleep study. *This has to end.*

She found a large Band-Aid printed with butterflies in the cabinet and applied it to her hand. Today was a Marilla day, and she wasn't going to be late because of more crazy sleepwalking.

Sara rehearsed her day. Second semester, senior year. This was it. Soon the grind would be over. She would be in the Real World, with her bachelor's degree. If she graduated. She splashed water on her face and brushed her teeth.

Science elective, yuck. Sara had never been good with formulas. Luckily, her work at the Tank counted as a lab. She also had to meet sometime soon with Polly Worden, her advisor. Sara ran a brush through her hair as she checked her ancient clock radio. It was never set right. She always messed up the time when she hit snooze. It flashed now, 3:16. Light dappled the high-ceilinged room from tall transom windows. The iron radiator hummed.

She was going to be late.

Sara jumped into her standard wardrobe: jeans and a long-sleeved tee shirt with black Chucks. A bit of lip gloss and she was out the door. She fumbled with her keys in the cold, cursing. Her coat, hat, scarf, and gloves were in the car, a temperamental '72 Karmann Ghia. Sara finally opened the door. She gunned the engine and threw on her coat and gloves, praying for warmth as the car slowly slid away from the curb.

Ornate Victorian homes reproached her like grand Southern belles, offended by her noisy car. The stone lion next to her building stood sentry in the gray morning light, frost coated. Her car coughed once as she passed it, coughed again, and settled into a purr.

The nursing home didn't really smell fetid, but she still breathed through her mouth in self-defense. The Nero Care facility off Highway 71 was top-notch, world famous.

But it made her cringe.

Sara buried her head in the bouquet she carried as she ambled past the nurses' station. She gripped the doorknob to Marilla's room. She breathed. This was a moment of hope. In her mind's eye, Marilla sat up, made fun of her like she used to, demanded ice cream. Coffee fudge ripple, her favorite.

Sara pulled the heavy door, and hope vanished, destroyed by the reality of coma. Monitors beeped, measuring her twin's heart, her breathing, her blood pressure. Marilla lay pale, unresponsive, like she had since D-day. Eight months ago. Sara blinked away tears and made a beeline for the vase on the side table. She pasted a smile on her face and forced her mood into submission. She would be cheerful. *Happy thoughts. Rainbows. Butterflies.*

"Hi, Rilla! Mellow greetings! Sorry I'm late," she said. "Traffic was hell, and I had those weird dreams again. Remember how I used to dream when we were kids? I've totally gotten worse."

She eyed her sister before walking into the adjoining bath. The fading mass of daisies went into the trash. Sara chattered while she worked, washing out the vase, refilling it with water and adding flower preservative. Flowers calmed her. It's why she worked at the Tank. She claimed the roses and grabbed scissors from the room's small desk. "This time was a doozy. I even scored a new wound." Sara held out her injured hand. It throbbed. Marilla's eyes didn't open. She had read Marilla heard her, anyway. She kept talking.

"Probably sleepwalking. I'm dreaming about gnomes. Can you believe it? Gnomes. Definitely have been listening to Peter drone on about dragon flicks too much.

"The weird thing? I do remember how I got the splinter. I saw an old table with a banged-up corner. I couldn't resist touching it. You know how I love texture? The table gave me a splinter. It was so real."

Sara concentrated, trying to remember anything else. The only sounds were the soft rhythmic beeps of Marilla's monitors and the rasp of her breathing.

Sara listened, letting her heart remain open, reaching for answers.

Maybe it was real.

She threw up her hands, confessing aloud to banish the thought. "I'm visiting a parallel universe in my dreams. You know? Sleepwalking isn't crazy enough for Sara Moore. No, I have to do the entire artist crazy. Lose my mind completely. Maybe I'll cut off my ear. Maybe then Mom would get it, finally admit I'm a real artist. Would she think my art matters, then?"

She shook herself. Enough. It wasn't real. Sara returned to her task. She filled the sink with warm water and dunked the stems, clipping each on a diagonal before placing them in the vase. "Brought cottage roses. Your favorite.

"I'm doing twenty hours a week now at the Tank, helping with the hybrids. It's changing how I work with clay. The plants inspire me. I only have Practicum and Organic Chem this semester. Chem is with Peter, so that's fun. He says hi, by the way.

"Let's see, what else? Dad is MIA, as usual. Probably has a new bimbo. Lunches with Mom are the usual. Lots of her telling me it isn't too late for a real career. I can still be just like her. No life, all work. I can still go to grad school. Yada, yada, etcetera.

"Oh! You'll never believe who's in my art class. Remember Chantal? Snooty diva from Prospect? The one who used to talk smack about us? She went to Assumption? Yeah, her. Anyhow, she's in my senior practicum. You'd think she'd have learned to be nice in four years, you know, be an adult and everything, but no. She hasn't. I heard she went to RISD. Tough school.

"I don't know. Funny to transfer home midsemester, the year before you graduate, and move all the way back from Rhode Island, don't you think? She came in a month before break last year. You think she failed out at RISD, and they accepted her here, anyway? Her daddy donates heavily to the school."

Sara made a face as she came back to the room with the vase. "There. These should last awhile."

Sara placed the arrangement in a shaded nook next to the window. She settled into the hospital-blue recliner and picked up her paperback. "Okay, where were we? Chapter two? I thought we were farther along?"

She looked at Marilla, watching for a change. Breathing. Beeping. Anything. There was no change. Not for the first time, her eyes caught on the print above the bed, a framed inspirational quote with a dramatic photographed landscape.

A sky full of lightning glowered over the scene. Shelf clouds resembled a monster, reaching for the farmhouse below. The verse highlighted beneath read:

The Lord answered Job out of the storm
- Job 38:1

Why is that inspirational? Religion is so weird. Sara leaned back in her chair and began to read aloud. Sunbeams cascaded over her shoulder. Two chapters later, she was jolted out of the story by a tap at the door.

"It's time for her exercises," the nurse said. "You can keep reading if you like."

"Thanks, Phoebe. I have my first classes today, and I'm probably already late. I better go."

Sara stood and bent to kiss her sister's cheek. "I'll be back soon. You wake up, Marilla Moore. I miss you. I really do. I'm sorry, I'm so, so sorry for everything."

She placed the book on the nightstand, pointing the bookmark toward the window.

4

The *Bell and Rider* was as well-known for its keeper as it was for its mead. Both were lively spirits.

Dane walked in, and Bell tilted her head, her eyes narrowing. Her small hand tightened into a fist. She released it, collecting mugs from the bar as she swept toward the kitchen.

"Lile will serve you," she called over her shoulder as she passed him. She retreated. Indignance pulsated from beyond the door after it slammed behind her.

Dane claimed a bar stool. Well, she was angry after all. *Why are women so confusing?* He signaled Lile for an ale and nodded a greeting to the man beside him. Not anyone he knew. Lile plopped an ale in front of him.

The man pulled a pipe from his belt pouch, not acknowledging him. He tapped its contents onto the straw-covered stone floor. Soon, the air was scented with a sweet aroma. Smoke wreathed the stranger's angular face and floated away. He was bearded, with fair hair and dark eyes. Maybe he was from Perrhil. The stranger spoke as if launching into a thrilling story to an old friend. "Faisant," he said. "The fae."

Dane nearly spewed his ale. He caught himself and swallowed it down, his nostrils burning. "What about them?" It was madness to discuss children's stories with a stranger, even knowing they were true.

"What do you know of the fae?" the man asked. He took a draw from his pipe.

Dane eyed him, gauging his sobriety, before answering. He could just be a talkative traveler passing time. Dane made the sign of the arc, automatically warding off evil.

"I know what every child knows, milord. The Festival of Lights is held at midwinter, our songs inviting the fae to come. They bring gifts for babes to find on First Morning. They speak only to children, gnomes, or the pure in heart. If you sing with them, you'll become a majister. Or so the old tales say." Dane finished with only a trace of bitterness. "In some stories they play tricks. They lie. They disappear. I've never liked those stories, though."

"Aye, they disappear, lad," the man murmured. He leaned forward, propping his elbow on the bar. "But what if they did not?" He took a long draw from his pipe.

Bell burst from the kitchen, eyes flashing daggers in Dane's direction. She bustled across the common room, flouncing onto a bench with her back to him. She tapped her foot. Clearly, she expected an apology. Now.

The stranger tracked Dane's gaze. "A friend of yours?" His mouth twisted, wry.

Dane nodded, miserable.

"Odd for a young, unmarried woman to hold her own property."

"You're not from here. We see women as the gnomes do. Bell is respected. Her family has run this inn for as long as anyone can remember. Her father passed away midwinter last. But she has Jax there. And everyone knows better than to anger a gnome."

Jax sat on a small stool in the corner, still as a small statue.

"I had best go make amends with his deemling." Dane welcomed the opportunity to free himself from the odd conversation, even if he did dread what was coming next.

He threaded his way through the benches and tables to reach Bell's side.

"Good evening, Bell."

His voice didn't croak or squeak, a small victory. He cleared his throat, not trusting his luck to last two sentences. "I need a room for the night."

Bell whirled, facing him. "The stable," she said. "All of our rooms are full."

Dane blinked. The common room was only half full, and several of the doors lining the balcony upstairs were open, a sign they were available to rent. Scratching the back of his neck, he considered for a moment. Softly, so Bell had to lean in, he said, "All right. I can bed in the stable. I'll just be here the one night and be gone in the morning."

"Half silver," said Bell, rising to her feet.

"That's outrageous!" Dane spluttered, forgetting his remorse. "Even if it includes supper and a bath, a half silver is more than you ask for three nights. I know, I've stayed here enough."

"You have previously enjoyed a price extended to friends," Bell said, her face reddening. She stamped her foot for emphasis on the word friends. "And I'll tell you what is outrageous." Her voice shrilled as she stamped again. Her index finger stabbed his chest. "What's outrageous is promising a friend you will visit, and then not showing up for weeks." She stamped and stabbed his chest again. "What's outrageous is making her wait, not knowing what happened." And another stamp and stab. "What's outrageous is expecting that girl to treat you"—poke—"as a friend. As a loyal, valued customer. Instead of as a horse's bottom! Half silver." She stamped her foot again and crossed her arms.

Dane had the sense to look ashamed. He tried not to feel all eyes in the room on him. Thunder take him, Poll would get a tale tonight, for certain.

"I'm sorry, Bell. I really am." He lowered his eyes and continued in a rush. "I had a surprise order come in for work and had to travel north for more hardwoods. I just returned. I hadn't time to send word. I have little time to finish this job, but it catches me up on..." He grimaced, not wanting to discuss his taxes in front of the town. "This will set me right for the winter." He summoned the courage to look at her. "Can we go somewhere else and discuss this?"

Bell's mouth twitched. For a moment, Dane thought she might laugh, but her mouth settled into a grim line. She stood, marched toward the kitchen, and out the door to the alley outside. Whoops followed them, along with shouts of encouragement, toasts, and offers of physical protection. He hoped that wasn't a bet being laid in the corner. Then again, his money would be on Bell.

She rounded on him as they stepped into the alley and pushed him roughly against the building. "Don't you ever." Push. "Do that." Push. "Again."

The wall was rough against Dane's back. Not for the first time, he wished he could sink into it like a gnome.

"Where were you?"

"I told you, I had to go into the forest for a special job that came in suddenly. Seasoned wood to be brought from the Heye. Then there was much work to be done, and I couldn't spare two days to ride here and back. I needed the money. Things have been hard since Pa passed, you know. I work sunup to sundown, running the workshop alone." Dane measured her reaction, waiting.

Bell had lost her father not long before Dane's parents passed. She sometimes understood his struggles. It was one of the reasons their friendship had deepened.

"And I needed to think."

Bell's eyes widened.

"Because we kissed and..."

Bell stepped back, drawing herself up to her full height and schooled her expression into a prim mask. "It was one kiss, Master Whitley. Not a proposal. Not a promise. And blast if you get another. One kiss and you run away?" She shook her head. "Friends. Friends we have been since we were wee children, and friends we remain."

"I think we are more than friends, Bell." He watched her closely. *Stars, I'm not good at this.* "I want to be."

Bell continued as if she hadn't heard him. "I won't tolerate friends who don't keep their promises or disappear. I've had enough loss in my life. Next time you decide to run off into the forest when you are supposed to come into town, let me know. Send word. You live in the wilderness on the edge of the Heyegrove alone with one gnome. I know Pezzik is well able to watch over you, but I still worry. Anything could happen!"

The door never opened. Jax was just there suddenly, next to Bell. His beard lent his mischievous eyes wisdom as he looked them over. "You two about done, then? And Dane has no bruises." Jax eyed him. "I'll let Lile know he lost five coppers. And who was the gentleman you were chatting with then, young Dane, if you don't mind my asking?" He hooked his thumbs around the edges of his vest, rocking back and forth. His cap quivered.

Dane had forgotten the stranger. "I don't know," he said. "Odd sort. He seemed to be in his cups, chattering about children's stories."

Jax nodded and vanished into the stone wall as suddenly as he had appeared.

"I wish he wouldn't do that," Bell complained. "It frightens outlanders."

"You think he is bad, you should see Pezzik during harvest. She's everywhere." Dane looked into her eyes. "I promise I won't disappear again, Bell. Really."

Bell's eyes softened. She bowed her head. A mane of dark curls tumbled around her face. "I can't stay angry with you. I'm glad you're safe."

Dane let out a slow sigh of relief. "Are you still going to make me sleep in the stable?"

"I should." Bell glanced up at him, withdrawing her hand. "But no. First door on the left after you climb the stairs. Standard rate. I have to go see to business now, but we can talk more later."

"I look forward to it," he said. And he meant it. Dane followed her back inside, waving at the roar of approval that greeted him as he entered the inn unscathed. Dane saw the stranger had departed. He'd likely gone to sleep it off. Dane checked the satchel he'd left under his chair. The wrapped package was still inside, though it seemed some wrappings had loosened. The contents threatened to spill out. He sighed, glad the bag hadn't been taken. Today he'd been lucky indeed. He had escaped a sermon, endured the wrath of Bell, and kept his pack, despite being careless. He murmured thanks to the Storm King as he made his way upstairs to stow his gear.

While normally Dane would make his own strings, time constraints for his present job would not permit it. Gut strings, Indra ink, an assortment of fine thin blades for the detailing of the rosette, and the frippery Pell had spoken of. A small quantity of mother-of-pearl and a bottle of blue dye. He couldn't be sure his tunebells would cure in time and would not risk it. It was all there. He repacked the satchel and hung it on a hook. Yes, it had been a lucky day. He felt like dancing.

Dane reached the bottom of the stairs and spied the stranger. He was setting up near the hearth. Jax stood with him, the two deep in conversation. The gnome stooped and unclasped the man's lute case, pointing and nodding. The bard smiled, dark eyes crinkling as he listened. He picked up his lute and handed it to Jax. Jax handled it reverently. Jax listened, his head tilted, and plucked the strings one by one. He handed it back to the bard, saying something that made the man laugh. Dane watched with equal parts amusement and trepidation as he resumed his seat.

If there was a song playing, a gnome would be the first to join in singing, his voice lifted in perfect harmony. Music pulsed through a gnome's speech. There was a cadence in their step, their hammer blows—all their work. It was said in old tales that gnomes were born from the Song long ago, charged by the Storm King to watch over and guide the children in their care, their deemae. A gnome was always humming, tapping, whistling, or singing. Musicians welcomed gnomish companions and considered them good luck. A gnome could accompany any melody, and it was a rare treat to sing with them.

However. Jax was a singular gnome.

Bell slid into the stool beside Dane, nodding toward Jax. "That's why he was interested. The stranger is a bard, I should have known."

Gnomes were rarely seen outside the Heyegrove and its surrounding hills these days. Musicians came to Dohnavur hoping to meet one and were directed to the inn. While several local families were deemae, adopted by a gnomic guardian and protector, only a few were seen in public.

"Ah, the stranger's nattering about fae makes sense; he's a storysmith. He's likely composing," Dane said. "Did you get a chance to warn him?" He nodded at Jax and raised his eyebrows.

"Warn the bard about Jax? No, I thought I'd let him find out on his own. Besides, Jax really has improved. He practices for hours every morning."

Dane raised a mug to his lips, thankful for the strong brew in light of what was coming.

5

The crowd had grown while Dane was upstairs. The two barmaids pushed through it, serving customers with patience and laughter. As the bard took up his lute, the room quieted. More than a few locals glanced at Bell with knowing expressions and suppressed smiles. Most gave their attention to the bard and the gnome.

The bard's lute gleamed; its neck, rosette, and bridge were the standard black. The intricately carved rosette was a round Conclave design. The songs played would be approved melodies. The man was Bindery-trained. Odd for him to speak of fae. But then, even Bindery bards loved stories. It was their trade.

The bard tapped a beat against the soundboard of the lute, letting it fill the room in a steady driving rhythm, the sole accompaniment to his verse. Dane smiled as he recognized "The Suitor Song."

Once there was a deemae, a deemae, a deemae
Once there was a deemae, who had a pretty smile
And she met a young man, a young man, a young man
And she met a young man, whose wits she did beguile.

The young man bent to kiss her, to kiss her, to kiss her

The young man bent to kiss her, his plans they went awry.
The young man met her deema, her deema, her deema
The young man met her deema, and he did learn to fly.

Dane laughed as the bard winked and played the traditional folk melody. He sang the round and gestured for Jax and the crowd to start the next verse.

Jax stepped forward and belted it out.

Once there was a deemae, a deemae, a deemae

Dane had to give the bard credit. His hands didn't stumble on the strings. Jax's melody veered in and out of tune. The beat never faltered. What Jax lacked in talent, he made up for in enthusiasm.

Once there was a deemae, a deemae, a deemae
Once there was a deemae, she was a pretty lass.

The locals, used to the gnome's voice, laughed and clapped along. But some children put their hands over their ears. The smallest started crying.

And she met a young man, a young man, a young man
And she met a young man, and he loved her...sass!

Jax roared the last word, his hand thumping the stool in emphasis. A dog under one of the tables began to whine as if in pain.

The young man went to hug her, to hug her, to hug her
The young man went to hold her, and life it went askew.

The crowd had joined in now. They muffled the sound of the cacophonous gnome.

The young man met her deema, her deema, her deema
The young man met her deema, and now he cannot chew.

The bard visibly winced as he struck a major chord while Jax's voice dipped perfectly flat. The song had twenty verses, and likely more, but the bard rushed to finish. He launched into the traditional last chorus.

So if you love a deemae, a deemae, a deemae
So if you love a deemae, and you must true love bring
Your only hope my young man, my young man, my young man

Your only hope my young man, is to stop and sing!

The bard gestured, using his lute to point at Dane. Bell flushed but laughed with the rest as the song ended amid cries of "Sing, Dane! Sing!" Dane raised his hands, protesting, but Lile grabbed his arm and dragged him to the makeshift stage. Dane heartily wished he'd had more ale.

"I believe you need to sing, sir," said the bard.

So I can rescue you from a tone-deaf gnome...Dane wasn't keen on singing solo in public. He was dewin. If he sang by himself, without a crowd to mask his voice, the consequences could be dire indeed. But it was expected after the "Suitor Song" for a young man to sing. Dancing would follow. Besides, it might help fully mend things with Bell. He really did want another kiss.

"Do you know 'The Rose'?" Dane asked.

The bard nodded assent, adjusting the pegs on his lute. Dane gulped and faced the crowd with a smile.

"A rose," he said, bowing, "for the lovely deemae." Dane sang, modulating his voice to disguise his gifts.

The bard played a full set of dances after Dane finished his song. Tables were pushed back, and townfolk whirled across the floor like flower petals tossed by the wind. Dane and Bell danced with the rest before collapsing at their table. Bell did not pull her hand away when Dane cupped it with his, twining his fingers through hers. She smiled, and a happy glow enveloped Dane.

"Careful, my deema might see," Bell said, squeezing his hand.

"I think he already has," Dane said. He leaned in. "But I think he likes me."

"Perhaps," Bell said. "Did you see the bard's face when he started to sing?"

"You never tire of that, do you?"

"Never," Bell said. "These minstrels travel so far from the Bindery to meet a gnome. I love the looks on their faces when they sing with Jax. The last one faked an illness. It's the most common way to escape, suddenly develop a stomach cramp, or lose their voice."

"Broken strings," Dane said. "I saw a minstrel break four strings at once. No idea how he managed it. It can backfire, though. Jax found his tambor and demanded the man sing a set a cappella. I thought the poor sap's head would burst."

They were still chuckling when the bard found them and claimed an empty chair. "That was not what I expected." He signaled to one of the serving girls for a drink. "But I appreciate the chance to play with Jax, all the same."

"Your ale is on the house, sir," said Bell, smiling. "Thank you for your kindness to my friend. He loves meeting new musicians." She paused and added, "I'm Bell."

"Aric," the bard said.

"Dane. Where are you from, Aric?"

"Originally from Baehnt. More recently from Bestua. This is my first time this far north."

"Are you planning to stay long?" asked Dane.

The ale arrived, and Aric drank a long pull before answering. "A few days, perhaps more. I'm collecting songs and lore. I had planned to visit the Heyegrove. You must have many who pass through to do the same."

Bell sniffed. "This past year, few. Jax was particularly happy to see you."

A sudden crash came from the kitchen, and Bell stood, excusing herself. "Good to meet you."

Aric nodded in answer. He watched her walk away, then added, "I'm here to collect stories. That's true. But I also hoped to retrieve a package for a friend. A delicate package."

Dane raised his eyebrows, instantly wary. "Oh?"

Aric nodded. "Trystan is a good mate. He told me to find a young cabinetmaker named Dane. He thought you might have stories for me. I've known him since we were children. He also asked me to give you this"—Aric set a pouch on the table—"and I'm to wait for his package and deliver it to him when I return." Aric paused. "I need to travel quickly, so I'll travel night and day. The moon will be new, but I can see by starlight."

Trystan's name set Dane to near panic. The way the bard emphasized the word "starlight" nearly pushed him over the edge. Dane looked at the pouch on the table, calculating. This Conclave bard was trying to get him to admit to building enchanted lutes. Tricky. His forehead wrinkled in confusion. He lifted the pouch, weighing it, and slid it back across the table. "While I enjoy gold as much as the next man and am the only craftsman meeting your description, I'm afraid there is some mistake." Dane shook his head in apology. "I have never met anyone named Trystan. My next shipment is a fine cabinet, bound for Bestua by flatboat. It was ordered by Lord Tabor Demitri a month ago, and I'm hard pressed to finish it. I came to town to pick up final supplies for the inlay."

Dane smiled more easily than he felt, gesturing to the common room. "Perhaps your friend has me confused with someone else. What did he order?" He worried Aric would hear his pulse racing. He slowed his breathing, thinking quickly.

Dane leaned forward. "I can help you find the person you seek. Elkere? He is the town chandler. If you're traveling at night, you might need candles or one of his oil lamps. Shrinnik? He is the cooper." Dane nodded to a table where a large man sat playing dice.

Aric arched a brow at Dane but reclaimed his gold. "I'm not sure what the package was," he said. "Only that he needed it immediately. He didn't say why."

Dane emptied his mug and shrugged. "I'm sorry I can't help you."

Aric sighed. "Ah well, thank you for your time." He stood, offering his hand. "It was good to meet you."

"Likewise."

Aric retreated through the crowd, toward the stairs. Dane tracked him, watching until the bard retired to his room. Dane stood, looking for Jax. The gnome was perched behind the bar on his stool, assisting Lile. He smiled when he saw Dane.

"Tell Bell I'll be back soon?"

Jax's smile faded, but he tapped the side of his nose and nodded.

Dane strolled into the town square and headed toward the docks. He digested what had just happened as he walked. A mist had fallen, draping the buildings in white. A cantor knew about his lutes. A breeze ruffled his mop of hair as he moved down the street, making him shiver in the damp. There was no telling when, but Aric would show up on Dane's doorstep. The mist swirled. Dane's back prickled. He turned left, away from the main street and onto a narrow alley. Was he being followed? Taking the next right turn, he quickened his steps, and ducked into a lane parallel to the main street. He needed to talk to Mod. He followed the lane for a few blocks, seeing no one. He heard no footfalls. He turned left again toward the river, passing a few of the Watch, the local baron's men. They paid him no heed. Whew.

Dane stopped at a small whitewashed stone cottage. He knocked twice, two more times, and four times again. The door opened inward, revealing a small old woman with kind eyes and a warm smile.

"It's good to see you, Dane, I was expecting you tomorrow morning."

"Likewise, Mod. I'm sorry. This couldn't wait." Dane bent to kiss her cheek. "I can't stay long. I have to ride back tonight; I think we are in trouble."

Mod nodded and shuffled to her kitchen. Intricate hand-worked lace doilies cushioned warm-hued earthenware. Copper pots gleamed, hanging from the hooks that dangled from the crossbeam. The smell of beeswax and lavender mingled as a kettle steamed on its hook over the wide stone hearth. Mod gestured to a bench along the table. "Sit my dear. Have a spot of tea."

Dane knew better than to refuse. "Thank you. Someone tried to collect my latest shipment early. I think I'm being watched. The buyer will be in danger."

Mod peered at Dane briefly but focused on the kettle as she poured a cup. "You haven't finished it yet?"

Dane shook his head. "I knew I would be cutting it close."

"What did he look like?"

Dane described the man, sketching with his hands. "Medium height, light brown hair, and cleft chin, scruffy but no real beard. A full bard. He claimed to know Trystan. He offered gold openly at the inn. He was speaking of the fae before I'd properly introduced myself, and he tricked me into singing in public. I thought he might be just another storysmith out hunting old tales. But he tried to obtain the lute himself. It was bold. He called himself Aric."

Dane cupped his hands around the teacup, letting the warmth flow into his fingers before raising it to his lips. The steam curled upward, and he breathed in the scent of honeysuckle. "And there were jackdaws on my hedges today."

Mod clucked to herself, settled into her chair and picked up her teacup.

"Conclave. He'll be paying you a visit then."

Dane nodded. "He said he was headed to the Grove."

Mod pursed her lips, considering. "We've sent fourteen of your father's lutes out over the years, Dane. I canna remember anyone trying to intercept them. We thought we had a close call seven years ago, when you were just a boy, but the lute made it to its owner. The person turned out to be a merchant traveler. We've never had anything as bold as this."

"Could it have been a trap? Was there anything odd about this order? It's the first lute I've built on my own, Mod. Stars."

He didn't even know what he was doing. What if he was captured?

The penalty for performing with an enchanted lute was severe. The penalty for making them was worse. Much worse. Never mind the fact he was dewin. *Storm King, help me.*

Mod shook her head. "Everything was in order, and one of my boys met Trystan himself, scried him in a mirror. He was genuine. Trystan dan Tenkor is not just a bard. He's a prince. He's respected, not fully bound to the Conclave like most. Independently trained in Pelegor, not molly-coddled. He is making his Journey to become a full Bindery master, but he had the proper tune. He was genuinely sent to us."

"I don't know then. I'd best get home. But Bell..."

"Never mind the girl, lad. I'll get word to her. You slip away."

Dane nodded briefly, meeting her eyes. "Tell her to stow my things. I'll come back for them." With a wave, he headed back out into the mist, striding toward the inn stable.

It was going to be a long ride home.

6

Mid-January in Louisville, Kentucky wasn't subzero weather, but the walk across the campus green still made Sara wish she'd chosen a school in Florida. Peter swept in not far behind her and parked his athletic frame into the seat next to her. He carried a beverage tray with two steaming cups of coffee.

"Here you go, Rudolph," he said. "One vanilla latte."

"My hero." Sara sipped slowly, careful not to burn her tongue. "Are my ears red too?"

"Vermilion," Peter said. "But you look great, milady." He bowed, somehow managing not to seem awkward, though he was seated. Peter didn't look like a nerd. He looked like a singer from a boy band, with a smile that could melt even her cold face. His ice-blue eyes and crooked grin always made her feel better.

But he really was *such* a geek.

Sara narrowed her eyes. "Have you been larping again?"

"Belegarth is not larping. In my case, it's exercise. But no, it's too cold. We won't meet again until spring."

Sara said, "You pretend to sword fight. That's larping." She laughed.

"Larping, milady, is when you dress up and pretend to be in another world. It's live action role play." He tapped the desk in front of him. "Belegarth is just pretending to fight with padded swords and armor. It's exercise." The room began to fill with other students. Peter paused and added, innocently, "I did watch Princess Bride again last night."

Sara rolled her eyes, swiveling her legs under her desk. Professor Kent strode to the podium and welcomed them. She listened, taking notes and pointedly not reacting to Peter's antics as he doodled in the margins of his syllabus.

It was their first class together in ages, like freshman year all over again. Peter certainly hadn't changed much.

As the professor droned on about what they could expect, Sara snuck a look at Peter, who had given up on his drawing and was listening, taking actual notes. He'd been her rock these past few months. Late-night phone calls, lazy days hanging out listening to music, pizza study sessions. It had all cemented their friendship to the point that he was family. Sometimes she wanted more, imagining what he would be like as her boyfriend. Peter was a good person. *Too good for me.*

"Pizza tonight?" he asked as class ended.

Sara shook her head. "I have to work at the Tank."

"Okay. What are you doing Friday night?"

"Friday..." Sara thought for a minute, then flipped her phone open to check her calendar. "Friday I'm at the library till six, then free."

"Cool. I'm taking you on a date."

"A date?"

Oh no. Oh no. No, no, no, no, no, no.

"A date, milady." Peter's eyes twinkled. "Dinner and a movie. I expect you to be on your best behavior."

Sara looked at Peter. A movie quote flew out of her mouth. It was one Peter knew and would begin the bit they did sometimes. It would also tip him off. Big time. But she needed to stall him.

"You remind me of a guy."

"What guy?"

"A guy with power."

"What power?"

"The power of woo-hoo."

"Woo-hoo?"

"Hoo-do!"

"Who do?"

"You do."

"Do what?"

"Remind me of a guy."

"What guy?"

"A guy with power."

"What power?"

"Give up?"

Peter's expression transformed from playful to serious to uncertain as they traded the lines. She was anxious. Crap. Could she go out on a real date with Peter? Geek, brother-like man child? Really cute geek. She couldn't deny it. But he was her friend. That was rare. And safe. His sister was her roommate. She didn't want to screw this up, too. Besides, Peter never dated anyone for long. His last girlfriend had been a year or so ago, what had her name been? June? Sara had met her twice. That was before D-day. Before Rilla.

But she couldn't hurt him.

Coward. I'm such a coward.

Peter would keep at her too, if she blew him off. He wasn't the type to let it go. She could think about it this week, then talk to him on Friday at dinner. No need to blurt things she might regret, admit to her confusion. Not here, not in class with people streaming out of the room around them.

"Okay, pick me up at eight. And no dragon flicks."

Peter's grin was relieved. "Wouldn't dream of it."

The Senior Practicum at the Hite Institute for the Arts was an intensive class with a studio component. A juried showing at the end of the semester counted for half their grade. Very important. Sara needed to get there early. She claimed a space on one of the couches lining the front of the vast loft-like space. A converted chapel, the building featured high ceilings beamed with golden oak. Overstuffed couches formed an informal enclosed meeting space.

By this point in the program, most students had either dropped or moved on to more practical studies. The twenty Material Arts students who remained knew each other well.

A huge screen dominated the wall in front of the sofas. It flickered with a slide cast from a feeble projector. The aroma of coffee and the faint smell of burning metal reached Sara as she read.

Internship with Wryneck Workshop.

Sara frowned. Actor's Theatre had an internship up for grabs every year. The highly coveted arts internship program was open to schools across the country. Interns helped fabricate props and sets, some worked with sculpted fantasy costumes or elaborate makeup. There were only a few open positions, and exposure also included travel to New York or Los Angeles to work with professionals in major markets.

The class had competed for the internship in September. Sara had submitted her application packet, and like everyone else, received a polite rejection letter. The Wryneck Workshop was a very famous design and effects company in Hollywood. Famous. It would make an internship with Actor's look like kindergarten.

Miranda Vine settled into a cross-legged position, resting against a couch and settling her skirt around her. Sara nodded to the slide and raised an eyebrow, sipping from her travel mug. Miranda peered at it and shrugged.

"No telling," Miranda commented. She pulled a sketchbook and pink gel pen from her bag.

Chantal Goddard was one of the last to arrive. Small, wiry, sharp faced, with close-set eyes and a large mouth, her lips curled in disdain as she surveyed her seating options. Barely pausing, she swept over to Sara, looking at her pointedly until she made room. Chantal proceeded to ignore Sara. Sara pretended not to notice.

Their teacher and mentor, Polly Worden, bustled in...and she wasn't alone. Bastien Crowe. *The* Bastien Crowe strode in behind her.

"I'd like to introduce Bastien Crowe," said Polly. "He's here to discuss this semester's first practicum." She gestured to the lectern in front of the screen and claimed the large overstuffed armchair reserved for the professor. Nonchalant. As if the most famous designer on the planet attending her class was super ordinary.

Bastien Crowe. Young, hip, but sure of himself. He didn't act self-important—not what Sara expected at all. He sidled up to the podium and stood in front of it.

"This year a feature film is being shot in the hills of Kentucky. We start in six weeks. I have family here and came out during the location scout to visit. For those who have not seen my work..." He paused, his blue eyes crinkling before he turned to the screen.

Images of amazing creatures, soaring sculptures, large-scale models, and fantastic vehicles for the latest ten blockbuster film releases faded in and out behind him. "Those are some pieces built at my shop.

"We'll be filming here for several months, first for a small television pilot, then for my film. The film is urban fantasy, and we'll need a lot of help. But we have one spot—one special place for one extraordinary person—on the design team."

He looked at Sara. Her breath caught in her throat as he continued.

"This job will let you explore your craft in a paid position with my shop for, at minimum, one year. Your job interview includes one piece and a design presentation. If you secure the position, your internship will end with a job offer. Your deadline is in a few weeks, with the winners announced on Valentine's Day. Questions?"

Chantal raised her hand. "Who will conduct the interviews?"

"I will," he replied briefly, nodding to the next student.

"Are there any size requirements?" a boy on the other side of the room asked.

"Bigger is better," said Bastien, grinning. He was known for the scale in his work outside of the film industry. "But there are no requirements. One piece. Show me your best."

Questions continued. Slides must be presented. It had to be shot with proper lighting. Staging for the piece could be creative. As the questions died down, Sara raised her hand, her small arm slipping up as if clutching at something. Sara turned pink as Bastien focused on her.

"What are you looking for?"

He might not answer, but she wanted to know. It couldn't hurt to ask. Bastien rocked back on his heels and broke into another easy grin.

"Originality doesn't really say much, does it?" He stepped away from the podium. "I think an example might help. It's better to show, not tell."

He cycled through the slides. "This is Max." A ninety-foot-tall gargoyle rose from the middle of a deserted landscape. Mountains and a sheer cliff face rose in the distance behind him. Now a tourist attraction in Australia, he reigned over the landscape.

Max's features reminded her of DaVinci's grotesques. He was playful and stern, majestic and alive all at the same time, faintly comic. He was ugly. He was part gargoyle, part mountain, a force of nature that blended perfectly with his surroundings.

"Max was a dream of mine. Look at him closely." He zoomed in to show the detail. Max's skin had texture. He wasn't smooth like polished stone. More like leather or hide. The room was completely silent, focused.

"He took two years and a team of people to finish. It was very important to me that Max be permanent," Bastien said. "If you understand why I made him, you are a good candidate for our new hire."

The lights rose again.

"That doesn't mean that you have to build a ninety-foot sculpture in a foreign country. But I need to see what matters to you. And the piece itself needs to tell me why."

"So we need to be geniuses," Sara said.

Bastien laughed along with the other students, then answered with surprising intensity. "No, but you do need to meet your heart's inner fire and master it."

Sara blinked. Crap. Meet your heart's inner fire and master it? How did Max show Bastien's heart? Really? This was the big thing she was supposed to understand? Max disturbed her; she didn't quite know why. She'd seen pictures of him before. Maybe seeing him so large, with his creator, had unsettled her. It burned like an itch in her brain.

Polly rose, thanking Bastien. She dismissed the students to sketch ideas.

Chantal jostled Sara as she clambered to her feet. "Don't bother, sweetie. I've got this," she said. Her tone held a veiled threat. She'd heard it before.

Sara's most saccharine tone oozed out, automatically, a normally nonexistent Southern drawl rising to the surface. "Bless your heart."

She held Chantal's gaze for a moment. Chantal looked at her watch, covering the anger in her eyes. She clucked and scooped up her bag. "Meeting my boyfriend," she said and flounced away.

Miranda stopped in front of Sara, her eyes bright, amused. "That one is sure of herself."

"Something like that."

"Hey, you got a sec? I've been meaning to ask you something."

"Sure, what's up?"

Miranda pulled a neon pink piece of paper from her bag and pressed it into Sara's hands. "I'm trying to start a group to work with Somalian refugee kids. There's a huge community of them in government housing not far from here. I thought an art program might help them integrate, learn English, you know? Give them a leg up. You interested?"

Sara took the flyer, a plastic smile fixed to her face as she looked over the details, bordered by clipart butterflies and bees. *Good grief. I can't help kids. I'm a total mess.* She feigned interest and clamped down on the butterflies in her stomach. Nervous. A movie misquote flew out of her mouth before she could stop it.

"Have you ever been stung by a dead bee?" Sara murmured, tracing one of the fat bees on the paper with her finger.

Miranda blinked and tilted her head. "Have you?"

Sara grinned. Miranda Vine knew Bogey and Bacall? "You're all right," Sara said.

Maybe there is more to Miranda than do-gooding and perfect grades?

Sara folded the paper carefully and slid it into her pocket. "I might be interested. You know, let me see how this week goes, and I'll get back to you. I'm a little worried about my course load. I don't want to overcommit."

Miranda nodded. "Gotcha. Think about it. I think you'd be great and really make an impact."

"Sure, thanks." Her? Make an impact? Uh. No... She'd beg off because of her chemistry labs later.

Turning to pick up her bag, Sara met Polly Worden's soft smile.

"Sara, a moment? We have your semester advisory still to finish."

Sara nodded. The advisory was routine, but time with Polly was precious.

"Great, I'll see you in ten minutes in my office."

Nine minutes later, Sara was in Polly's warm office. The same light from the nave flowed here, glimmers touching five metal sculptures that lined the large room. Lovely plants of all sizes perched on bookshelves, surrounding an informal seating group on one side and a glass desk. A carved stone water-wall stood in the corner, filling the room with a musical gurgle. A pillar candle burned at its base.

...a great cloud with fire flashing forth continually and a bright light around it, and in its midst something like glowing...

Sara puzzled out the words carved as a border on the water-wall. They seemed out of place. A quote about fire on a water feature. It didn't make sense, even with the candle.

She shrugged and took a seat in front of the desk, relaxing as she listened to the water.

Polly strode in two minutes later, dropping her bag under her desk. She plucked a file from a neat stack, slid on her glasses, and studied it, then removed her glasses and looked at Sara. She didn't speak.

Sara waited. She'd done this before. It was sort of like playing chicken. If she spoke first, the rest of the conference would not go well.

"What are you working on, Sara?"

Sara slipped large photo prints and sketches from her portfolio. "This is my latest design." The sketches depicted a large abstract form. It writhed and twisted, like a tornado in stone. It reminded her of a stalagtite born in a womb-like cave set free to dance. Glorious. Alive. Whirling. Dangerous. Detailed inset sketches revealed a polished surface broken by areas with a mottled texture reminiscent of bone. Pieces of metal skewered the form, as if it had been pinned down but had ripped itself free. Raw power pulsed from the mass. "It represents the earth and nature being affected by the work of man." She pointed to the metal rods and coils. "These shapes for a halo and fencing for the... I think of him as an earth elemental?"

Polly frowned at the photos. "They're good. It's good," she said. Her voice throbbed with unstated criticism. She paused and pursed her lips, pointing. "Glass?"

Sara nodded. She folded her hands to halt their trembling. "For parts like the hair. You think I should change it?"

It's not good enough.

I'm not good enough.

Polly gave her a level look and plucked another file from the stack in front of her.

"Sara, this is good, better than good, even. But it doesn't show me you. And for this year's practicum? I need to see you. Your grades from here forward will need to be exceptional if you want to graduate. We've made allowances because of your family circumstances, but your work has not been satisfactory. You know it. Were you listening to Bastien?

"I need to see your heart. The piece you are planning, while it fulfills your requirements...it's only adequate. Impersonal. For you to shine? You need more. You need to push yourself. And I believe—no, I know —you have more in you."

She slid the file across her desk at Sara. Within was a black-and-white sketch of a woman. Her form snaked, thin, elegant and beautiful. But her face was screaming. Frozen in pain of such abject agony, it was hard to look away. It wasn't like the Scream by Edvard Munch, not in the slightest. Munch's Scream was all organic shape and suggestion, the humanity leached from his figure, the power of his piece fueled by color. In contrast, the lack of bright color in this sketch made it more powerful. The details of the screaming woman's face and body were distorted by pain, but there was an immense power in her, and it underscored the horror of her circumstance. The details left no doubt of her personality, her clear personhood.

The throes of her pain struck Sara like a blow.

The piece was fantastic. It was Chantal's. Her name was in the top right corner. Sara looked at it for a long moment, unable to breathe. A single tear escaped her. She took a ragged breath, forcing herself. Another.

Stupid. Stupid. Stupid me. I can't. I'm not good enough. Oh my God, I suck.

"Are you okay?" Great. Just what she needed, to break down in front of Polly. The professor reclaimed the file folder, sliding it smoothly back to her stack.

Sara blinked rapidly. She forced a smile and unclenched her fist.

"I-I'm fine," she lied. Her voice was calm, at least. Sara reached for her bag and stood. "I understand. I'll rework my idea. I have to go now." She backed toward the door.

"All right." Polly waved Sara away. "Check in with me soon."

7

Lord Tabor Demitri, clad in a formal blue velvet surcoat trimmed and embroidered with silver thread, stood in his entrance hall receiving guests. He bowed over Lady Aracine's gloved hand. His cadence was clipped. His tone was nasal, in the most recent fashion of Bestuan dandies. "Milady, methinks you are a picture of unmatched elegance. And your dress!" He straightened and stepped back to take it all in. "Simply perfect."

Lady Aracine, an older woman, blushed and tittered behind her feathered fan. Her green silk gown, trimmed with seed pearls and lace, glowed in the ocean of candlelight. "You're too kind, Lord Demitri. I had it made special for this evening, of course. Your Spring Fête is the height of the season."

"My compliments to your dressmaker, madam." Tabor bowed again and clicked his heels together. Next to him, Lady Bronwyn Demitri, Tabor's younger sister, curtsied. Her heart-shaped face nodded, eyes sparkling, as she murmured appropriate compliments. Tabor played the noble fop to the hilt, always remarking on jewels and lavish attire with perfect empty-headed aplomb.

When the throng of guests had filed past, they filled the large ballroom beyond where a full chamber orchestra played. Hundreds of candles shimmered from candelabras while couples whirled across the polished parquet floors. Even the Watchers mounted at the central hearth were unusually beautiful, a gryphon poised to take flight sat next to a winged horse.

Tabor searched the large room. A crowd of giggling ladies

surrounded Bronwyn. He smiled indulgently. His sister shone like a gem among them, radiant. He spotted Trystan, arched an eyebrow, and nodded. As the ensemble played a pavane, couples lined up to dance the intricate steps. Trystan dodged a particularly buxom partner, excusing himself, and wandered over to Tabor.

"My dear Lord Tabor, you certainly know how to entertain." Trystan greeted him with a shallow bow.

Tabor smiled and returned his bow. This was the first time he had seen the bard in a moon. It was past time to show him what owning a starbound lute meant. It was well past time to bring him into the Spinners. "Well met, sir." He sniffed delicately into a lace-edged handkerchief and gestured to the musicians. "Have you found our players perform to your standard?"

"Indeed! They're all Bindery trained. I made their acquaintance at court last they played there but knew some of them from my classes. Prince Hector was very keen to have me directing when I finish my Journey," said Trystan.

A servant approached with champagne flutes. Trystan and Tabor both plucked one from the tray, turning to survey the crowd. Tabor asked, "Will you complete your Journey soon? You have just returned from Siarad? I daresay you look as though you tumbled from a cart." He tutted and brushed at Trystan's shoulder, as if dislodging a piece of straw.

Trystan nodded, flushing. He ran his hands through his cropped blond hair and shifted his belt around his richly embroidered tunic. "I'm nearly finished with my composition. Cyntae willing, I'll be performing it this month."

Tabor nodded. "I really must get you to my tailor," he said, waving his lace-trimmed sleeves. "You'll need to be presentable when you finally gain your gold ring. Everyone knows I have the best tailor, my ribands and silks are envied by all. We'll go tomorrow and see what new things he has in from the north. He's been bragging there will be some that mimic spun gold." Tabor paused significantly. "I'll have my man take us straightaway in the morning. So tonight you will sleep here. Bronwyn will be thrilled."

"Thank you, milord." Trystan bowed again. Tabor observed him closely to see if the lad caught his meaning. Gold. The word was a signal. It meant his lute was ready. Spinner business at hand. Little did Trystan really know what would be required of him. After tonight, he would understand. The ball was but a ruse.

"Enjoy the ball." Tabor dismissed him as he drained his champagne glass and handed it to a passing servant. He drifted off into the crowd, only pausing once to air-kiss a gaudily jeweled overweight matron.

Trystan wandered out of the ballroom, looking for a quiet place to wait. Tabor would send for him soon. He'd been to the manor several times in the months since he first met the baron, but the halls branched, and the many rooms still confused him. It was worse than the cavern halls of Mos Tevis. Watchers decorated the mantels of every room he entered, all of them elaborate and detailed. Finally, he found the library. He stepped inside, closing the oaken doors to shut out the revelry. A fire crackled cheerily. Above the mantel, the Watchers perched, inert. Trystan read some titles. The collection was massive, worth a king's ransom.

The Secrets of the Sea sat next to a copy of *Impossible Creatures from the Fells and Fenns*. *A Treatise on Resonance* was shelved with other esoteric philosophy. There were even books in other languages. He found a book of ancient maps and settled down to pore over it. The maps were rough, hand drawn on the lined vellum. They sketched the world before the Breaking, cities and towns now fallen to dust.

The roads were still there, though some were in ruins or had fallen into disuse. The Lohewelde was shaped very differently, and the Sundered City was whole. Citraehne, it had been called then. All the Aeries were clearly marked along with ten or twelve Burrows. Trystan was counting them and trying to relate them to the modern shape of the land when the library door burst open, and Tabor's sister fell in, laughing. A tall girl with elaborate brunette braids and a lavish purple gown followed close behind her.

Both girls approached Trystan with more decorum, curtsying formally, their eyes lowered. "Trystan dan Tenkor," Bronwyn murmured demurely. "Might I introduce you to my closest friend? She is known as Lady Gwyneth dePaul."

Trystan rose quickly and bowed over Gwyneth's gloved hand, only looking at her closely as he straightened. He gasped. "Stars above."

Tabor's eyes glittered back at him underneath artfully arranged brown tresses. His mustaches were gone, his chin close shaven, and his face painted so unless one looked very closely indeed, Tabor appeared to be a woman. He winked at Trystan and tittered, raising a glittering fan.

"Bronwyn has told me so much about you, milord." Tabor spoke in a voice that was rich and undeniably feminine. His eyes flicked to the Watchers and back, his meaning clear. Dissemble.

Bronwyn nodded. "I'm afraid Gwyneth's escort for the evening has had too much wine. I would insist that she stay here, but her only living aunt is very aged and will worry. Would you be a dear and escort her, ensure she gets to their estate safely?"

"Of course, milady." Trystan was at once the courteous prince. He glanced at the Watchers. Their heads now turned in his direction. Gallantly, he offered Tabor his arm. "But I must insist the beauty in distress pay me with a dance."

Tabor shook his head slightly, blinking, as he took Trystan's arm. Trystan gently led them back to the ballroom. "Oh no, I insist. It is so rare for me to meet a lady of such poise and refinement. I must have a dance."

Bronwyn looked both amused and relieved. "I'll leave you in Trystan's most capable hands then. Fare thee well!"

Trystan followed in her wake. He clasped Tabor lightly about the waist, an evil grin lighting his features.

"I'll step on your feet," hissed Tabor as they proceeded down the hall.

"You will not." Trystan steered Tabor to the dance floor. "This is happening, *milady*."

After a rather energetic set of courtly dances, Trystan finally relented and led his partner to the courtyard. A carriage awaited, and he helped "Lady Gwyneth" inside. He climbed in after, his expression bland. "Are you comfortable?" he asked, as the carriage lurched into motion.

"If I don't get out of this dress, I'm going to vomit," declared Tabor in his own voice, his expression black. He tore the wig from his head, revealing a bald pate. "Hand me the bag at your feet."

Trystan obeyed.

Tabor rummaged, producing comfortable sailor's garb, the costume he had been wearing when they first met. He kicked off large satin slippers and pulled on black trousers under his skirts, then presented his back to Trystan. "Unlace me."

Trystan clucked. "So forward, milady. We've only just met."

Nimble musician's fingers made quick work of the lacing. Trystan leaned back in his seat, entirely too pleased with himself.

Tabor only grunted in reply. He pulled the dress off, his muscled back flashing before he slid a fresh black undershirt over his head. A black tunic and belt followed, along with black boots. In the satchel he found a rag, a flute, a glowstone, a waterskin, and a hand mirror. Tabor poured a thin stream of liquid from the skin onto the glowstone. He took up the flute and played a quiet tune. The glowstone slowly began to shine as if lit from within by a flame.

Trystan watched with interest. "It's still unnerving, seeing you do that."

"What? Become a woman? Act a fool? I can't believe you made me dance. I will have my revenge." He soaked his rag with the same liquid from the skin and proceeded to scrub the paint from his face.

"No. I meant you use the Song like an acolyte." Trystan said. "We have glowstones in the Bindery, but cantors set them alight."

"I use the Song like a Spinner," Tabor said, correcting him. "Storm King willing, you will do the same. Tonight, we're going on a small quest to prove your mettle."

He reached into his bag and removed a kerchief, which he fashioned into a tight headwrap, covering his bald pate.

"My lute isn't here? I thought we were going to retrieve it." Trystan couldn't mask his disappointment.

"Patience." Tabor's tone was sharp. "While the nobles of Baehnt are occupied, we have an opportunity that needs seizing. The Lady Aracine has an unusual scroll in her library, and we are going to liberate it."

Tabor fished in his bag again, removing another black undershirt and tunic, along with a large coil of rope. "Here, put these on. I hope you can climb." He tossed the clothing to Trystan and flashed a broad grin.

Trystan sighed and began removing his finery. "I can climb well enough, I grew up in the mountains, remember? Large rocks. Climbing." He pulled the dark clothing on, his voice muffled by fabric as he asked, "What scroll?"

Tabor waited until Trystan's head emerged from the undershirt to answer. "Remember how I explained the Spinner's mission?"

Trystan nodded. "You're all maintaining a web formed with the

Song. The web feeds Songlines, which radiate from the World Tree. They carry power and grace throughout the kingdoms. I still don't understand how the Broken Song is safe to use." He sighed.

Tabor brushed this away. "I'll show you soon. For now, this is enough. We are working to combat Dissonance. We perform other tasks as well, but 'tis our most important purpose. It is dangerous, make no mistake. But worth it." He leaned forward. "The scroll we are going to retrieve was once housed at Anach, in the Tower."

Trystan whistled. "It's from the Majisterium?"

Tabor nodded. "Very rare and important to our mission."

Trystan nodded. "Just tell me what to do."

Tabor grinned again. "You're going to climb with me to the roof of the estate and keep watch while I retrieve the scroll. Simple enough."

"Do you know where we're going?" Trystan asked.

Tabor winked and leaned back to look out the window. "I know the estate well. Lady Aracine is, after all, my only aunt."

An hour later, the carriage stopped on the roadside, pulling off into a small grove of trees with enough underbrush to mask it from view. They slipped into the night, joining the driver and footman. Tabor spoke softly to each of the manservants, who nodded and faded into the shadows.

"They'll keep watch." Tabor gave a low call—*dubdubdub*—and received one back in return. "If the call sounds twice, we need to run."

Trystan nodded and took up a coil of rope. "How do we avoid Watchers?"

"We don't," Tabor said. "We'll need to be very quiet. There is no moon, we should be safe enough. If all else fails, I have a plan."

Trystan eyed Tabor until he explained.

"I have Conclave robes to don before climbing. If the Watchers report, they shall have a lowly acolyte to describe." Tabor whisked his kerchief from his head and assumed a pious position of prayer.

Trystan laughed and said, "You make a better cantor than woman."

Tabor hopped into the carriage driver's seat. He tossed down a leather satchel. "My tools," he said. "All right, let's go."

They slipped through the hedgerow and approached the manor from the west. House Aracine wasn't as impressive as Tabor's family estate, but it was large. There were no outer walls. Instead, it was protected by a moat. The drawbridge was down. They crossed quickly, keeping to shadows. The house loomed tall and menacing as they approached.

At the base of the manor. Tabor produced a grapple and tied it to the rope. He tossed it over the battlement, tugging to secure its grip. He scrambled up, hand over hand, bracing against the wall with his feet. In minutes, he was on the roof. Trystan followed.

Tabor coiled the rope and pointed to the tower. Trystan nodded, not daring to speak. The outline of a Watcher perched only fifteen feet away. It wasn't moving. Tabor threw on his robes and set off for the tower. Trystan settled down to listen and wait.

8

Sara struggled not to wither under her mother's Southern stare. Catherine Moore assessed her with a tiny mouth. *Bad sign.* "You're slouching," said her mother, crisply. "Sit up straight, you'll feel better."

Sara's palms sweated. She muttered. "No manners, just got no couth."

Her mother's eyes narrowed. The movie quote game Sara played pricked at Mom's half-healed wounds. Sara knew it. She didn't particularly care. *That's what she gets for judging me.*

"*Born Yesterday*? You're reaching deep."

Sara slowly drew her shoulders back. She kept her eyes on her plate. A salad. She hated salads. She also knew better than to order anything else when eating with her mother. *I will get through this lunch. I will be civil.* She stabbed a crouton. It flew off her plate, landing on the white tablecloth. Sara's mother granted her a level look. Violin music wafted through the restaurant, muffling the hum of other diners. Sara held onto it like a life preserver, willing herself to relax.

"How is school?" Mom said. Without waiting for an answer, she continued, "I've heard there is a new internship? Polly mentioned it at the last Women's Club meeting."

"It's fine, Mom. Great," Sara said. "I have a piece I'm preparing." You're checking on me. Awesome. I wonder what you tell Dr. Carol. The two women were friends.

"Good. Then you will graduate. Have you thought any further about your plans?"

Sara took a bite. They always had the same conversation. Every

71

week, lunch on Thursday. Every week her mother asked the same questions. She gave her standard answer. "I'm looking at grad school. I've been accepted to a few programs already. I plan to get a master's and teach."

"You know you could look at law. Or even medicine," Mom said. "These days a fine arts degree gives you so many options. It isn't like it was when I was in school. Back then, you had to have a degree in history or biology to enter one of those programs. Now you can have it all." Her perfectly penciled lips curved, aping a smile. "You should think about it."

"I've been thinking about it, Mother. I'm pretty sure I want to teach," repeated Sara. *Teaching is safe.* She fiddled with a leaf of lettuce.

Her mother continued as if she hadn't heard. "Marilla always thought you should go into medicine, you're so good with your hands. She said you could be a surgeon."

"I saw her yesterday," Sara said. "We're reading a Sue Grafton mystery. Did you know Sue is from Louisville?"

Her mom's mouth softened. She sipped water from a sparkling goblet. "I'm glad you're reading to her, Sara. But you mustn't get your hopes up. Focus on yourself right now. We must accept the pain life brings and do our best to move on."

"Yes, Mother." Sara kept her face a mask. Lunch was almost over. She only had to hold it together a little while longer.

"You know I love you both," Mom said. Her voice shook but did not break. She cleared her throat. "I'd give anything to help her. I've had the best specialists evaluate her. I've researched. I've done all I can do. We must keep living, Sara, for Marilla's sake. She would want that."

Sara saw the tears in her mother's eyes. She reached across the table, took her hand, and held it.

"I know I must seem demanding or cold. But the truth is holding it together is difficult. I'm doing my best."

Sara squeezed her hand. They sat in silence for a moment, joined by pain. *She misses her too. Maybe I'm too hard on her. Maybe...*

Mom coughed, releasing her, and shifted in her seat.

"Peter and I are going to a movie," Sara said. "Not a real date. But I'm going out."

"That's wonderful, Sara. He's a fine young man, a good person." Her mother genuinely warmed, seeming relieved to be talking about something as normal as boys.

Encouraged, Sara continued. "And I've decided to do that sleep study. Dr. Carol says it might be good. I'll be going for the weekend next month."

"University Hospital?"

Sara nodded. The violin music faded, and an orchestral piece began. Sara recognized it. "Fate: Allegro con brio."

"I know the attending on that unit. I'll give him a call and ask him to take special care of you."

"Thanks."

"If you went to medical school, you could end up working there," she said, smiling. "You never know."

Sara's temper flashed hot, their fragile camaraderie broken. *Mom just had to go there, had to keep pushing, keep dismissing her dreams.* She took a deep breath, keeping her voice even as she replied. "Mom. I love you. I know you mean well. I know you want what is best for me. Please hear me. I love my work. You have to stop pushing me. I love my studio. I understand I likely can't support myself as a sculptor full time, but I have ideas and dreams of my own."

Sara struggled to control her temper and lost. Her voice began to rise.

"I do not want to be a doctor. That was Marilla. Not me. She wanted to be like you. I'm Sara. Likely to end up a teacher, but I have to try to make it first. I need you to support me. Sara. My dreams." Her fist thumped the table, making the silverware rattle. Other diners looked in alarm, then looked away.

Her mother drew back, stung. Her face a mask, she said, "I know who you are, Sara. I raised both of you. You're just like your father with his cello. You with your art."

Sara stiffened. She was *nothing* like her father. "I'm surprised you could even tell the two of us apart. You were at the hospital working more than you were at home. You never saw me, you never heard me. You never heard Marilla...either of us...unless we said what you wanted.

"Marilla did. She was much better at pretending than I was, and you never really knew her. But even she could only fake it for so long. Perhaps if you or Dad had been home that night? If you had been there, Marilla wouldn't have nearly killed herself."

The words hung there, ringing through the room like a slap. The other diners were very quiet. Their waitress, who had been approaching with a smile, shook her head slightly and veered away.

Her mother's face was so pale. Everything was moving in slow motion. Her mother whispered, "Excuse me." She reached into her purse and placed cash on the table, rose, and with great dignity, looked down at Sara. There was no trace of warmth. "Selfish, just like your father." She strode away.

Sara's breath came in quiet shudders. She took a drink of water, her hands trembling. *That went well.* She rubbed the pendant Carol had given her, feeling the engraved words. Maybe it could keep her mother away.

She counted back from ten, letting her breath slow. She named the colors in the room. Brown table. White tablecloths. Blue walls.

She had actually held her ground, told the truth. Pete would be so proud. She signaled to the waitress.

"I'm going to need chocolate cake. The biggest slice you have. And coffee." Selfish, her mother called her. A folded neon-pink piece of paper thunked softly on the floor, falling out of her pocket. Sara bent to pick it up. A clip art butterfly perched on the page. Miranda's flyer. It must have gone through the wash. She slid it under the napkin on her plate for the waitress to take away. They'd throw it out.

An opportunity to make a difference, and I toss it in the garbage.

Sara covered the folded pink edges with her napkin to hide the paper. She pushed the plate aside and called Peter. It rang three times before he answered. "Pete, I need backup."

"Your mom again?" he asked.

"What else?" Sara picked at the cloth napkin. "I'm at Porcini's, come quick?"

"I'll be there in ten. Save me some cake."

Peter slid into her mother's chair, brandishing a fork. "I told you to leave some for me," he said, stabbing the cake and mercilessly scooping up the last bite. He chewed slowly, rolling his eyes in mock ecstasy and groaning.

"If you do a full-on Sally, I'm leaving," said Sara. Peter could reenact the famous diner scene from *When Harry Met Sally* on cue, especially if he thought it would make her laugh.

"Come on, Sara," Peter said, mumbling through cake. He swallowed. "I kill that scene."

"There are children here," Sara said, nonplussed. "But take me to

Joe's, and I'll wander with you." She needed to be in a happy place. A place with no pressure. She was still reeling from the fight with her mother but refused to show it. Not here. Not now. It would mean her mother might be right. Maybe she should give up her artwork. Make it a hobby. Sara wasn't about to explore any of that. She stuffed it away.

Peter was on his feet in an instant, keys in hand. "What are we waiting for?"

Joe Heye's was an antique store, six stories of Victorian madness where merry-go-round animals and life-size tin soldiers guarded vintage cupolas and gazebos. Wrought-iron ladies danced next to fanciful fountains, all just inside a tall fenced courtyard.

When you actually entered the building, time stood still.

Joe's was sacred space.

Several peacock-feathered headdresses from Vegas showgirl costumes lazed underneath a crystal chandelier. A flint arrowhead mounted in silver bore an intriguing label—Thunderstone. Sara barely saw them. She was in no mood for elegance today. She needed to be where the history was.

Remnants of other lives, fully lived, made Sara's problems seem manageable. Every object told a story, some hinted at heartbreak, like a torn and stained Victorian wedding dress. Some spoke of hope.

Sara grabbed Peter's hand and crossed the creaky wood floors. She took a right, then veered left down a ramp lined with life-sized carousel horses. Sara liked to linger and talk to each one. But today, she just wanted to lose herself in the otherworld depths of Joe's basement.

Sara didn't need to speak. She communed with the piles.

Peter didn't let go of her hand when they got to the bottom of the ramp. He laced his fingers through hers and walked with her. He waited. They meandered.

When Sara did talk, it was easier in the dim coolness. "It was bad this time."

Peter stopped. He leaned against a table, facing her and grabbed her other hand. He began swinging both gently in a calming rhythm. "I'm here."

Sara sighed, feeling tension seep out of her. "I told Mom that she never listened. I told her that she was lucky that she could tell the two of us apart. I told her that it was her fault, Dad's fault..."

And the tears started.

Peter pulled her into a bear hug. Sara relaxed and wept. She cried for Marilla, for herself, for her father, for the look on her mom's face, and for the chasm between them all.

Peter smoothed her hair, and when she snuffled, supplied a neatly pressed handkerchief. She accepted it, blowing her nose and pushing away from him. He was too close. "You must think I'm a mess. I should be over this by now."

"Bah," scoffed Peter, grabbing her chin and turning her face to look up at him. He looked her over, eyes twinkling. "I like you with your nose red and blotchy." He leaned in and planted a peck on it. "You're cute. Besides, if you weren't around, who would I impress with my handkerchiefs?"

Maybe it was the way Peter's hair flopped down in his eyes. Maybe it was that she felt so alone. Sara very much wanted to kiss Peter. She couldn't deny it, no matter how it scared her. Peter was more than her best friend. Sara felt herself moving forward. His eyes were so kind, and when he looked at her that way...

She stiffened, dropping her hands and took a quick step back. "I-I can't believe you iron them," she said. Sara held up the sodden white fabric like a shield between them. "I think I've ruined this one."

"Keep it." Peter hesitated, but claimed her hand again. He pulled her into the next section of the vast space. Huge shelves contained every sort of bottle and trinket from times gone by.

"How did your mom take it when you told her all that?"

He stepped carefully around a pile of magazines, leading her back around large wooden monkeys. A carved wooden palm tree leaned over the monkeys, daring them to climb.

Sara shoved the handkerchief in her pocket. "Mom left," she said. "It's her classic move, the one she's really good at."

"Is your dad home or gone?"

"He's in London, playing for some music festival. He'll fly home next week," Sara said. "It doesn't matter. When he's home, it's like he can't stand to look at me. I know it hurts. He sees Rilla. Heck, I see her when I look in the mirror. I think he and Mom might finally divorce, but she's too wrapped up in work to care that he's not around. They keep going, because it's easier than dealing with it."

Peter let go of her hand and faced her. "You ought to reach out to your dad."

Sara sputtered, but Peter held up a hand, halting the tirade he knew was coming. "Yeah, I know. Your dad was always gone. He found another girlfriend, hurt your mom. But they stayed together. You've told me. I've been here for you, remember?"

"He was never there when you needed him. And when Rick and Rilla broke up, Rilla nearly killed herself..." Peter didn't finish. "I get it. I do. I know you think it's their fault. But the thing is, they probably think that too. So tell your dad, talk to him. Yell at him, scream at him, have it out. Don't hold it in.

"You did great today, finally saying it to your mom. Make them talk to you."

Sara shook her head.

"You don't understand, that's not how my family works. Everything must be perfect. Everyone is doing great. Always. Problems? No, the Moore's don't have problems. If we do, we deal with them on our own. We don't argue. We don't ask for help, and we don't speak of anything unpleasant, especially in public." Her laugh was bitter. "I committed the unpardonable sin today. I made a scene. Mom probably won't ever speak to me again."

"I doubt that. But I do know that sometimes you have to fight with people to love them. Sometimes the love is the fighting."

"Well if that's true, I have the most loving and yet the most oddly hateful family on the planet." Sara shrugged. She looked into Peter's eyes, holding his gaze, her lower lip trembling. Sara backed away. In another moment she would kiss him. "Come on, we better go. I gotta work tonight. I'm okay now...and Peter? Thanks."

It would take half an hour to wind back through the maze. Sara's hoodie caught on a gargoyle that loomed on a shelf, bringing her up short as she tried to escape. She unhooked herself from its stone fingers. "Race you to the ramp," she called behind her, and took off running. She laughed as he clomped at her heels, cursing when he bumped into a sharp corner.

"I'll catch you yet, Sara Moore," he yelled. "You just wait and see. I don't give up."

Sara burst into her apartment and threw her keys on the side table in the entryway, shimmying her boots off as she half ran to answer the phone. Jane had a night class on Thursdays; she wasn't there to get it. It could be the long-term care home. She nearly yanked the thing off the wall.

"Hello?" she answered, out of breath.

A rich bass voice on the other end said, "Sara? Honey, is that you?"

"Hi, Dad." Sara slumped into a kitchen chair. Of course it was him. She forced herself to try, but couldn't resist a dig. "How's tricks?"

"The performance sold out, if that's what you mean," he replied, his voice gaining an edge.

Awkward.

"Great, Dad, that's really great. And you'll be home next week?"

"I will. Listen, your mother asked me to speak to you. I don't have much time. We have decided to move Sara from the Nero facility to that long-term care place on the East Coast where she will be more comfortable. It's better suited for her condition. The costs will be manageable."

"Marilla, Dad. You've decided to move Marilla." Sara was proud of herself for not shouting. "I'm Sara. I'm here, you're talking to me. The person in the bed who doesn't move or speak? She looks like me, but she is my twin sister, Marilla."

Sara's voice rose in pitch and volume as she continued, "I know you haven't seen her in six months, but our names have not changed. Her condition has not changed. I have not changed, other than I do speak and move. I hear you loud and clear. You want to move Marilla to a place fourteen hours away, where she won't remind you of how you have failed us.

"Mom was a coward for not telling me herself today, she could have. She hid it. She knew. That's a lie. She lied to me. You guys are not moving her!"

Now Sara really was shouting, but she didn't care.

"I have to go," he said.

She was shaking. A click on the other end of the line. Typical. He would deposit money in her bank account next week, the latest in a long line of guilt gifts.

Somehow, her dad thought money would undo every mess he made. It never did. Sara pulled Peter's handkerchief from her pocket and wiped her eyes. She looked at the linen square, tracing his monogrammed initials with her thumb. Then she took a deep breath.

Sara named the colors in the room. She took more slow breaths, counting back from ten. She waited for the shaking to stop. Slowly, she got up and wandered into her room, pulling on sneakers and a hoodie. She had to get to work.

I refuse to waste tears on Dad, she thought. *Him or Mom, either one, they're not worthy.*

Sara went to the sink, splashed water on her face, and filled a glass. She took a long drink. She named the colors in the room. She took ten more deep breaths. She could do this. She could pull herself together. Go to work. Act normal. She could be strong. Not fall apart.

But what was she going to do about Marilla?

9

About a quarter of an hour passed before Trystan spied Tabor, running. His white robes flopped open, revealing black garb underneath. Tabor's bald head shimmered with sweat.

Trystan watched, mystified as Tabor stopped in the middle of the roof, pulling a tunebell and a small flute from his satchel. He began to play. The scent of the bloom wafted into the night. The tunebell chimed softly. The Watcher tracked Tabor. "Identify yourself."

The Watcher's voice reminded Trystan of rocks falling down a hillside.

Trystan hoped desperately it had not woken any servants or house guards—or worse.

The flute's gentle lilting filled the air. Trystan tore his eyes from the gargoyle and watched Tabor. *What was he playing?*

Tabor played peace. He played joy. He played a soft gentle breeze and a cool springtime sky filled with stars. He played birdsong. He played children's laughter and a message. *All is well. All is well. All is well.* Soft starlight coalesced around him. Trystan could see it shimmer in the air, forming a web.

The Song.

The Watcher turned away.

Tabor kept playing for a few more minutes and let the tune fade. He slipped out of the acolyte's robes, stowing them in his satchel and threw down the rope, hitching his bag over his shoulder. He shimmied down. Trystan followed. *Tabor just used the Song with an enchanted instrument, only this time he controlled a Watcher. What else could he do?*

Trystan could almost feel Tabor brooding. The carriage rumbled along the road, creaking and swaying, with Tabor huddled in a corner. They hadn't exchanged more than a few words since escaping the manse.

Finally, Trystan could stand it no longer. "You acquired the scroll?"

Tabor looked up, as if surprised he was not alone.

"What? Oh, yes. It might be more valuable than we originally thought."

"And the Watcher didn't rouse an alarm. We're safe then."

"Safe? Safe?" Tabor gestured to the widow. "No, I only delayed the hunt."

"I don't understand. The Watcher turned away. We escaped."

"The Watchers in the Lady's quarters saw me. There's no doubt it raised an alarm even though I wore these robes. When I played the flute, I only interrupted them.

"They will be...questioned...regardless. My features may be examined. If a chymaera investigates, it will see what occurred through the Watcher's eyes. I could be identified. However, if only a Conclave monitor investigates? They will receive only something like a sketch, not much more. My chances improve much if chymaera are not involved." He sighed. "I just hope they are all otherwise occupied."

Trystan exhaled, leaning forward. "The chymaera work with the Conclave. They did in Bestua as well, but I wasn't sure they did everywhere."

Tabor nodded, his face a grim mask. In the dappled moonlight, Trystan saw it only in flashes. "What do you know of them?"

"Not as much as I'd like to know. We've collected lore over the centuries. The shape-shifters themselves say very little when they are among us. No matter how anyone tries, they get little information. That's why we must liberate pertinent documents." He pointed to his satchel. "In every city, chymaera come and go, working with the Watchers, Takers, and Speakers. Rumors persist of skycarts, but I don't know if 'tis true."

Trystan nodded. "I met a few. They would come in to use our library but were always silent. I've heard rumors they are feared by country folk."

"More revered than feared," said Tabor. "If a chymaera is threatened, of course it can transform and rip you to pieces. So would you attack one?" He raised an eyebrow at the idea. "Even the lowest, most base of men hesitate to try. There have been reports of a few bravos starting a fight, but not one ends well for the man."

Tabor looked out the carriage window. They were moving along the outskirts of Baehnt now, passing ancient crumbling ruins. They passed the city gates and headed southeast. Tabor looked at Trystan, his gaze somber.

"I'll ask the chymaera, when I present this scroll, if I was identified."

Trystan's mouth dropped open, but for once he was speechless. His mind whirled. "You retrieved the scroll for the chymaera? But they don't work with men outside the Conclave. I thought they despised us."

"Some do," Tabor said. "We retrieved the scroll for our own archives, but yes we're allowing a chymaera to borrow it. You'll meet him soon enough," Tabor said. "Lady Aracine would never relinquish one of her precious artifacts without inconvenient questions. The theft couldn't be helped."

Trystan shook his head, marveling.

"What? Spinners have important work to do. It isn't all galas and thievery." Tabor pulled a black tricorn hat from under his seat, placing it jauntily on his head. His voice slurred, his posture relaxed, and he took on the mannerisms of a common sailor. "Aye, sirrah. 'Twill be a daisy morn, it will. Buck up milord, yer gettin' yer shiny stuffing right enough."

"Stuffing?"

Tabor straightened, speaking again in his true voice, "Stuffing means contraband. In this case, your lute. We speak in a cipher, the Spinner's Cant. You'll learn quickly. We have a lot of training to do, but you've passed your first tests with flying colors."

Trystan's eyes narrowed as they rolled up to a warehouse.

"Tests?" Trystan said. Nothing made any sense. He shook his head, refusing to be put off. He had joined in with Tabor's mad errand without question, trusting it would all come clear. Instead, he only had more questions.

"Of course. You didn't think we were just going to let you buy a truly starbound lute and waltz away with it, did you? You'd be captured or killed, or both, within a week. No. We watched you for a while, then offered you a small mission. Now your training begins in earnest. You didn't panic. You kept your head, avoided the Watchers. You followed instructions. Trusted me. You did well. In particular, the bit of fun you chose to have at my expense. Making me dance." Tabor chuckled and adjusted his hat.

"You're not the ugliest I've had to partner."

"It was well done. Quick thinking. If any had suspected us, it would put them off our game. And you made my sister laugh."

Trystan's lips twitched. "Glad to be of service."

The carriage slowed. Tabor's shoulders relaxed, and he sank back into his sailor persona, opening the carriage door to clamber out. Tabor pivoted and affected a sweeping bow.

"Congratulations, milord, you have officially become an apprentice Spinner."

Trystan entered the half-timbered warehouse via a side door, passing large wooden shelves and racks. Barrels and crates rested in neat rows. Tabor held the glowstone aloft. In one corner, wooden stairs led up to a loft area. Tabor stopped before the stairs and asked Trystan, "What do spiders regret?"

Trystan thought a moment, recalling the lyrics. "Mercy. They regret mercy."

"Remember it. 'Tis the greeting we exchange. By this, we know each other."

The wooden stairway flipped upward, revealing another passage that descended underneath. Tabor led the way down. The staircase dropped into place behind them. They descended a short flight of steps and reached a landing. Tabor stopped and looked up. There, perched on a high shelf, was a small man. He waved jauntily and winked.

"That's Seth, guarding the door today. You'll meet him later," said Tabor. He returned the wave and continued down the stairs. "The Spinners' main nest is here in Baehnt. We have others throughout the Weldenlands. Baehnt was built on top of another, far older city, destroyed in the War during an earthquake. However, a few comforts survived. We have put them to good use."

They turned down two more flights of stairs. As they descended the third, Trystan smelled the sea. The stairs opened into a massive landing that gave way to a vaulted chamber. Buttresses fluted into branches like trees. Between these flutes, the vaulting formed lacy and intricate lines that interconnected in the pattern of a spider's web. Marble floors stretched underneath, while hundreds of glowstones flickered from sconces on every pillar and wall. Rows of tall wooden shelves filled most of the huge expanse, filled with books and scrolls. Individuals moved among the shelves and shadowed arches led out of the large chamber.

"This must honeycomb half the city. The spider spun a home, indeed," breathed Trystan. "It's amazing."

Tabor nodded agreement. "There are tombs as well, at deeper levels. We believe the majisters reinforced this structure with the Song, which is why much of it held up. Portions have collapsed, but we managed to dig out and reclaim many. All of this was once under the protection of the Majisterium. The Conclave mimics their old structure in a way."

Tabor flashed a smile and beckoned for Trystan to follow. He strode along the edge of the cavernous room to the nearest arch and turned down a wide corridor. They passed several closed doors before he stopped. They entered a sizable room, furnished with thick carpets and overstuffed furniture.

Tabor flopped in an upholstered chair with a sigh and pointed to the settee.

"Now, tell me what you have been doing on your trips to Siarad."

"I've been getting to know the guards. High King Tenneth rotates them every few weeks, but I've made a few acquaintances and have learned more regarding the Cursed City's local customs, about the Caprices and their oracles. I've been working on my composition as I can. The path from here to Siarad, through the Puzzlewood, grows darker each time I take it. Shadowkin. I feel them even when I can't see them. I'm Forge-bred yet have little songsteel. If they attack me en masse, I'll not survive."

Tabor pursed his lips. "You of all people should have a songsteel blade. They're made in the Forge."

Trystan winced. *If only you understood. We are desperate.* "I have one I do not use. It is irreplaceable. The Forge has been unreliable at best for the past few years. The blades they sell are made at a much higher cost. Pelegor is simply fortunate there have been no massed attacks. Since the steel degrades when used, they've focused more on producing arrowheads, throwing knives and spears, less on making swords.

"The last message I received from father said the Forge had gone completely cold."

"What does that mean?" asked Tabor.

"It means that the songsteel we have is all we will *ever have* unless the Forge can be relighted. It means Pelegor could be overrun with Shadowborn. Everyone dead. It means the Weldenlands and the world, are likewise vulnerable. Without dewin, without songsteel, we are completely reliant on the Conclave for defense against all the forces of Dissonance. Shadowkin. The other monsters and Shadowborn. Goblins and the like."

Tabor shuddered. "A grave problem, indeed," he said.

Trystan nodded. "Father was sending an envoy to the High King and to the Tree to see if any solution could be found or even an explanation given. He believes the songlines have been blocked in some manner. The songlines radiate from the World Tree to send power to the Forge. Its flame cannot be sustained apart from them. A lordling from Perrhil named Gisle de Clelland visited and seems to have influenced his thinking."

Tabor snorted. "As well he might—de Clelland can be most emphatic and persuasive. He travels the breadth of the world with a small army, hoping to convince any who might listen of his views. High King Tenneth allows it. I believe he enjoys tweaking the arch cantor's nose.

"Gisle believes the Conclave to be corrupted beyond imagining. He is correct, unfortunately."

Trystan settled back against the settee. "How do you know that?"

Tabor stood, retrieving the scroll they had stolen the night before. He unrolled it and began to read aloud.

My dear Petros,
Your last message was heartening. We know Modric conspires to shift the Song into Dissonance and rewrite the Lorica. Your work is vital, preserving the Song in its true form. Starlight carries our hope. Guard the aural nexus, guard the Lorica, and carry on. I will come to you soon, but I fear things are worse than we first understood. Remain vigilant.
-Jamis Ivor

Trystan's eyes widened. "Jamis the Wise?... the famous majister? One of the locals I spoke to in Siarad mentioned him. He said his ancestor saw Modric and Jamis enter a skycart on the day of the Breaking. They flew to the Tree together. I assumed Jamis perished in the battle, but this..."

Tabor said, "Jamis and his assistant, Petros, suspected Modric well before the War. It was Jamis who set the Spinners to their tasks, while Petros created a web of starlight to preserve the pure Song. Something about starlight having originated in the past made it work.

"Our most sacred lore is only spoken, a strict rule. We need pieces like this one"—he pointed to the scroll—"to convince those outside our ranks. They do not wish to believe in such treachery from Modric."

Trystan understood all too clearly. "The chymaera don't want to accept Modric has betrayed everyone and conspired with the Wyrm to create Dissonance."

Tabor shook his head. "They do not. They trusted him after the War, you see, and they trust him still. We have men like Gisle de Clelland who wish to reject the Song completely in their hatred for the Conclave. So he rejects all the Conclave represents, even the cyntae and the Song. If the Song is not restored, if Dissonance is not held back and even reversed, all is lost."

"If what you say is true, the Bindery is also compromised."

Tabor shook his head. "Perhaps not. Nearly everyone was deceived. They are not evil, just misguided. The songlines spring from the Tree's root system. If the Tree dies, they fail.

"After the War, Modric remained. Only Modric, the last majister, full of answers. He rescued us, gave us the Arcanum. And what did he tell us?"

"He said the Storm King sacrificed himself on the Tree to save us. The Wyrm is held captive beyond the door of the moon, and the cyntae sustain the Song in place of their master, carrying on his work. They sustain life, the Song, and all worlds beyond," said Trystan.

"And we must join them by Canting. And so the arc of the moon became the most holy sign of our faith. We Cant morning and evening to strengthen the cyntae and hold back the Wyrm. Strengthen the Song. As if we could. The faithful and devout attend Camber each Moonday. Dewin are captured lest they kill as they did before. Instruments that wield the Song are forbidden and songflowers are sanctioned." Tabor's eyes flashed. "All power has been given to the Conclave. All based on lies, creating more and more Dissonance. As each lie begets more lies and the false Canting rises, the Dissonance grows. Now we give our devotion to the cyntae, an abomination. The only cyntae who appears? Doran, the Lesser."

Tabor fell silent. Trystan mulled his words over. A suspicion, like an itch, formed within him. It burned, turning to horror as he grasped the truth. Modric had lied about everything. Modric could not be trusted.

Modric was trying to destroy everything. With Doran?

Tabor nodded as if Trystan had spoken aloud. He continued. "The Storm King is alive. Cyntae do not visit the Aeries as they once did.

The cantors say they cannot, kept from us by their work. I know otherwise. The Lorica was not destroyed, but hidden for safekeeping. The Song can be restored, the Shadowborn driven back. The Storm King shall return. In the meantime, we Spinners must play the true Song. That is our purpose. The Conclave will do anything to stop us. We are the defense, the only true defense, against the Dissonance."

Trystan straightened. "My sword and my lute are at your service," he said.

Tabor bowed from the waist, accepting his pledge. "Your studies shall take place here. You shall have what you seek. We will train you in the use of the pure Song, and our good luthier will provide you with your own lute. In the meantime, you may train with our instruments."

Tabor removed his flute from his waistcoat, waving it at Trystan.

"Your lessons begin now."

10

Dane stared at the lute. It had taken most of the day to finish. The wood gleamed, ready to receive its final coats of varnish. The inlay was a wonder.

Last night under the stars, with the scent of Essence strong in the air, he had unrolled his father's scroll, reading the verses within, yet again. He'd listened to the rhythms of the wind, heard his own heartbeat.

He had listened for the Song. It came when he called, and he sang the tune he heard in his heart. He sang those ancient words, over and over. As he continued, starlight shimmered and solidified, forming a web. Dane had rested the lute carefully within this cradle.

Where the light kissed the wood, it coalesced. It pooled, glowing ever brighter until he had to look away. He kept singing, and the light did its work. Fae had flickered, flashing. Their shapes glistened. Some had smiled, others crinkled their brows in confusion or dismay. They had noticed him. Like flames, they shifted and were gone.

When it was over, curving shapes wrapped the instrument. The shapes shimmered, like mother-of-pearl. Only he and Pezzik knew the truth.

Starlight, pure and pale, had fused with the Song, transforming into a solid material that wrapped and climbed the neck. It would imbue the tone with a strange sweetness. All music from this lute would ring with the Song itself. Under certain conditions, it would become capable of mighty power.

Conclave luthiers could mimic his work with their crafting, but never equal it.

It had been foolish to worry he'd need extra supplies. His binding had taken hold, just as it had for Pa.

Chance, Dane's dog, slept at his feet. Dane whistled as he applied the Essence varnish. It was one of the things Pa had first let him do. Dane grinned, thinking of the first time his father had let him witness a binding. His mind clouded with more memories. It always did when he worked so much with starlight. Starlight was pure memory.

Visions from his childhood drowned the present.

His mother cautioned him to not speak or ask any questions. She led him past garden hedges, Chance at his heels. The northern terrace edged the rear stone wall. Built high and strong, it was a shield against any danger in the wood. But if you walked through the barred wooden door in the wall, toward the forest, on the other side was a wide stone platform. An eight-sided pool glistened in its center, reflecting the night sky

The web formed from starlight. His mother, Maggie, held Dane's hand while Pa recited. Dane focused on the glimmering web and the fae.

Mother answered his questions.

"We live on the edge of the grove away from prying eyes. The stories you learn are not the ones any other folk know. You can never ever speak them until you have a child, not even to Poll. Others do not see fae as you do. You are dewin and shall have a very long life. No one can ever know. Dewin are feared and misunderstood."

Dane blinked as the vision faded. Despite all he had known about the long life of dewin, his father and mother had died of a sudden unnatural fever last year. He could not heal them. That failure stalked him daily. Dane's training hadn't been complete. Now he was tentative. Careful. Pezzik could fill in many gaps. Today, working with the Song, Dane was groping his way along the edge of a cliff, unsure and about to plummet. He had so many questions. *Storm King, have mercy. Help me.*

Tears ran down his face. He wiped them away as he finished sealing the lute and was shocked to see the shimmer of a fae. It was the girl again. He frowned.

The same girl had floated near the kitchen hearth. He'd seen her many times now. She was always more distinct than the rest of them. She didn't flicker away. She hovered, watching him. Dane kept working, drawing the octagonal Sign over the lute with his hands while he sang the refrain again.

The Dark One ascends,

Eight shall turn him round...

His voice chimed as he sang, the words of the Lorica ringing in the air like bells. Dane saw the octagon he had marked out glow in the air and rise. He hadn't slept. Could he be asleep now? The Sign drifted to the fae, like a smoke ring made of light. It surrounded her in a halo of color.

The fae stiffened. She solidified, no doubt about it. Color from the Sign seeped into her at the edges of her form. She no longer shimmered. She looked at Dane in wonder. She saw him. Finally, she spoke with a broad accent.

Chance whined and pricked his ears.

At first her words made no sense.

"Small choices shall rule large kingdoms as the Day draws ever near. Do not lose hope. The jackdaw shall linger, and the storms shall begin. Each shall flee to his place. Your work does matter. Do not give up. Do not falter. Those below shall be as above. Shadows will fall across fen and glade and forest. The game is not a game. A tiny word can move a seeker toward his doom..."

The words trailed off, and the fae stretched as if she were waking. She focused on Dane.

"Why do you glow?" she said.

Melody spilled out behind her voice, barely there. Chimes infused her words, filling him with peace and joy. The Song.

Dane set his brush down, swallowing the knot in his throat. Grounded. This fae was grounded. She was here, physically. Flesh. She could interact with him. Dane wasn't sure exactly what he had done. Was it... the sign and the verse together with the Essence? Flame it all. He would have given anything to have his Pa there.

He answered in hushed tones. "You see my heartfire, milady. What is your name?"

He gulped, reaching for anything his father had ever mentioned about grounding fae. Only done by majisters or those beginning a Harmony Bond. The creature's name was important in old fae tales. If he knew its name, it could not harm him.

"Sara," she said, without hesitation. She was watching him, her eyes wide in a small face. "That is lovely." She nodded at the lute. "Do you play?"

Dane froze. Playing a starbound instrument was perilous for dewin. He knew how to play, of course. He'd been taught from childhood on a normal lute, the battered instrument in the corner.

This was a grounding. He dared not deceive the fae in any way.

"I cannot, milady," he said. "Its varnish is still wet."

"Oh!" She jumped back, startled. She stiffened, and her face went slack. *"Knock, knock, he is coming. Fire. Fire everywhere. Run."* Sara's eyes widened in horror. The melody wafted toward him, intensifying, making it difficult to understand her words.

The fae vanished, leaving only dust motes drifting in the afternoon sunlight, dancing to the far-off trill of birds. A jackdaw cried. He sat, varnish forgotten. *Run? Who was coming?*

Chance nuzzled his hand.

"You're right, boy," Dane said.

"Pezzik!" Dane yelled. "Help!" He sprang into action, hastily gathering up the supplies. The fae had warned him. He had to hide everything. *Now.* True, it could mean nothing.

Dane would not take chances.

The gnomemother popped out of the wall and assisted without a word of fuss. She removed a large tile from the floor, threw a short ladder down, and scrambled to receive the jars and bottles Dane passed her. Pezzik placed the tools and Essences into the room-like space. She flashed in and out of the stone itself, alternating between catching items and carrying them through the stone.

A special shelf for drying claimed the instrument. Dane clambered down and placed the lute himself. It needed at least eight hours to cure before he could move it again. He hoped fervently he would have the time. His father's box with its ancient scroll went next to it. He scrambled back up the ladder and repositioned the tile. Dane pulled levers, and his furniture transformed, back into a cabinet maker's shop. This finished, he ran to the garden.

What Dane needed to do worked best in starlight. But no, the light was waning; it was only late afternoon. It would be hours before full night.

He'd never cast a glamour. Pa had explained it at length. "The secret," Pa had said, "is to imagine how the scene looks. Hold it steady in your mind. You cannot for a moment waver, and you cannot be distracted. Inhale the flower's scent. You will feel the Song, its power and strength moving through all things. The refrain releases the Song. The image in your mind will hold."

Some fae could cast like breathing. For dewin, it was dangerous. He could draw attention from the wrong type of eyes. Shadowborn. Much of what he knew was only theory.

Dane looked at his garden, its careful rows of flowers. They were all flowers he needed to make his lutes. Each one possessed a delicate auric nexus, a Virtue, prized for its energy.

Not long after his first binding, Dane's father had given him a painting of the garden, planted with ordinary vegetables and herbs. His mother had painted it.

"Look," he said. "Look long, until you can call up this image, every detail, in an instant."

And Dane had looked. He had looked at it for hours over the years until every line was familiar. He brought a tunebell to his nose and inhaled. He exhaled as he imagined the scene and rotated it in his mind. He saw it from every angle. He let his senses expand and heard the Song. It thrummed in the wind's whisper, the call of the birds and the whirring of insects. He joined them, singing the melody as it formed in his mind.

The Dark One ascends, Eight shall turn him round

The scene transformed. The light curved.

The garden was normal. It mirrored his painting. Shadows fell from the house, bees humming. Dane wanted to crow. He wished he could show his Pa. Dane's longing for his parents swelled. But he had no time to wallow. Slowly he turned, slipping the flower into his sleeve, and headed for the kitchen and the main hearth.

He didn't make it to the fire before two raps at the door came.

Pezzik plucked the tunebell from his sleeve and thrust it into the stone wall next to him, her face placid. "You can't burn such, boy, it will fill the house with scent, then where would we be?"

11

Dane jerked the door open. Jax stood with Aric, a horse hitched to the post behind them. Chance wriggled past Dane, running to greet the horse.

"Dane," Jax nodded and pushed past him into the small entry. He hefted Dane's satchel over his shoulder and dropped it before continuing to the kitchen. Aric stepped in behind the gnome, stamping his feet.

"I'm on my way to the Heyegrove, and Jax offered to introduce me to the Burrow. He said you had left your satchel behind, and this was on the way."

"Of course. Welcome, welcome," Dane said. "I think Jax has already found Pezzik, but we'll be more comfortable in here." He glanced at his dog, still inspecting the new horse. He shook his head at Chance's hospitality and closed the door.

Dane led the way to his sitting room. A massive stone fireplace welcomed them with a cozy fire. A chandelier illuminated a framed map above the hearth. Upholstered chairs, a small lamp table, and a bench crafted by his grandfather were scattered about. Shelves lined one wall, displaying paintings collected over four generations along with no small number of books. A thick bearskin covered the stone floor. A spinning wheel idled in a corner.

Dane chose his favorite chair while Pezzik bustled in carrying mugs, trailed by Jax. She pushed a mug into the bard's hand before handing one to Dane.

Pinning Jax with a stern look, she announced, "Dinner will be ready soon, and in the meantime, ale should refresh you. There will be pie after. I do not need any help." Pezzik's cap quivered. With a flounce, she returned to the kitchen.

Jax settled himself in one of the smaller chairs and chuckled. "Your Pezzik is a treasure," he said. "Her pies have no equal."

Dane agreed. "I'm sure she'll feed us well to thank you for your kindness. Though I must say, you didn't have to bring my satchel all the way here. I planned to come for it tomorrow."

"Bell thought you'd need it. She was surprised you left so sudden."

Jax's flat look spoke volumes.

Dane gulped his drink to stall for time. *Storm King, help me.* "I discovered my shipment needed to leave earlier than planned. I had to hop to finish, so I panicked." He flashed his best apologetic smile. "I barely made it, but I did complete the job."

Jax nodded, satisfied. "You'll still likely want to bring a gift to Bell when you come to town. A pie perhaps." His eyes glittered. Dane laughed.

"Did you make all of this?" Aric gestured to the furniture.

"My family made most of it, my father, his father. I've made some. Our family has lived here for generations."

"It's fine work, I can see why nobles order from you."

"The Guild usually orders," Dane said. "I know where the pieces are bound. But they handle sales and shipments and take their due. It makes my work a bit easier. Direct orders can be demanding. The forests here source the finest wood. Crafting here before shipping downriver means a finer quality piece, provided they are well crated."

"And your varnishes?" Aric stroked the wood of his chair. Dane forced himself not to stiffen. *Is he probing to see if I have Essences?*

"I make them," he said.

"Beautiful."

"You're bound for the Burrow?" Dane asked Jax.

"Aye, and I had hoped to make it by nightfall. I met a squirrel on the road who said bears are hunting..." the gnome trailed off.

"You will stay here," Dane said. "You can't travel or camp in the forest at night. That's settled."

"The bears would not bother you?" Aric asked.

"No," said Jax. "They honor gnomes. Most forest folk do, and I could ask them to leave us both alone, but this wood shelters more than bears." The gnome's face was grave. "Best not to risk it. If bears are a-hunting, dark things will be abroad. We need to avoid traveling at night. I could descend," he pointed to the stone below their feet, "but you could not."

Pezzik rattled dishes in the tiny dining room. Dane stood and excused himself. "I'll go ready your rooms and see to your horse."

The cottage sprawled with five bedrooms, the workshop, and a barn. Though in truth, one room was tiny, little more than a closet, only used for storage. Dane's great-grandfather had added on two rooms because he'd sired five children. They were mostly unused, but Dane walked back and aired them out.

He quickly dusted and checked the chamber pots. Dane fetched and carried ewers to the pump for water. Chance had finished with the horse and reappeared, trotting at his heels. Dane filled the ewers and placed them in the rooms with matching bowls and clean linens. He tried not to worry about the lute. The bard would be their guest for the night. He hurried to stable the mount.

Dane returned to see Pezzik ushering the guests into their dining room. A small feast was arranged there. The aromas made Dane's mouth water. Bowls of carrots, peas, beans, parsnips, and tiny potatoes nestled next to a wooden block. It held a huge roasted mushroom. A large wedge of cheese, a steaming loaf of bread, and saucers of creamy butter completed the meal.

"Thank you for all this, Pezzik," Dane said, settling into his chair. For Aric's benefit, he blessed the food. "Lord of All, bless these gifts which we are about to receive from thy bounty." Their visitor would assume he addressed Domini, rather than the Storm King himself. Dane dug in.

"This is delicious," Aric said, eyes wide with appreciation. He passed butter to Jax, who perched on a high stool.

Pezzik blushed, her cap bending in pleasure at the compliment. Aric said, "I really must thank you for your hospitality."

"Nonsense." Dane dismissed his thanks with a wave. "We rarely have visitors, and 'tis a welcome change. You can give us a song after dinner, 'tis thanks enough."

Pezzik brightened at the mention of music. Her fork clinked against her plate.

"I'd be most grateful for some of your stories," said Aric. "Gnomes are uncommon outside this region. I know a few tales, but I'm finding reality to be much different."

Jax sniffed, raised his bushy eyebrows, and cleared his throat.

"Different?"

"They say you're twelve inches high and live in underground tunnels. You ride dogs or cats like we ride horses and can speak to every animal. You sing like cyntae."

Jax blushed and coughed.

"And you never sleep. You can travel through earth and stone. You live a thousand years and carry babies away in your caps."

Pezzik snorted. "Most of us are closer to three feet tall, not counting our caps. Some are smaller, and of course our babes are very small."

"We rarely ask an animal to carry us. 'Tis a children's game. Adults prefer small ponies. Our Burrows aren't caves." Pezzik's lips thinned, and she drew herself up, indignant. "They're very comfortable homes, as comfortable as this cottage. They're connected by tunnels, built in a ring. There is a central Burrow-Moot where the community works and feasts."

Jax said, "We can speak to most woodland animals, though bears aren't particularly friendly. It's the bees, you see. They want the honey, but we guard hives. Makes 'em terrible angry. Birds just chatter nonsense, but we get along."

"We do sleep, but not as men do. We sleep once a month for a full day. And we carry nothing in our caps you would be able to see, other than perhaps seeds. Certainly not human children. We enjoy music, but most of us know many crafts," Pezzik said. "The rest is true enough."

"How and why do you choose deemling?" Aric asked. "I've found nothing recorded."

Pezzik shifted on her stool and grew very still. The pause stretched, uncomfortable. Dane's face warmed, embarrassed. It was an intimate question, surely the man understood?

"I'm sorry," Aric said, "I mean no offense."

Pezzik bowed her head, accepting his apology. She answered, looking into his eyes. "Tradition."

Aric met her gaze and held it.

"I am an Order Bard," he said. "I was tested at a young age, brought to Bestua, trained at the Bindery. After, I trained with the cantors. I serve now within the Bindery. I'm studying rituals and traditions of other races." Aric paused, pursing his lips as if weighing his words.

"When the Majisterium fell, more was lost than just majisters and their wonders. We lost understanding of many peoples. Some fear it will never be recovered. I'm doing my part to gather it again."

Dane exhaled. *Then why was he looking for the lute?*

Pezzik took a small bite of her cheese, chewing in contemplation. "Conclave rules protect us, eh? Anyone with a musical knack, like you," the gnome nodded at the bard, "is tested and trained. Some serve the Conclave all their lives and some go on to entertain or teach, not touching the Broken Song." Pezzik's eyes rested on Aric, watching for reactions. "Am I correct in my Arcanum?"

Aric leaned forward. "The bardic calling doesn't encompass studying the Broken Song. Most perform. Some are archivists, some build and repair instruments. Bards who work with the Song take Arcane vows." His smile was self-deprecating. "A few of us travel."

Jax said, "A deemling is chosen by rhythm. Deemae are chosen, you would say, at random. The choice is in our rhythm."

"Gnomes move in a cadence, much like your Canting, but expressed in our breath, our step. And so we choose deemling." Her eyes sparkled.

"Is the choice truly random?" He leaned forward and laughed easily. "I'll wager that's where stories of stolen children come…"

Dane bristled. "Will the Conclave sanction deemae now? Cantors take children, not gnomes." He shook his head. "Nadir enjoys telling us how far cantor reach extends. We can all be purified at any moment if we step out of line. Just the fines are burdensome, even if no one is taken."

"Nadir is a jackdaw serving on the edge of known civilization for a reason," said Aric, his voice snapping like a whip. "Most of us who serve are not threatening. The Conclave exists to make the world better." He spread his fingers wide. "Perhaps I have been sent to the edge of civilization alone to keep my dreams in check. My master doesn't know what to do with me."

Pezzik finished the last of her meal and hopped down from her stool. "Well, you're a welcome change," she said, plodding into the kitchen. "And now it's time for pie."

"Refills, anyone?" Dane asked, picking up his own mug. "I have tea or cider if you'd rather have that."

"Cider." Aric handed his mug over. Jax just shook his head and turned his full attention to his unfinished plate.

Dane followed Pezzik into the kitchen and whispered urgently, "What do you think?"

Pezzik shook her head. "I think you'd best be gone before dawn. I'll make excuses."

"What if he is watching for me to run? What if he is telling the truth and actually is what he says he is, just has more love of lore than most? Could he be telling the truth? But the fae said to run. She saw fire and said shadows would fall across fen and glade and forest."

Pezzik sliced her pie and placed generous pieces on small plates. "This man is seeking dewin, or I'm a potato. True, it's been a long while since we've seen such here. But I remember. They choose their words very carefully. Questioners are careful not to lie." Her cap drooped. "The problem is, he might pose a danger to Bell."

"And Jax," Dane pointed out. "Though really, why are our families chosen?"

"Each has our reasons and now isn't the time to discuss it. We're safe enough as long as we can see him, and he's alone. Don't forget your cider."

Dane sighed and went to the sideboard. He poured two mugs while Pezzik balanced plates. He followed her with cider. He placed a mug in front of Aric and regained his seat. Pezzik went back to the kitchen, returning with two more plates of pie.

Aric launched into a raucous story about his journey upriver involving a mule, a large rat, and a fat bargeman. Soon they were all smiling and laughing. The pie was excellent, and everyone had second helpings. Aric's uncomfortable comments faded with the laughter. Dane let himself relax. Perhaps everything would be all right. The fae could have been speaking of something else.

Dane excused himself. He fed the chickens and goats and tended to the horses. He ordered Chance to stay with them. The dog settled in a corner, turning around and around to make a nest for himself in the clean straw.

Dane went about his duties. The moon was higher when he went to the pump. He washed his hands and checked his glamour before returning to the sitting room. Jax and Pezzik both smoked long pipes while Aric played his lute.

Dane stood in the doorway, watching, his heart warming. For a moment, he saw his mother rocking in her chair. His father would sit and play for hours. Dane shook his head to clear it and joined them, drinking in the music.

12

After a while, Aric put his lute back in its case. He looked at the sleeping forms, waiting to see if they would wake. His sleeping song was ancient, and if the boy actually was dewin, he should have noticed it. Aric frowned and leaned forward, steepling his fingers. He waited, watching them breathe, listening to soft snores while the fire crackled. Finally satisfied they were fully enchanted, he stood and slipped out.

Aric strode into the kitchen. The boy's words were all innocence, but the bard must *make sure* there was nothing to find. After years of waiting for rumors of another dewin-wrought lute, years of careful planning and watching, he had finally gotten word. Trystan had led them to their prize unwittingly. The Conclave had dispatched their best to the four corners of the Weldes to find this luthier.

Aric inspected each cabinet, looking for telltale signs of dried herbs, oils, or Essences. Nothing. Nodding to himself, he continued to the back door. He had to be thorough.

The moon was full: the Wyrm's Eye was open. Aric snorted softly to himself, imagining the Wyrm's gaze upon him. Still, he stepped carefully in the moonlight, surveying the rows of vegetables and herbs.

Craftsman did have leave to grow plants for the oils used in varnishes. He saw these immediately, closest to the door. Aric began to inspect the rows. He methodically stepped down each row, bending close, inhaling. He was nearly finished when a wind gusted, blowing a cloud over the moon. In the wind, a soft sigh of chimes.

Aric stilled.

The wind blew harder, and the chimes rose up, surrounding him.

Aric felt nausea rise. He didn't know how smell and sight had been hidden, but he was certain now. He was standing in the midst of a tunebell garden. He palmed his forehead, rubbing his temples. Aric calculated even as his heart sank. He had half hoped they were innocent. He'd had no idea of the boy's true skill. *If this hiding was any indication...*

He didn't finish the thought. He could not consider it yet. No, he had to focus. He could keep to his charade, sleep and wake, going to the Grove with Jax the next day. This would give him essential knowledge of the exact location and means of entry to the Burrow. The village itself would have to be purified, that much was plain.

However, traveling to the Burrow would also give Dane a chance to run. Aric decided. He couldn't risk it, he needed Dane alive, captured, and the lute intact.

It was not too late. *Not yet.* A weight settled in the pit of Aric's stomach, knowing what purification would mean for Dane. Such pain. There was too much at stake. The chymaera. The local Chapterhouse must be alerted. After, he could ride back with cantors and trained acolytes before the sleepsong faded. *It should hold through midday.*

Decision made, Aric silently prayed to the cyntae, knowing he was heard in spite of that evil moon.

The eye of the moon followed the bard as he slipped back into the cottage, carefully picking up his pack and instrument. It followed him, unblinking, as he stepped into the stable and back again, leading his horse. It watched him gallop down the road, toward Dohnavur.

Aric gave the moon no more mind—he had work to do.

Pezzik woke with a start. Dane's dog Chance was nuzzling her face, whining and licking. The fire was burning low. Her ears and cap twitched as she inhaled and listened. The crickets were singing. A few hours to dawn yet.

She glared at Jax and Dane, snoring in their chairs, as angry with them as she was at herself. The bard was gone as sure as her cap was tall. She knew it in her bones. Pezzik popped up and shook Jax.

She shouted as she leaned into Dane's ear, "Dane, wake up!"

Dane stretched and looked around, confused. Jax sat up, hair and eyebrows bristling. His cap had fallen off as he dozed. He looked naked without it. A piece of pie rested near it on the floor. Obviously it had rolled out. Absently, the gnome scratched this scalp, and fumbled to retrieve the pie, shoving it back into his cap.

"What...what time is it? How long did I sleep? Where's the bard?" Dane looked behind the upholstered chair and stood to check the other rooms in the cottage.

"A Conclave bard wants to visit our Burrow and asks those questions about deemae." Jax shook his now covered head, speaking softly to Pezzik. "Not good, not good. I liked him well enough. He might even be telling the truth. But I'll be happy to see him gone, no mistake."

Pezzik tilted her head. Without preamble she asked Jax, "Does Bell know the truth?"

Jax shook his head, swallowing. "She's been raised proper, but like most deemling except that one, she has no idea." He nodded at Dane.

Pezzik clucked, hushing him. "All right, go and check the horses. The man might have returned to the Chapterhouse, and if he did, we need to know. I need to speak with Dane."

Jax wheeled and walked through the outer wall.

Pezzik found Dane in the hallway, his eyes panicked. "He's gone. The fae I spoke with said she saw flames," Dane said, continuing breathlessly. "And the bard knew the name of the man who ordered the lute. He tried to get me to talk about it and take gold from him."

Pezzik's breath caught, but before she could answer, Jax rounded the corner. "His horse is gone," he reported. "Your mare said he left a few hours ago."

Pezzik eyed Dane. "Tell me exactly what the bard said to you from the moment you met, all of it."

Dane plunged in. When he finished, Jax whistled. Pezzik began speaking in gnomic. Jax nodded assent and headed down the corridor.

"Jax will scout the road and rouse the wood. We will run. My guess is the bard will go to the Chapterhouse and try to capture you shortly after dawn. We don't have much time. We won't return for a long time, Dane. Pack what you can."

Dane's eyes darkened. "I have to go alone, deema."

"Nonsense." She waved the idea away.

"No. I do. I have to find Trystan and warn him. They'll be coming for him as well, not just for me. I can make it to Baehnt...or wherever I need to go...by river, Mod can help me. The Conclave will be searching. A man traveling with gnomes? People will remember that outside of Dohnavur and the Heyegrove. You know it. The fae saw flames. They will come, search and fire the grounds. You and Jax have time. You can get the Essences to safety, some flowers. Warn the Burrow."

Realization dawned within Pezzik as Dane spoke.
"Deema, if they capture me, you can stage a rescue, but you can't be caught with me." He said the last in a gentle voice that seemed to melt her protests.

Pezzik's cap drooped. Tears filled her eyes, and she raised her hands, helpless. "You are like my own child, Dane."

"I know, deema, I know." He bent to hug her, feeling their roles suddenly reverse. She was as small as a toddler in his arms. "Chance will stay with you. I'll come home to you both."

"I can't believe I gave that man pie." her voice was gruff, choked with her tears. She pushed him away. "All right, enough, get moving. Warn Trystan. But after, you go to Siarad. Go to the Caprices. Tell them your full name. They'll help you. I'll send word as soon as I can."

13

Dane finally rested. The shelflike bed in his tiny cabin felt welcome, indeed. His mind spun, revisiting every detail of his escape. It all happened so fast. The events of the day rolled before him in fragments. Frenzied packing. Crating the lute. The short cart ride to the mountain lake, sunlight dappling the road as it filtered through leaves overhead. Loading the weathered dinghy he used for fishing. Saying goodbye to Pezzik.

While Jax drove to town to rouse Mod, Dane glided through the first hint of dawn. Mist was rising. Lily pads covered the lake's surface like a carpet before giving way to deeper waters. The call of geese in the distance broke the hush.

Dane's anxiety mounted with each oar stroke. At the docks, he kept his hood up, speaking little to the shipmaster. The note he found waiting had been curt, written in haste.

"This time of year, the passage to Baehnt will be long. Look for piece men. Dance the shadows. T will be safe."

Dane mulled over the cryptic message. Trystan would be kept safe until Dane could deliver the package. Hide as best he could. Mod would send further instructions. *How would she know where he was?*

He hurriedly stowed himself in a tiny cabin with his precious cargo, while the flatboat pulled away from the dock. He shredded the note and dropped it over the side. The pieces floated on the surface of the water like petals. As they disappeared, a shadow fell on his heart.

Now he could not shake it.

Dane lay in his bunk and thought about the fae, Sara.

Was she sent to help him? Truly? The only wisdom she'd uttered seemed so unspecific. Irrelevant. The game is not a game. Do not give up. Your work matters. There were other things she'd said, most of it fading from his memory despite his desperation to hold the words sent from the Storm King himself.

He whispered a prayer, hoping the Storm King would listen.

"Keep Pezzik safe and watch over Bell. Help me to remember the fae's message when I need to. Guide my path."

Dane changed vessels several times, avoiding notice. The barge finally reached the Thwn Channel. He boarded an actual ship at Bridgeton. Its mast seemed huge, though he was told the ship itself wasn't large. Dane was pleased to find he didn't suffer from nausea. He began to enjoy the journey. This channel flowed all the way to the Sundered City and the open sea.

He spent hours watching the landscape, the forests and fields separated by low stone walls. Occasional towns and the odd fisherman drifted past. He sketched them in his journal and scribbled what he remembered of the fae's message, committing it to memory.

He wondered about Trystan, this bard who would receive his first lute. *What was the man like? Was he worthy? Would he understand what he had? Could he be trusted?*

Dane's attention was consumed by the view. As the ship drew closer to the delta, fresh water flowed into salt. The halves of the World Tree towered, glowing like giant pillars on either side of the channel. The Tree was enormous, bone white, its top shrouded. It had split perfectly down the center, like the city just beyond. Clouds served as the Tree's canopy. They poured down the trunk, wrapping it with a thick, patchy fog.

Men called the Tree by many names. Ceffyl Brenin, Wyrmfell, the Blood Tree. The World Tree. *It was so immense and important it needed many names.* Dane imagined the Wyrm scaling the Tree, winding around it. He shivered.

Dane glimpsed the Tree's ivory bark and its legendary sap as they slowly entered the rift that flowed through, gliding between its two halves. The blood red sap had been exposed to the elements for five centuries, a hardened, glistening scream. Wider than a palace. It looked like it was still bleeding. *How could it possibly be alive?*

Yet it was.

Dane shivered again and rewrapped himself in his cloak. The sap put him in mind of passing through a womb. Or a scar. The power of the Storm King, Lord of Lightning, had done this thing. Here, where it had happened, Dane could only glimpse a tiny portion of the power expended in that battle.

"The dark one ascends," Dane whispered.

The words escaped before he realized what he was doing. Dane stopped himself with an effort. Suddenly, the murmurs of the other passengers rose to a cacophony. Many made the sign of the arc. Dane tore his eyes from the Tree and hastily arced himself as well. Both halves of the Sundered City shimmered in the distance, its terraced hill split into perfect sheer cliffs, mirroring the riven Tree.

The ship docked on the Ciclaehne side of the Sundered City. The captain let them know he would be there two days and two nights. After, they would sail around the coast to Baehnt. Dane couldn't miss the chance. He knew about this fabled port only from Pa's stories. He had to see it.

As soon as he stepped off the boat, Dane noticed the torso of a giant stone man, richly carved and eerily animate, jutting from the stone retaining wall. The lower half of his body was contained in the wall. He dominated the exit from the wooden piers into the main city. A monocle covered his stone eye.

The grotesque held a carved book in one hand, which he looked at now and again. Anyone exiting the docks stopped to speak with him, and soon a queue formed. Dane watched the others. He expected the Speaker's voice to boom, but it did not. Nothing but rumbling murmurs. Dane listened closely, trying to glean cues as to proper etiquette. While Dane had seen a few inert Speakers in Bestua, he'd never been this close to an active one.

Dane joined the line of people seeking entrance, watching those ahead carefully. Each interacted with the Speaker for a few minutes before passing on through the large gate, the Wharf entrance.

A man apparently said something the Speaker found Dissonant. The giant motioned and two grotesques approached, gliding up to flank the now-panicked man. "Take him to the guard," said the Speaker. The little group moved through the gate. They disappeared into a large building, where, presumably, the City Guard would uncover his chicanery.

The next person in line moved forward.

Dane quickly abandoned his plan to pass off Poll's name as his own and instead rehearsed a truthful response to the giant. The line shuffled forward again. Dane shifted from one foot to another.

And it was his turn. A stone gaze pierced him, blinking down through a monocle. "Your name?"

"Danethor Thomas, sir." Dane said, giving his full first and middle name. He dared not give his surname but also dared not lie. The Dissonance of an outright lie could land him with the guard. Idly, he wondered why the creature needed to blink. For that matter, why have a monocle? Surely that was some sort of chymaera joke.

"The name of your vessel?" asked the Speaker.

"The Thundering Wave," said Dane. "I'm stopping here for two nights. I've come from Teredhe, making a delivery in Baehnt." All technically true. He was taking no chances. The Speaker paused, noting these details in his book.

That couldn't actually be a book. It was made of stone. But the Speaker was recording his answers somehow.

"Do you have any need of direction or assistance?" he asked. This seemed to be the last question on Monocle's list. He'd dismissed the man in front of Dane after asking it. The others had all declined, but Dane grabbed the opportunity.

"Yes, sir," he said, flashing his best smile. Speakers couldn't be persuaded or even like people, but the smile covered his anxiety if nothing else. "Could you direct me to a good inn?"

The stone man regarded him. He motioned to an imp perched on the roof of the closest building. "Follow that one," he said. It was a dismissal. Dane gulped, trying not to show his obvious childlike wonder. But then again, he was just a country rube.

The imp climbed down the building and raised its wings in greeting. Dane could see a ridge of stone ran down the edifice and lined the street. Each building had this raised ridge, and creatures moved along it. Most were whimsical imps like the one meant for Dane, but some were not. Dane stopped to watch as a half eagle met a rather terrifying lion-bat. They melded together when they met, passing through each other before continuing in separate directions.

Some just descended, melting into buildings.

They must have been going inside. They were a bit like Pezzik. He knew he was gawking, but only in the Sundered Cities were Speakers so numerous and active.

All of the cities in Canard were like this once. Now the Speakers were only here.

We lost so much.

Dane's guide spoke when he got close. "Danethor Thomas, you have need of direction?" Its tone was dignified and formal.

"I need to find a place to stay the night, not too costly, but clean and comfortable," said Dane.

Wordlessly, the monster gestured for him to follow. He glided down the ridge alongside the cobblestone street. A few carts were passing through, but most folk were on foot.

"What's your name?"

The wizened face looked at him, his expression unchanging. "We do not have names, sir. We are simply Speakers."

Dane harrumphed. "All right then, mind if I call you Hodges?" He was an ignorant, obnoxious peasant arriving in the big city, and he intended to play the part with abandon. The gargoyle hesitated but bared his teeth in what approximated a smile. He inclined his large head.

"As you wish."

"So, do you help with directions all day, Hodges? Or do you do other things?"

"I guard," the monster said. "We're bound to the stone but keep peace in the city. We carry messages and protect the innocent from rogues." He gestured toward the shanty town, south of the lowest walls. "For the most part, the crime within city walls is limited."

"Aren't you stuck on that?" Dane pointed to the ridge.

"We can travel on any stone for short periods of time, but it is unpleasant. Eventually movement becomes more difficult. We remain on this lodestone way as we can. However, if you were attacked, I could leave it to defend you."

Dane was fascinated. "And you're made by chymaera? How old are you?"

"I am young, sir. I'm only one hundred years old. There are others much older here in the city. I was made in the Wyn Aerie, sir, the Gryphon." Hodges pointed to other shapes. "Most gryphon work is in my form, but there are other sigils." He pointed to a lion-bat. "Made by the Draig, in the Fells."

Dane inquired, pointing to a spindly little troll-man with an impish expression. "And that one?"

"The March, you might know them as Equis," replied Hodges. "They tend to be pranksters." His tone showed disapproval.

The creature turned a corner and continued gliding down the cobbled street while Dane followed, lengthening his stride to keep up. The buildings here were ornately carved. Arches, rosettes, flowers, and leaves gave the street the look of a carved garden. Dane marveled at the craftsmanship.

Eventually, they stopped in front of a three-story building with a sign that read "The Flaming Guardian."

"Thank you, Hodges."

"My pleasure, sir." It bowed and turned back toward the docks. Dane shook his head, still marveling, as it glided away.

Dane wandered down the stairs and into the common room. Dinner was included with his lodging. As much as he longed to explore the rest of the city, he dared not risk it. However, the common room would have novel sights. Perhaps Dane could glean information, if he were careful.

He took a seat in a dark corner and sipped a tankard. The ale was refreshing. He relaxed, enjoying the hum of conversation while surveying the other diners. An elderly man and his wife sat together, quietly eating. Several families chatted and laughed across tables.

A very tall, very thin person with close-cropped silver hair stood up from the bar; Dane's breath caught. *It was a chymaera.* His gaze traveled quickly from the odd silken garb to its eyes, searching for their distinctive tilt and a gold or silver color. Its eyes were amethyst blue. The creature blinked and stared back at him. Dane saw a shadow cross its eyes vertically just before its bottom eyelids rose to meet the top. Dane looked away quickly.

Dane hoped it couldn't read his mind. He fought himself not to make the Storm King's sign. Feeling the weight of that eagle gaze, he understood why folk feared them. Dane tried to make himself smaller, cursing inwardly for attracting the creature's notice.

He focused instead on sailors in their distinctive blacks and oiled leathers. He heard several odd accents and languages. Dane tried to guess where each person hailed from. Veiled Fenn Folk sat close to the fire, their heads together. There were even a few Northmen, obviously from Pelegor, with white-blond hair in long braids.

Dane blinked as a dwarf stood from the Northmen's table and approached the bar. He'd only seen a few dwarves before. Taller and sturdier than every gnome Dane knew, dwarves could be mistaken for them, nonetheless.

But dwarves don't wear caps. Gnomes do. Dane chuckled at the thought of the dwarf in a gnome hat. His surprise magnified when the dwarf hesitated and approached his table, leaning over and slamming a mug down with a thump.

"Bellin," he said, by way of introduction, glaring over the top of the mug.

"Danethor," answered Dane. "Pleased to make your acquaintance."

The dwarf raised an eyebrow and harrumphed. "My companions and I need a fourth. Stones." He nodded toward his table. "Do you play?"

"Passably well."

He rose and followed the dwarf, trying not to spill the two tankards. He glanced over his shoulder. The chymaera was gone.

"You have your fourth, Birgir. His name is Danethor," the dwarf said to the largest man as he settled into his chair and gestured to the empty seat. "Now your boasting will reap its just reward." Bellin's eyes gleamed. He tossed two coppers in as an opening bid and said something in the Northern tongue.

Dane stiffened, sure he was the topic of the exchange, but placed his ante next to Bellin's and scooped up his allotment of square stones. He placed the first on the board, wordlessly. The opening move for the game was prescribed, and he took it. He was wary but determined to know the real reason the dwarf had been so friendly.

The huge Northman called Birgir raised a mug, his deep voice booming. "Well met, Danethor. My thanks for joining us in battle, ser. My brother Harald"—he nodded to the other bearded Northman, who was studying the board—"and this wretched son of a mountain have challenged my honor. I can best both with any partner. That would be you, in this case. And this"—he gestured to the stones board—"this is the proving ground."

Harald snorted, not raising his eyes. He took a sip from his mug and carefully placed a rounded stone. Satisfied, he leaned back in his chair, nodding to himself slowly. His eyes remained steadfastly locked on the stones.

Birgir quirked an eyebrow at his brother and placed his square stone diagonal to Dane's.

At this Harald glared at Birgir, astonished, and shook his head, muttering. He went back to his furious study of the board.

Bellin placed his rounded stone to support Harald's.

Dane placed his stone to flank Bellin's. *Best to attack first.*

"Is it your first time in the City?" Dane asked, looking from the dwarf to his companions.

Harald appeared to not notice the inquiry, so fierce was his concentration.

Birgir replied, "No, we represent the Forge and travel where they send us. More times than not they send us here." He pulled a pendant in the shape of a dagger from beneath his jerkin, the token of the Forge.

"I am a woodcrafter, cabinets and tables, mostly," Dane said.

"Aye and a deemling too, unless I miss my mark," said Bellin. "'Twas what led me to your table. Rare to see, even here, but it means you know your game." He winked and nodded at the stones board.

Dane's mouth opened, aghast. He would not deny what the dwarf obviously knew, but was horrified to be so distinct when he wanted nothing more than to blend in. As a country craftsman come to the big city, he was forgettable. As a deemling, he could be remembered. Did the chymaera see as well? He set his jaw and fixed the dwarf with a questioning stare.

Harald placed his stone to flank Dane's, a riposte. He answered the boy's unspoken question. "The dwarf says you're marked." He raised his eyes, meeting Dane's gaze. "I canna see it, nor can my brother. But he said," Harald jerked a thumb at Bellin, "and we have learned over the years to listen."

Dane matched Birgir's nonchalance, covering his initial horror with self-mockery. "We don't have horns like the old stories say, but stars, what'd she do to me?" He ran his hands through his hair, searching.

Birgir's eyes flicked from the dwarf to Dane, amused. he placed his piece, flanking Harald, and captured two round stones. With a flourish, he placed them in his waiting purse and collected the bid coppers from the other players. They all replaced their bids automatically.

"Lad, never underestimate the cunning of a gnome, especially a female." Bellin shut his eyes and grimaced, obviously speaking from experience. He pointed to Dane's left boot. Its buckle peeked from under his trousers, gleaming in the lamplight.

Pezzik had crafted his boots, as she had for his whole family. The buckle, normally round, had eight sides and a rune inscribed on it, the mark of her Burrow. "Your deema marked you for any who know Burrow crafting. Those who do not, would not take notice. Those who do will take heed." He tapped his nose. "We are duty bound to make you welcome. 'Tis a simple enough message, but subtle." Bellin placed his stone.

Dane sighed, shaking his head. He shifted his feet deeper into the shadows pooling under the table. This mark was easily hidden, for now, but he would have to find new buckles in the morning. "She worries," he said. "'Tis my first trip alone since my father passed." Dane studied the board in front of him. He placed his stone in a safe position.

"You get to know a man's mettle," Harald announced, "two ways. Swords and stones." He nodded to the board. "You're a thinker, you are. And cautious, but smart. How you play a game is how you live. You'll do well enough on your own." He placed his own marker and took a swig of ale.

Dane decided to trust any dwarf who knew Burrow lore was indeed an ally, or at least a person who respected the wrath of gnomes. They talked idly of rising prices, the joys of haggling, and the perils of sailing in the last month's almost continuous storms.

Dane watched as Birgir controlled every round, masterfully escaping traps set, laying his own snares, and scooping up his winnings. As the eighth captured set and the end of the game approached, Dane was thankful to be part of the larger man's team and not his opponent. He made safe choices and followed the Northman's lead.

While the ale flowed, the game wound down. Bellin fixed Dane with a hard stare. "Have you seen the World Tree lad?"

"We passed through it as we came downriver, of course. It...I..." He fought to find words to describe the experience.

The dwarf silenced him with a wave. "Aye, lad. I know the sorrow." He lowered his voice. "Few dare to approach it on foot, but we plan to make the pilgrimage in the morn. You could join us."

Dane took a swig of his ale, considering. He had to get new buckles for his boots. He couldn't hope that only friendly folk would see Pezzik's mark. A deemling was possibly as rare as a chymaera to anyone outside the Heyegrove. But after, the day promised to drag, long and empty. He'd be confined to the inn from caution.

The safe thing was to stay in his room—even the Common Room had proven itself a risk. Yet he'd always longed to touch the Tree. To actually approach it on foot, study it closely? That would be wondrous. And it would be madness.

"Going on a picnic?" he asked, placing his stone.

Harald barked a laugh and patted the knife hanging at his belt. "More like a hunt," he said, baring his teeth. "The Tree and the Song."

Birgir and Bellin repeated it. "The Tree and the Song," they said, in unison.

Bellin snorted at Dane's confused expression. "We must report back to the Forge, lad. We've been to meet the local cantor, but this inspection must be thorough."

"Inspection?" Dane knew more than he could dare admit. Even so, his excitement was rising. He only just kept himself from holding his breath, waiting for the answer.

"Your Conclave guards the Song and its power, tending the Tree, nurturing what remains after the Breaking. The mists that surround it lead those who seek to come near astray. Enchanted. All who try are led to the Chapterhouse. We have leave to approach. To inspect the Songlines proper, we must. They radiate from the Tree's roots to all people, carrying power. We need to see them." He slammed his mug on the table in punctuation.

It was Birgir's turn to snort. "The power for our forges is fading. We can use normal fire, but those will not make blades that kill Shadowborn. The water-leapers and other foul beasties. Shadowkin." He shook his head, his hair a mane of braids. "They tell us there's nothing to fear, but we've seen naught to confirm it. High King Tenneth lies dying, wasting away. Welden noble houses are full of whispers. Tales have made a journey north. The Weldes are ripe for a war of succession, while the resonance is weakened. We cannot be shut off."

Dane tapped the table, frowning.

"War? Surely the Conclave will confirm the succession."

Harald lowered his voice, leaning forward, the game forgotten. "If our power is failing, theirs is dying as well. There will be no confirmations, no Cantings, no power but the fist and the blade." His eyes flashed. "Fear of enchantment or even piety, those will only hold back unrest for so long. In the countryside, peasants are already asking why they pay so many taxes. Crops are small. Tempers run hot. If the Takers and the Watchers both fail and all the water is fouled? The merchants looted?"

Bellin nodded solemn agreement.

Dane wished his head wasn't so muddled with ale. "But the Takers and Watchers are only in cities. Peasants aren't affected by ebbs much. Aren't we taught there's waxing and waning in the Song? Isn't this just waning?

"And since the Tree was broken, the Conclave has known this could happen. The Tree could fully die. They always have said that our faithfulness sustains the Song."

Dane paused and considered, finally admitting the obvious. "If the Tree dies, it affects all living things. No Song."

Birgir slammed his tankard down with a thump, interrupting. "Exactly. Not all believe the drivel the Conclave spews, or even that the Wyrm was real." He shook his finger in Dane's face. "But if the Conclave isn't prepared for the worst, then war might be the least of our problems. The Song stops flowing. Dissonance reigns unchecked. Death, disease, insanity, famine. The end of all we know."

Dane sat back in his seat, horrified. "Storm King save us," he murmured, shaking his head. "How long do we have?"

Bellin answered, his face grim. "That's what we are here to learn." He looked up at Dane, his eyes bright. "Do you want to go with us?"

Dane shook his head with regret. He dared not walk into the largest Conclave chapter, not until his lute was delivered. Now, more than ever, he realized how urgent his task was. His lute might keep death at bay.

"I would," he said. "But I have pressing business that will not allow it."

Birgir pointed to the board, triumphant even in the face of certain doom as he captured the last set of stones for the victory. "Never fear lads, all is right in the world for now. I've won again."

Bellin's eyes didn't leave Dane's face. They dimmed with disappointment at Dane's refusal, as if he sensed his reasoning somehow. Bellin reminded Dane of Pezzik.

Bellin's heavy expression faded, replaced with a mask of good humor. The dwarf forced a retort to the smug victor. "You're the son of a wyrm, Birgir, and no mistake. Again!"

Birgir laughed as he reset the board. "See what comes of teaming with legend, lad? And there's even more to gain and learn, you'll see."

The Forgeman's confident boast, while brash, pushed at Dane. An idea, like an itch started to form.

The game is not a game.

He'd followed Birgir's lead on the stones board.

Am I meant to follow him to the Tree? Could I, without being caught?

If the worst had already occurred, his home was gone, and his village was being purified. The people could be interrogated and fined or their homes taken away. Dane gulped. Speakers may already have spread his description far and wide.

But the game is not a game. Did the fae mean this game? And if she did, what were the consequences if I do not follow the path?

He had to heed her message.

"More ale!" Dane called, gesturing for another round. He turned his attention back to the board, his path decided. It felt right.

"I'll go with you," he said. "But I have to finish my business early in the morn ere we leave. Also, I'm going to need a small favor. I'll tell you more about it when my business is concluded."

The dwarf did not mask his delight, pounding the table. "Thunder and stone! Glad to have you. A deemling can be a sure help to us at the Tree. We'll leave in the third hour after dawn."

Dane grimaced. The hour was already growing late.

Catching his expression, Birgir winked and scooped up his stones. "We'll just have to win quickly, lad. We'll just have to win quickly."

14

Near the Burrows, only a faint whiff of char marked the loss.

Pezzik's cap quivered as she pictured Dane's workshop. Her kitchen. The gardens. All of it. Gone.

The acolytes in their white robes and hoods would have come like ghosts, silent and deadly. But by that time, she was gone. Pezzik had been far into the forest when the burning began, her mare and Chance both loaded down with all she dared carry. Smoke from the cottage billowed into the sky. The wind caught it, smearing sooty clouds across the Heyegrove, raining small bits of ash. The smell was acrid. The sky had turned black beyond the forest canopy.

Her home was purified. There would be nothing left.

She allowed herself to feel the anguish, to mourn in this moment, for three breaths. On the fourth exhale, Pezzik released her pain into the sky, like a dove. She would do this many times over the next weeks, sometimes many times an hour.

It was not her first war with rage.

Pezzik led Chance and the pony to the ring of toadstools in the center of the Heyegrove. Once there, she stopped and listened, still as only a gnome can be.

The grove rustled in answer. In this forest, the tallest man barely attained the height of a tree's smallest roots. Gnomes seemed tiny insects in comparison. They were not insects, of course. They were the heart of the grove, its pulse.

"*Repu*," she sang.

It sounded like a bird call. In a few moments, she heard a trill, an answer. She walked across the clearing toward a giant hollow log and passed within.

She followed the natural tunnel and approached a large hole. She spoke to her mare. "There will be someone up to get you shortly. Just wait here."

The mare neighed assent and swished her tail. She ambled away, back toward the mouth of the log tunnel.

"You have to go this way," she said to Chance, pointing to the hole. "I'm going to go with you. Just follow me."

Pezzik crept to the edge and sat down, waiting for the shepherd dog to join her. She grasped Chance's right forepaw and shoved herself off, unable to contain a whoop as they slid together down a long spiral. They landed at the bottom on a moss cushion with a thump.

The gnome on duty rushed forward to assist her.

"Pezzik!" he said. "Are you well?" Concern painted his large nose a rosy pink. Hair needled from his ears, and his bushy eyebrows wriggled as he inspected her thoroughly, concerned. His cap tilted forward, dangerously askew.

Pezzik waved him away. "I'm right enough, Ortie, but I do not fancy a climb back up. Could you send someone to see to my mare? Her name is Misselthwaite."

"Of course." Ortie signaled to a shadowed corner. A very short fat gnome waddled out and bobbed a bow before hurrying from the room.

Pezzik removed her cap and checked its contents. She patted the pack strapped to Chance and nodded to herself. "Thank you, there may be others along directly, I expect. Watch for them."

As the sentry took up his position, Pezzik followed a winding passage, Chance at her heels.

The passage widened. It was clean, carpeted with springy moss and lighted with glowstones. Pezzik strode quickly, impatient to see Thurial. When the passage opened into the Burrow-Moot, she barely slowed. Sunlight shafted down through several holes far above.

The Moot was abuzz with activity, bustling in the underlying rhythm thrumming through each individual gnome. Pezzik paused to survey the scene before diving into the fray.

The daily cadence of her kin created a rhythmic music startling to anyone not accustomed to it. She stepped around two tiny tangled giggling gnomelings. She hopped past a group of grunting girls pulling taffy into long twists. Nodding gnomefathers sat at a stones board, pebbles clicking as they played. A bossy gnomemother ordered several squirrels to haul a net full of nuts into another passage. She stamped her foot. Young gnomes hefted hewn walking staves, tapping the tiles as they trooped out. Tiny children of all ages danced, dodging their mothers and their chores. The Burrow's badger snored near the warm central fire, pretending to be a bear. All of the sounds combined, drumming together so perfectly, Pezzik ached to dance. For Pezzik, it was a heartbeat. It meant she was home.

Rows of tables and chairs dominated one side of the Moot. Here Pezzik spied her prey, a tall thin gnome with a floor-length beard, high-peaked cap, and curled mustaches. She swept toward him. "Thurial, it's time!" she shouted.

"Eh? What's that? Time for what, dear girl?" the old gnome regarded her kindly.

Pezzik sighed and picked up the large ear trumpet next to Thurial, twisting it in her hands. She placed the small end into the gnomefather's ear and shouted into the large end. "It's time to move to a new Burrow, Thurial. The Conclave is burning Whitley Cottage, and they will come here soon. It's time to leave. We have to go now."

Thurial snorted. He picked up his pipe and tapped it on the table, gesturing for Pezzik to sit across from him. "Tell me from the beginning," he said, "And have a spot of tea." Thurial rang a bell beside him three times.

Within a few minutes, more bells were ringing, and the Burrow was preparing to move.

The Chapterhouse held its secrets close. All villagers knew acolytes lived under the building, their refectory and dormitory built into the clay and stone. Tunnels and vaulted chambers extended out from the central underground living area. Beyond that, crypts five centuries old held the dignified remains of prominent village families.

High Cantor Nadir gestured for the next penitent to be brought in. The acolytes ushered her to the high-backed chair in front of him, not gently. Nadir's eyes flicked from his list to the young woman. She was older than he recalled.

"Bell, is it?" he said, leaning over the ancient black desk.

"You know right well it's me, Cantor. You've known me since I could walk." Bell glared at the acolytes who had dragged her into the chamber. Her disheveled hair and clothes hinted she'd been roused from bed for questioning. She had spent the wee hours of the morning and early dawn in a stark room, alone, waiting to speak with the cantor. Every second had stoked her ire. She was nearly snarling when the time finally came.

"You're a deemling, aren't you?" Nadir leaned forward, looking at Bell as if she'd suddenly sprouted wings. The unexpected question silenced her, chilling her fury.

Bell blinked, suddenly uncertain. "Your Grace, you know Jax. Yes, I am a deemling."

"Where is the little fellow this morning?" Nadir asked, his voice quiet, measured. Something in the cantor's voice shook Bell.

"He took the new bard to visit the Burrows. He won't return for a few days." She tossed her head. "Is there something you need from him?"

Nadir shook his head and leaned back in his chair, regarding Bell with a satisfied expression. "Do you know why deemae are chosen, Bell? Do you know what the Apokrypha says?"

Bell froze, her mouth agape. "Deemae aren't mentioned in the Apokrypha, Cantor," she whispered. "Not anywhere."

"Not directly," Nadir agreed. "They aren't. Your friend Dane is a deemling too, isn't he? And young Stu Callin. Mary Planor, the Frenner family, the Smiths, and the Hodges. Only a few of you now. There used to be scores."

Nadir rose and moved out from behind the ornately carved desk. He leaned against it, looking down his thin nose, his eyes hooded in the blazing torch light. The cantor's mouth twisted. His next words reached out to caress her in a much too intimate manner.

"But you are, of course, mentioned in the Apokrypha. It's just the passage in question is a mystery only revealed when you reach enlightenment. Before that, a mind cannot hold the truth, and it will fade from your memory within an hour. Would you like to know what it says about deemling?" Excited like a child, he leaned forward. The flickering light reflected from his eyes.

Bell cautiously nodded.

Nadir walked behind Bell's chair. He leaned forward to whisper directly in her ear, enunciating distinctly. "It says that you are dewin." His hand clamped on her shoulder, holding her down as an acolyte held her from the other side. She did not resist. A bell tolled, and the scent of decaying roses filled the room.

It was a long time before Bell stopped screaming.

15

Sara kept her hood up as she rushed into the Tank. Late. She grabbed her clipboard and scanned it. Tonight she was harvesting, this time a different strain.

Sara grabbed her cutting tool and gloves. She headed through the vast main greenhouse toward Annex B, a smaller pod used for the varietals. These needed to be sequestered so they didn't cross pollinate. The entire annex was full of the alternative hemp strain, with hundreds of plants. Large narrow troughs in the floor formed aisles, with each seven-foot plant set into the trough in its own pot.

Scott Black rhythmically hacked in the next row over, grunting with the effort. He laid large stalks on the cart next to him to be dried and retted. Sara waved as she entered, resisting the urge to retreat further into her hoodie. She headed for the far corner of the building, grabbed a cart, and chose a row as far from Scott as possible. She craved alone time.

Sara jammed her headphones into her ears, cranked up her Paganini CD and got to work. The music soothed her raw emotions. By the time it got to the fifth track, she was humming along and dancing in place. She picked up a large stalk, twirling right into Scott, who stood eating an apple at the end of her row, watching with a decidedly amused grin.

"Good grief!" Tearing her headphones out she scrambled to regain her dignity. "There you go again, standing where I'm going," she snapped. "I thought you'd learned your lesson."

Scott laughed. "Sorry, I heard an angel and had to see where the music was coming from. Then I saw you. Do you want to help me find the angel?"

Sara made a face and whacked Scott on his head with the hemp stalk. "Shame on you, spying on me," she said, placing the hemp on her cart. "I've had a rough day, am quite content to take it out on the hemp and not on you."

"Yeah?" Scott arched a brow at Sara. "I've got just the cure for a rough day. It's almost time to clock out. Do you have any plans for tonight?"

Sara's lips quirked in a smile despite herself.

"I guess I do now."

Scott's car was a pristine blue Mazda RX-7. He held the door open. Sara curtsied, lightly mocking, before sliding into the passenger seat. "Such a gentleman."

"I am, really." He closed the door as if he were tucking her into bed, rounded the car, and settled himself behind the wheel.

"I'm still not used to this car, got it for my birthday," Scott said. The headlights flipped up as he turned the key in the ignition. "We're not going far, but I think you'll like this place. I go there sometimes to think after a hard day. You'll dig it."

"Are you from here originally?"

"Yeah, I grew up in the Highlands, went to Trinity."

"Hm, I am surprised we never met. I went to Sacred Heart, right down the street," said Sara.

"I was a football player...didn't have time for much, outside practice and school."

"Oh." Trinity was one of the best football schools in the state. She looked out the window as Scott maneuvered the sports car through campus and on to Eastern Parkway. They passed the mansions lining the wide street, many of them converted into student apartments. One had a yard overrun with garden gnomes.

Were the gnomes waving? No. Just my imagination.

"So we're going to the Highlands? I've been there, you know. Hippie central."

Scott glanced at her and grinned. He shook his head. "I told you, I'm looking for angels."

He turned left. Large Tudor homes lined these streets. They passed a small park. A stone wall towered on the right. They continued for blocks before turning onto a drive blocked by massive wrought-iron gates. Scott pulled up and got out of the car, leaving the engine running. He walked over and pressed a button embedded in the wall. He spoke quietly into a speaker. A buzz answered, and the gates swung inward, opening. Scott jumped back into the car and inched it inside. The massive gates shut behind them.

They crested a steep hill, and Sara gasped. She couldn't tear her eyes from the massive angel-topped monuments and gothic mausoleums everywhere, each more ornate than the last. Dark shadows held mysteries, overhung with ancient trees. Moonlight kissed marble, and the stones glowed. Sara's arms prickled with goosebumps.

She itched to touch the markers, to explore the carving and detail with her fingers. She whispered, "Can we get out?"

He parked at the top of the hill next to a forest of obelisks.

"St. Louis Cemetery. It used to be a fort. From here you can see all of it," Scott said, pointing. "You usually can't get in at night, but it's my favorite time to visit, and I know the groundskeeper pretty well. I thought you might like to see the statues."

Sara twirled in a circle slowly, absorbing the eerie landscape. "This makes you feel better after a rough day?"

Scott rummaged through the hatchback until he found what he wanted. "Sure it does. I used to walk here and think when I was growing up."

"You know I'm a sculptor, right?"

Scott handed her a flask. "I didn't know. This will help keep you warm, it's chilly. Let's go explore and see what you think, Madam Sculptor."

Sara took the flask and unscrewed the top, taking a small sip. She coughed. "Bourbon?"

"What else?" Scott said, grinning. "Take another drink, it's smooth."

Sara wrinkled her nose doubtfully but looked around and threw caution to the wind. She took a larger drink and swallowed. "Thanks."

"Keep it. Come on, I want to show you this." He pivoted and headed downhill toward the mausoleums.

Sara followed him into the shadows. Scott stopped in front of a large obelisk. "Why do you think we mark graves with stone?"

Sara stood, rapt, examining the intricate carving at the base on up to the angel that topped it. It held a trumpet as if sounding a warning. A stone pavilion beside it marked another grave. Inside, the figure of a man rested. His stone eyes stared into the night, seeing nothing.

"It's been practiced for centuries. I think we all want to leave something, so we're remembered. We want it to last. It's a message for those who follow us."

She traced the message carved into the stone and read it aloud.
"Afflictions are but the shadows of God's wings. His way is in the whirlwind and the storm, and clouds are the dust of his feet."

Sara shivered as she thought of Marilla and took another sip from the flask.

"The symbols mean things, you know. Most people think the obelisks were Masonic, but there was a huge interest in Egyptian symbolism in the early 1900s," she said. They turned together and walked down the road that circled the hill. As they walked, Sara pointed to different markers. "That person was a Mason." She pointed to a marker with a compass. "The anchor means hope. The anvil represents creation, the forging of the universe. The empty chair? It's for a child."

"You know a lot about this."

"Art history. I study a lot about symbolism. I use it in my work." She spied a particularly beautiful marker, a cast metal statue of three children. She studied it, pointing out the style and explaining how it had been created. She walked on in comfortable silence, relaxing as the bourbon and moonlight took effect. Scott grabbed her hand.

They stopped at the base of the hill, near an especially ornate family crypt. This one resembled a miniature classical mansion, complete with pillars and pediment. An angel perched on the roof, wings spread. Gargoyles surrounded the angel, their marble faces at once noble and imperious. Carved into the pediment was a single word—Black.

"This is my family." He picked up a pebble and set it in the doorway, adding to a large pile of pebbles nestled there. "My mother. I like to think she hears me, walks with me."

The beautiful angel and its gargoyle attendants framed Scott as moonlight fell on his face.

"When did she pass?"

"I was in high school," Scott said. "That's when I started coming to visit."

Impulsively, Sara leaned in and kissed him.

He looked at her, surprised, and pulled her into a warm embrace, kissing her gently. As the kiss broke, his eyes softened. "What was that for?"

"It was a thank you for bringing me here, for sharing this place," Sara said. "And for opening up. I do feel better." She looked into his eyes and kissed him again.

"Any time I can be of service, Miss Moore, you just let me know." He leaned in, but his phone buzzed. Scott pulled away and looked at it. "Damn," he said under his breath.

"What?"

"We'll have to pick this up another time. I gotta get back." Scott's disappointment painted his face.

"No problem. I have an early class tomorrow, anyway."

Scott tapped out a reply on his phone, nodding. "Okay, I definitely want a rain check though."

"That can be arranged."

Sara bounced into chem class, her eyes sparkling. Her makeup was perfect, and she had spent time on her hair. Her black shirt hugged her figure and in place of her usual denim and Chuck Taylor's, she wore a black pencil skirt, black leggings, and midcalf black boots. Chunky silver jewelry completed the look. She was humming as she slid into the seat.

Her eyes fell on Peter.

Her stomach lurched.

"Whoa," said Peter, looking up from his notebook. "You look great. You know our date is tonight, not today, right?"

Sara shrugged. "I felt like dressing up. I'm in a good mood."

Was in a good mood. She had totally forgotten their date but wasn't going to admit it.

"Glad to hear it." Peter opened his mouth, about to say something else, but Professor Kent walked in. Peter stopped, muttering under his breath, "After class."

Sara didn't listen to a word of the lecture. She was too busy freaking out. Scott, his kisses, and the magical sculptures had driven everything else from her mind.

Should she tell Peter what happened? Should she still go out with him? She didn't want to lose Peter. The truth was, she'd nearly kissed Peter yesterday. She'd barely pulled away.

Why? Why did I make out with an almost complete stranger instead? What is wrong with me? Maybe I am selfish. Maybe I'm just using Peter. No. She did care for Peter. She knew that much.

Sara had never felt so confused in her life.

Peter glanced at her and winked. She forced a smile. Sara had nearly decided to come clean when her phone buzzed. She flipped it open and saw a text from her mother.

Moving Marilla today.

Sara tapped back a reply.

You can't do this, Mom.

The display flashed again. *It's done and I'm not discussing it further. It's time to let go, Sara.*

Things were happening too fast. Sara shoved her books into her backpack and grabbed her purse. The professor had fallen silent at her interruption. "I'm sorry, sir, I have to leave, family emergency."

She stormed out.

16

Jax spared precious time to speak to squirrels, asking them to spread the word throughout the forest. Danger was coming. The forest might see fire. Many offered to help, and he left it to them, riding hard for the village. Perhaps the squirrels could convince birds to dive at Aric's eyes and drive the Conclave off. Jax could only hope.

When Jax reached Dohnavur, he led his pony to a tree on the edge of the main road.

"Wait here for me," he said. It whinnied assent.

Jax went to Mod's house first. She wasn't there; the house was shuttered. Bell will be safe. We will escape. He ducked into a side alley, heading for the inn.

Jax stepped into a darkened doorway as acolytes in white robes and hoods appeared. They herded a few bleary-eyed villagers down the cobblestone street toward the Chapterhouse. None of the citizens resisted. They did as they were told, quiet as bones. Jax absorbed the scene, waiting until they passed to emerge from the shadows.

He dodged a few other acolytes accompanied by watchmen. These carried tools. A large censer swung as they walked, spreading billows of aromatic smoke. One held a large bell. Another carried a candle.

Purification. They were purifying the village.

He followed. They entered one house, then another. They only lingered inside for a few minutes but left behind a smoky haze that spread. Soon it would blanket everything.

Satisfied the monks had not progressed far into their ritual, Jax ran for the Bell and Rider. It was deserted. The rooms upstairs had been emptied, all doors flung wide open.

Heart pounding, Jax rushed to Bell's room, not bothering with the door but popping directly through the wall.

Bell was gone.

The Conclave Chapterhouse was formed from stone, like most of the larger structures in Dohnavur. It was large, much larger than the dock warehouses or the inn. The uninitiated might not have noticed that the huge reinforced door, and the single arc window made it defensible by only a few acolytes.

Jax was not uninitiated. He was fully alert and very angry.

Jax approached the Chapterhouse from behind, stilled and listened carefully. He paced, footsteps falling in a soft rhythm, three times, up and back along the wall. He walked over to a spot nine paces from the south wall and sank slowly into the packed earth.

The chamber Jax dropped into was unlit, its air close and stale. Jax sensed rather than saw the stone slabs in the room. They held human remains of long-dead villagers. He tapped the walls until one rang hollow.

Jax poked his head through the wall, blinking in the flickering torchlight. The passage was empty. He crept through, careful to step quietly.

He trailed one hand along the wall and hummed. He walked a few paces and hummed again. He kept to his rhythm, moving methodically down the passage. Step, step, step, step, step, hum.

When the passage was paced off, he moved to the next, always to his right. Jax refused to think about the choice, trusting his instincts. He searched for what felt like hours, not meeting any other person.

When the resonance of Bell's aural nexus finally echoed back to him, it was very faint. But it was enough. *My deemling.* Jax's cap quivered. His step quickened as he headed toward the source. He turned down one vaulted passage, and another, dust rising behind him. At intersections, he stopped and hummed. Finally he stepped through a wall, into a small room.

Bell lay on the floor, tossed onto a small pile of straw like a rag doll. Jax ran to her and held his hand before her mouth. She breathed.

Jax opened one of her eyes, and another, peering. Jax removed his hat and pulled out a small bottle. Uncorking it, he held it under Bell's nose. She coughed and gasped but did not revive. Jax stepped back and scratched his head. He leaned next to Bell's ear, whispering.

"Bell, it's me. Your old Jax, I'm here. It's all right now, my deemling. I've come to get you. You're not alone." He brushed her hair from her face and waved the bottle under her nose again.

Bell's eyes fluttered. Jax stepped back and corked his smelling salts, a wave of relief washing over him as she sat up. She looked at the gnome, saying nothing.

Bell's eyes were empty, blank. Her jaw hung slack. Drool dribbled from one corner of her mouth. She groaned, the sound of a wounded animal, and lifted her hands, reaching for him. She mewled like a helpless, newborn kitten.

Bell had been Purified.

For most, the process of purification produced no ill effects. For dewin, it was a violation and a torture. Jax didn't know if this could be reversed, but he clung to hope. His Bell would live and be whole. She had to.

Jax almost didn't pick up the shuffling outside the door. Quickly, he scurried up the stone wall until he was nearly level with the ceiling. He pressed his body into the wall like a dagger entering a sheath. Carefully, he pressed his face back through, exposing himself enough to spy.

Aric stood below, with Nadir, studying Bell as she scraped her hands ineffectually on the stone floor.

Jax shook as wrath flooded him.

"Take her back with the others," Aric said. "Provided all goes well, we should be able to restore some of her faculties. She might be useful again, and even if not, we can still perhaps learn much. My master shall be pleased."

Nadir dry-washed his hands, tutting. "She will survive the travel back to Bestua?"

"She should. We'll take her to the Rift Chapterhouse in a skycart. Our other subjects live there. She'll get the care she needs. I will remain here long enough to make sure the effects have taken hold with the rest of the village, while you finish the work at the Burrow."

Nadir held up a hand. "I expect the Burrow to be empty. These gnomes are cunning, spiteful, and cowardly. They will run at the first hint of a problem."

Aric seemed amused by Nadir's statement. "Really?" he said. "I seem to remember one of them beating you soundly."

Nadir's ears turned red. "That was a long time ago, Master. They are inordinately strong for creatures of their size. Even the most low of creatures, when backed into a corner, will fight."

"And even the most educated of creatures can bleed," Aric said. He leaned forward, his face perfectly unchanged, but a new quiet menace tinged his tone. "Make sure you do not forget it, Nadir. I know you. We need to discover how the gnomes are enhancing those with a knack and creating dewin. These deemae are not to be touched or harmed further in any way, or I'll make sure you wish you had never been born."

"Yes, Master," Nadir said.

Jax could see the high cantor's hands behind his back, clenched into fists, his knuckles white.

"Good," Aric said, leaning back and clapping Nadir on the shoulder. "I'm glad we have an understanding. The purification Essence will not harm most of the village. Indeed, they will feel refreshed and at peace. Agreeable. We will suggest these unfortunates have gone traveling, left on their own. They will not question it." He turned to the door, guiding the cantor out. "Now when you approach the Burrow..."

The rest of his words were lost as the door slammed shut. A bolt slid into place. He waited a few minutes before extricating himself from the stone, emerging and climbing back down. He gathered Bell in his arms, hugging her tight.

"I'll be back," he whispered. "I'm going for help. You hang on. I know you understand me. I know you'll fight." He released her, doffed his hat again and pulled out some bread. "Eat this, love, I'll bring you more as soon as I can. I'll be back."

Bell took the bread from him, stuffing it all into her mouth. She licked her fingers when it was gone and crooned with pleasure.

"I'll be back." Jax climbed into the wall, and up toward the sunlight.

Jax knew Mod had vanished, all traces of her presence removed from the village she had called home for so long. Purification would create holes in the memory of many townsfolk and aid her flight.

The Burrow would already be on the move. By the time he warned them of the cantor's plans, it would be too late. Bell would have vanished too. He might not be able to find her again.

Jax headed to the inn for supplies, knowing he had no other choices. He had to find a way to help the Burrow, but he still had to save Bell.

Jax rode a short way into the forest and dismounted, leading his pony into a clearing. The trees here were smaller than the giant trees in the Heyegrove, normal oaks, elms, and maples. He located a beehive in a maple on the west side, hanging from a low branch. Jax shimmied up the tree and whispered to the hive. He cocked his head, listening, as four bees emerged. They buzzed around him.

"You're going to make me do this the hard way then?" Jax said. "All right, I will. But remember this the next time you wish to know where the best flowers grow."

He built a fire under the beehive and waited for smoke to envelop it. After a few minutes, he shimmied back up the tree. He pulled a knife from his hat and set to work. He opened the hive near the bottom. He spied the dark-brown brood area and sawed a large chunk off, leaving the bigger portion for the bees.

He applied leaves and sap to the opening he'd made, sealing it. Jax thanked the hive. He wrapped the honeycomb in leaves, placing it with the knife into his hat. He scrambled back down the tree.

He instructed his pony to remain in the clearing and set off into the forest, heading north. An old enemy hunted there. It was time to make amends.

The hemlock was just as he remembered. It soared into the sky next to a woodland stream gurgling over large stones. This time of day, the black bear lazed. She raised her head as Jax approached, her voice a low rumble. "Son of stone and Song, you are bold to visit me."

Jax bowed. "I came to honor you, great one. To ask a boon." He stepped forward and placed the honeycomb between himself and the bear and waited.

The bear sniffed and levered her huge body up, grabbing the package with a massive paw. She flicked the leaf cover off the large chunk of honeycomb and inspected it. She popped it into her mouth and chewed.

Jax waited until she finished. "I also promise to bring you two full nets of fish if you will but hear my need."

"Why should I trust you?" the bear said. "You have sent squirrels and birds to pester me, you have stolen my honey, and worst of all, you have stood outside my cave in winter singing. Your song is like trees crashing, like rocks falling, like the stench of a month-dead horse. Be glad I do not eat you. Fish? You owe me that and more, stonefriend."

She stood and swayed, her words a fearsome groan to anyone who didn't speak Bear.

Jax regarded the huge beast. "My family is in danger, great one. You are right to be angry. It is true, I sang to you in winter. But it is also true I have kept jackals from your cubs in springtime and left fruit and nuts so you could find them.

"If I sent my friends to pester you, kept you from the path of the hunter. My song piled snow high to hide your cave from prying eyes. If it made you howl, and I laughed? You remember, children of the Song love merriment and joy. I meant no harm. I call on you now only in great need."

The bear bent, her eyes searching his face. She snuffed loudly, smelling him. Jax stood motionless under the weight of her gaze, meeting it. Her hot breath smelled of honey, and he could see her sharp teeth, but he did not flinch. Finally, she sat up and gestured for him to sit.

"I will hear you," she said.

"Mighty queen, a clan of tall furless two-legs with metal teeth and evil songs are coming to my Burrow. They might overcome even your greatness, so I do not ask you to attack them directly. But you might frighten their horses or startle them, lead them astray, put obstacles in their path, and give my people time to run."

The bear rumbled when Jax mentioned the tall two-legs. She had no love for them. She regarded him for so long that Jax began to worry she might indeed be considering him as a meal. She answered with a groan. "It shall be done, son of stone. I will require that in the future, you not sing at my door."

Jax nodded in agreement. "Thank you, great one." He stood, bowed again, and returned to his pony.

It was time to rescue Bell.

17

Pezzik, Thurial, and other leaders inspected the ranks. Rows of gnomic warriors stood ready to defend the Burrow dwellers. Soldiers would scout in advance and defend the rear of the Moot as they travelled to their new home. Several families had already been dispatched to prepare.

Pezzik peered into the face of the gnomefather before her. His banded steel battle-cap stood proudly at attention. At a little over three feet, he was taller than most in the line. His armor, a combination of cleverly worked small steel plates and chainmail, shone. Sword and bow looked to be in good condition, the quiver well supplied. She nodded and inspected the rest of the line. Finished, she took her place atop a dais.

She pitched her voice to be heard, even as Gully, their tiny captain, rang the bell for attention.

The Moot quieted.

"Thank you for your attention. I will be brief. The squirrels have sent word. Our enemies are on their way. Conclave cantors and their acolytes can be disrupted, their allies confused. A confrontation need not end in battle. Listen well for orders. If you are unarmed, be prepared to go beneath the earth for protection until the stomping signals you to surface again. Good luck, and I will see you again in our new home!"

Gully spoke to his rank-leaders. Though very respected, he was one of the smallest gnomes. The leaders listened and began whistling. The ranks obeyed the whistles, dividing into six groups. Two trooped out,

131

while others prepared to wait for their enemy.

The escape plan was sound. The hard part had been convincing Thurial and the others to agree on a destination. Burrows were plentiful throughout their forest. Gnome numbers had diminished, so many now lay unused.

Pezzik clambered down from the dais and approached Thurial. His cap quivered. "You won't go with us?"

Pezzik shook her head. "I must find Jax. He should have been here yesterday. The squirrels saw him. He went to find Bell. A skunk carried word. He has asked the great bear to aid us. Something is not right. Bell has likely been taken. My place is at his side."

Thurial nodded and handed Pezzik a package.

She tilted her head, her cap curling as she turned it over.

"A number of Essences. You will need them," he said. Thurial took both her hands, squeezing them. "Be well, my sister, until we meet again."

Pezzik pulled him into a hug. "I am always careful."

She broke the embrace, waved farewell, and hurried to her pack. She needed to reach the village quickly. The fastest route overland was blocked, with the forest readying for battle. She would travel below, out of sight.

Pezzik shouldered her pack and pointed herself toward Dohnavur. She stepped into the stone wall and began her trek, careful to stay just under the root-line of the trees.

Pezzik strode through the earth at a steady pace. Occasionally she came upon a rabbit hole or fox den. She always apologized and passed through. When the tree roots thinned, she was close to the village.

She surfaced on the eastern side of Dohnavur. The stars twinkled. The moon's soft light fell on thatched roofs.

Pezzik lingered under the trees, watching the village for signs of trouble. Houses lay dark. Few chimneys belched smoke. Villagers should still be gathered at the inn's common room, playing stones, telling stories, and drinking their mugs. Some might be walking home.

It was too quiet. The streets were empty.

She set off for the *Bell and Rider* to see what was what. Her footsteps pattered in the quiet. Hair prickled on the back of her neck, but she saw no faces watching at windows. She quickened her pace.

She rounded the corner and made for the inn stables. Empty, Jax's pony and Bell's mare were both missing. The stable boy, Kellen, was absent. No other horses waited in the stalls.

The village had been purified before, but never had the outcome been so devastating. Deema had always protected their charges, hiding them away until the danger passed. The acolytes did a sweep with their incense and Camber the next week took an extra hour or two of Canting and confession. Those who needed to did penance. Life in town went on.

This time was different. They all had been caught unaware.

Pezzik crept through the wall of the inn, coming out in the kitchen. The inn's round cook, Lola, swept the floor, jumping when she saw Pezzik. She kneeled in front of the gnome.

"Pezzik! What are you doing out? They will see you."

Pezzik tilted her head. "The cantors?"

Lola nodded, her ample chins wobbling. She pushed a strand of dark hair that had escaped her kerchief. "Thank the cyntae you are all right. They have set Master Lile in charge of the inn. There is a curfew until the rites are complete. Pezzik, they have taken all the deemling, and we're to report the sight of any gnome at once. They say you are dangerous."

Pezzik sniffed. "I'm only dangerous to fools. Where is Bell?"

The cook shook her head. "I've not seen her since the purification began. It was terrible, all the acolytes in the streets with their hoods, those bells ringing. We thought certain the madness was falling again, only this time it had fallen on the cantors. Most townfolk have been afraid to set foot outside, and that's a fact. The cantors are watching the common room. Several acolytes are in there right now." Lola's eyes pleaded with her. "You have to hide."

Pezzik patted her arm. "Do not fear for me, good woman. Have you seen Jax?"

The cook gestured toward the door to the wine cellar. She looked from the kitchen door to the cellar, as if frightened of discovery. Pezzik nodded. She opened the cellar door, sliding into the cool darkness. As Lola shut the door behind her, Pezzik heard her answering a muffled query.

"Who were you—"

The question was silenced as the heavy door shut. Pezzik hurried down the steps.

Rows of casks rested in the vaulted cellar. Pezzik walked behind the first row of casks and found Jax. He stood, lost in thought, on top of a stool. He had fashioned a barrel into a makeshift table. Sheets of paper were spread on it, and he was busy writing, every now and again, stopping to read over what he had written and nodding to himself.

"Where have you been? What is happening? Where is Bell? Is she all right?" Pezzik demanded, the questions coming rapid fire as she settled on the other stool to rest.

Jax jumped. "I've been working out how to save Bell," he said, gesturing to his papers. "She's in the Chapterhouse tunnels along with the other deemling. None of them are free. They've all been purified with some Arcana I've never seen before. It affected Bell as if she is fully dewin. Mod has vanished."

Pezzik clucked. "So they're risking the wrath of all gnomes, then? Bold as bears and no mistake."

Jax nodded. "It took a while for me to find Bell, and when I did, it was too late. She doesn't respond. I can't get her to the surface alone. They are set to move all the deemling tomorrow. A skycart is coming to take them south. Aric leads this effort. He sent Nadir to the Burrow this morning."

Pezzik sniffed. "Fat lot of good that will do. The forest is ready. Our warriors will prevail, they always do. But a skycart? The aeries are aiding these tyrants? We haven't seen cantors behave so for centuries. The chymaera did not aid them before, why do they now?"

Jax shook his head. "You must feel it. The Song has been fading. This isn't the normal waning we see in midsummer, 'tis more. The vile son of a beetle, Aric, might have deceived the chymaera as he deceived us."

Pezzik set her jaw. "What of the other deema? If all the deemling were taken, then their deema should be tracking. Bolly? Tonk? Popple? Noorie? Dodd? All should be here."

Jax squared his shoulders. "I sent them out to spy. They're preparing special gifts for our hooded friends."

Pezzik raised an eyebrow.

Jax rubbed his hands together and laced them, turned them backwards, and stretched his arms to their full length in front of his paunch. "Let's just say tomorrow will be a very bad day for the cantors. A very bad day indeed."

Nadir trotted along the forest road, not quite at the head of the company. The trees were growing enormous. They were nearing the

Grove. He had fifty men, mostly trained soldiers from the baron's watch. All were mounted and under his sole purview, with Baron Pickell away at court. The men were more than enough to make quick work of these nasty little vermin. Insufferable monsters, with their beady eyes and their unusual strength. Nadir entertained himself as he rode, thinking about what he would do to the wee beasts. He could ride them down. He could burn them out of their Burrow. He could...

Nadir's reverie was rudely interrupted when the group topped a hill. His horse reared, nearly throwing him. The other horses in the company also spooked. It took several minutes to get them back under control. When they did, a line seven feet deep of armored, steadfast gnomes blocked their path forward.

Nadir barely took in the full extent of the gnome army before a large black bear emerged from the forest in front of the assembled troops. A tiny wizened gnome perched between her ears. The bear's size commanded attention. Nadir's horse sidestepped and whinnied. The bear stepped closer until the gnome and the cantor's horse were face-to-face. Nadir fought to control his horse.

The gnome regarded Nadir, gravely. He turned to Nadir's horse. "Fear not! I'm sorry, madam, we mean you and your kin no harm this day, But, if you persist in following my people, I must insist on defending them. It will be very unpleasant, and likely fatal for all of you."

The horse neighed.

"Yes, ma'am," replied the gnome. "Indeed, it isn't intelligent to ride horses if you go to war with gnomes. I will let him know that. I do much prefer to negotiate with the most reasonable members of a party. You horses seem more mature than your riders. If you don't mind my saying so. But I shall defer to your wisdom."

The gnome bowed slightly.

The horse whinnied and pawed the ground.

The gnome addressed Nadir. "Ser. My name is Captain Gully, and I command the Heyegrove Burrow Regiment. I must object to your further intrusion into our grove. If you take one more step, your horse assures me she shall throw you. My troops will then cut you down like curs. This bear and all of the forest animals will likewise defend us."

As if on cue, a number of foxes, badgers, otters, and even snakes emerged from the woods, coming to stand in front of the gnomes.

"In addition, you will promise never to harm or meddle with any of our kind in the future. Turn around and you will be allowed to return to your homes, unharmed. All of you." The gnome was speaking now to Nadir's little army. His voice was pitched to carry.

Nadir pulled himself up to his full height and laughed in the gnome's face.

"How dare you, you venomous little..."

Nadir's horse reared, promptly throwing him into the dirt. She immediately joined the line of animals with the gnomes.

Nadir lay in the road. Slowly, he got to his feet, checking himself for injury—his dignity, bruised.

Captain Gully and the local watchmen barely stifled amusement. The rest of Nadir's troop sat waiting for orders, carefully expressionless and unmoving.

Ungrateful wretches. I should have brought only the acolytes. This was that peacock Aric's fault. I could just Cant, and kill them all, but the watch would rebel or carry the tale to the twit baron, Pickell. No, it has to be the sword.

Slowly, Nadir clapped. "Well done, well done my small friend. I will accept your terms, you leave me no choice. After all, what other choice do I have when faced with such a company, except to...attack!"

With that, he charged the bear, drawing his sword. The few acolytes with him pressed into the fray, urging their horses forward.

The watchmen held back.

Every single man who moved against the gnomes was thrown from his horse without ceremony or hesitation. Each riderless horse took up a position behind the gnomes.

Nadir received a cuff on the head from the bear while being shot full of small arrows. He fell in the middle of the road, unconscious.

The others, seeing Nadir fall, laid down their weapons and backed away.

Captain Gully turned to the man still on horseback directly behind Nadir, the officer of the watch. "Sir, our terms still stand, if you choose to accept them. We have enjoyed a long friendship with the men of Dohnavur and with the baron. We have no wish to be at war with you. Should you proceed, war you shall have."

The captain bowed in his saddle. He saluted the bear and the other forest animals. "Retreat at once!" he ordered.

While his men loaded Nadir's body carefully on one of their horses, the now horseless acolytes mounted behind other soldiers. The last man was nearly out of his sight when he turned back to the gnomes. They still stood in formation, blocking the road.

"Thank you, Captain, and please accept my deepest apology. This will not happen again. I give you my word. Your families will remain safe," said the officer. "I will speak to the village council and send word to the baron."

Captain Gully nodded and bowed to the man. "Your apology is accepted. Go with grace. May the Song lead you home."

18

Noorie looked from Dodd to Popple. They were younger gnomes, only in their sixties, not yet grown into their beards and caps. Dodd, with his dark hair and slow, thoughtful manner, was likely safe to leave on his own. But Popple? Popple was thin, quick, and tricksy. His cap was never properly clean or sitting straight. His clothes were always rumpled. He was overconfident. Popple could get caught. But the Conclave had taken his deemling too. It was time to go to war.

Tonk and Bolly were planting itching powder and nettles in the boots, pillows, and beds of every cantor and acolyte in Dohnavur. Perhaps Popple should have joined them. Too late now. These young bravados were needed to gather information. Usually when Noorie wanted to know something about the Conclave, he would simply follow the cantor, Nadir. The man was a fool who loved to talk to himself. But Nadir had ridden off into the forest that morning, leaving this new cantor, Aric, in charge.

"We can't follow Aric around inside the Chapterhouse openly, we'll have to move between the walls and ceilings. Best to split up and meet back at the inn. Report to Jax in three hours. Learn what you can, and don't get caught!" Noorie explained, tugging his beard for emphasis.

With a nod, Popple grinned and pushed his disheveled cap up on his wide forehead. "We need to know when the chymaera will be here and where the skycart will be? Anything else?"

"Just anything you can learn about their plans will help," said Noorie.

Dodd nodded slowly. "I'll explore the lower chambers."

"Popple, you should follow any of the cantors or their acolytes about town, stay hidden but watch and listen," Norrie instructed. "I'll take the other floors inside."

With a wink and nod, Popple was scrambling up the side of the townhouse beside them. He disappeared over the roof line even as Dodd sank down into the earth.

Noorie sighed and crossed the street. He climbed up the stone wall of the Chapterhouse. He wouldn't worry about Popple. He had too much of his own work to do.

The stone felt cold, chilling Noorie as he sank into the wall, through to the other side. He entered near the ceiling height of an inner chamber, poking his head in to listen.

"Cows give milk, but it's sour as my pappy's spit. Been like that nigh on a month now. And I come to Camber proper. I pay my taxes. This purification 'tain't helping," said a farmer earnestly to a cantor.

The young cantor nodded, writing notes on a scroll before him. "We expect to see the changes take effect within a week or so. Be patient. In the meantime, take this and sprinkle it on the fields where your cows graze." The cantor handed the farmer a pouch.

Noorie shook his head and moved on, backing out of this room and creeping along the wall to the next one. He pushed through again and watched. Here ten cantors sat, rehearsing the Cants for Camber on Moonday. Noorie slipped out of this room as well.

In the next room, he saw rows upon rows of flowers drying. It was empty. A woman covered in festering sores lay in the room beyond, moaning. Acolytes attended her. Three chambers contained more of the sick. Several were townsfolk Noorie recognized. All seemed to be suffering from a kind of pox. He quickly retreated.

Noorie nearly left the next room immediately. It appeared to be empty and dark. Before he could retreat, the door opened, and glowstones came to light. A bearded man dressed in common garb strode in and sat at a desk. He pulled out a piece of parchment and began writing. Noorie settled in to wait. A half an hour later, the man folded and sealed the parchment. He rang a handbell on the desk. An acolyte entered the room in response.

"Take this message to the docks. There will be a man there named Sartor. You will find his vessel docked with a blue flag. He is expecting this. Let him know that this must get to the Conclave Chapterhouse in Bestua immediately. He is to give it to Modric only. They will admit him when he tells them it is from Aric. He must put this in Modric's hands himself. Is this understood?"

The acolyte nodded, turning deathly pale.

"Repeat the message back to me," Aric ordered.

The acolyte stammered, his bald head shining with sweat. "G-go to the docks, find Sartor. He has a boat with a blue flag. He is to give this to Modric at the Cantorium—"

"At the Chapterhouse," Aric corrected. "It's behind the Cantorium. The campus is large. But he must go to the Chapterhouse. Again from the beginning."

The acolyte repeated the instructions word perfect this time. With a wave, Aric dismissed him.

Noorie quickly climbed out of the office, climbing into one of the empty rooms. He found blank parchment and scribbled a quick message. He folded it, sealing it with the wax and seal on the desk. He stowed it within his cap and scaled the wall again, popping through the other side. He scrambled to the roof. He spied the acolyte messenger plodding slowly down a side street toward the docks.

Noorie caught up to a nearby pigeon. He instructed it to fly to Popple and ask him to swap his parchment from the acolyte. He could see Popple hanging from the side of the cobbler's shop. The pigeon cooed, agreeing, as Noorie grabbed his own parchment from his cap, along with a bit of thread and a needle. He threaded the needle through his message and tied it carefully to the pigeon's foot, bidding it to hurry.

The pigeon took off as Noorie watched. It circled Popple. He spotted the parchment hanging from its leg and followed it to the roof. When he reached for the parchment, the pigeon pecked at his hands. Popple listened to the bird and grinned, turning to look for Noorie. Seeing him, he waved and nodded. He detached the message from the bird's foot. Popple scurried along the tile rooftops and ridgepoles till he was at the end of the last row. The acolyte must pass that way just before he reached the dock. Popple carefully crawled down the side of the building.

Noorie held his breath, certain the acolyte would see Popple. Popple sank into the stone of the building until only his long nose and the tip of his cap were visible. As the acolyte walked by, his long arm shot out filching the packet from the acolyte's pocket. The man kept walking, oblivious. Popple cast Noorie's parchment into the street and shimmied back up the side of the building. He waved again and started running toward the inn's roof, jumping the gaps between buildings.

The counterfeit parchment blew in the wind and settled onto the cobbled lane, like an injured dove.

Noorie scrambled down a gutter, not waiting for the acolyte to retrace his steps and find the false parchment. Whatever Aric's message said, it was certain to help them rescue their deemling. Even better, the note Modric should now receive would go down as one of Noorie's greatest exploits.

Chesed climbed the tower stairs, his steps ringing through the aerie. The wind whistled through fluted spires. Tonight the wind sang of choices and longing. For too long it had carried only hopeless fear aloft. Dissonance had colored the wind's tune. Chesed was grateful for the hope, the change in tone.

The moon watched Chesed as he stopped on the landing and entered the translucent pavilion. It bathed the stone, painting it with a pale glow. The light fell on a towering copy of his own likeness, his signet. Two legs, two arms, nearly human in appearance, save for the unnatural height and too-thin build that marked an unwinged chymaera. The stone figure had hair so real it appeared to ruffle. Marble clothing mimicked his own, the texture of loose linen, not the silk most of his fellows wore. Chesed's eyes shone pale Profi silver, while the stone was only gray. Yet the marble expression captured his heartfire. Chesed walked around the signet, contemplating. It waited for him, waited to merge with his Profi form in the ancient Quickening ceremony, the rite which would finally grant him wings.

His signet had been waiting for over three hundred years.

Chesed knelt and sang to the Storm King. The song began as the wordless cry of an eagle, changing to reflect what he had heard tonight in the wind. He sang about his choices and longings, his failures and fears. He took the wind's melody as his own and offered it back to the Storm King with humility and thanks. Everyone claimed the Storm King was dead, but Chesed refused to believe it. His faith fueled his resolve, even as it isolated him from the others. I know you are at work, my Lord. Even now. He dared not share this hope with anyone else yet. He apologized for his cowardice and finished with another eagle cry. He rose and walked around the form again. It had changed slightly in response to his song. It always did, though the changes were miniscule. The hair had moved; the eyes were uplifted. Seeking the wind's hope.

He grasped the two hands of his signet briefly. They warmed under his fingers, his heartfire kindling communion between them. He smiled at it. It smiled back, mirroring him, much as a Speaker would. He wished—he hoped to Quicken. He gave silent voice to his longing, reaching toward his elders, the cyntae, in his heart. No answer.

He turned and began his long trek back down the stairs.

Some of his brothers had forsaken the daily rite in despair. These had abandoned their signets and joined the Pryf, their silver eyes turning blue or green. Not Chesed. He would never turn his back on the Storm King.

Chesed loped through the branching passages that riddled the Aerie. Some were huge, where trees grew, and gardens bloomed. Some were so narrow only one person at a time could squeeze through. Carved by Song, the Aerie was a wonder of delicate towers and intricate whorls, lacelike formations. Trees blended with stone, growing entwined with the karst spires. Their root systems adorned the lower passages, branching into and out of the stone itself before burrowing greedily into cold pools of water. Steps twined around the spires like vines, leading up to the flight platforms and aeries of the Derbyn, the accepted.

The Profi, the unproven, and the Pryf, the rejected, were assigned to lower passages, earthbound.

Chesed turned through the labyrinth, captured by the play of moonlight on lacework stone. He slowed and absorbed the beauty, adding it to his heartfire. He moved on, turning toward the heart of the Aerie, the songpitches. The massive Cyntaf, a giant stone gryphon, towered over this open field. The field was divided into octagons, or pitches, each connecting to the next like honeycomb, bordered by diamonds. Chesed smiled as he watched the other Profi working by moonlight, like bees. He was sure they would not appreciate the comparison.

The Profi labored, one to a section, wrestling with the Song. In front of each was a block of marble. Some used tools, as men did, singing as they worked. The more learned used only Song, mouths working silently. The pitches contained all sound, allowing none to escape. Impish, whimsical figures took shape under each voice. The best of these would adorn the quarters of Derbyn, feeding their heartfires.

Some would become Speakers, replacing the failing or inert grotesques in the Aeries, as well as those in the human's Sundered City. Each lesser form might serve as a Watcher or a Taker.

Chesed found an empty pitch and entered, singing the names of the cyntae to bond it and keep his song from spilling out. He signaled to a black-winged Derbyn. The gryphon lifted a piece of stone gently into the pitch. Chesed sang a thank you. The gryphon inclined his massive hawk's head in response and flew back to his perch.

Chesed stared at the stone. He touched it, feeling its inner form. He caught a glimpse of the figure lurking within the stone, closed his eyes and reached for his heartfire. He sat, listening. He had barely begun to see the form of the shaping song when a shadow fell across his face, blocking the moonlight.

It was M'ra, eldest of the Derbyn. She entered the songpitch quickly. Her ancient eyes gleamed golden. She was unwinged, wearing a silken gown to cover her slim ivory limbs. Long hair flowed over a finely shaped head and long neck. It was a sign of deep respect, to appear so before a mere Profi, unwinged. Chesed was humbled. He bowed deeply.

"M'ra." Chesed covered his heart with his hand, indicating the gift of his heartfire. M'ra bowed and covered her heart in reply.

"Walk with me, Chesed," said M'ra. Her command brooked no argument. Chesed sang the names of the cyntae again to unbond the pitch. As they left the space, another Profi entered, taking his place. The Profi sang before silence fell, separating them from the work.

M'ra led Chesed out of the songpitch field and into a large park just beyond. Trees here soared, growing so close together with vines and moss they nearly hid the stone walls. A waterfall cascaded into a large pool at one end. Paths wound around low grassy knolls and flower beds. Starlight seeped through the leafy canopy above.

"Did you hear the wind today, little brother?" asked M'ra. Chesed answered quickly, his pulse racing. "Yes, lady. It sang of hope."

"Why do you think it sang so?"

"I do not know, eldest."

"I do not know either, little brother. But I would know, and I would see through your eyes. I would know as a Profi knows and see what a Profi sees. You shall travel with me as I conduct my work, little brother. You shall ride and talk to men. You shall be ears and eyes to me. I would know what your heartfire gathers."

Chesed was stunned. It was unheard of for a mere Profi to leave the Aerie, and in such exalted company. "Why, M'ra?" The question left his lips before he could stop it.

M'ra regarded him with amused eyes. "We Derbyn have sought for truth and solutions for five centuries. Still our Cyntaf does not quicken with the voice of Renato. Only Doran comes, and that, rarely. We cannot perform your Quickening, however perfect your signet might be. You long to see the shape of your true form at last. You seek to fly. You see more clearly perhaps, because of this desire. You are still young and have not been shrouded with the pain we know."

Chesed bowed his head.

"Watch the Conclave cantors, listen as we serve them. Tell me all you hear. You shall speak your thoughts to me alone," M'ra said. She looked at him, her ageless face glowing softly in the starlight. "Meet me here at noon tomorrow. We shall begin our journey of new eyes. May the cyntae bless it and give us what we seek."

Pezzik waited. Jax read Aric's message slowly, his bushy eyebrows drawn. This message might hold the key to Bell's freedom. She bit her tongue, willing herself to silence and patience. It's his deemling, she told herself after a quarter hour had passed. Jax grunted, turning the page over and kept reading. Pezzik cleared her throat and settled noisily in her chair. Jax didn't look up. She cleared her throat again.

"I'm trying to read this. You just made me lose my place. Now I have to start over." Jax leveled a look at Pezzik. He looked at the parchment again, but before he could focus, Pezzik lost her grip on patience.

She plucked it from his hands. "You see here, Jax na'Timmon"—she waggled a finger under his nose, waving the parchment for emphasis —"You are not the only gnome to have lost a deemling, and the proper thing is to read this aloud. As you're too addlepated to do so, I'll help you." She fixed him with a glare, challenging him to protest.

Behind her, the other deema nodded and fidgeted, murmuring.

Jax sputtered, objecting, but his complaints died under the weight of her indignation. "Go ahead," he said with a sigh.

Pezzik began to read.

Master Modric,

All is proceeding well. As you suspected, some of the deemling are indeed dewin, though not all responded to the testing we administered. These are still being held for observation. Our experiments will continue when we have them safely at the Rift Chapterhouse with the others. Their proximity to one another and exposure to a cyntae should give exciting new insights. We plan to leave at dawn on Whensday and will arrive no later than midday. Should everything go well, we will proceed to the Tree. I will be exposing them to measure the effects.

Our trap has sprung. We have discovered the source of the cursed instruments. The luthier's workshop has been purified, though he did escape with the lute meant for Trystan. Danethor had several strains of tunebell I've never seen before. I shall send a specimen along shortly. We have plans to acquire several gnomes along with Trystan. They should help us locate Danethor. I am confident we will do so. However, because the instruments will no longer be crafted, rest assured, your plans will be hindered no longer. Enclosed you will find a drawing to identify the luthier.

Pezzik looked up, her eyes angry.

"It's signed, Master Crafter Aric Miller, The Bindery." She held up a sketch of Dane, drawn on a separate parchment and tucked in with the note. It was a good likeness.

"Thank the stars this did not go to the Conclave," she said, shaking her head.

Noorie stepped forward. "Dawn tomorrow is well and good, but where will the skycart be? And how shall we take the deemling from them? Perhaps we could get one away, but fourteen of them?" His pointed cap drooped.

Dodd cleared his throat. "I saw the deemling, all of them. I also heard where they are taking them to meet the skycart. The Willow Bottoms. Stu was all right, he could talk. I told him we were planning a rescue. Little Mary Planor was like Bell. The Frenner family except for Jess were all well and the Smiths and the Hodges likewise. They were held separately but seemed whole enough."

Popple and Bolly exchanged glances, relief flooding their faces. Noorie's cap drooped. Mary was his deemling. Tonk kicked a cask of wine in frustration.

"Jess has only fourteen summers. It 'tain't right," Tonk's voice broke. Jax's face set with determination. "We will restore them, brothers. We will."

The other gnomes agreed, bustling around Tonk and Noorie to show their support. Pezzik hugged them. Popple slapped their backs. Dodd and Bolly tipped their caps. Jax paced, thinking.

"The Willow Bottoms are south of town, we should get there as soon as possible. They could travel by boat or on foot, but I'll wager they use boats. We can rescue them at the shore before they reach the skycart. We will need help. We have no idea how many they will take as guards, but a boat would limit their numbers."

Pezzik frowned. "The beavers and otters would be close by, and likely a few water rats. We could ask for support. We can speak to any horses."

Jax went to his map. "Our best hope is to have our own boat waiting and outrun them. We are agreed that we need to take them to the Caprices for healing? The Conclave cannot enter Siarad."

The gnomes nodded as one.

"All right, we load them into our boat. We take the River Alyn as far as the Thwn Channel and float past Inner Siarad to the village."

"What about the chymaera?" Dodd asked.

"They shouldn't be assisting in this outrage," said Popple.

"Will they attack us?" asked Tonk.

Bolly said, "Stu and all the others will fight with us."

"What if they enchant us?" asked Popple.

Pezzik shook her head. "Floating past the island at Siarad won't be simple, the Dread falls thick."

Jax waved the questions and worries away. "We shall ask the Storm King for aid, do what we can do. Tonk, Bolly, Pezzik. Go to the mercantile in town, find Poll. Tell him what we need. He will help. Ask Lile for coin to pay for the wares. Meet me at Mod's house, geared and ready.

"Noorie, go to the Bottoms with Popple and seek the beaver clan. They should be nesting this time of year. Ask them who else can help. I will take Dodd with me. We will meet you at the largest willow after midnight."

Chesed woke, blinking as sunlight streamed into his rooms. He dressed quickly and packed a woven bag with essentials. He loped down the stairs to meet M'ra.

She was winged today. Her plumed ivory form filled the small meadow. Her massive tail twitched in greeting. She extended her foot and lowered her head, bidding him to ride.

We have much to see, little brother. Her communion was sudden and intimate. When winged, M'ra could sense general emotion from anyone. Chesed could not properly reply as he was not yet Derbyn, so he held grateful thoughts as he climbed onto her neck and settled into the slingback.

They flew first to retrieve the skycart, a small rectangular building, richly embellished with filigree. M'ra grasped the roofpole in her talons. She spoke to Chesed again, communing.

N'khum will also take a skycart to the Tree to carry dignitaries from Pelegor and bring mad dewin to be healed. Modric has promised a breakthrough for us. Doran will give us a Quickening ceremony. He claims the mad dewin can assist. We go to fetch them. Yet I am uneasy and would see what else we can learn. We will seek to understand the wind's new hope.

Chesed kept his heart and mind open, peaceful. It was the only reply of trust he could make, but M'ra seemed to accept it. She rose into the clouds, and he gripped the slingback, his face turned into the wind as if he could catch its hope and drink it.

They stopped just outside Ciclaehne so M'ra could shed her wings and rest. The next flight would be long. They were headed deep into the northern Welde. They entered the city and turned through the streets, ignoring the stares of men until they reached M'ra's favorite tavern, The Stone Guardian. While many of the patrons eyed them warily, they were treated with deference and respect.

M'ra instructed Chesed as they finished their meal. "Men see us come and go to Conclave Chapterhouses and sometimes the palace. But none of them understand the difference between Profi, Derbyn, and Pryf. When you are alone, if threatened, simply sing, or call to one of the Speakers. They will help you. Most of the time the singing is enough."

Chesed raised his eyebrows, shocked. "They would attack us?"
"It has happened before. A Derbyn can transform, but you are not yet Derbyn. Best not to take chances. I will have you with me always, but I want you to be careful and ready. Stars know, things can go awry when we do not wish it so."

M'ra gestured to the men and women around them. "The Conclave cantors will have long black robes with arc pins at the collar. Their acolytes wear white and have no hair. Not short, but completely removed."

Chesed picked at his plate, scooping up crumbs. "What of the other races?"

"In the human cities you will see dwarves. They are very short, no larger than four feet tall. Their cousins are gnomes, but I have not seen one in two hundred years. They are even smaller. Gnomes and dwarves love the Song and are usually friendly. In the wilds creatures of shadow thrive. Giants, goblins, spiders, water-leapers. There are other Shadowborn, but we shall not speak of them here." M'ra fell silent and rose.

Chesed followed. As they walked through the city, he glimpsed Speakers serving men. Many of them were Wyn crafted, but he noticed some from the other sigils. They made him feel more comfortable in this city, surrounded by so many smaller folk.

M'ra transformed in a field outside the city gates, and once again they flew. She followed the channel, and they passed close to the World Tree, circling. Chesed had never seen it before. It filled his heartfire to overflowing.

M'ra winged onward, more swiftly. They flew for hours, with M'ra occasionally breaking into communion to teach him a thing she thought he might need to know. They stopped outside a smaller city called Teredhe and ate again. They winged their way toward the Draigor Mountains and the River Wych. As they neared a mountain lake, M'ra began to circle.

I will land outside the town. We are meant to be here in secret, tomorrow. We will not announce our presence, but if we are seen, we shall not hide. I will learn more than these Conclaves wish to say.

Along the river, south of town, a large grove of willow trees bordered a small estuary. A meadow lay beyond. It was a place of uncommon beauty. Here M'ra settled as the moon rose high into the sky. Crickets sang anxiously, disturbed by M'ra as she set the skycart gently down and transformed. Fireflies danced around them, pretending to be stars.

"It will be difficult to go unnoticed, eldest," Chesed ventured. "Will we go to town?"

M'ra nodded. "This late, most will be sleeping. However, we might chance upon someone who has a tale. Come little brother, let us seek to learn more of these cantors."

As she set off toward the willows, ready to follow the river to Dohnavur, the crickets' song grew merry, welcoming. Chesed took up his bag and followed her, listening to the wind and watching the arc of the moon as it began to descend.

Suddenly, the crickets went silent.

19

Dane woke, surprised his head wasn't pounding from all the ale he had consumed the night before. It was dawn. He hadn't really slept, but he was alert. He dressed quickly, emptied most of his purse and hid the contents under his thick feather mattress. He needed a new pair of boots, quickly. For that matter, he really needed to change his entire appearance. He had pondered the problem the night before, brooding.

He ducked out of his room and down the stairs.

Dane's description could have been passed throughout all Conclave chapters by now. At the larger Chapters, there would be questioners, skilled at detecting Dissonance. Lies could be almost scented by a questioner. And if there were no questioners? This was Ciclaehne. Each active Speaker had the talent.

Dane had to come up with a method to hide his identity from the Conclave, while not rousing suspicion from the Northmen or the dwarf. He must manage to deceive questioners, all without overtly speaking a lie. Thorny.

He shouldn't go. This was madness. He was just guessing what the fae meant with her babbled phrases. *The game is not a game.* It could mean anything. But he had already committed. If he didn't show up, the dwarf would look for him.

It was early, yet the streets bustled with activity. Dane traced his way back to the shanties below the outer wall. Beyond the gate, rows of pavilions, shacks, and other makeshift shelters crouched, haphazard. Like drunken sailors, they lurched and leaned into each other, leaving no space between them. Where space did open, shadows pooled. Dane surveyed the scene, impassive, before heading into their midst.

Dane was relieved to find a likely tinker after only a short walk. He lounged on a low stool in the shadows of a makeshift storefront.

"That'll be a one and a ha'penny, young sir," the tinker said to Dane, handing him nondescript pewter buckles. Dane paid the man, pocketing the buckles with a murmured thanks and continued down the tented path on the lookout for a barber. Children played in the distance, chanting an old rhyme.

One two three, Lord Domini
Four, Five, Renato is alive
Six seven, Miah is in Heaven, Eight,
nine, Faron is Father Time, Ten,
eleven, who falls from Heaven. Twelve,
thirteen, fourteen Solimon 'n' Lalo are
courting Fifteen takes all
Tieson breaks the Fall.
Doran turns, turns, turns
The Wyrm burns, burns, burns
Cyntae bright, cyntae might
Keep us safe till morning.

Dane stopped, listening. He felt a pang of homesickness and shook his head to clear it. No time to wallow today. His eyes fell on a painted white pole wrapped with bloody linens, two shacks down. Perfect. The mottled bell on the door jingled as he entered.

"Good morning, young sir." The barber smiled from behind a large wooden chair. "How might I be of service? Do you need a shave? A tooth pulled? An illness cured?" He motioned to the array of instruments behind him, some rather fearsome. Pincers, claws, knives, scissors, and razors all neatly shone on trays.

"I need a shave," said Dane. "I need you to shave my entire head." The barber beamed. "The fashion of acolytes! Are you bound to the Chapterhouse then?"

Dane nodded, returning the smile. "Aye, I'm due to go today."

"Well, say no more, I shall make you suitable in two shakes of a lamb's tail."

"Also, I do not wish to have my tooth pulled, but believe a packing of garlic and fabric would help one in the back. 'Tis bothersome. My mum taught me the trick," Dane said. "Might I get a bit of clean packing?"

"Certainly, young fellow, and the garlic as well. 'Tis a remedy I myself employ to save a tooth. Your mother is a wise woman."

"Yes, she was. She was."

When Dane emerged from the barber's shack, his boot buckles had been replaced. His thick shock of black hair was completely gone, and the right side of his face was packed with garlic and linen. The pungent odor made his eyes water, but the smell would deter the curious. He'd venture even Pezzik would not know him on sight.

He purchased gently worn garb, a linen tunic, a cloak, and a leather jerkin. Almost ready. He returned to his room and quickly donned his new clothing. He belted the tunic, covering all with the hooded traveling cloak, and then headed back downstairs, preparing to explain his transformation. This was the thorny bit.

Dane was directed to the stables behind the inn, where he found Bellin, Harald, and Birgir saddling their mounts, preparing for the day's journey.

"Can I help you, sir?" asked Bellin, as Dane approached.

"Aye," said Dane in a passable rendition of the dwarf's thick Northern brogue. "I need to know if you've seen a thieving scamp of a weevil by the name of Danethor. Lad has made off, breaking a promise to a fine young lass. I mean to uphold her honor and bring him home."

Birgir stepped forward, ready to defend his young friend, but Harald pointed at Dane and began laughing.

Birgir stopped, glaring at Dane and back again to Harald in confusion. He peered more closely. "By Lalo's right tit, you're a proper knave!"

He walked up to Dane and squarely punched him on the nose. Dane reeled, taking a step back and did the only sensible thing. He crumpled to the ground, unconscious.

Dane revived suddenly, sputtering as Birgir doused him with a bucket of water. "Solimon's balls!" he yelled, trying to roll out of the deluge. He immediately regretted moving as his head swam. He coughed, wiped his face on the sleeve of his new tunic, and gingerly felt his nose. It didn't seem to be broken, but he could feel his face swelling. He spat out the garlic packing and glared at Birgir, who only laughed.

"Since you're dodging a woman and likely a wedding, you'll be glad to have your face changed," Birgir said. "I only tapped you."

He handed Dane a wet cloth. Dane stood and wiped the blood from his lip.

Bellin said, "Can you ride, Danethor?"

Dane shook his head slowly. "Not after that wallop. I'll just slow you down." He felt a need to vomit. His head hurt and vision swam. Stars, but the man's fist was huge.

Bellin, Harald, and Birgir conferred for a moment, heads together, and came to an agreement. Bellin pulled a small pouch from his saddlebag and tossed it to Dane, along with a water skin. "Take one pinch," he instructed. "And wash it down. 'Twill set you to rights."

Dane eyed the pouch with frank suspicion. "You lot have tried to kill me twice now. What is this?"

Harald snorted. "If we'd tried to kill you, you'd be dead. It was just a tap."

Birgir laughed and thumped Dane on the back, a little too hard. "Harald thinks a punch is a kiss, it's his way. And that," he pointed to the pouch, "is willow bark and ginger. 'Twill help your aching head."

"You'll be able to ride," said Bellin.

"Why is it so important that I come along, Bellin? Do you really think a deemling is going to give you any information at the Tree you might not have yourself?" Dane was serious. He took a pinch of the powder and quickly washed it down, then tossed the skin back to the dwarf.

"We have time for the entire tale. It will take a bit for the potion to help you," said Bellin. "Listen and after, you tell us what's what." Bellin claimed a hay bale in the corner, gesturing for his companions to join him. Harald sighed, produced his pipe, and settled on an adjacent bench. Dane and Birgir arranged themselves between.

"We told you our forges are failing. The truth is, folk believe the Conclave is a festering ball of pus controlling nations, and the Song itself needs to stop flowing," he said. "They teach when the Tree fully dies, nothing will happen.

"These perfect fools do not believe in the Breaking or the events directly after. They've stirred unrest in smaller towns from Mos Tevis to the Fells," said Birgir, his face darkening.

"One of these fine young radicals is a lordling named Gisle de Clelland. He and his cronies visited the Forge at Mos Tevis in the weeks before we left for this mission."

"He mentioned two things to our Forgelord, Tenkor, of particular import. Firstly, Gisle told Tenkor the true reason for our troubles wasn't due to the Tree. He said it was Conclave interference. Secondly, he said gnomes might have the key to ridding us of our dependence on the Conclave. When pressed, he would say no more, but he was very keen for any lore we might have.

"We looked into our records, and indeed, there are many accounts of gnomic crafting. They do not use songlines as we do. We are interested to learn more. Burrows have fallen silent over the years." Bellin lit his pipe, puffed and continued. "But the true reason we feel you might be a help to us today is one we almost dare not mention."

Here, Bellin leaned forward and looked at Dane with a solemn expression. "I don't want to alarm you lad, but you might have a knack. And if you do, we'd like to find out."

"Knack?" Dane tasted the word aloud. He recoiled in shock and half stood. "I'm not mad, Bellin, I only shaved my head. You haven't met Bell and her deema."

Bellin put a placating hand on his arm. "No, lad, don't misunderstand. We aren't hidebound Welden folk. We do not believe every bleating of the cantors. You're obviously a good lad in his right mind. We're not saying you are dewin. Before the Breaking, deemling and deemae often served the majisters. They had prized skills and talents, knacks. Some were small, finding water. Others were rarer and more prized. Understanding languages and the like. When the dewin went mad," Bellin said, "anyone who had worked with the Song was taken by the Conclave. Taken, watched, and purified as needed. Most deemling were eventually sent home. Most, but not all." He tapped the side of his nose.

"So you think deemling have a talent with the Song, and if I get close to the Tree...I'll see something?"

Birgir and Harald nodded.

"What if I can't help you? What am I supposed to do? What sort of thing might happen?" Dane's voice stayed low as he faced the three Northerners.

Bellin cut him off. "We do not know, but 'tis worth walking through a dark tunnel to find out what lies beyond, since, by the cyntae's grace, we met you. Just come with us, look at the Tree and say what you see. You do not have to do more. The old knacks were cottage helps. Some could find water easily. Others could tell the weather. Might be you have none, or it will be of no use at all. Mayhap you will see something we can use. No matter how the stones roll, we aren't asking you to do anything to cause harm."

Dane pursed his lips, weighing his thoughts, and slowly said, "I have always wanted to see the Tree. My deema said I am daft as a rock, make no mistake. I'm unlikely to be able to help you. But I will try."

Harald beamed and thumped the bench. "Good lad."

"One other thing," Dane said. "I told you I would need a favor before we went. It's a small thing but will set my mind at ease."

Bellin nodded, encouraging him to continue.

"I need you to hire me. I'll only charge you a copper." He shifted uneasily. "It's just so if asked, you can truthfully say that I am one of your servants. It's about the girl, you see." Not an outright lie. Bell could be hurt if he was discovered. Still, he was walking a fine line.

Bellin grunted and walked over to his pony's saddlebag, rooting in it for a moment before coming up with a small object, which he tossed to Dane. "You're hired."

Dane looked in his lap and gawked. There in his lap was a small ruby.

Birgir got up and went to locate another horse for Dane.

Bellin barked a laugh at Dane's expression. "Don't worry, my boy. Before this day is done, you will have earned every penny."

20

Chesed and M'ra both halted, listening.

The silence had been broken by splashing, muffled curses, and enthusiastic shushing coming from the largest willow, the low buzz of conversation. A pointed cap poked out from the willow fronds, then vanished.

Chesed strained to make sense of what was being said.

"...sure the otters know the plan. They'll need to have the slides built by...Noorie, you and Tonk will have th...at the end...ready to...the deemlings. Pezzik and I are going to go...and see...guess...cart will be...yes, Popple?"

"Pardon, Jax, but...two chymaera over there, I thought you ought to know." The voice was loud. Excited.

"Two?" A row of red caps popped through the curtain of willow branches in succession.

Chesed counted seven of them. M'ra smiled in delight upon seeing the gnomes. Their earnest faces reflected varying degrees of consternation and wonder at the sight of her. She took a slow step forward. Her long white hair flowed unbraided over alabaster skin, gathering moonlight until it glowed. She knelt to examine the gnomes but did not speak. She simply waited. Chesed took a step forward to join her.

The gnomemother stepped out and cleared her throat. She marched up to M'ra and curtsied deeply. "Greetings, Children of the Dawn, I am called Pezzik," she said, her voice clear and resolute. She motioned the others forward. "These are fellow deema from my Burrow. Jax, Tonk,

Noorie, Popple, Bolly, and Dodd." She pointed to each in turn as they emerged from the sheltering branches.

"Thank you for the gift of your names, cousin. I am M'ra, Derbyn of the Wyn Aerie. This is Chesed."

Chesed bowed from the waist, his eyes crinkling as he smiled. These gnomes were less than half his height and reminded him very much of his impish grotesques. It was delightful to meet living examples.

Pezzik's brow furrowed. She cleared her throat. "We normally live in the Heyewood, not in the Willow Bottoms. It's been an age since we've seen your folk, but I do remember a few. I was but a wee lass."

Chesed squatted next to M'ra, to put himself on the gnomes' level. "The hour is late, and you are far from your Burrow."

Pezzik nodded, looking at the other gnomes, as if she hoped someone else would explain. One stepped forward, and the others drew in closer, but they didn't speak. Her conical hat curled to one side as she spoke. "You see our deemling have been taken by the Conclave. We are deema. Guardians. We are here to rescue our charges as they will be moved tomorrow."

She crossed her arms and eyed M'ra.

"What we don't understand is how you folk came to help the cantors do this thing." The gnomemother's tone was sharp.

M'ra blinked. "Your deemling?" She tilted her head, considering, and stood, straightening to her full height.

These creatures have no right to judge the Wyn.

"We are here to bring mad dewin to a place where they can harm no one and perhaps be aided. We know nothing of deemling." M'ra's voice chilled. "If your deemling are our dewin, they must be kept from violence."

"My Bell has harmed no one," said one of the taller gnomes, stepping forward. He crossed his arms, mirroring Pezzik. His cap quivered. "These cantors have hurt her. They were all right as rain before they were purified. Now some can't help themselves or speak."

Horror stuck Chesed like a blow as he heard the gnome speak. He saw it mirrored on M'ra's face, quickly replaced by pity. "It is always so with dewin. They must be disabled. Do you remember the days just after the Song was broken, and the darkness fell? Gnomes live nearly as long as we do. Do you recall how the dewin raged?"

Do you feel it little brother? Dissonance. Never have I heard Dissonance in the voice of any living creature... other than true dewin as they sing. This gnome carries their blight. All who meet him should be affected. Yet clearly they are not. A mystery.

Jax nodded, tapping the side of his nose. "Not all raged, lady. Elsewhere, they did. The gnomes of the Heyewelde were warned before the War. We trained with Majister Jamis himself to prepare and kept our dewin from madness. These and their descendants became our deemae, watched and guarded by the most brave, the most daring."

M'ra looked at Jax, her face icy with rage. "You lie, there is Dissonance in your voice."

The gnomes all looked truly frightened...all except Pezzik. "He is not lying, lady. 'Tis true," she said. "Yes, some deemling may be dewin but most are not. Those with the full gift are rare. Yet when they do have it, we ensure they never succumb to Dissonance. Not one under my watch has gone mad in five centuries!"

M'ra dismissed her claim with a wave, shaking her head. "You have not truly had dewin. They all go mad. I hear them, you see. I heard them on that last day. I heard them in the months after, and I would hear them now, if I were close enough. I will hear them tomorrow. Madness, gibbering meaningless madness fills their hearts. It consumes, and they lash out. It has been so since the Tree was riven to now. We thought the last dewin we transported died centuries ago, as mad as the rest."

She studied the other gnome, Jax, for a long quiet moment. "You might not know you lie. But there is a Dissonance in your voice. I feel it. You cannot speak truly."

Chesed stood, his voice low and smooth despite the upset he felt. When the male gnome spoke, his voice twisted. It was palpable.

"The lady speaks what she feels, and I feel it as well. I hear Dissonance in you, gnome. I didn't see the destruction they wrought, but I know dewin murdered many of my people with music on their lips. They sang as only they could. So many died. We grieve their loss with you."

Pezzik stared down the two chymaera, her voice steady but rising in volume. "How do you think we saved the dewin, Children of the Morning? Do you think we forced stone to take their pain? Lured animals to be targets for their rage? No. We took their Dissonance into our very bones. What you feel from Jax is not untruth. 'Twas his heart that first found the way. The learning of it affected him. That is what you sense. He is as true a soul as you would ever know."

M'ra laughed. "No one can take madness from another nor

Dissonance. We sought for centuries to find a shield. You could do what we could not? No. Little cousins, you have done what you could for the unfortunates, and for this we give you thanks. You truly believe lies. You have carried them long. This might be the source of Dissonance in the one you call Jax. For that reason we shall let him live. We do not wish you harm. But we shall take your friends, your dewin, and keep them from harming others. We shall aid the Conclave, as we have before."

It was a dismissal.

As one, Chesed and M'ra turned away.

"Wait!" The gnome called Jax was running after them, his face desperate, his cap nearly falling off his head. "You said you could hear dewin?"

M'ra nodded.

"Then let us have those you cannot hear and take them home. They are no threat to anyone. If you do not hear them, they are not truly dewin."

M'ra hesitated, looking at Chesed. He gazed into the eyes of the wizened gnome, admiring his courage. *As true a soul as you will ever know.* Pezzik's words rang within him like a shaping song in his pitch, despite the Dissonance in the other gnome's voice. Chesed held his impressions fast, making them as clear as possible for M'ra to read. Mercy.

Perhaps we shape your signet in this place, as well as in our home, little brother, M'ra said.

M'ra spoke to the gnome aloud. "What you ask is permissible. It shall be done."

"And let us go with the others. Pezzik and I," said Jax. His small figure stood solemn, immovable. Sweat beaded on his forehead. He removed a handkerchief from his cap and mopped his brow. "We shall not interfere. We need to know where they are being taken, so—"

"You shall have nothing more to do with dewin." M'ra seemed to grow taller, her features hardening into marble. She did not raise her voice, but her words slashed forth. "Do not try my patience. Innocent you may be, but Dissonant you are. I should by all rights end you. That I do not is a sign of my mercy and faith that you are indeed harmless. Do not test it. If you try to take the dewin, you shall die by my talon."

The gnome did not bend under the chymaera's threat. He returned her gaze, uncowed.

Chesed intervened, lest M'ra change her mind and rip the gnome to shreds. "We shall send the silent deemling to your willow at dawn. Good evening."

He stepped forward and took M'ra's hand, leading her away toward the village. As they disappeared into the shadows, Chesed heard the gnomes whispering of their foolish defiance.

Quietly Chesed prayed to the Storm King, knowing M'ra might understand, even if the Lord did not answer.

Please, give these gnomes the wisdom to walk away. Let them live.

Gisle de Clelland watched the scene unfolding in the Willow Bottoms with great interest. He could not hear what was said, but it wasn't important. He had eyes only for the small figures in their conical caps, speaking with the chymaera.

Gnomes. Some do yet live.

He signaled with his hands to his scout, Brock, silently. *Move forward, listen, report.*

That done, he leaned back and waited. It was too dark to see expressions. He dismissed the tableau, turned, and walked back to his camp, two miles away from the river. His guards, Rennet and Martine, followed.

Gisle's travel pavilion was small, but adequate for his needs on the road. A small cot, a chest, a folding chair, and an oil lamp were all he required. His guards left him, taking up stations around the perimeter. He pushed the fabric panel that served as a door to one side. His was a soldier's camp. His was a soldier's life, despite his noble birth. Discipline. He crossed to his cot and sat, pulling a weathered book from under his mattress. Gisle traced a map marked with gnome burrows. His generous mouth pursed as he considered their position. His company had landed south of the Heyegrove, intending to spend time in the village and restock while they considered their next move.

When Brock reported unusual activity in Dohnavur, they had regrouped. The reconnaissance mission tonight had been meant to discover the lay of the land. Gisle had not been prepared for so many cantors and acolytes this far away from larger cities. Very odd.

Gisle did not like being unprepared. The gnomes, so near and easily accessible, were an unexpected boon.

Brock cleared his throat.

Gisle looked up, unsettled. The man was a ghost, silently appearing. It made him the perfect scout, but also made him singularly overweening. He positively enjoyed startling his master, Gisle was sure of it. He would not give him the satisfaction. Gisle kept his face calm, meeting the scout's gaze.

"Report."

"There are seven gnomes, sir, planning to meet the chymaera at dawn and take custody of villagers rather than letting them go with the cantors. They have a flatboat ready and stocked. They are in league with local vermin, sir. Otters and beavers. Two gnomes plan to sneak onto the skycart and rescue the incapacitated. This is against the female chymaera's expressed wishes. Their plan is not tenable, sir. They will be killed. The chymaera believe the villagers are dewin."

Gisle snorted. "Nonsense. There are no dewin."

"That fact will not stop an angry gryphon, sir."

"Two gnomes against a full party of cantors and two chymaera. Advise."

"Advise to intercept the gnomes, sir."

Gisle nodded. "Plan accepted, work out details, and wake me in two hours. Prepare the others. Dismissed."

Gisle turned and doused his lamp, laying on his cot for a short rest. These cantors and their pets would not keep him from his goal. Nothing would. He would free his land from this blight of Conclave tyranny.

Chesed and M'ra found the village inn with little trouble. A few older men and one younger one, deep in their cups, sat at the bar while a weary maid swept up straw, herbs, crumbs, and dirt from the stone floor. Clean rushes lay in a basket at her feet, ready to be strewn. Two acolytes sat in a corner drinking tea. M'ra swept a glance at the large, nearly empty room with its huge fireplace and gleaming tables.

She chose a table near the bar. As she sat, the men turned, staring openly. Chesed met their gaze with his silver eyes, steady and unafraid. One man dropped his eyes, muttering, and swiveled back to his mug. The others turned away more slowly, casting furtive glances over their shoulders.

The barmaid approached. She attempted an awkward curtsy and

asked, "What can I get you?"

M'ra blinked both sets of eyelids, reacting to the girl's unease. "We would like two cups of tea, please. Is there any food left?"

The girl's eyes rounded. "Half a pie, my lady."

"We'll have some of that as well."

The maid bustled away, nearly tripping over an acolyte. His bald head shone in the light of the oil lamps, white robes dragging through the pile of abandoned sweepings. He stopped and straightened, waiting. Chesed smiled, but M'ra held up one hand before the acolyte could speak. "No," she said. "Not you. Go tell your master we have arrived."

The acolyte bowed and spun, robes flapping. He hurried to obey.

A tall, skinny man with a big nose, his curly hair tousled as if he had just roused from sleep, brought spoons and forks. "I'm Lile, the barkeep, er, the innkeep. Will you be needing rooms?"

He gestured to the stairs.

"Two, please. The cantors shall pay you."

Lile's green eyes widened, and his mouth turned down at the corners. "Of course," he murmured. "The first two rooms at the top of the stairs are ready for you. If you require anything else, let me know."

M'ra looked at the innkeeper, taking in his rumpled clothing. "Some cheese and bread if you have it, for the morning. We shall leave very early."

"I'll wrap it and leave it in your room." He lingered a moment as if he would say more, then slowly backed away and strode back to the kitchen.

Chesed settled in his chair, taking in the people, the faint smell of herbs, the crackle of the fire.

M'ra watched his expression. "What do you see?"

"The men have never seen our kind before. They are sharing stories about us, most of them nonsense," said Chesed. "The maid has hidden herself until our tea is ready, she watches from a crack in the kitchen door. The acolyte watches us as well, though he would rather not. He is afraid."

"Well done," said M'ra. "What else?"

"The innkeeper does not approve of cantors and would like to warn us. Likely he cannot without drawing unwanted attention from the acolyte."

"Do you believe the innkeeper is friendly with the gnomes we met?"

"I do," said Chesed. "The name of the inn is the Bell and Rider, and the gnome mentioned a captive named Bell. If she is dewin, as the gnomes claimed, likely those who care for her will be unwilling to do what must be done. It is unfortunate."

M'ra's golden eyes fixed on Chesed. "What can dewin do?"

Chesed frowned, thinking. "They access the Song with their voices alone. They do not need an instrument or Essences to use its power. But how are they different from majisters?"

M'ra answered quickly. "All majisters were dewin, but not all dewin were majisters. Those who wished to become majisters dedicated themselves to a lifetime of study and discipline, and submitted to a series of trials, ending with the harmony bond. A bonding with fae. This bond transformed mere fae into faisant, makers of marvels. 'Twas the bond which made a majister.

"Nearly all villages would have at least one dewin serving, healing others. They handled day-to-day needs of farmers and craftsmen. Majisters were rare and lived apart, in their tower of Anach. They were dedicated to the Storm King, above all."

She lowered her voice. "These deemling the gnomes spoke of? It is true they existed before the Song was broken, assisted dewin or the majisters. However, most only had knacks. They could locate the best place to build a well or make a birthing easier."

Chesed's brow furrowed, hearing this. "What if the gnome spoke truly, eldest?"

M'ra shook her head. "It cannot be. You felt his Dissonance. It was odd, a reverberation shifting. Perhaps he has merely lied to protect and defend his deemling. 'Tis why I let him go. His love for this Bell is admirable. We may show him mercy, but Dissonance cannot ever simply be ignored. I must return after our task is complete to learn more."

Chesed closed his eyes, remembering the feeling that had washed over him whenever the little gnome had spoken. He examined the effect. Panic. He was undone by panic. "I have no experience with men, so I cannot compare. His Dissonance overwhelmed me. I am grateful he did not sing. It would have been unbearable."

"And yet you ask if he spoke truly?"

Chesed nodded. "In spite of Dissonance, I am not certain. I also felt the Song."

"Can believing a lie make it true?" asked M'ra.

"Here we are," said a cheerful voice. The barmaid carefully set her tray on an adjacent table and set two pieces of pie and two cups of tea before them. She laid a small bowl of honey for their tea and a crock full of cream in front of them.

"Will there be anything else?" she asked.

Chesed shook his head as he dolloped large spoons of honey into each cup in turn. The barmaid backed away and escaped back into the kitchen.

They were halfway through their pie when the door opened. A tall man entered, searching the common room with dark eyes. He wore a blue hooded robe, not the white or black M'ra had described.

It is the robe of a Bindery master. He is a bard. He is also a full member of the Arcanum and ranked above a high cantor. His name is Aric. Watch and listen, little brother.

M'ra's expression did not change as she spoke in Chesed's heart, but Chesed sensed a new wariness all the same. Aric stopped at their table and placed his hand over his heart, bowing. M'ra rose from her seat and inclined her head, accepting his obeisance.

"We meet again, Master Aric. I apologize for the late hour. This is my brother, Chesed."

Chesed rose, murmuring a greeting.

"Please, join us."

The barmaid hurried in with a third cup of tea and a plate of pie for Aric. He smiled as she set them down, his eyes crinkling. "Thank you, Minnie, give Lola my compliments."

He gestured to the pie. "The inn's cook is amazing. I'm glad you get to taste this. It—all greatness—adds to your heartfire, does it not?"

M'ra nodded. "Every fine work sustains it. You are learned, Master Aric."

Aric waved away the honorific. "Just Aric, please. Yes. At the Bindery we have little lore about your people, but I have studied all I could find. I am particularly honored to spend time with you before our task tomorrow. Thank you for the opportunity, 'tis unexpected."

"We wished to see gnomes if possible. 'Tis rumored they live in this remote country," M'ra said.

Aric stopped midbite and set his fork down, his face painted with sorrow.

"Would that you could, my lady. Many of the dewin we are transporting are actually deemling. It's a special role. Gnomes see them as family. The dewin have been...altered. They are greatly affected by the purification we give them. The gnomes have rebelled. The main Burrow actually took arms against our local cantor and the village watch."

M'ra tilted her head, listening. "They should support your cause, Master Aric. All know the danger of dewin. Were one to go mad, innocents would die. Curious, the gnomes do not fear such."

Aric nodded and picked up his fork again. He gestured with it. "Your people are connected like no other to the Song and the cyntae. Gnomes share your connection to the Song in their rhythm. If you are with two or more, it becomes very noticeable. Their cadence. I believe the Song's ebb has affected their wits, leaving them unable to make wise choices." He shrugged. "I hope not, but it's the only theory I have at the moment. We will try to study them, learn more."

Chesed blinked. "You plan to take them to the Rifthouse?"
"If we can find one or two, yes. I do not expect them to go willingly. They seem to believe we are evil." His laugh was self-deprecating and somehow disconsolate. "I suppose, seeing the dewin in their current state, they are justified. Bell owns this inn. She was especially beloved by gnome and townfolk alike."

Do not mention our encounter with the gnomes. The warning sounded like a whip cracking in Chesed's mind. *I do not trust this cantor. If only we could hear Dissonance from all those touched with evil.*

M'ra sipped her tea. "Perhaps we shall see in the morning."
"I believe we will. I expect them to stage a rescue."
Chesed straightened in his chair. "You will force them to come with you?"

Aric set his fork down and steepled his fingers, bowing his head to rest his lips on his fingertips. He held Chesed's silver gaze with his own dark one for a long moment. He dropped his hands.

"We will defend innocent people from the threat of dewin and fight for your heartfire with every means at our disposal. We will do what is necessary, whatever that means." Aric made the sign of the arc. "Pray to the cyntae we need not hurt the gnomes."

Lord Gisle de Clelland slept for exactly two hours, rose, and summoned his officers. Their party, though small—only twenty men and horses, still commanded respect. They were well armed, well trained, and well mounted. Throughout his travels across the Weldes, Gisle had yet to encounter a force equal to them in discipline. Most villages had a watch, funded by the local baron, duke or prince. But since nearly all of the nobility were in Bestua, circling the throne of the dying High King like vultures, Gisle and his men were rarely challenged. Peasants obeyed nobles, any nobles. Better yet, they listened.

Now if only his scout would listen, perhaps he could accomplish his objective. The thought brought a wry grin to his lips.

"Report, Brock."

Brock took a stick and drew in the packed dirt floor of the pavilion. He drew a box, a wavy line, and several circles.

"We have located the skycart here. The river is here, approximately two leagues away. Gnomes and their allies have taken positions here, using willows as cover. Their boats are hidden here."

He pointed to the circles, then drew two small x's next to them to indicate the boats.

"If the victims are transported down the river, we expect the gnomes to mount an offense and rescue the prisoners here."

He drew another x.

"In order to gain the trust of the gnomes, we will assist them in their objective, liberate the captives and defend them as they escape. Then we will follow. When we encounter them again, we shall offer guidance and protection. We can achieve our objective and obtain the information we need."

"Insertion point?"

Brock pointed with his stick. "Here. We'll station the men in three squads with archers, two at the river and one at the skycart."

Sundin cleared his throat. Martine shifted from foot to foot. Rennet stood frowning at the makeshift map.

"Yes, Sundin?"

"Beg pardon, sir, but the gryphon will defend the cantors and the so-called dewin."

Gisle's eyes glittered as he paced in front of the map. "Do whatever is necessary. Defend these gnomes, gentlemen. They are the key to our freedom, to our very lives. Their lore can undo the Conclave and restore our Weldes to balance, to freedom. We must, at all costs, achieve our mission. We have been handed this opportunity. Do not squander it. Understood?"

The men nodded.

"Spare the gryphon if you can and keep all gnomes off that skycart. You have your orders, gentlemen, move out."

21

Outside the city gates, the landscape unfurled. Neat hedgerows separated the crushed stone road from gold and green fields. Dane's mare trotted behind the Northmen's stallions. Bellin paced Dane on a stoic, thick-kneed pony, only falling behind when the track narrowed.

Eventually the road branched west toward Baehnt and northeast toward the Tree. With a shout, Birgir spurred his mount to gallop northeast. The others followed.

Dane concentrated on riding. Farms gave way to thin brush and heather. He saw a few abandoned steadings. Some looked as if they had burned. He caught glimpses of them through gaps in the tall unkempt hedges lining the road.

Folk had not lived here in centuries, yet the way was maintained. Dane wondered idly if the chymaera assisted.

Soon, forest shadow loomed, embraced by wisps of fog. When the road dove into the gloom, the fog thickened until they could no longer see, slowing them by degrees to a walk. The mist dampened Dane's skin, chilling him, making his shirt cling. He wiped moisture from his brow, blinking as it dripped into his eyes.

Bellin whickered, calling his pony to halt and dismounting in one smooth motion. Dane recognized the distinctive roofline of a Conclave watchhouse.

The official who emerged must have been expecting them; he directed them to a small stable immediately. The watchhouse gate arched across the road, barring further traffic. Trees gathered beyond the gate like sentries. Their branches faded into the mist and formed an impenetrable roof that blocked the afternoon light. The result was a permanent dim twilight.

Dane dismounted and led his mare to robed acolytes. They accepted the reins with shallow bows in silence, leading the mare away. They were eerie. Too pale. Their eyes seemed empty.

His companions were subdued, adjusting their sword belts and clothing with muffled grunts. Harald eyed Birgir, Bellin, and Dane, nodding sharply at each in turn, and headed toward the waiting cantor. A hooded figure stood with the guard and cantor, impossibly tall and silent. His white garment shimmered even in the half light.

The cantor stepped forward with a bow from the waist. "Welcome, friends." He nodded to each in turn, arching an eyebrow when he got to Dane. Dane did his best to adopt a humble expression, eyes lowered.

Birgir smiled easily. "Thank you, High Cantor Siles. Good to see you again. You remember Harald, Bellin. This is our young servant, Danethor. He's newly recruited, allegiant to the Forge."

The cantor smiled at Dane, his expression concerned. "Your training looks to be taxing, my son."

"My lessons are well learned, Father," answered Dane, "and valuable indeed."

Siles' laugh echoed in the gloom as he gestured to his hooded companion. "And this is N'khum of the Wyn, who will be your escort today."

N'khum's voice reminded Dane of a mountain lion's low growl. "Well met, I am honored to serve you, men of the Forge, sons of the flame."

Dane and the others murmured inarticulate thanks before Birgir interrupted. "You will not be joining us, Father?"

A shadow crossed the high cantor's eyes. He hesitated to answer. "I shall be here waiting when you return," the cantor replied. "Our acolytes along with Brothers Bren, Flyn, and Master N'khum shall complete your party. May you find what you seek." He bowed, gesturing for them to follow N'khum.

Birgir thumped his right fist to his heart in respect. Harald and Bellin followed suit, with Dane awkwardly mimicking the gesture. As he straightened, Dane lifted his eyes to N'khum's face. He saw golden eyes flashing from beneath the deep cowl.

Of course. Wyn. N'khum is chymaera.

Dane saw the alabaster skin and distinctive markings of the Wyn when N'khum doffed his hood as they followed a path behind the watchhouse. Like the one he had seen in Ciclaehne, this chymaera was tall and very thin. Dane averted his eyes so he would not stare, studying the outpost instead.

Despite the fog, he could see a large complex extending beyond. More of a fortress, really. A full Conclave Chapterhouse and large shadows of buildings he didn't recognize. Most were marked with the arc and the distinctive steep-pitched roof. N'khum kept silent, gliding forward in his silken robes.

Brother Bren more than compensated for his silence. "We have so few visitors to the Tree," he said. "Not just anyone can visit of course. We must protect what remains." At this, all of the Conclave folk made the sign of the arc automatically, a tiny ritual. "We'll fly around the Tree so you may inspect it from the top down along its length and give you time to commune on the ground. When you are satisfied, we will return. There are a few protocols important to observe."

The path had taken them through a large formal garden and beyond the complex to a vast cropped lawn and a rectangular wooden building, topped with a tube railing. Both the building and the railing were ornately decorated with filigree embellishments, gold and silver.

Bren stopped and continued his monologue, hardly stopping for breath. N'khum kept walking, into the mist beyond their sight.

Bren held up one finger. "First, when we arrive at the Tree, please refrain from any music or singing of any kind. The aural nexus is volatile, and we are careful not to disturb it. While the likelihood of your accessing the broken Song is very small"—his smile was nearly sickening in its condescension—"we can never be too careful."

Brother Flyn tutted, good natured and round, his honest face red from the walk. "Won't do, won't do." He repeated the warning, shaking his head solemnly.

Acolytes busied themselves with the air of those who had heard the lecture many times. They opened the skycart door and folded down panels, revealing windowlike openings in the sides.

Dane itched to examine the mechanisms. His inner cabinetmaker was amazed. He thought all skycarts had fallen into disuse.

Brother Bren continued, "Secondly, the path around the Tree is clearly marked. Please do not stray from it. You might see odd visions when we get close. These are normal. I assure you they are not harmful. Stay on the path to ensure your safety. If you wish to examine something not on the path, we will escort you. Stay well clear of any roots. Any accidental contact with a songline could cause injury, so please stay close."

A strong breeze began to whip at Dane's cloak, and the mists cleared. A whooshing, like a rapier slashed at the air. He looked up and saw a huge gryphon land gracefully behind them.

N'khum regarded them, his ancient eyes unblinking. He was easily four times the height of a man, with midnight blue and golden feathers, extending down to his black foreclaws. His powerful feline hindquarters and tail were a glorious gold that blended with long blue and silver feathers flowing down his back. The creature shimmered, light clinging to it like raindrops. He settled atop the skycart to wait, perching not unlike the jackdaws on Dane's hedges at home.

He had been taught about chymaera, of course, but had never thought he would see one in actual winged form. They rarely transformed in front of men. This was breathtaking.

Thank you, Sara, he silently blessed the fae. *This was worth the risk.* N'khum's head swiveled immediately, his gaze fixing on Dane like prey.

Dane swallowed hard and forced his attention back to the cantor, who was still speaking. He tried to think very hard about anything but fae.

"Keep your hands and arms inside the cart, and if you have questions, any of us can help you," finished Bren. "And now, if you will enter the skycart, we shall proceed."

They filed inside the large box. Inside, they sat on cushioned benches, looping their arms into the soft, thick, velveteen straps as directed. Bellin elbowed Dane. "Quite a day, eh, lad?" He winked.

When all were seated and enmeshed in their straps, he heard scraping. The cart shook. With a jolt, the box lifted into the air. The wings of the gryphon sliced the wind. For a moment, emptiness yawned below, vast and deep. They were above the trees. Above the mists. The sun was shining down on top of the fog, transforming it into a sea of glowing light. The scene dazzled.

With an enormous cry, N'khum swooped forward. Harald cursed roundly, but Dane exulted. They were soaring at a high speed; it was cold. The wind rushed past, and he couldn't help whooping. He held onto his straps for dear life.

Bren shouted above the wind. "It won't be long now. You should be able to see the Tree soon."

N'khum looped and glided north until the trunk rose from the mist like an island from the sea. Its trunk glistened through mists. The vast crevasse between the two sides shone, blackened, wet from bloodlike sap. It striped the exposed heart of the Tree's majestic trunk. They could clearly see the two sides, mirroring against each other with bonelike branches that reached up to the heavens.

The branches had leaves, despite all the horrible damage. It yet lived.

Dane drank in the sight, his heart expanding as he remembered his old oak tree at home, the hours he'd spent as a child playing at battle with the Wyrm. The Storm King had vanquished his foe, saving the world and the Song at a terrible cost. Looking at the Tree, he was filled with awe. He was dewin; this place sang to his blood.

He hadn't known how much this visit, the full view of the Tree, would affect him. The sun shone through the rift in the trunk, the wound ripped open and left to bleed. A shaft of light fell across Dane's face. Softly, Dane whispered words he'd known since childhood—all of them.

He Canted the verses on his father's scroll, the sacred words from the lost Lorica. The wind was rushing past, roaring. Dane mouthed the ancient verses, reverent, overcome by the moment. He could not stop himself.

The Dark One ascends,
Eight shall turn him round.
One from the heartfire
One beneath the ground,
One stone rider,
One who cannot hear.
One claims the Storm King,
One Names the Fear.
As the Last begins to sing
One may be reborn
Speak the words of wisdom
Sound the golden Horn.

Heedless heartless helpless
Blast, blast away
Lone fire lighted
Truth cannot stay
When the heartfire kindles

All that is writ
The King will spend the knight's blood
Bone fells Spirit

As the Last ends refrain
To die fade away
Duty binds the heartfire
Dullard shine, play
Fire sears the Melody
Sorrow, Sorrowfish
The Storm King returns
Wyrm to vanquish

He sang the last phrase of the Lorica's refrain. Absolute silence fell. No wind, no whisper touched Dane. The stillness was absolute.

Only then did it occur to Dane what he had actually done.

22

The world stood still. Everything stood still. They hung in the sky, suspended, unmoving. The skycart, Bellin, Birgir, and Harald, all of the monks, the acolytes, N'khum's wings…even the wind was still.

One chime. Another. The chimes rang in Dane's mind. *The Song?*

The Tree was no longer enshrouded; the mist had vanished. Instead, the white bark glowed not with a usual pearlescent reflection of the sun, but with an intense brightness. It appeared to be whole.

No great rift separated the two sides, no crevasse or blackness marred the beauty, the majesty of its massive canopy. Glow swept up and down the Tree, flashing. Bells chimed and a massive sweep of music flowed. It was as if the sky and the Tree and the moon themselves sang for joy.

The unseen stars, far away, sang counter-melody, and all of it echoed through Dane's bones, calling him. They spoke of his mother and her eyes and his father's strength, his wisdom. He saw his home in his mind's eye, his friends. Pezzik stood in a cellar with Jax. Bell lay on a cot, sleeping. A blond man stood in front of a rain barrel. He saw the fae, Sara, behind all of it, weeping alone.

A figure formed from lightning fixed him with a burning gaze and spoke his name. The images shone within a brightness. Light enveloped the Tree as the music rose to a crescendo.

Abruptly, the light flashed and was no more. The Song faded and only silence remained. Stillness. Tears streamed down his face. One heartbeat. Two heartbeats. He wiped his eyes.

And the wind once again howled, rushing past the windows.

Bellin prodded Dane. "Are you all right, lad?"

Dane gasped and put his head in his hands, trying to regain control of his raw emotions. "Not used to this," he mumbled, waving at the window, his voice trembling.

"Did you see the light? Did it blind you?"

Dane looked up, staring at Bellin, and turned to the window. The monks were conferring at the front of the cabin near the doors, heads close together, their voices hushed. The wind was so loud they would not have been heard in any case. He nodded assent to Bellin and focused on the Tree.

Before the light had flared, the lower branches had borne leaves. Now there were more. Many, many more. Leaves bristled from thousands of small branches in a thicket of color, bright green against white bark. The rift between the two sides of the Tree was no longer black. Red sap coated the entire interior of the rift. The heart of the Tree, which had been exposed to the elements for centuries, striped in sap, now stood completely coated, fresh, bright red.

Dane took it all in, wonder mixing with dread, and leaned toward Bellin, raising his voice enough to be heard. "Did you hear it?"

Bellin's eyes widened, and he shook his head.

Stupid, stupid, stupid. What have I done?

Dane had sung a refrain of the lost Lorica—the entire refrain—at the World Tree. Never mind he had only whispered it—he had done it. Whatever had happened, it was surely his fault. His fault alone. *What was I thinking?* He hadn't thought. He had only responded in near ecstasy to the overwhelming urge to utter those words. He knew better. His Pa had cautioned him, over and over.

When he was first given the ancient vellum scroll, his parents had cautioned him never to speak the words without utmost care. Never ever in public. It was too dangerous. The Lorica was the most important tool of the Majisterium. With all the refrains of the Lorica, a majister could create. The Lorica was the Song, pure and whole. Those words were potent, absolute truth from the mind of the Storm King himself. They contained His own power.

Dane's most important job, his primary duty, higher even than manufacturing lutes, was to protect this refrain and pass it on. It had been entrusted to his family. Dane's father had taught him, and his father's father had taught his Pa before that, all the way back to the time of the Wyrm.

And he had spoken a refrain of the lost Lorica at the World Tree.

Stars, why? He had not been himself. It was as if he were enchanted.

He had failed. His disguise was for nothing. Dane wanted very much to take off running into the forest, to run from everyone and everything and never return. But it wouldn't undo anything.

His companions pointed and stared in wonder at the changes in the Tree. The brothers still conferred. The skycart landed, and they all disembarked. Cantors streamed from the Chapterhouse, joining them, along with a number of acolytes. They gestured to his little party, talking excitedly. He knew what was coming. It might not come quickly, but they would certainly question him, and any Dissonance would unveil him.

On the ground in front of Dane lay an acorn. He picked it up, looking at it for a long moment, lost in memory. He placed it in a pocket of his cloak and straightened his shoulders. Muttering a prayer to the Storm King, he approached Bellin.

Dane cleared his throat and pulled the dwarf aside. "Bellin, you were right in a way about me. Now there is no time. I need your help."

The dwarf looked into his eyes, searching.

"There is a package on my ship bound for Baehnt. You must ensure it gets delivered. Promise me. No matter what else happens, I need you to promise. The Thundering Wave. It leaves in the morning and should get there within the week. Find a man named Trystan in Baehnt and tell him what has transpired. Make sure he gets the package. It should be given whether I am there or not. But this is very important," he said. "It might be all right, I might make it back to the ship, but if I do not..."

Bellin's eyes hardened with resolve. "You will get back to your ship lad, I promise you that. And we will speak of these matters further. Now is not the time." Firmly, he repeated, "Now is not the time—"

"There may never be another time. The songlines can be restored, and so can the Tree. Do not put any trust in the Conclave if you love life. But your Gisle fellow was wrong, too. The Tree matters, it all does. You're part of this now, and I'm sorry. I'm so sorry. Find Trystan, he's a bard." He took the acorn from his pocket and pressed it into the dwarf's hand.

Bellin's eyes widened. He accepted the seed, a small enough choice. He put it in his belt pouch.

"My deema is Pezzik. Give this acorn to Trystan. Tell him to give it to her. She will understand. That's all I can say." He gestured toward the priests. "Tell the cantors everything they ask of you, except these things. They should let you go." Dane hoped it was true. It was all he had.

He started running for the Tree and its rift. An acolyte pointed, shouting for him to stop. Dane ignored him, aiming straight for the Tree, which was still wondrously free of all enveloping mists.

Dane zigzagged away from the paths, deliberately avoiding them. He was dewin, a songline would have no ill effect on him whatsoever. Other than making me lose all sense of propriety. But that was hardly worrisome now. If he could reach the channel, he could float downstream to safety. There were too many acolytes, at least ten of them. Maybe twelve. Maybe more. One rather athletic man would be on him quickly, and Dane wasn't sure he could fend him off.

Dane saw the Tree's smooth white bark. Thick roots emerged from the ground like fish surfacing from the deep. The ground near them was bone white, as if the earth itself had been leached, drained. The pattern reminded Dane of lightning in the sky. Songlines. Can the others see them? He saw other things too. Fae flickered everywhere. The chimes of the Song floated through the air, faint and continuous. They reminded him of the tunebells at home. He stopped, looking back at his pursuers. Dane nodded once to himself and vanished into thin air.

Brother Flyn seemed to have remembered Bellin and Birgir finally and spoke in earnest, effusive tones. "Can't be sure of your safety until all has been examined. Most unusual, most unusual. Of course we need you to return with us and share what you saw and heard with the high cantor. He will have many questions—"

"The boy has gone mad. He wants me to go to Baehnt with an acorn." He pointed to Dane's retreating figure. Flyn jumped, seeing the mad dash. He hurried after him, muttering, "Oh no! That won't do at all." He shouted for his brethren to stop Dane. Every acolyte gave chase, though they all kept to the marked paths.

Bellin, Harald, and Birgir watched as if it were a festival play, dumbfounded. There was no accounting for the boy's behavior.

"I thought he had a knack, had no idea the Tree would drive him mad," murmured Bellin, rueful.

"You cannot blame yourself," answered Harald. "You did not know."

"They'll put him right when they catch him," added Birgir, crossing his arms. "You'll see he will be right as—"

Dane suddenly vanished. They all gaped, as one, and fell into stunned silence.

"He will be tortured for any information he has. Purification, they call it. They will twist his soul and use him for their purposes," said a low voice, growling behind them. "If he is caught. Your fate will not be better, now he has confirmed what he is. Therefore, we must go." N'khum stepped forward. "You must follow me and do exactly as I say if you wish to live."

Harald sputtered. "We're representatives of the Forge! No one would dare harm us. We're known to be here, sent by Tenkor himself."

N'khum regarded Harald and the others with sorrow. "You have brought dewin to the World Tree, the first in over half a millennium, and he is not mad, but trained. He has healed the Tree more than any. They will not rest until they have wrung every last ounce of knowledge from you. You will be discarded like old bones lest others understand the truth of their treachery and lies."

He pointed at Brother Bren, who was approaching, a group of acolytes in his wake. "Do you wish to live? Choose."

Bellin decided. "Lead on, Child of the Morning."

N'khum said, "You'll have to ride." He spoke a single word, like an eagle's cry. The chymaera's body stretched, growing in bulk and height. His distinctive garb seemed to flow as well, becoming a sling around his torso as N'khum assumed his true form. His face distorted and nose elongated, becoming a beak. Only the eyes remained the same. N'khum's hands curled into claws, sporting talons, while his hindquarters lengthened and rippled into massively powerful feline legs. N'khum bent and faced the Forgemen, extending one massive foreclaw, his meaning clear.

Harald wasted no time, clambering up and grabbing the silken wrappings. The gryphon was large, big enough for two men and a dwarf to ride upon. They ignored the shouting acolytes and slid their arms under the silk, barely seated before N'khum was beating the brethren back with his enormous wings. They rose into the air. Behind them, the World Tree soared, white and red and impossibly green with new growth. They circled it once, twice, and disappeared into the clouds.

23

"Pete? It's me. Yeah. They already moved Marilla. I can't believe it."
Sara sat in her car, staring into the distance. She was in shock. Of
course she had called Peter. "I drove straight here, but she's gone. I
won't be able to see her without a fourteen-hour drive. She'll be living
with strangers. Why?" she yelled into her phone, beating the steering
wheel. "Why would they do this?"

He sighed. "I don't know, Sara, I really don't."

"I'll tell you why," Sara said. "If there's a problem, we don't deal
with it. We hide it, lock it up, cover it up, put it away. We don't talk
about it. We sweep it under the rug and forget about it. That's how my
parents deal with problems. All problems. And they think I'm selfish?
They just rug swept my sister!"

"What are you going to do?"

"I guess find a lawyer and fight it," said Sara. "I don't have a lot of
money, but I do have a little in savings. I don't know what else to do.
Move there? Move to South Carolina?"

"Are you headed home?"

"No, I was going to do an emergency session with Carol, Dr.
Sherman. Sometimes she gives really good advice. I've got to run over
and talk to Polly today, too, and let her know why I missed Practicum.
I'm going to need an extension on my project. I'm already on thin ice
because I've been late with other pieces."

There was silence on the other end of the line. Finally, Peter said,
"Do you want to just watch TV tonight? I'll bring pizza. I figure you
won't feel much like going out."

Oh God. Our date.

"Honestly, Pete, I just want to go to bed early. There's no one I'd rather hang out with. I need some alone time. I may go to the studio and work a little, but I need to figure things out."

"That's cool. I understand. Just...promise me you aren't leaving."

Sara sat back in her seat and ran her hand through her hair. "What?"

"You said you might move. South Carolina. I know you, Sara. You'll take off, hit the road, and go find Rilla. Don't do it. Wait. If you need to road trip to see her, I'll go with you. Don't leave. If you have to go, take me with you, okay?"

"Okay," said Sara.

"You promise?"

"I promise," said Sara.

"Okay then," said Peter. "I don't want to push you, Sara. I'm here for you, whatever you need."

Peter's relief came through over the phone. "I'll be okay, I won't do anything rash. I'll call you later, I promise."

Sara sank into the plush chair in Dr. Carol's office. All of a sudden, she felt completely drained. As she waited for Dr. Carol, she inspected the room. It was a bright space filled with overstuffed furniture and wall-to-wall bookshelves. Photos of Dr. Carol's family hung on one wall, next to her diplomas. A framed poster proclaimed,

"He calms the storm."

Bongo drums rested in a corner, silent. Sculptures and artwork from all over the world rounded out the decor.

The door opened, and Dr. Carol pushed through, squinting at a clipboard through her rectangular black readers. She looked up, saw Sara, and smiled warmly. "How are you, Sara?"

"I know we weren't on the schedule for today, Dr. Carol, thanks for fitting me in. I didn't know what else to do. I need to talk to someone."

"Of course. I'm here for you. You know that. How can I help?"

Dr. Carol sat in the chair across from Sara, concern painting her face.

"They moved Marilla," Sara said.

"Who did?"

"My parents. My mother and father. They moved her to a less expensive facility on the coast. As if they don't have enough money to support her. They do." Sara stood and began pacing. "I won't be able to see her now without a fourteen-hour drive." Sara whirled. "Can I get a lawyer and fight this? Do you know?"

"What does an ideal outcome look like for you?"

Sara frowned. "What? You mean what do I want to happen?"

"Yes," said Dr. Carol, taking off her glasses. "If Marilla doesn't wake up, what's the best outcome?"

"For me to be where I can see her, read to her, help her," Sara said. "I need to be close to her. She's my twin. We've always been together. I need to help her get well. She has to get better. I can't face the world without her."

It was her fault Marilla was in the coma. She had to save her. She couldn't face the world without Rilla.

She froze. She finally saw it.

She was using Rilla. She was hiding from her own stuff, all her issues, and using her twin sister to do it.

Dr. Carol's eyes were full of sympathy and unspoken answers. She waited.

"Oh God. Am I being selfish? Is it selfish to want to keep her here?"

"Not necessarily. You might be right, believing she needs to be close. She shouldn't be left alone. I can't argue with that. But it's really important you realize…that even if she wakes, she may very well need special care for some time. As I understand it, your mother reviewed all the facilities in the country to find the best for Marilla's condition. And she's given notice at the hospital. She quit. Did you know that?"

Dr. Carol's practice was in the same hospital her mother was a department head at, University Hospital; she and Sara's mother were colleagues.

"My mother quit?" Sara's voice rose to an unbelieving squeak. She would never quit. She worked on holidays, missed our games growing up. They had a series of nannies. Who had a nanny in Kentucky? Or rather, Au pair. "You're telling me she quit? Just quit?"

Sara sat down.

"Your mother is going to South Carolina," Carol said. "She's going with Marilla. There's a hyperthermia treatment this facility does for coma patients. No one else does it as well. It might wake her, and they're going to try. She was afraid to talk to you about it because she thought you'd insist on going. She wants you to graduate. She called me this morning, worried. Your mom gave me permission to share these things with you if I needed to. Apparently you had a stressful lunch this week."

Sara gave Dr. Carol a flat look. "Stressful is an understatement. She acted totally normal and never mentioned moving Marilla. I had to find out from Dad. It was underhanded. It was dishonest."

Carol nodded. "I think you're completely justified, feeling betrayed and angry about this decision, not being consulted. But I also think your mother might not be the monster you believe she is. Or perhaps she has changed."

Sara didn't know what to think. She just felt numb. "Why didn't she tell me?"

Dr. Carol leaned forward, looking in Sara's eyes. "I think she tried and just shut down. From what I gather, she is in terrible pain."

Dr. Carol leaned back, tapping her pencil against her clipboard. "The biggest gift we can give anyone, ever, is forgiveness. Everyone makes mistakes. Sometimes we react selfishly because we are hurting. Not because the intent is to harm. Even parents are just human. They hurt too.

"You've been processing a lot of anger, but don't remain in that anger. It's important to identify how you feel and to name it. But you have to make choices and decide what to do with your feelings. You don't have to be ruled by them. You can make choices, in spite of how you feel. Think about it, okay?"

Sara nodded again. "How do I stop being afraid?"

Dr. Carol's smile was warm. "None of us ever really stops being afraid. We just learn how to cope with fear as we mature. Courage means doing what you must, even when you're afraid."

Sara drove to the School of Art mechanically. She pulled into the parking lot and walked toward Polly's office, her eyes red from weeping. She didn't know what was right anymore. She was still angry, but she now was angry with herself, too. She pushed away the real reason.

Maybe she should just leave. She could go to South Carolina and stay with Mom.

But if Mom was going, Marilla wouldn't be alone. And she needed to graduate. She really didn't want to live alone with Mom.

The truth was, as much as she hated to admit, she was scared of this semester. She was scared of graduating, of being finished with school and plunging into the real world work force. She was scared of never finding a job in her field. She was scared of never making it as a real artist. She was scared of Peter. She didn't deserve any of it. She was scared of...

Sara's litany of cowardice came to an abrupt halt. A blue Mazda RX-7 was parked, its motor idling, in front of the Material Arts building. Her heart skipped a beat, and she quickened her pace. Scott was waiting for her?

She was just about to call out to him when Chantal Goddard came skipping down the steps. Sara stopped, watching as Chantal cooed. She ran to the car and jumped into the passenger's seat. Chantal and Scott kissed.

She stood there, dumbfounded, as they drove away.

Chantal Goddard had a boyfriend. Chantal was kissing Scott. Scott was...no. Yes.

Scott Black was Chantal Goddard's boyfriend.

Sara swiveled, headed back to her car, and drove home. She ran up the stairs, threw her keys on the table, and went straight to her room. She dove into bed and pulled the duvet up over her head. She needed to not think. She couldn't deal with all of this.

It began to rain outside. The droplets rattled at her window as the wind blew. She lay there, thoughts whirling, listening to the storm until fitful sleep drew her under.

Dane filled with relief as he watched the gryphon carry his friends away. The chymaera were mysterious, unpredictable. However, it seemed in this case, N'khum was friendly. He pondered this as he watched the Conclave monks and acolytes. They congregated near the Tree, pointing and talking among themselves, appearing shocked. The one called Flyn took over, giving instructions Dane could not hear. The acolytes began to search for him systematically, following the safe marked paths.

Dane stood perfectly still, hardly daring to breathe. The glamour he had thrown up shielded him from sight, but this was no carefully prepared enchantment he had cast. Desperate, Dane had seen his peril and improvised. Now he was hidden, but there was no way to know how long it would last. He didn't know if he could move, either.

He decided to wait and trust in the Song. Whatever he had done, it had been in the shadow of the World Tree, and the Storm King had somehow given him favor. He would not panic, he would watch. His moment would come.

Two acolytes passed close to him, speaking in low tones. Tunebells chimed softly, and suddenly it was as if Dane was standing next to them. He heard them clearly. One acolyte was round, his pudgy face gleaming with sweat. The other was taller and had large ears that protruded on both sides of his bald head like wings.

"...immensely powerful, unlike anything they have ever seen, even with the dewin they have held at the Hermitage." The fat acolyte gestured to the Tree, its inner surface.

"The Tree has certainly changed. We need to question this dewin and find out how he did it, his intent. Was he trying to set the Wyrm free? We must *find those Forgemen*. When the king gets wind of what happened here, there will be panic at court. There is no hiding it. The first boat to pass through the rift will carry the tale."

"We cannot enter an Aerie uninvited," said the fat man. "Not even Cantor Siles would attempt that. If the Wyn took the Forgemen there, they are lost to us. No. Our masters will be kept busy explaining this to noble houses for months, calming fears."

The taller man's ears nearly wagged. "Why would this Wyn risk so much? You forget, Siles can cut the Aeries off from the Song whenever he wishes." He nodded to the surrounding ground, indicating the songlines.

"I don't think he will do so, no matter how much this Wyn has betrayed us. Whether he likes it or not, we need the chymaera as much as they need us."

The fat man sighed and continued down the path, and the conversation passed out of range. Dane was tempted to follow but decided to remain where he was. He mulled over what he had heard while he waited for nightfall.

They thought that he would free the Wyrm? Why?

He had so many questions. But first he had to get out of the reach of these men. He would wait, and try to escape under cover of darkness. It was his best chance.

Sara blinked. The park stretched, green and welcoming. Men and women ran to and fro around it, all of them bald and wearing white robes. Other shapes, ghostlike, flickered among the robed figures.

They looked like those monks in Nepal. They were looking for something. Like an Easter egg hunt.

Wide gravel avenues poked out from what appeared to be an enormous tree. Half of a mammoth tree? It was torn in two, each half standing. The middle, where the core of the tree should be, was bright red. Sara shivered, looking at it. It reminded her of an open wound. That tree was taller than a skyscraper. Tall as a mountain.

Someone on her left stood nearly shoulder to shoulder with her. He was tall and sported a shaved head, like the monks. He wasn't running. He wasn't wearing robes either. Ghostly images flashed thick around him. He seemed familiar. He had a long nose. He watched the monks intently.

"Hello," she said.

The man nearly jumped out of his skin. He looked at her, slack-jawed in amazement. Now she could see he was hurt. He looked like he'd lost a bar fight. "Sara, what are you doing here?" he whispered. Without waiting for an answer, he motioned her away from the park. He reached to encircle her, drawing her toward the tree line.

"You know my name? Why are we whispering?" Sara whispered.

"Those men want to hurt me," the man answered. "They might catch me if they see you."

"Why do they want to hurt you?"

"They think I'm crazy," he said. "I'm not, but they don't know that. They think I want to destroy the world. I don't." He kept herding her toward the tree line. They were close now. The shadows reached for them.

"Can't you talk to them and explain? Did they do this to you?" Sara's voice grew louder with outrage as she pointed to his black eye and swollen lip.

"They won't listen. They probably won't give me a chance to say anything at all. But no, my friends did that."

Sara harumphed and stopped. The long-nosed man's encompassing arm passed right through her. She looked down at herself. "Those below shall be as above," she said. Her voice chimed in the night air over echoes of haunting music. *Why did I say that?*

She gasped as a large man appeared behind her battered friend. The long-nosed man was so focused on her that he didn't notice the new man. Sara didn't have time to scream before her world went black.

Sara sat straight up in bed as lightning flashed outside her window, bright as day. Thunder cracked immediately. The worst of the storm was close. It matched her mood. Black and violent. She grabbed her journal automatically and wrote, scribbling quickly.

Monks. Big Tree split in half and still upright. *Am I the tree? I feel broken. Why monks?*

Her phone flashed, lighting up with messages. She reached for it, tossing her journal aside. Three voicemails from Peter. She pushed away shame and put the phone back on her bedside table next to Scott's flask.

The flask sparked as the lightning flashed again. It was monogrammed, engraved with his fraternity symbol. She hadn't noticed before. She picked it up and swished. Nearly full, it held enough to silence her anger, confusion and guilt. She opened it slowly and took a sip. Bourbon burned down her throat. She picked up her phone again and flipped it open to text Peter.

I'm okay, just went to bed early. Will call you tomorrow.

Sara looked at her clock. Eleven p.m. Scrambling up, she quickly changed into jeans, a *Keep Louisville Weird* tee shirt, and a black hoodie. She threw the phone and flask into her satchel. She ran through the rain and started the car. Classical music poured from the radio. Sara snarled, turning the dial. That wouldn't suit her at all, not tonight. Tonight she needed rock-and-roll. Metal.

The rain made visibility difficult and though Sara hadn't drunk much, she knew alcohol would be on her breath. She didn't drink often. It would take very little to make her tipsy. She was extra careful as she pulled out. It was only a few blocks to her studio. She could walk back if needed. She was going to throw herself into her sculpture. Polly wanted to see her heart, her true soul? Well. Tonight Sara would make it happen.

She was raw. She was going to pour her outrage, every ounce of it, into her sculpture.

The main floor of the building was locked, but all students in the program had a key. Sara opened the door and took the stairs two at a time, to the fourth floor. Strains of music drifted down the long corridor. Others were here working late; she wasn't alone. Quickly, she strode to her studio door and opened it, flipping on the lights. Plastic shrouded the figure. She tuned the stereo to the college station. Angry music poured forth with cookie monster vocals. Satisfied, Sara unveiled him.

The column was as she had left it, features still blank. Carefully she approached the figure and began to carve a face, eyes. She added scaly patches to the skin texture she had formed in her last session. Sara added slip and new clay as needed to build the features until they were part serpentine, part human. She moved quickly, working with passion. No thought menaced her now. The music blared, its rhythm fueling her. She drank as she worked.

Carving, drinking, carving. Finally she abandoned her tools and began to work with her hands and fingernails.

The slimy clay writhed under her fingers. The snake eyes she had carved gleamed wetly as she built ridges up around them. Thoughts stayed under the surface—but she could feel them there. Sara wouldn't let them manifest. She refused to think. Still, she felt the truths in her deepest heart. She couldn't escape them.

Marilla was gone. Mother had hidden it from her...but...she deserved this after what she did. Marilla was unconscious, but she the one who was drowning. It was all her fault. She should've been the one in a coma. Or dead.

She drank. The eye ridges were mostly formed now, so she attacked the ear area, smoothing the ear shapes down until they were imperceptible.

She had blown Peter off before she found out about Marilla. Why? For what? For a guy who was cheating on his smug, catty girlfriend. And the sick part was, she still wanted to see Scott. She shouldn't. But there it was. She was using Peter too. She was selfish. Just like her dad. She cheated, just like him. But she didn't have half his artistic talent. She was just a faker. Toxic.

Sara drank more. She felt a little dizzy now. Scott was a snake, she was sure of it. She wouldn't see him again. All men were snakes. Her dad was a snake. Maybe all people were snakes. Maybe she was a snake. She looked at her Storm King. He was no longer a Storm King. He was a snake. A worm. A pathetic lowly belly-crawling lowlife. She was going to have it out with this betrayer, here and now.

"Snake!" she yelled. "You're a liar and a snake. All you care about is YOU. You don't care who you hurt. Selfish, evil, ugly snake." Sara was filled with more fury than she'd ever known. She was angry at everyone. Most of all, she was angry with herself. She beat the sculpture with each word, punctuating. Then her fists pummeled the figure. She felt pieces crumbling as she raged.

The serpentine head didn't turn and look at her, but a voice answered in her mind, scratchy and sibilant.

"Are you talking about me? Or are you describing yourself?"

The world began to spin. Then she was falling. A pit yawned beneath her.

24

Jax waited for the Conclave and the chymaera, three otters at his side. They were coming.

The birds sang their dawn chorus, though light had not yet begun to reach into the eastern sky. Otter and beaver slides ran down the steep sides of the riverbank where their flatboat was moored, just south of the line of willows. The current raced, tugging it. The boat would have no trouble escaping once it received passengers.

Just north, a smooth stone outcropping with natural steps formed an inviting landing for the Conclave's party. Just inland, nine large willows guarded the shore. The captives would have to be led through to reach the meadow beyond and the waiting skycart. The five deema waited within the willow's sheltering branches, prepared for battle.

The Conclave vessels emerged from out of the darkness, full of acolytes. Two chymaera stood in the front of the first vessel, with Aric. As they landed, a ramp extended to shore. The acolytes disembarked in a flood, fifteen or twenty men and women swinging incense burners. They Canted, spreading out to blanket the area with toxic fumes. The incense spread like fingers, tendrils of a fog. Jax gulped fresh air as the fog wafted closer. He was tempted to sink into the earth where it could not reach him. He dropped flat to the ground and held his breath. The fog rolled harmlessly over him.

He heard thuds as otters and beavers fell, unconscious.

Chesed and M'ra stood with Aric on the rock shelf waiting for the second boat's occupants to disembark. It released twenty more acolytes and watchmen, with prisoners in tow. Bell was tossed over the shoulder of a burly bald man like a sack of meal. Two other men carried little Mary and young Jess. The fog remained outside a protective circle surrounding them, moving as they moved.

Jax counted quickly. All the deemling were there. He whispered to an otter crouched nearby and sent him on to Pezzik, signaling her to be ready. He took another gulp of fresh air and stood, knowing the fog would take effect quickly, but stepped forward to deliver his message. As he did, the Canting stopped. Muffled sound of thumps came from the trees behind him.

"Child of the Morning, have you listened to these prisoners?" Jax's voice rang clear even over the noise of the small throng. Noorie appeared from under the nearest willow canopy. The other gnomes stepped out in turn, deema come to claim their own.

M'ra nodded and walked the line of those in chains, touching all who could walk on their own. Stu Callin, Jon Frenner, and his wife, Sal. Cap and Tera Planor. Hal and Fran Smith and their four children. Ben Hodges and his wife Cora with their young son, Trent. All were silent, unseeing and mute as they stood awaiting their fate. Each had been well dosed.

She swept down the line, walking quickly, and spoke to Aric. "These are not dewin. Release them immediately."

Aric crossed his arms and regarded M'ra, his dark eyes shadowed. He said something in a low voice that Jax could not hear. Chesed, standing next to her, stiffened.

M'ra drew herself up to her full height and repeated. "Release them, or you shall see the end of our patience."

The tree branches rustled and behind the gnomes, armored men with scarves tied across their noses and mouths appeared, bows drawn and arrows nocked to fly. More stepped from behind these, dragging unconscious acolytes, their empty incense burners bouncing. The soldiers dropped the acolytes in unison as their archers took aim. The largest of these soldiers stepped forward, his voice muffled by his scarf. He held up his right hand, palm out. Quickly he swept it down.

Jax watched this in wonder, dizzy from the effects of the fog. "By Lalo's right hand, who are you?"

The soldier winked, gray eyes twinkling. He handed Jax a wet scarf, motioning him to tie it over his face for protection. "Friends with common goals, come to assist. Let's help your villagers."

Jax tied the scarf over his nose and mouth, considerably heartened, though his mind raced. He was glad of the help and muttered his thanks for the Storm King's aid. This must have been His work.

Aric ordered the acolytes to release their prisoners. Tonk raced down the gentle slope to them, accompanied by two chattering otters. Pezzik and Popple followed. Together they herded their families down the riverbank, where their boat waited. A few of the mysterious soldiers broke off from the main group to escort them.

Popple peppered one with questions. "Where did you come from? Why are you helping us?"

M'ra bent, speaking urgently to Aric and gesturing to the three unconscious dewin.

Jax frowned. She was telling him the gnomes wanted to join them or get them free. They were going to take Bell away.

"Stop!" he roared, pointing stiffly at the acolytes who were gathered, prepared to carry Mary, Jess, and Bell. He wasn't sure if the soldiers behind him were prepared to fight a gryphon, but he was willing to risk it. Arrows flew and landed in front of each acolyte, thudding into the damp ground with deadly accuracy in a long line that blocked their way forward.

Apparently, they would fight. The archers nocked more arrows. Jax smiled grimly.

M'ra stepped forward, her eyes blazing. "I have kept my word, gnome. You will not hinder the cantors further. I warn you. Take what you have been given and walk away, or face my wrath."

Jax stood his ground, his cap quivering under the heat of her ire. The chymaera towered over him even in unwinged form. He gulped, raised his chin, and looked her straight in the eye. "Bell is my family and no threat to you or anyone else. If we can accompany them, there need be no blood shed today."

Aric leaned forward, speaking to M'ra. He laid a hand on her shoulder.

M'ra softened at once and nodded. "Go with Chesed, he will escort you to the skycart."

She stepped forward into the open space between the two groups, and with a loud eagle's cry, her body shifted. She stretched, and her arms lengthened. Wings sprouted from her back as her legs thickened. Her face shifted, its angles and ridges sprouting feathers. She grew as she shifted, filling the space. A majestic ivory gryphon stood where she had been. With another cry, she launched into the air, circling, flying up over the willows to the marshy meadow beyond.

Jax, Dodd, and Noorie, and a few of their small otter friends, walked over to the remaining chymaera. Chesed waited for them, impassive. A row of soldiers broke off to follow. They remained a few paces behind. Chesed bent over Jax, speaking softly. "The Eldest is very displeased, and Master Aric will wreak vengeance if you go with him. I am sure of it. He has a darkness in his heart. My heartfire bids me help you escape. When we reach the trees, you must resist."

Without waiting for a reply, the chymaera led the party toward the trees, following the three acolytes who carried Jess, Mary, and Bell.

The ring of metal on metal sounded as they passed through the first fronds. Acolytes wielded short swords and knives, attacking the other gnomes. Jax roared a warning and drew his own blade, stabbing at the robes of the acolyte that held Jess. Chesed splayed his hands, placing them over this acolyte's eyes from behind. The acolyte slumped to his knees, Jess sliding from his shoulders.

"Noorie!" yelled Jax. "Take him!"

The two acolytes, both burly farm boys, ran toward the meadow. Bell and Mary flopped over their shoulders. Jax didn't wait; he followed, shouting for the otters to trip them. Arrows flew, hitting one acolyte in the leg and the other in his buttocks. Both fell. Jax reached them as Bell tumbled off the acolyte's shoulder. He broke her fall. Jax grunted and pushed Bell aside. He sat up in time to see Aric hold a blade to the tall chymaera's neck.

"We can end them," said a soldier.

"No!" shouted Jax. "Do not harm the chymaera." Why didn't he transform and rip that blackguard to pieces? Blasted gryphon.

"Drop your weapons," instructed Aric, evenly.

The soldiers obeyed.

"You, carry the girls. Take them to the skycart. Quickly."

The acolytes bent to lift the deemling. Chesed raised his hands and twisted in the bard's grip. Aric's knife slid, slicing into the flesh of Chesed's neck. Blood began to trickle down his body, but Chesed fought to place his hands over Aric's eyes. The soldiers picked up their weapons, rushing forward to attack Aric and defend Chesed. Aric wrestled free from the chymaera, stabbing wildly.

Red stains bloomed like flowers on the Chesed's flowing white garment.

Chesed fell.

Behind him, Aric was running, acolytes close on his heels. The girls bounced in their arms. The one carrying Bell shifted her on his shoulder.

Aric shouted, "Treachery! Chesed is dead, lady M'ra, fly!"

And Jax was up, running after them. The acolyte carrying Mary fell, downed by an arrow. Jax leapt over him and fixed his eyes on Bell's limp form. She flopped over the shoulder of the remaining acolyte, who had gained speed. They reached the waiting skycart and dove inside. Aric slammed the door behind them. As the cart began to lift, Jax dove for the door handle. He caught it and held on, bracing his legs in the ledge formed by the doorway. He rose with the box as it lifted and risked a glance down to the meadow below.

The tall form of Chesed, dressed all in white, lay in a pool of blood and did not rise.

Pezzik watched the skycart, swinging gently as it rose, and the gnome-capped figure clinging to it, from her perch on the flatboat. *Storm King, keep Jax safe and grant him wisdom.*

The boat rocked in the water, as the others bustled, readying to launch. She faced the soldier beside her, who had doffed his scarf. Mustaches curled around his nose. They made him look older, but she guessed he wasn't many years over thirty, still young. His short, immaculately groomed beard and calloused-but-manicured hands told her he was nobility before he spoke.

The man gave her a shallow bow. "Lord Gisle de Clelland, at your service. We have travelled long to make your acquaintance."

Pezzik's cap tilted forward in surprise. "My acquaintance?"

Gisle nodded. "Stories of gnomekind have been shared by the fires of my homeland, near Perrhil. Our forests no longer shelter your Burrows, I fear. Once, there were many. So we travelled to find you. We witnessed your exchange with the gryphons. Once we knew your need, we planned to assist you. Our mission is to rid this land of the creeping darkness of Conclave rule. We believe you can be of some assistance in this matter and came to seek your boon. There is only one thing I must know. I have traveled very far to ask you."

Pezzik regarded the man, wide-eyed. "What's that?"

Gisle hesitated, then his words came in a rush. "Is Doran the Wyrm?"

Pezzik looked at him, keenly. She nodded. "He is. Jealous of Domini and bound to that form in judgment.

"I appreciate the aid, Lord de Clelland. We must leave immediately and transport our charges to safety. We shall make for Siarad. The Conclave cannot enter the cursed city. We cannot be of much immediate help to you, I'm sure."

The lord's eyes bulged. His eyebrows raised, his mustaches quivering.

Pezzik stifled a laugh at his expression.

"You have a long journey through rough country, but you travel toward my home. My company could join you. The Conclave has helpfully left us extra boats. Will you grant us the honor of escorting you? We can speak more of these matters."

Noorie and Dodd slid down the embankment to the chirps and nickers of approving otters. They were followed by a soldier who helped to catch Jesse and Mary. Pezzik frowned, thinking.

"We are well supplied and shall of course respect your privacy," said de Clelland. "We have travelled the country you must cross. Shadows are falling across fen, glade, and forest. It is not safe. Please, gnomemother, accept our escort."

Pezzik's mouth twitched as the man's words tugged at her memory. Shadows are falling across fen and glade and forest. The man echoed the fae's warnings to Dane. He must be the Storm King's aid.

She nodded, acquiescing. "My name is Pezzik. I'm pleased to meet you. We shall accept your kind offer. How soon can you leave?"

"Instantly. Many thanks. You shall not regret this."

The man clicked his heels together, turned and began shouting orders to load the boats and care for the wounded. Pezzik watched their progress. The soldiers nearly had the first boat loaded when two straggled in from beneath the willow branches, dragging a makeshift stretcher behind them. Chesed lay on it, bloodstained, his breathing shallow.

Pezzik grabbed her satchel and hopped down from the boat, running to reach the injured chymaera. She leaned her head on his chest and listened. His heart was beating, but it was very slow.

"I need water," she said, pulling scissors from the satchel to cut crusted linen from his wounds. "Water and clean linens."

Chesed moaned.

Pezzik leaned in, her tone fierce. "I won't let you die, Child of the Morning. I promise."

In the distance, an eagle cried.

Pezzik labored over Chesed, cleaning each wound carefully, applying Essences as a balm.

As she worked, she prayed to the Storm King for the chymaera's life. Shanna, Gisle de Clelland's healer, helped, applying pressure to the wounds and supplying clean needles with cotton thread. Pezzik worked as quickly as she could, sewing up each gash and cut.

In the end, despite her promise, her efforts were in vain. Shortly before noon, Chesed stopped breathing. He opened his eyes and gazed at Pezzik and took her hand in his. A smile lit his face.

Then he was gone.

Pezzik closed Chesed's eyes and snapped clean sheets over his rigid form. She had to use two because he was so tall. Tears rolled down her face, and she muttered under her breath as she worked, cursing Aric.

"You did all you could, Pezzik" said Shanna. "He just lost too much blood. Nothing could have saved him from that neck wound. Now 'tis time to care for those he died to save. Do you know the chymaera burial custom?"

Pezzik shook her head, numb. "I've no idea what their ways are. Surely M'ra will come back for him. When she does, we need to be well away. The bard, Aric, has laid Chesed's death at our feet. The chymaera may hunt us."

"Leave his body," said Gisle, coming up behind her. "If we leave the body, the chymaera may take their beloved home and mourn him in their own way. You may ask your otter friends to watch over him."

"We might need to abandon the boats. If we stay on the rivers, we could be too easily found," said Pezzik.

Gisle tipped his hat to the gnome. "We have been planning while you worked and have already chosen a possible alternate route over land. We shall mourn the noble Chesed and be on our way."

In the end, they laid him on his makeshift pallet once more and dragged him under the largest willow. Pezzik placed a rose blossom in his hands, and they covered him. The gnomes gathered round and sang a mourning song, their five voices rising in harmony. The song drifted over the river and into the meadows beyond.

Pezzik stepped forward. She cleared her voice to address the group.

"Today Chesed died so our loved ones might live. We pledge to hold him in our hearts and share his story to our children and our children's children. His name may never be forgotten. His song has ended, but his life shall continue, in those he died to save.

"We thank you, Storm King, for this bright child of the morning and commit him to your care."

Not one person made the sign of the Arc, not even the men and women in Gisle's company. Noorie and Dodd bowed and walked away. The others followed their example. All were solemn as they boarded the flatboats and pushed off from the mooring.

M'ra stood over Chesed's body as the sun rose the next day. She had flown all night to return so quickly. She gathered him in her arms and wept. Her shining hair covered his still, broken form. She kissed his cheek and dragged his pallet to the skycart, placing him carefully inside.

She spoke as if he could hear, seeking absolution. "I needed your eyes, little brother. I did not seek your life. Your heartfire burned so bright. You shall be avenged. I vow to bring justice to those responsible. I will spend my life hunting them and shall show them no mercy."

She sat with him, weeping, until she had no more tears. She rose and gathered meadow blossoms, covering his lifeless form. That done, she shifted, transforming into her true shape. The enormous white gryphon lifted the skycart and carried Chesed home to his final rest.

Sara wiped her eyes with the back of her hand and looked up. She blinked.

Sara watched the gnomes sing. The tall lady came and took him away. Chesed, they called him. Sara saw the lady weeping. Sara stared in wonder as the lady transformed into a gryphon. Tears streaked Sara's face as she tracked the white gryphon's flight, not understanding why she wept.

Sara was suddenly in a large cave, next to a massive statue of Chesed. He stood next to her as well, alive. The living-Chesed fell to his knees and raised one arm, begging her for help. He was silent. In fact, everything was silent. She couldn't hear at all. No wind, no rustling, not even her own breath or heartbeat.

Am I deaf? She felt curiously detached. Dreaming.

Sara smiled, relieved to see Chesed alive. She took his hand in her transparent one and helped him rise to his feet. His hand felt solid in hers. She touched the statue. Music played.

The statue moved. It bent on one knee and put one hand on its heart, while the other reached out in supplication. Sara could not see the living-Chesed anymore. All she saw was the statue.

"So strange," she murmured aloud. She shifted in bed, pulling her blankets up under her chin.

Sara rolled over and drifted back into a dreamless sleep.

M'ra took the stairs to Chesed's quarters, her feet ringing each hollow step like a bell. Chesed could not have been more explicit if he had written her a letter. M'ra marveled at the energy and the grace it must have taken to control his signet from such a distance while dying. Never before had such a thing occurred.

The moon watched her enter the pavilion housing Chesed's signet. The stone figure contained so much of him. It was kneeling, one arm outspread, beseeching. The other covered his heart. Its message was clear. *Remember love and mercy. Listen to your heartfire.*

She stood, contemplating the signet for a long time. It accused, humbled, rebuked, and challenged her. She took it in whole, absorbing its Virtue into her heartfire. When finished, she touched it and sang. The signet crumbled into dust as her voice rang out in sorrow. She returned the way she had come. She took the same path, but in a very real sense, she was not the same person she had been.

M'ra had found a glimpse of grace.

25

Sara's head pounded. She stared blearily at the clock, at herself. She was wearing the same clothes from the night before but had no recollection of walking home. She sat up in bed. Her shoes had been neatly placed next to her dresser. She groaned. Her phone lay on her nightstand. There it was, a text from Peter.

—*Got someone to let me in last night and found you. Brought you home. Nice flask you have there. We need to talk.*

Without even thinking about it, Sara dialed his number. He answered on the third ring.

"It's me. I'm so sorry, Peter. I lost it yesterday."

"Yeah, you did," said Peter. "I saw your sculpture. You okay now?"

"I don't know," said Sara. "It's not about Marilla. It's really about me. I realized yesterday. Mom is going to try to get Marilla real help. She quit her job. She's going with her to do some crazy treatment. She didn't tell me so I wouldn't try to go with her, so I could graduate. I've been hiding. I've been hiding from my life and from my artwork and from decisions. It all came clear yesterday. When it did, I tried to run away."

"Did part of that running include a fraternity guy? You had a flask with Phi Kappa monogrammed on it," Peter said. "Who is it?"

Sara exhaled slowly. "I hung out with Scott Black after work the other night. He gave me the flask. We kissed. That's all. Yesterday I found out he has a girlfriend."

The silence on the other end of the line stabbed Sara.

"So you never meant to go on our date," Peter said. "I know you,

Sara. At least tell me the truth. Just spit it out."

"I was running from you, too, Peter," Sara said. "I need time."

"Okay," said Peter.

"Please don't give up on me. I..."

Peter laughed, and even over the phone, Sara sensed how hollow the laugh was. "Hey, I know when I'm being friend-zoned. I've seen you do this before, remember? In high school, to other guys. Why would you be different with me? I gotta go. I'll talk to you later."

The line went dead. It felt like a verdict.

Sara's studio looked like a storm had blown through it. Her sculpture was in pieces. She fiddled with her amulet absently, surveying the damage, and set about cleaning the mess. She walked over to her stereo, popped in an instrumental soundtrack from one of her favorite movies, and trekked to the supply closet for trash bags.

Marilla had always been the brave one. She was the outgoing one, the fearless one. Marilla and her boyfriend Rick met in high school and were inseparable. They both wanted the same things. Rick had proposed to Rilla at Christmas. He had been almost a brother to Sara.

Now she couldn't bear to be in the same room with him. He knew Dad cheated on Mom. In spite of that, he had...cheated on Marilla. Marilla never should have been in that accident. Maybe she tried to kill herself. Or maybe she just swerved into the oncoming lane because she was upset. The result was the same, either way.

Sara swept the floor, beating it with her broom. She stooped and picked up a large piece to throw away. A reptilian eye shone out of the fragment, part of her angry drunken sculpt session. Sara stared at it.

Snake.

She tossed it in the bag and sat down hard on her stool.

Marilla was gone. Even if she came back, it would all be different. She'd never be the same. It was time to accept her own crap. Peter scared the hell out of her. She leaned on him and gave little back. She knew what he wanted. Part of her wanted it too.

She didn't know.

You must find your heart's inner fire and master it. The words rose up within her. Bastien Crowe had said it during his presentation. Sara wondered if she could. She didn't know what she loved the most. She didn't know who she was without Marilla. There wasn't anything she could call her heart's inner fire.

The door opened, and Chantal swept in. Her smirk was triumphant, surveying the destruction. Sara balled her hand into a fist. The jagged shard of clay bit into her palm.

"I heard there was a problem with your piece," Chantal said. She stopped just inside the door, one hand on her hip. "Just wanted to check and see if you needed any help."

"No, thanks." Sara's voice sounded clipped, strange even to her own ears.

Chantal shook her head, her mouth pursing as she took in the full extent of the carnage. "Too bad. I thought you might be able to give me a run for my money. I do love a good challenge."

"I don't know what you're talking about," Sara said. She stood, her cheeks flushing.

"The internship?"

"You don't need to worry. I'm not out of the running yet," Sara said.

Chantal's laugh tinkled as it bounced around the room. "Aren't you just a peach? You really think you can beat me now?" She shook her head, looking at Sara with something like pity. "Well..." She waved her hand over the mess and shrugged. "Good luck with that."

Her narrow-set eyes gleamed.

Sara's rage rekindled. But now it had focus. She had fallen. It was true. But she could get back up.

"I will not only beat you, I will beat everyone else and win the internship," Sara said. She felt a strange resolve fall on her. It almost felt like peace. "Now get your bony butt out of my studio."

Chantal rolled her eyes, and left, still smirking. Her scorn remained, hanging heavy in the air as the door clicked shut behind her.

"I gotta deal with my mess. But I will beat you," Sara said. She picked up another piece of sculpture and spoke to it. "I will win. I can do this. I may not understand my heart's inner fire yet, but putting that witch in her place is a heck of a start."

Sara flopped on the couch in her apartment and arched a brow at her roommate. Jane was wearing a red dress and heels. "Hey stranger. You look hot."

"Hey lady, thanks," said Jane. "I'm sorry I've been gone so much this week. You know how it is. Last semester of school. I'm a wreck."

"Yep, I get it. Listen, I'm going to catch up on my Practicum project and will be at the studio all weekend. I just came home to grab food and sketch. But I didn't want you to worry."

"Cool." Jane's blue eyes rested on Sara. "How's Pete? I haven't seen him lately."

Sara sighed. "He asked me out on a real date," she said. "I screwed it up, bad."

Jane leaned forward. "He finally asked you out? What did you do?"

"I ended up blowing him off. Mom moved Marilla to South Carolina behind my back..."

"What?" Jane interrupted. "Are you kidding me? How could she do that?"

"Well, it turns out, pretty easily. But it's not what you think. She quit her job. She's actually going to take care of Rilla. Anyhow. I freaked out and blew Peter off. And I sorta kissed this other guy."

"You what? No way." Jane's eyes widened.

"Yeah, I did. And he has a girlfriend." Sara's chest felt heavy as she confessed. "I didn't know when I kissed him, I swear. Anyhow I told Peter about all of it, and it's a big mess now. He's really hurt. I screwed up. Please don't hate me. I hate myself right now."

Jane shook her head. "What happens between you and Peter is between the two of you. I gotta stay out of it. But yeah, you screwed up. On the other hand, Pete has seen you breaking hearts since we were in high school, so..." Jane shrugged. Her eyes narrowed. "Who's the other guy?"

"Scott Black, I work with him at the Tank," Sara answered.

Jane visibly recoiled at the mention of Scott's name. "That guy is a jerk. Cute, but a real slimeball. He went to Trinity, and I had a couple friends who went out with him. He thought he was a big deal, because he was a football player. But he always tried...well, you know. More than he should. Didn't like the word no."

Jane glanced at the clock. "Listen, there's more to that story, but Daniel is picking me up any minute now. We have dinner with his parents tonight. I'll be back late. Are you okay, though? I can cancel if you need me. I'll stay here with you."

Sara waved her away. "I'm good. I may just stay in and sketch. Go into the studio tomorrow. Making tea and watching old movies sounds really good right now. I'll be fine."

Jane looked at Sara as if weighing her, uncertain, but nodded slowly. "Okay, but if you need anything, call, okay? I'll come home."

"I'll be fine, mama," Sara said. "Get outta here."

Sara put on sweats and slippers, popped a huge bowl of popcorn, made a pitcher of sweet tea, and settled in on the couch with her sketchbook. Sara flipped to a clean page and started doodling. She didn't know her own heart, but maybe she could come to understand it by exploring.

She drew Max, the gargoyle Bastien had shown them. She dreamed about them enough. As she drew, she thought about gargoyles, reviewing what she knew. It wasn't much. She flipped open her Mac and searched, making notes as she read.

Gargoyles were originally ornamental architectural features, part of a gutter system on building. They literally carried water runoff. The water they carried would spill out of their mouths. Later, gargoyles that had no water spouts became popular. These were known as grotesques. They were added to churches and other buildings in Europe to teach about the inhabitants of Hell. Some thought they were put there to guard or protect the inhabitants by scaring away evil spirits.

Sara sighed.

Bastien said that if she understood Max and why he was made, she'd be a good candidate. But she didn't have a clue.

Sara stared at the figure she had drawn. It was a good likeness of Max. She'd studied him a lot since Bastien's presentation. Now, sketching him was simple. He didn't look so much like a demon as much as he resembled a whimsical imp. His face was sly and wise at once. He sported wings, like many creatures who adorned gothic buildings, but he stood on his own. Unattached to any building, he gave the impression of a resting mountain.

A guardian?
A resident of hell?
A teacher?
A warning?
A representation of inner darkness?

She scrawled the questions under the sketch and made a few other notes.

Styrofoam carving

Concrete coating

Paint

She could create a new piece in a week if she used foam carving rather than clay. Plus, the piece would be created as theatrical sculpture. It should win her points. Sara set aside her notebook and grabbed a handful of popcorn. She stared at the fire.

She could make a big heart and have flames inside it and call it heartburn.

She laughed and thought about Bastien's work. Gargoyles were symbols to scare away evil, protectors and guardians. He had done much within the film industry but had also done large-scale installations across the planet. All were designed to call attention to a social issue and raise awareness. He had created a series of huge plastic pink kapok trees to call attention to the deforestation of the Amazon. The installation had stretched across a desert out West somewhere. He'd wrapped a huge corporate building in Tokyo completely in quilts.

No telling what that meant, but it was probably profound.

Sara doodled for a minute and then wrote *Heart's inner fire = a why?*

Sara flipped open her laptop again and typed in *gargoyle*. A book cover with a gargoyle on it came up in the search results. She clicked and scanned a quote. The excerpt made her sit up and take notes.

… a writhing awareness of the superiority of others will kick off an angry, defiant denial...Envy can drive a person, but it will devour your soul.

Sara was shaking.

Marilla. Envy.

She closed her eyes, remembering Chantal's sketches.

I too am not a bit tamed—I too am untranslatable...

The Walt Whitman poem had always spoken to her. The line floated through her mind like music. Right now Sara felt untranslatable. Absently she tapped a new search into her browser. She clicked on the first result, reading an interview with Bastien. "An artist's path is a hero quest in a very concrete way. The monsters we face lie within us." She copied the quote into her notes.

Sara yawned and kept doodling, trying to concentrate. Her other idea, a dragon, took form. Snakelike, sinuous, it writhed across the page. She fiddled with her pendant, pulling it idly back and forth along its chain. Her eyes got heavier and heavier. She fell asleep sitting up, the pendant in her hand.

26

"So I need a dispensation."

"Do you need a full or a partial dispensation?"

"Full, please."

"All right. That will be ten gold."

"Ten gold? That's outrageous."

"For ten gold you get a perfect excuse. No holes in your story whatsoever, guaranteed not to cause Dissonance, will resonate true even when used near a grotesque. It won't raise a fuss among family or friends, will last a lifetime and keep working long after you stop. It's the perfect solution. Now if you want a partial one, it will cost less, but will not hold so neatly. May unravel a bit, wear thin over time. But if you're a gambling sort…"

"How much for the partial?"

"Five gold. Effects will last a lifetime."

"And no Dissonance?"

"No Dissonance felt," the cantor said. "You'll receive it along with an indulgence to keep it from spoiling. You'll need to carry it with you at all times, however. It might make you occasionally uncomfortable. Which will it be?"

"I might only be able to afford the indulgence, how much…"

The voices became muffled as they haggled. Dane grimaced through his gag. Stuffed into an enclosure behind one of the confessional nooks near the Chapterhouse Quiet Room, he could still hear everything. The patter of the cantors as they dealt with their flock's needs turned his stomach.

With a dispensation, an untruth could be spoken with no effects, undetectable by normal means. No grotesque would feel the Dissonance. Dane thought they were only granted in great need, perhaps to prevent a war or save a child. He was wrong.

Lies created Dissonance, whether anyone felt it or not.

Dane shifted in his bonds, uncomfortable with the thought. It pushed at him, heavy with portent. He needed to explore the idea further, but right now he had to escape.

He'd woken, bound hand and foot to a chair and gagged tight. At first, he tried to kick and scoot, to alert the penitents of his predicament. He couldn't reach anything. The chair would not budge. If anyone heard him, they gave no sign. He'd finally given up and begun merely waiting.

Dane searched the nook with his eyes for the hundredth time, looking for anything that might help. He wriggled, working against his bonds again.

A new voice spoke within the confessional. A woman's voice, it rang clearly in Dane's compartment. "Bless me, Brother, for I have sinned. In the name of Domini, Lord of All and His servants. It has been three days since my last confession."

The responding voice was new. It sounded smooth, like velvet. It comforted, wrapping around the hearer like a warm blanket. "May the cyntae, who enlighten every heart, help you to know your sins."

"Amen."

The cantor continued, "Worship all the cyntae, they are Many and worthy to be praised. Fear them and suppress all desires in your heart, listening only to the Apokrypha for all guidance. By your offering, receive forgiveness. Judgment is swift for those who will not dona... er...obey."

The penitent answered. "Cyntae bright, I am sorry for my sins. In failing to obey, I have sinned against You. I firmly intend to give my penance. Our Lord commands me to give that I might be forgiven. Please do not let me fall ill because of the Dissonance in my life."

The small window in the confessional slid open. Coins clinked.

The brother said, "Domini, Lord of the bright, sent the Conclave among men to receive gifts for the forgiveness of sins; through the Conclave He gives you pardon. I absolve you from your sins in the name of Domini and all cyntae."

Bells tinkled in the air, hanging there. Almost visible. Dane recognized a form of the Song. Something like the Song; it was changed. Empty. Something was missing, as if the tones had shifted. The difference was palpable. It wasn't good. It wasn't good at all.

The woman said, "Amen."

"Give thanks to the cyntae, for they are good," intoned the brother. "The cyntae have freed you from your Dissonance. Go in peace."

"I won't be sick again, Brother?"

"No, child," he assured her.

Dane stiffened, growing more angry with each word. *Paying gold for forgiveness and relief from Dissonance? Absurd! Dissonance causing sickness among common folk as if that were normal? Outrageous. Petitioning the cyntae. Cyntae cannot forgive. They should never be worshiped. They're telling falsehoods! But of course, they teach the Storm King is dead. So they have replaced Him with the cyntae. And lies.*

Footsteps faded away. He pushed harder at the knots holding his hands. The rough rope tore at his wrists. Now he was desperate. He didn't know what the Conclave cantors had planned for him. He didn't want to find out.

Brother Bren and Brother Flyn barely fit in the nook where Dane waited. They made the best of it and picked him up, chair and all, carrying him to a nearby chamber. The chamber was very large, with vaulted ceilings and abstract colored-glass windows. Elaborate tapestries told the story of the Broken Tree as they softened the walls. The ceiling, painted with the likenesses of the eight cyntae, arched over rich cherry furniture and a thick Fennish rug.

The High Cantor Siles appeared not long after Dane arrived. The door locked behind him. Brother Flyn prepared censers, filling them with a sweet aromatic, while Brother Bren began Canting. His rich baritone dissipated in the large space as background noise.

Siles walked around Dane's chair, examining him from various angles. Dane stared straight ahead, impassive and resolute. Siles drew up a low ottoman and settled himself, black robes billowing.

"Danethor Thomas." He tapped his finger on his mouth, tracking Dane's eyes. "Danethor Thomas...Whitley, isn't it?"

Dane winced as he realized what the possession of his full name meant. He glared at the cantor.

"Ah, yes. The young cabinetmaker from the lovely village of Dohnavur. Tell me, Danethor, how is it you became apprenticed to the Forge? An odd choice to make, since your business is so profitable. It's been in your family for generations, has it not? You even build custom pieces for nobility."

Still gagged, Dane couldn't answer if he tried. The cantor didn't seem to care. Brother Bren kept Canting, a droning monotone sound. It reminded Dane of a bee's buzzing. Dane wondered what the Canting was supposed to accomplish.

"Don't mind Bren, he is just making sure we have privacy. It's so important to have privacy for a dewin, isn't it? There are so many things you need to keep hidden. To be honest, we have been protecting people from the likes of you for centuries. I've met many dewin. Do you know what you all have in common, Danethor Thomas Whitley?"

Dane relaxed into impassivity, determined not to respond in any way, not even with a facial expression. He fixed his eyes on the cantor's pin, worn at his collar.

Siles leaned in as if relating a secret. "All dewin lie. Every one of them. They all tell outrageous stories, and they lie. Tell me, do you worship the Wyrm? Do you Cant to Him the way we Cant to the cyntae?" Siles searched his face, looking for answers. There were none.

"It isn't Brother Bren who should concern you, you know, it's Brother Flyn. What is he mixing, I wonder? What sort of thing shall you be inhaling? Something to disable you? Keep us safe? Purify you? Or should we even bother trying to help you find a path back to wholeness? Should we just put you to death?"

Siles waited. Dane refused any thought of fear. His fate was in the hands of the Storm King alone. The Storm King had brought him here.

His eyes remained solely fixed on the pin on the cantor's collar. It was eight sided and shone golden in the glowlight. It looked exactly like Dane's binding sign, the sign of the Storm King.

"One of the dewin we've met is from your village. I think you know her. Bell Pennyweather? She's a lovely girl. So delicate. When Dohnavur was purified, of course we detained her. She didn't take the purification process well." He paused, letting the words strike home. "Shame, that. Nadir was always a bit enthusiastic about these things."

No, not Bell. She couldn't be gone.

Dane lifted his gaze, looking into the high cantor's eyes. He was telling the perfect truth.

"Ah, that's better. I can see your true self, the man you are, in your eyes. You need not speak. She means something to you. Interesting. She's here. You can see her. She's quite diminished, I'm afraid. She's conscious, healing and can speak, but she tires easily. Nevertheless, it's so good to see her improving. I'd hate for her get worse. It's quite repugnant to see a beautiful woman drooling and soiling themselves, don't you think?"

Dane looked up at the cyntae painted on the ceiling. The two lovers, Solimon and Lalo, stared at each other. *She was alive. He could save her.*

"Dane, normally we would immediately disable you. But you obviously have had training. We cannot risk the threat you pose to common people. Whether you accept it or not, there is madness in you. When you begin to fail, it will happen quickly, and you will destroy all who surround you. You will kill them. You will not be able to help yourself.

"We have two options. We can force you to use your gifts in our service. You would be under our power. We would give you Essences to keep you docile. You would not be able to think for yourself, but you could still be very useful, I think. However, it would also diminish your abilities, and those seem considerable. We think it would be rather better if you simply cooperate. We could train you to avoid madness, in time, and restrain you before you hurt anyone, if needed. We'd like to offer you the chance. Do you understand? Nod if you do."

Dane nodded. He exaggerated the motion so there could be no misunderstanding. He would rather cooperate than become mindless.

"You've been lied to Dane. Likely you've been lied to your entire life. Everything you think you know isn't true. It might contain seeds of truth. Believable lies always do. As you come to accept truth and serve us and the cyntae from your heart, you will gain more freedom. I hope in time you will come to love the Conclave and serve her as you would Bell." Siles held up a hand. "Flyn, you may stop. Release our new acolyte."

Brother Flyn stopped. He turned and approached Dane with a dagger, cutting his bonds. He left the gag in place. Dane sat, waiting.

Siles eyes rested on Dane's bald head. "You have already adopted some of our ways, I see. You'll need to shave your head daily. Bren will take you to your rooms and guide you. You'll begin your instruction today. Your voice has power, as you know, and so we command you to utter silence at all times, whether alone or in the company of others. If you disobey, we shall remove your tongue. That would be unfortunate.

"I don't have to explain to you, Bell Pennyweather's fate rests in your hands. Should you disobey at all, she will suffer. In time you'll come to see this precaution was necessary. It's for your own good."

Dane nodded.

Brother Flyn removed his gag. Brother Bren stopped his Canting.

Siles stood, lifting Dane to his feet and wrapping him in a warm embrace. He leaned back, regarding him with the pride and affection of a father. "Enough of the unpleasantness. Welcome to the Order."

Siles released him, stepping back and signaling Flyn, who presented Dane with a small slate and chalk. "You're not the only acolyte with a vow of silence. Use this when you need to speak. All are accustomed to them. You can read and write, can you not?"

Dane nodded again. He shifted from foot to foot, letting blood flow back into them.

"I imagine you are hungry. Go with Bren. He will see to your needs."

Dane followed Bren into a vaulted passage. They walked through a labyrinth of hallways and stairs, arriving finally at a long corridor filled with doors. Bren stopped at the end of the row and opened one into a small cell.

"You'll find robes. Change out of your clothing and place them on your bed," said Bren. "I'll have food brought. Vespers are held at the sixth bell. Be prepared to join us. You will, of course, remain silent through them."

Dane nodded and bowed, then entered his cell. The door to the tiny room closed. A lock clicked.

27

Trystan listened intently. Tabor pointed to his own head, where a mop of dark hair curled under his sailor's hat. "This is a wig," he said. "As a Spinner, we often need to disappear. One of the best ways to accomplish this is a disguise. Disguises should become second nature, easily adopted or discarded. A few simple preparations will aid you greatly. The first aid for the disguises we employ is to keep your hair close-cropped or shave it completely. We have several barbers in the nest, and many throughout the land are friendly to our cause. They create our wigs."

He walked around Trystan, inspecting him. "'Tis a blessing you don't have the braided beards of your countrymen. Those would be costly to replicate.

"The shaved head is your first line of defense in subterfuge, hiding, and freedom. Need to capture the eye of a soldier and distract him?" Tabor whipped off his hat and wig and took up another from those arrayed on the shelves in the narrow mirrored room. Long, curled tresses framed his mobile face. He simpered at himself and Trystan.

"A pretty face can quickly lead a guard from his post."

He leaned forward and tapped Trystan lightly on the shoulder. "But the best thing is to blend in. You want to not be noticed. A selection of wigs for every occasion and clothes to match. That's what you'll find in the Spinner's nest and in a Spinner's pack. Try for nondescript cloaks, hoods, and of course, a variety of mustaches.

"All right, you have five minutes. Create a disguise to fool me and escape the nest," he said. Tabor left the room, closing the door behind him.

Blend in. Trystan set to work. He assembled a sailor's black tunic and breeches, a standard uniform in the nest. He stuffed a cloth in his boot to give himself a limp. To this he added a long brown beard and matching mustaches. A bit of clay and some paint lengthened his nose. A few dabs of dark powder in the right places made him look older. He topped his cropped blond hair with a medium-length brown wig and added a broad-brimmed hat. He put on a pair of spectacles. Lastly, he picked up a large sack filled with flour and hoisted it on his shoulder.

He was ready.

Trystan fixed his eyes on the floor, using the flour bag as a shield to hide his face. He struggled to keep his limp consistent as he made his way to the lift. Seth didn't give him a second glance as he manned the lift pulleys. Trystan stumped through the short hallway to the main warehouse. *Almost there.*

"Here, let me help you with that, sir." Tabor's voice was friendly. He pulled the flour sack from Trystan's grasp with a wide grin. "Well done, you nearly made it on the first try."

"Has anyone ever bested you?" asked Trystan.

"No," he said, clapping Trystan on the shoulder. "But I have a lot of fun letting them think they've fooled me. The limp caught my eye, by the way."

"Great."

"Next time, stoop and don't drag your leg. It changes your height. All right. Ready for the next lesson?" Tabor placed the flour bag on a nearby shelf.

The cell was cold. Dane stifled an exclamation as he shucked off his Northern garb and donned a white robe. The robe branded him as an acolyte to the Conclave, theirs to do with as they pleased. He detested it already. His stomach growled. He scanned the windowless room, looking for anything he could use to escape. The stone walls were bare. A single bed with a threadbare quilt had a table next to it, topped with both a candle and an oil lamp. A ewer and bowl sat in one corner, filled with clean water, a battered wardrobe, and a desk and chair.

There was no Watcher here, a small solace.

Quickly, Dane took the meager contents of his cloak pockets and put them in the desk. He had the small bottle of Indra ink he'd purchased from Poll before he left home, a quill, the old buckles from his boots, and the jewel given to him by Birgir as payment. Everything else was gone. He folded his clothes slowly and set them on the bed as instructed.

Two raps on the door broke the silence. Brother Bren entered, carrying a tray of food. The monk set the tray on the desk and gestured for Dane to eat. Dane sat and focused on the simple meal, brown bread and cheese. He chewed slowly and washed down the dry crust with a mug of spring water as Brother Bren waited. When he finished, Bren gathered up Dane's discarded clothing and commanded him to follow. Dane scrambled, scooping up his slate and chalk and closing the door behind him.

"You're already shaven," Bren said, looking at Dane's bald pate with approval. "I'll walk you to the baths. Our barbers serve the entire community in a workshop adjacent to them. Acolytes shave as a sign of subjection, chastity, and honesty. You are expected to bathe and shave daily." Bren pointed out toilet facilities as they passed through the hallways, along with the symbol carved into the doors to mark them.

They descended several flights of stairs and entered a large room with pools of steaming water. The air faintly smelled of rotten eggs.

"The baths," said Bren, gesturing to encompass them. "They're fed by hot springs and drain continually. They smell odd, but you will get used to it."

They passed through several arcades filled with pools. Bren briefly walked through the barbery, greeting the barbers as they shaved a few acolytes. He glanced back at Dane and marched up two flights of stairs, coming out into a walled courtyard. They passed under an arch dripping lavender wisteria blossoms into another courtyard, ringed by benches. Several acolytes sat listening to a cantor lecture.

Bren nodded to the cantor and murmured to Dane, "Acolytes have eight hours of training and work, eight hours of service to the cyntae, and eight hours of sleep. Ours is a life of knowledge. As you learn our mysteries, you will progress and perhaps become a cantor."

Never. He smiled respectfully, turning to listen to the lesson.

"Songlines formed by the root system of the Tree are infused every night with strength from the cyntae. Our Canting provides the connection. As we Cant Matins, Vespers, Compline, and the little hours, we strengthen the trickle we have."

An acolyte held up his slate. The cantor leaned forward to read it, then nodded. "Yes, good question. We have been seeking to strengthen the songlines even more for centuries. Much of the work here is aimed at that very purpose. Your training will allow you to join us in this research. Many of our higher teachings may only take hold in your memory as you ascend in your learning and train your mind. For this reason, you must work as hard as possible to further your studies."

Dane stifled a snort. It wasn't the songlines that needed strengthening, it was the cyntae who needed finding. The Storm King needed the cyntae, and they were missing. Except for Doran.

He wrote on his slate, the chalk squeaking in protest. *Has anyone talked to Solimon or Lalo? Do they come to visit? Can they help?*

The cantor stiffened. "All cyntae, including Solimon and Lalo, are giving their full effort to maintain the Song. The nexus they inhabit has changed because of increased Dissonance. Only one is able to work with us directly, but he imparts the wisdom of all. This cyntae, Doran, speaks only with the Arcantor Modric, of course."

Modric was the cause of all of this. He could never be the cure. Did they really not understand? Dane bowed and folded his hands together, humbly.

Looking at the other acolytes, Dane saw no sign of distress, no skepticism or questioning. All so trusting, they believed what they were taught must be true. But why shouldn't they? He wrote another question on his slate. He knew he would get the same answer he had been given as a child during Camber, but he had to try.

The teacher took the slate and read aloud.

"Where is the Storm King?"

The cantor raised his thin blonde eyebrows. "Have you never been to Camber? The Storm King sacrificed himself on the Tree to save us from the Wyrm. The Storm King is dead, and The Wyrm was cast out of our universe, into the void beyond the door of the Moon. Its arc is now our seal of protection." He tutted and shook his head, and the other acolytes smiled, some stifling laughter.

Dane erased his slate and inscribed the question no one ever asked, the most important question. *"How do you know this?"*

"The Cyntae Doran told us, he told the Arcantor Modric himself," the cantor's spoke with the measured tones reserved for simpletons and irritating children.

Dane knew he was treading a thin line, but he didn't care. He shook his slate to repeat his question, but Bren held his hand, stilling him.

"Thank you, Brother Kain," said Brother Bren. "Our new brother has much to learn. He was raised without benefit of a Chapterhouse. It is good to be reminded of our basic tenets. Thank you for disrupting your class for us."

He bowed and took Dane by the upper arm, guiding him out of the courtyard. When they were out of sight, he hissed, "Are you trying to get yourself killed? Do you not understand? High Cantor Siles is taking a terrific gamble with you. You have been given a boon, unheard of, yet at the first opportunity, you try to throw it away. You will learn the price of such questions, wyrmfriend. We shall purge you of all evil lies." He pushed Dane toward another set of steps down into the stone belly of the compound. "A new lesson. You're going to learn about the sacrament of flagellation."

The ugly whip, a wicked scourge with three tails, snapped across Dane's back.

"Again," ordered Bren. "In rhythm with my Canting. Accept the pain and allow it to cleanse you."

Bren began to Cant. At the end of each phrase, Dane cracked the whip across his own torn and bloody back.

Hear our prayer, Cyntae bright
Bring your servant to the light
Strike each lie from his bones
Let our Cant lead him home.

Dane's eyes watered. He struggled not to cry out. He raised his head at the end of the verse and squinted, unsure if Bren would continue. Inexplicably, he saw the fae. Sara stood behind Bren, shimmering. Tears ran down her face. Dane swallowed.

He was not alone. It was enough.

Bren paused and picked up the slate and chalk, passing these to him in exchange for the scourge.

"Where is the Storm King?" he asked.

Dane sat on his haunches and wrote slowly, his vision blurring. He wiped sweat from his eyes. Gingerly, he handed the slate back to Bren, gasping even as he prayed with all his heart. *Let him believe.*

"The Storm King wrestles the Wyrm from beyond the door of the Moon. He lives. He will return."

Bren read the slate aloud and let out a black, enraged snarl. He took up the scourge and thrashed it across Dane's back, punctuating his words. "The Storm King is dead"—thrash—"The Storm King is dead"—thrash—"The Storm King is dead"—thrash.

Each fall cut deeper, burned longer. Blood pooled around his knees as it dripped from his torn flesh, his arms trembling too much to hold him upright any longer, he slumped forward and knew no more.

Bell opened her mouth, accepting food. She chewed. A man in a white robe spoke to her. She tried to answer, but her mouth fell open, and the only result was a low moan. Spittle dribbled down her chin. The man gave her another bite. He wiped her mouth, patted her on the head and took the tray away. She was alone in a white room. Light streamed through a colored-glass window next to her bed. Her fingers twitched. She wanted to touch the light. Red. Blue. A tear rolled down her cheek. She fell into a fitful sleep.

Words spoken in hushed tones washed over her. "...aural nexus permanently damaged. We can try the healing song, but it is incomplete. We cannot be sure what will happen. We do have the new Essences found in Dohnavur."

Bell tried to open her eyes.

"Worst case?"

"The song could backfire on the person who uses it. It could affect all within hearing. At worst, it will kill her."

A door opened. "She is expendable, but we shall take precautions. If she dies, we will know what to do with the next one. Be sure to record all of her responses."

A door shut. The voices faded. She followed them into darkness.

Bell heard music and smelled flowers. She saw indistinct faces as she opened her eyes. Music washed over her, monotonous. Something was unsettling in its repetition, sinister. It went on for a long time.

She moaned...

It went on for longer still.

Bell heard cries of pain. She opened her eyes. The light stabbed her, carving with a thousand knives. She tried to scream but found her mouth gagged. She started to choke. Bile rose, burning the back of her throat, spurting into her nose. The pain was unbearable.

A voice again.

"Bell, it's Jax."

The words were whispered in her ear, soft words, trembling with emotion. She couldn't open her eyes, couldn't respond.

"What have they done to you?" His voice broke.

She wanted to comfort him and could not. She could not scream her rage. She could not speak to the only family remaining to her. At least he was alive.

"You hang on. Fight, Bell. Keep trying. Don't let go. I'm here. I'm with you. I will find a way to help you. I made it here. I'm watching. They're going to move you again, and I've found a way to go with you. I'll be here. Hang on."

More sunlight came. It burned. Bell opened her eyes. Two men were lifting her on a cot, carrying her through a huge courtyard. She wanted to yell, to scream. But she couldn't.

She couldn't move. The last thing she remembered was Jax's voice telling her to hang on, that he would be with her. White robes and black robes obscured her view, surrounding her. They carried her for a long while. She could see nothing but open sky.

Finally, they set her cot down. A mist-covered tree, as large as a mountain, loomed over her head. Her vision swam. She moved her fingers, weak as a kitten.

"Wa—" she croaked. "Water." She closed her eyes. "Need water."

A rush of footsteps, a bald head hovering above her, excited murmurs from her caretakers—she absorbed all of it slowly. Her head throbbed. It hurt to think. Someone helped her sit up, a strong arm behind her back. A bald, white-robed woman held a glass of water to her lips. She drank, water spilling down her chest. It dripped from her chin, chilling her more. She flushed, humiliated and feral.

A tall bearded man in a blue robe with dark eyes knelt before her. "Bell? Do you know me? Do you remember anything? Do you recognize this place?" He pointed to the huge tree.

Bell stared at the man. Familiar, but she could not place him. She shook her head and twitched, her body convulsing.

The man rose and pointed to the acolytes. "Take her back inside the Chapterhouse. We will expose her to the Tree daily. Keep records of all she eats, drinks, says, and does. She is very delicate."

He turned back to Bell and knelt again. "You've been unwell. We're helping you to recover. Obey and you shall not suffer further."

28

Bell woke slowly and smiled. Jax was singing to her. He sang to her every night like he had when she was a tiny girl. His voice was gravel and rocks, out of tune. It comforted her like nothing else. He was still with her. He was safe.

She sat up.

He was in the middle of her room, whittling a stick as he sang. The room was big and airy, with windows of thick colored glass. Her bed was narrow but comfortable. Flowers filled every available surface. Tunebells and delphiniums. Their scent calmed her and held her ever-present headache at bay.

Jax stopped, looking up from his whittling. He tilted his head.

"You look much improved, lass."

"I feel better," said Bell, running her hands through her hair. Someone had cut it. It was too short. "How long have I been ill?"

"You've been out for weeks," said Jax. "The Conclave cantors purified you. They named you dewin and took you, gave you something that hurt you badly."

Bell's eyes widened, and Jax held up a hand to halt her inevitable anger.

"They've also nursed you back to health, and they don't know I am here. I need you to be quiet and follow them, lass. Go along with what they ask as long as it doesn't hurt you or others. Lile is watching the inn for us. I'm planning to get you out of here. But first you have to be well."

"Dane," Bell whispered, her eyes filling with tears. "Where is he? Do you know? I remember now, they said I was deemling, and it meant I was dewin. Is he safe?"

The gnome's cap drooped.

"I don't know. We rescued all the others. Jess, Little Mary Planor, Stu, all of them. I followed when they took you to this Chapterhouse. I listen and sneak about, learning all that I can, but have not heard any word of him yet. He left before the Conclave came for everyone. I'm sure he is safe."

"I'm not able to do much, Bell. I can't leave you. That son of a wyrm, Aric, brought you here a few days ago. You've drifted in and out since, but have spoken. That's more than you were able to do for so long. I thought I had lost you forever."

"Do you know where we are?"

Jax nodded. "We're at the Rift Chapterhouse. They've been taking you every day to the World Tree, letting you spend time near it. You're getting better."

Bell considered this, taking in the sight of tunebells and the delphiniums. She had seen them before at Camber in the Chapterhouse during the Canting services. The cantor taught they helped strengthen the Song. She thought about what Nadir had said to her the last time she had seen him.

"Last time the Conclave really purified Dohnavur, I was very small. I couldn't have been more than six years old. You took me to the Burrow. Dane was there, and so were the other deemling. I played with Stu Callin."

Jax nodded.

"I've never been in the village when it was purified."

Jax nodded again.

Bell's face flooded with color as truth dawned. "I'm really dewin?"

Jax clambered up onto her bed and crawled over to sit on its edge. "Keep your voice down, you'll have the baldpates running in. Yes, Bell. You're dewin. But don't worry, you will not go mad."

"Why won't I go mad?" Bell's eyes clouded. She reached for the gnome's hand, desperate for comfort.

"Because I am with you. I will keep you safe, as I have since you were a wee babe." Jax tapped the side of his nose. "In truth, the talk of dewin madness was not strictly the whole story, but by the Storm King's blood, few would ever believe what really happened. I'll tell you more tomorrow. Now it is almost time for them to tend to you. It might be wise for you to feign confusion until you get your bearings."

Bell nodded.

Jax looked at her a long moment, his eyes bright. "It is good to see you as yourself again, lassie." He gathered her into a rare hug. Then, with a hop down and a wink, he was gone.

Bell stayed awake most of the next day and ate all her meals unassisted. She didn't wake when Jax visited. Tunesday arrived, and canting sounded throughout the compound, both outside as she was walked for exercise through the arcades, and inside as she rested in her room. The singsong melodies made her feel strange.

She tried to nap in the afternoon but couldn't sleep. After she had lain there a short while, the heavy door to her room opened and shut. Cosette, her cantor guard, had stepped away. Bell's arms and legs tingled, and her head swam, but she sat upright and then stood. She swayed, arms akimbo for a few minutes, but took a step. Slowly, she made her way to the door. It opened.

Cautiously, she wandered down the windowless stone corridor until she came at last to another bound wooden door. This opened into a walled garden. She sat heavily on a bench, spent. The world spun slowly, flowers and trees swimming before her bleary eyes. She began weeping uncontrollably, unable to stop. An age passed before Cosette found her and half dragged her back to the bed.

She slept through dinner.

When she woke, Bell had a new visitor. The visitor wore the black robes of a cantor. Pins at his collar proclaimed him the high cantor. He sat in a chair next to her bed. Bell had the distinct impression he had been counting her breaths. She brushed the thought away.

Bell squirmed, pulling the blankets up over her thin nightdress as she struggled to sit up in bed and rearrange her matted hair.

The high cantor signaled to an acolyte. He stepped forward, propping her up, arranging pillows behind her.

"Some water," the cantor said, mildly. "And a bowl of fruit, I think. Yes?"

"Yes," said Bell, her voice sounding small in her own ears.

"I am High Cantor Siles," he said. "You've been here a long time. I thought it was time that we met."

"Bell Pennyweather, Father," she answered. "Do you know what was wrong with me? No one will say. I ask the nurses, but they all just say I've been very ill."

"You're still not well," Siles corrected. He was wiry, with a thin, expressive mouth and intelligent eyes that seemed to read her very thoughts. Those eyes bored into her before he spoke again. They gleamed. Hungry. He looked hungry. "Bell, have you ever met a chymaera?"

"No."

"But you know of them."

"They change into other creatures. They can transform into gryphons or winged horses, winged lions. They make the gargoyles and other wonders."

"They haven't been able to transform as they once did, and it's made some of them very anxious and unhappy. We would like you to meet a few, when you feel up to it. Would you mind doing that? We will wait until after you feel better."

Bell gaped. "What was wrong with me?"

"You were given a tincture, the Essence of a very old tree and a mixture of some other plants in a form that you could breathe. When most people receive this mixture, they feel happy and want to please others. They listen well and obey us without fuss. We can help them then, keep them safe. When we gave it to you, your body did not respond in that way. You rejected the tincture. It was quite painful for you, but necessary both to test you and also to cleanse you from what we call residual resonant energy. Such could have hurt you and others."

Bell felt the color rising in her cheeks as he spoke. "You purified me." Her voice remained calm, but her hands were shaking. She shoved them under the blankets.

"We helped you. Would you like to meet with the chymaera?" The high cantor's voice, bearing, and eyes were all patient as a mountain.

He actually sounded as if he were offering her a choice.

"If I do not?" she asked.

"Then we will give you more of other tinctures, and you will likely suffer greatly. After that, you will not remember anything. If you wake up from it, I will ask you again. We will do this until you decide to help." High Cantor Siles's face was marble; his eyes were serpentine. His voice was as patient as a gravestone. His bearing was as mild as a lamb being led to slaughter.

Bell swallowed her bile and nodded. "I will help."

Siles smiled at her, his thin lips twisting. The expression did not successfully reach his eyes. "Good."

He rose and left without another word.

29

N'khum waited until he was on the outskirts of Baehnt to transform. He secured the scroll within a pouch sewn into his vestments. He reached for his true form, familiar after so many years, and his whole being filled with light. He expanded, flowed. He cried out in triumph and joy, took wing, and flew as quickly as he could back the Wyn. As he flew, he pondered what he would say to the Derbyn. M'ra was insistent they assist the Conclave in whatever ways they could to capture dewin.

Then there was G'der. He and others believed interaction with those who were not chymaera would pollute the aeries. They blamed dewin and the majisters for their current suffering. More than that, they taught that if the cyntae and the chymaera had remained apart from men, the Breaking would never have happened.

They blamed M'ra for the death of Chesed. They said he should never have left the aerie.

It was their reaction that N'khum feared the most.

N'khum needed to approach this matter carefully, or it was possible no one would give him a chance to commune and prove the truth of what he had experienced. Yet a call for deep communion with all of the others could be misinterpreted, taken as a sign of offense or weakness.

N'khum landed in the hippodrome. Its large, bowl-like platform was the official takeoff and landing point for Derbyn, not that they didn't vault into the sky from anywhere. When on official business, they landed here. N'khum needed to make sure his return was recorded.

The attending Profi hurried up to him, an older one. Savlahnut was nearly as old as Chesed. He likely would have Quickened not long after the war, had he been able, also like Chesed. He wore his hair long, tied into a tail. It whipped in the wind created by N'khum's wings.

Savlahnut stopped in front of N'khum, his hand held over his heart. "Great one, your presence is requested by M'ra the Eldest without delay."

N'khum shed his true form, humbling himself to speak with this Profi on the same level. It was an honor he always granted to one who should have already Quickened. It did not change their status, but it was all he could do to convey his respect. He checked the pouch in his vestments as he transformed. The scroll was there. Relieved, he lightly touched Savlahnut's back, steering him from the center of the hippodrome to the arcade that ran around the bowl.

"Savlahnut, what have you heard?" he asked. He kept his face impassive, steadying himself for the inevitable.

"They are saying you killed the World Tree and doomed us all. Others say you were captured by a mad dewin. There is one story you battled a dwarf, a cantor, and a hundred Northmen, and were killed."

N'khum stopped in front of an arch. He turned, watching the field as other Derbyn took off and landed. It was late at night, but there were more landing than taking off. Those who were launching had hunting and guarding duties. He recognized their colors.

"Where is M'ra?" he asked.

"In her tower. She is unwinged, great one. She mourns for Chesed and will not be disturbed. The Council honors her wishes, but they grow impatient." Savlahnut bowed.

"Tell me, Savlahnut, despite what happened to Chesed, if you were given the opportunity to travel outside the aerie, to see men and dwarves and cities, would you go?" The question was pointed.

Savlahnut weighed his answer. His silver eyes closed as he walked through the possibilities. He opened them and smoothed his silver robes. "I would wish to see it all."

N'khum nodded. "Thank you for your service. Go with the Song." He placed his hand over his heart.

Savlahnut returned the gesture and walked back to his station.

M'ra's tower was on the other side of the hippodrome. N'khum followed the arcade, passing carved fountains and Speakers created to beautify the arena as well as to serve. Most of the Speakers in this section of the Aerie were angels, though a few imps sat on benches or crouched in ceiling corners, held there by wings. N'khum smiled at them, remembering when all were active.

He took the stairs up into the cluster of fluted towers with parapets, bridges, and walkways. Most of the Derbyn lived here. Profi scurried along the paths, their eyes properly downcast. They gave him a wide berth and turned aside to let him pass if the way became narrow. N'khum acknowledged them with a smile as he made his way to M'ra's tower.

The tallest tower was proper for the leader of the Wyn. Each had a wide pavilion and platform from which to glide, should a Derbyn wish to remain winged. Many did, refusing to leave their wings, refusing to speak with any but Derbyn. M'ra was not so inclined.

N'khum paused, considering. A communion would strengthen his reception, as M'ra would see through his eyes. But it was the scroll he held she must see. He climbed the long spiral staircase to the platform at the top of the tower.

When he got to the top, the wind whipped through his hair as he pulled the bell on the door. A robed Profi answered and ushered him to M'ra's wingroom.

M'ra was unwinged on a low velvet couch, dressed in the red vestments and veil of chymaera in deep mourning. She stood when he entered and rushed to greet him with genuine pleasure, clasping him in a warm embrace. "N'khum. I've been beside myself. It was so good to receive the Speaker's message last night and finally know you were safe. Please, sit."

A silken-clad Profi entered the room with a tray of nuts, fruit, breads, and tea and set them on a small table. She left quietly, closing the double doors behind her. Sunlight streamed through the open pavilion doors, falling on thick carpets and marble. N'khum sat in the offered chair. "I'm sorry to grieve you, Eldest. It was not my intent. I acted in the best interests of the aerie. But this delayed me."

M'ra poured both of them tea, her face impassive. "Please." She gestured to the food. "Help yourself."

N'khum took a piece of sweetbread and placed it on the plate in front of him and added honey to the tea. "Thank you, Eldest. You are most kind."

"We heard from the Conclave immediately after you departed from the Tree. I would hear your story myself."

N'khum took the scroll from his vestments and placed it in front of her.

"Honored Eldest. I beseech you to read this before I give you the story. I also ask that we commune, so you may see through my eyes."

M'ra gazed at N'khum, her golden eyes filling with tears. "You think I do not trust you?"

"I trust you completely, Eldest. These events must be witnessed, not told."

M'ra picked up the scroll, now curious, and unrolled it. She scanned it quickly, gasping at the signature. She read again carefully, her face clouding. "Where did you get this?"

"In Baehnt. A Majisterium archive has survived the centuries. The man who gave me this scroll had much to say. I had much to learn. We have been deceived, sister."

"Show me," M'ra commanded. She went to the center of the wingroom and removed her veil. She transformed, red vestments becoming a scarlet cross upon her white feathers and fur. Her tail twitched as she waited for N'khum. N'khum rose and joined her, shifting into his true form. He crouched and stretched his wings, extending them toward her. She likewise extended her wings to him. With a cry of surrender, they were one.

N'khum guided M'ra through his memories. He let her see Danethor, the boy's intelligence and sanity. He showed her the dewin's ignorance and how he had reached for Dane's mind, testing him. He showed her the Tree.

As the Tree healed, M'ra started to shake. She nearly broke communion, so violent was her reaction of wonder and joy. She held on as the skycart's passengers disembarked, as the Conclave began to search for an intruder. She exulted when the boy disappeared and agreed with N'khum's decision to help the Northmen. She watched as they escaped and then flew to Baehnt, meeting Spinners named Seth and Mod at the docks. They visited the Spinner's nest, where N'khum received the scroll. When M'ra understood the message at last, the tears began. Keening, she let him finish.

In turn, she showed him memories of the War, five centuries ago, of the man who had penned this scroll. She showed Jamis. His kindness, his wisdom. She showed the boy, Petros, his assistant. A boy who could not hear or sing, much less be dewin. She showed him rows of dewin, in the aerie to celebrate a Quickening. He saw the killing begin, brothers and sisters falling from the sky. He saw Profi burn.

She showed him more recent memories. Chesed, fallen on the grass, lying in his own blood. Then she showed him Chesed's signet as she had found it, with its message of love.

The communion lasted for hours. When it ended, they broke and retreated to corners of the pavilion. The energy required for the connection was overwhelming. N'khum's heartfire guttered, utterly depleted, despite the wonders he had seen. He grieved with M'ra for the fallen Profi, for the blood shed through the centuries. He shifted, again, becoming wingless to rest more fully.

M'ra shed her wings. She sat unmoving, her hair a blanket for her face. Finally, she rose and once more donned her veil.

"This dewin, Danethor, he was not mad. He was trained. He healed the Tree," she said. "And Jamis believed Modric was plotting the unthinkable."

N'khum nodded.

"I must find the gnomes I met in Dohnavur. They spoke truly. I must speak with them again," she decided. "You heard the gnome, his Dissonance. But Chesed heard more. He trusted them when I would not.

"G'der plots to remove me from rule. The Conclave accuses us of treachery. They claim you affected the Tree and demand to have you turned over to them. Unwinged. G'der would have you named Pryf. He will not consent to communion. You were marked when you landed. They will expect us to descend and call a council now."

M'ra strode to the table and rang a bell. A Profi entered. M'ra scribbled a message and pressed this parchment along with Jamis' scroll into her hands. "Take this to Ts'doq and bid him keep them safe. Go directly to him. Speak to no one else. Place them in his hands, do not leave them with a servant. I must fly on urgent business. No one is to speak to the Conclave until I return, it is forbidden. Tell Ts'doq I invoke the full Law of the Wyn on this matter."

The Profi bowed, her hand over her heart, and left the room at a run.

Turning to N'khum, M'ra said. "The ones you met in Baehnt, they were looking for a gnome called Pezzik and had a network of others to assist in finding her?"

N'khum nodded.

M'ra ducked behind a folding screen and talked to him from behind it as she disrobed. "I released the gnomes from judgment to honor Chesed but had planned to locate them after my mourning period had been completed. Pezzik, she was the gnomemother in my thoughts. We shall find her together, quickly." M'ra emerged from the screen, clad again in white, her veil discarded. "I begin to suspect something, brother, I go to seek confirmation."

N'khum bowed, placing his hand over his heart. He followed M'ra to the center of the room and shifted. Together, winged and ready, they dropped from the tower, gliding on currents of air that lifted them toward the stars and into the deepening night.

The Storm King's Eye watched them fly.

30

"Teach me this Spinner's Cant, you blackguard!" Trystan tossed his stones away in defeat. Three games down, he was in no mood to lose more of his thinning purse to Seth.

Tabor eyed the bard. He lounged in a chair upholstered in red velvet, one leg thrown over the arm. He stood, pointing his index finger to the heavens. "I shall teach you the Spinner's Cant, and you shall teach me a song."

"Any song?"

"Aye."

"It's a bargain."

"No, milord, it's a bolliker. There's your first word. Bargain means bolliker. Now teach me a song."

Trystan tried the new word. "Bolliker means bargain."

"Song!" said Tabor. He flopped back into his chair, saluting Trystan with his mug.

"I get more words for an entire song," the bard protested.

"How many?"

"Thirty."

Tabor groaned. "Thirty words, thirty words? Really?"

"Aye," said Trystan, taking his own swig of ale.

Tabor sighed, stood, and began to recite, miming to rather comical effect.

An Abram man's a beggar, who only plays the fool.
Do not listen to his patter or believe it if he drools.

If I fling dust into your eyes
That is me amusing
Moon pigs are night watchmen
They are never snoozing.
A napper is a thief, young man.
An onion is a ring.
The pad is the highway, and
Only a snitcher sings.
A wiper is a handkerchief, and yellow tin is gold.
I've only told ten words by now, the poem's already
old. A bluffer is an innkeeper, a bawler is a cantor
A cannon is a pickpocket, but
The head thief is dimber damber
Dodgies are innocent, and they will never hang.
Fans are gloves, equipt is rich and all the dogs are
fangs. An uncle takes your contraband
Keeps it in his fencing ken
Now you have ten more words
And I still owe you ten.
When you dance the shadows, you disappear
Flag wavers just make plans
A tilted floor is a wall my dear
Get information from the piece man
Moon men are all Spinners
To be quiet means you're smooth
A coachman is a rattling cove
This poem wasn't a good move.
This ditty's been rum fun to say
And a reader is a purse
I've had a headache all the day
I think it's getting worse
Finally, my fine young friend, I'll leave you with a
twig. A twig means you realize something's odd
Always avoid the pig.

The Spinner bowed as Trystan clapped and cheered, "Encore! Encore!"
   Tabor blinked. "You must be joking, I have no idea what I just said."
Trystan laughed and hummed to himself, prepared to keep up his
end of the bolliker. But when he looked up, Tabor had fallen asleep in

his chair, with his mug still in his hand.

Trystan woke in a small room, in an actual bed, with no memory of how he got there. A lute was in its case, propped in a corner. He unpacked it slowly. It was beautiful, with inlays and the star mark on its bowl. Slowly, he strummed the strings. This was *his* lute. He had risked everything for this. Finally, it was in his hands. Trystan thought about the journey to get here, the long search. His initiation into the Spinners. Now he finally held the lute. *It was his.* It was here.

A ripple of melody leapt forth from his fingers, soft at first. The music spoke the truth of his soul. The notes reflected his soul and intentions, a musical mirror. He was testing the sound, and they tested the air. They soared and then hung back, hesitant, as if waiting permission before dancing aloft. More confident now, Trystan swung into a traveling song that made his own legs restless. It was uncanny.

His joy in the sounds made the notes even brighter as they skipped and bounced, echoing with a mad beauty. Trystan could smell a forest and feel the wind on his face—the music conjured them. Birdsong trilled the counter-melody and found its way to the strings. It was so pure, his hands wavered. He shook himself as he let the music fade.

He swung the instrument over his shoulder, unwilling to let it out of his sight. Hours had passed in an instant. He needed to find Tabor.

When he wandered into the hallway, Trystan saw he was close to the archives. He found his way back to the map room easily enough. It had been tidied but still smelled of ale. Trystan paled at the odor, promising himself to never drink another ale again.

Trystan's stomach complained. He grimaced and went in search of something to settle it.

When he got to the courtyard, Trystan found Tabor lying on a bench, staring up at the morning sky. A basket next to him held sweetbreads and fruit. He was dressed as a lordling fop today, with a brocade coat and lacy sleeves.

"You know what I wish?" Tabor said, in lieu of a greeting.
"I can't possibly imagine what you wish," said Trystan. He grabbed a muffin and sat down on the bench, bumping off Tabor's feet.
"Do share."

"I wish I had wings of my own. I hate traveling. It inevitably means camping. There are never enough inns, no matter what route I take to Bestua."

Trystan arched a brow at Tabor. "Why are we going to Bestua?"

Tabor sat up, sighing heavily. He waved his hand, sending lace fluttering in the morning breeze. "Because I spoke with Mod today. She delivered your lute, which I see you found. She also brought guests, who have come and gone. The chymaera was here with two Forgemen and a dwarf. She says your luthier has been taken by the Conclave."

"Taken? And so we must leave as well?"

"Dear boy, Mod said you have been watched, as we suspected. She believes that the Conclave actually used you as bait to capture the luthier."

Tabor gestured, encompassing the courtyard. "They knew who you were and have watched all of your movements. They used you to find this luthier, Danethor, in the first place. The dwarf had a message for Danethor's gnome guardian as well, but Mod will deliver it. You have other business.

"You've been missed while you've been in the nest. It's time to let the Conclave see you again. Preferably doing what you're supposed to be doing, while leading them away from the luthier. It's time for us to go back to Bestua. You will get your master's rank, and I shall cause a ruckus." He paused, reflecting, and qualified. "A small one."

"I thought I couldn't go anywhere without more training."

Tabor gave Trystan a level look. "Yes, well that's true enough. We'll give you an intensive course over the next few days and teach you on the way. Do you remember the boy, Gint? He will accompany us as your manservant. His skills shall be useful when we get to the capitol." Tabor grinned, widely.

Trystan leaned back. "Something amuses you?"

Tabor shook his head and took a large bite of muffin, nearly finishing it. "Well there's one bright side."

"What?"

"Training will give us something to do when we camp."

The afternoon light slanted on Trystan's lute case, leaning against a bench. Next to it, a flute nestled on a pile of flowers. Trystan's eyes widened when he spotted them. In the last two days he'd been crammed full of herb lore, basic lockpicking, pickpocketing, subterfuge, acrobatics, self-defense, and disguises. All fascinating subjects, but what he really wanted was to use the Song. Aside from a short demonstration session with Tabor's flute, he'd had no instruction at all on the topic. He ached to learn more.

Now, finally, the time had come.

Tabor walked over to his flute and plucked it from its bed, turning it to display a stamped mark on the underside of the instrument—three stars inside an octagon. His lute bore the same mark.

"My flute, found within the ruins below, two hundred years ago. We've recovered a handful of these instruments. Some have been made by the likes of the dewin luthier. They are passed down and guarded with our lives. You do not have to be dewin to use one, as you well know."

"Why? What's the difference? Does any music that I play on this lute create a spell? I've been worried that I'm making storms or causing stillbirths."

Tabor laughed. "No. If a dewin were to play, yes. But the likes of you and I need the help of a strong supporting force. These flowers and their Virtue provide it." He picked up a lovely blue flower that chimed. "This is a tunebell. It has a powerful resonance that works with our instruments. Along with this, the will of a player playing the right song can move mountains, quite literally. Delphiniums also may help, though not as well. These are the most effective and versatile. Different blooms have different effects."

"What do you mean by the right song?" Trystan's eyes narrowed.

"I don't mean the monotone Canting twaddle peddled by our robed friends," Tabor said. He frowned, thinking. "We've gleaned there are combinations of words and tunes that the cantors wield to manipulate the Song's power, but they're limited by songs they know."

Trystan nodded, frowning. "I can identify many of those words, but not the exact order. I must see or hear one to identify it. They're in a dead language I haven't studied. The Bindery teaches basics to every musician as a precaution, so we can avoid their use. They're songs from the Majisterium."

"Are they now?" Tabor picked up his flute and twirled it. "That's good to know. We've scoured the archives here and oddly enough, found nothing useful but references to the Lorica. Have you heard of it?"

"Lorica..." Trystan tasted the word. It felt familiar. "I remember reading a scroll where it was mentioned. Very old. I'd have to look at my notes to find the exact information."

Tabor nodded, then pointed to his lute. "Doesn't matter. We don't worry with words or even with memorizing certain songs. We just crush the bloom." He picked up a tunebell and crushed it. "We focus on the question or problem we have, then we listen for an answer."

"Listen?"

"Listen. We're not trying to control our circumstances. Instead, we surrender. Trust that the true Song creates harmony for all things, and you can touch it. These instruments we hold attune us to the Song as it is meant to be, to the melody that was lost. The flower boosts our ability to hear. Listen, and when you know the Song, play it. If you don't hear, remain in your question until you do. We work only with what we hear."

"So I'll hear it? Are you sure?" Trystan inhaled the tunebell scent and waited a few moments before complaining. "I can't hear anything."

Tabor spoke slowly. "Do you ever hear a melody in your thoughts, in your heart? Do you walk around whistling it? Humming? That is the key. The song which comes to mind is not random. It has meaning. The tune you need in the moment will come clear. Focus on your need, listen, then play."

"What if I hear the wrong thing?"

"You won't. Not with that lute in your hands. Try it."

Trystan thought about his greatest need and focused. He shut his eyes and listened. His mind whirled with questions, but the one weighing on him most heavily was his fear for his people. He let himself picture his father and brothers. He held the idea of their forges growing cold, the Shadowborn threatening. He breathed again and kept holding the idea.

And he heard. In his mind, a tune sounded. It was unfamiliar, so he listened. When it began to repeat, he lifted the lute and played. He played power. Strong and throbbing, it jumped from his strings into the air, building into a crackling dance of light. Tabor joined him, and together they played, the flute keening a descant over his strident, joyful melody.

Trystan saw his father, standing next to a group of dwarves before a cold forge, their faces downcast. The image floated before his eyes on the river of Song that poured from his lute.

He wondered if his father would be there when he returned. Trystan focused on the melody in his mind and kept playing.

The room that he saw held the main forge, one of the largest in Pelegor. It always burned. "Hotter than a dragon's fire," his father would say. It burned bright blue, the flame of the Forge. This flame was more than just the tool their people used to shape impossible weapons. The flame represented their people. Their calling, their heritage, their culture were bound to the flame. Without it, the Northmen would have to abandon their craft, shaping only common metals. No more songsteel would keep the Shadowborn at bay.

Esseylte.

They would all be slaughtered.

Trystan's chest began to ache. But he played on. He played fire and sparks and light. He played heritage and destiny. He played hope. The image held before him. He saw his father talking to the dwarves, to the other Forgemen. He saw him gesture to the hearth, cold and silent.

And as he struck a powerful chord, he saw a spark flame. Another. *My Lord. What am I doing?*

The flame which sprang up was tiny, but Trystan's father, Tenkor, saw it. A dwarf leapt into the huge space to nurture the fire. *I've set the Forge aflame. I did it. First try.*

Trystan's fingers and shoulders ached. The vision faded, and his tune died with it. He flopped to his knees, spent and sweating.

"I can see what you're seeing when we play together," said Tabor. He barked a laugh and flopped on the bench, perspiration rolling down his brow. "You don't start small, I'll give you that. You tried to light the Forge from here? And the Song was willing. Gods man, I said you could move a mountain, I didn't mean for you to try it. Smaller feats to start. Small. Miniscule. Little. Teensy." He mimed a box a half-inch high, and wagged a finger, admonishing. "You have to practice and build your focus...But you did...more than well. Honestly, your strength is astonishing. Unprecedented."

Trystan panted, trying to recover. He looked up, surprised at the last remark and grinned crookedly at his mentor. "I did all right, didn't I?"

Tabor chuckled. "You'll do for a Spinner, lad. You'll do."

31

Dane groaned and lifted his head, immediately regretting it. The cold stone of the floor leached the heat radiating from his wounds. He blinked, moving as little as possible. The cell smelled musty, but not unclean. He was bandaged heavily, huddled on the floor of a dark, windowless cell. He vaguely remembered being dressed, dragged here, and a tonic poured down his throat.

He grit his teeth against the agony and sat up.

Stars whirled in his vision. Pain engulfed him. Dane squinted, struggling to see. A thin line of dim light glowed from under the iron-banded door, revealing a ten-by-ten compartment devoid of furniture. Only Dane's wrappings and thin robe softened the stone walls and floor. Dane closed his eyes and inhaled.

"Yer a sight for sore eyes and that's a fact," said Jax.

Dane's eyes flew open. It was too dark to see his features, but the gnome's rough voice was unmistakable.

He licked his dry lips and groaned.

Jax interrupted him. "Did you take a vow of silence? No speaking. Save your strength. You cannot risk lies, especially not here. I hope we get you and Bell out before you have to speak to a questioner, but if not..."

The gnome didn't finish the statement. He uncorked a waterskin and held it to Dane's lips. Dane drank, slowly at first, then greedily.

"They've had you here for almost a day. They check on you every hour or two, but you're in the solitary confinement cell for prisoners, in the deepest dungeon and few ever leave these. I overheard the good brothers discussing your future. After your display in that class, they seem to think you can't be trusted. Some want to give it another go, try to convert you. Others want your wits purged."

Jax pulled the skin away from Dane's mouth, wiping it with his sleeve.

"You know Bell is here? Just nod or shake your head."

Dane nodded. Seeing Jax was such a comfort. He was not alone. He motioned to his mouth, wincing as he raised his arm.

"They used her to force you to vow." Jax's cap stiffened in anger as he guessed. "I understand. She's safe. I've been seeing to her as I can."

Dane nodded again.

"Do you understand you can walk right out of here, lad? You're dewin. I know you've been taught to fear your gift and never use it. I know you've almost never tried. But by Lalo's right hand, that nut has broken open, and there's no sealing it back. You have it within you to heal yourself, rescue Bell and leave. It's time to use the power."

He can see in the dark, Dane realized. All these years living with Pezzik, and he didn't know gnomes could see in the dark. He was so blind sometimes. The observation floated through Dane's mind. He couldn't leave without Bell.

He gestured for Jax to continue.

"All of them, each and every last robed devil, obeys their ringing schedule. You should be able to sing your way out tonight, after the small hours sound. They will have few guards stationed, but I can guide you. They rely on the Watchers, and those are everywhere. It's why I haven't come to you before.

"They have a room filled with tiny Watchers, monitored at all times. If anything strange happens, the little Watchers show them what the large ones see. I've managed to stay out of sight, I think."

So many cantors. They use the Song, too.

"The day you got here, Bell was being prepared to visit the chymaera. They didn't take her, of course. The Wyn flew away instead with your friends. Angered them to no end. Bell must be dewin too, but she's been woeful bad at every test they've given her. I explained to her how to use the Song, but she couldn't hear it. They keep her under lock and key now, guarded in a dungeon with no windows and three Watchers because now she's recovering and can speak.

"I spend my time searching for a way to get us out. There are hidden passages used by some of the higher-ranked brothers. I haven't yet found one that leads out. But I have this."

Jax doffed his cap and reached in, pulling out a carefully wrapped package. "From Pezzik, she said you would need them. They're Essences from your garden."

Dane took the package and unwrapped it with shaking hands. Inside were all the Essences he used in the creation of his lutes in small stoppered vials. He opened one and sniffed, smiling to himself for the first time in days.

The fae's words floated through his mind.

Those below shall be as above.

Sara had said this to him just before she vanished, the Song ringing through her voice.

He and Bell were both being kept underground. What did she mean? Be as above? He felt so woozy. Could he heal himself? His Pa and mother could not heal themselves when the fever took them. They had tried. Stars above, he had tried. How could he truly trust his power when it was so capricious?

He sniffed the vial again, stoppered and bundled it with the others, rewrapping it securely.

Those below shall be as above. Those below shall be as above. Those below shall be as above.

He couldn't get the words out of his mind. They echoed, insistent. Outside his door, he heard scraping as its bar lifted. Dane shoved the package of Essences at Jax and motioned for him to hide. Jax melted into the shadows as the door swung open. Brother Bren stood in the lintel, his narrow face, shadowed. He held Dane's slate and chalk in his hand. Bren stooped and handed them to Dane. He fixed Dane with a stern expression, his voice hushed and even.

"I trust that you have been cleansed of your lies. If not, the grace you have been given shall be utterly removed, and you shall be permanently disabled. We do not wish this to happen. You can be of great service to our cause. To all people. Do you understand? Consider your answer carefully, Brother."

He pointed to the slate.

"Where is the Storm King?"

Those below shall be as above. Those below shall be as above. Those below shall be as above.

The words positively roared in Dane's mind. He prayed to the Storm King, even as he leaned into the light falling from the doorway and wrote them on the slate. *Help me.*

Those below shall be as above. Those below shall be as above. Those below shall be as above.

A meaningless phrase, but if he answered the question posed to him directly and truthfully, they would kill him.

Brother Bren took the slate and read it aloud, stiffening.

"Those below shall be as above."

"Where did you hear this? How do you know these words?" he shouted angrily.

Dane stared at him, dazed and unblinking. He didn't have the slate and couldn't answer without breaking his vow. He shrugged, splaying his empty hands.

The cantor shoved the slate at Dane. "Where?"

Dane used the edge of his robe to erase the slate. He wrote one word.

Fae.

"Do you know the rest of it?" Brother Bren asked.

Dane took the slate again. Slowly he scrawled the entire message Sara had spoken to him.

Small choices shall rule large kingdoms as the Day draws ever near. Do not lose hope. The jackdaw shall linger then the storms shall begin. Each shall flee to his place. Your work does matter. Do not give up. Do not falter. Those below shall be as above. Shadows will fall across fen and glade and forest. The game is not a game. A tiny word can move a seeker toward his doom.

He handed the slate to Bren. Silhouetted in the doorway, Dane could not see the cantor's expression. He could only hear his voice tremble with emotion as he asked again. "Where is the Storm King?"

Dane accepted the slate and erased it.

I will not lie. He wrote quickly. *He lives beyond the door of the Moon. He yet wrestles the Wyrm. He will return.*

The cantor fell to his knees and read his answer slowly, as if seeing the words for the first time. Dane saw tears glisten in his eyes.

"What have I done?" he whispered.

Dane stared in wonder as his torturer wept.

Bren composed himself after his outburst, rising and smoothing his robes. "I will return. Have no fear. I shall not harm you further. This cell is one of the few places we may speak freely. I must hear what you have to say."

He left, returning a quarter of an hour later with a plate of food, a flask of tea and some glowstones. An acolyte followed with blankets, pillows, and a rolled mat. After lighting the glows, Bren gave Dane the plate. He prepared a makeshift bed in the corner while Dane ate in silence. The cantor faced Dane, sinking to sit on the floor and placed a glow between them.

"You cannot lie."

It was a statement, not a question. Dane shook his head. He wrote on the slate and showed it to the cantor.

Lies cause Dissonance. They can kill me.

Bren pursed his lips. "We have been told that dewin believe lies, whether they know they are lies or not. It has the same effect."

Dane shook his head and set his bread down. He wrote, *You believe lies. Telling lies can make me sick, kill me.*

Bren bowed his head.

"You see the fae. You speak with them, converse as you do with me?" he asked, quietly.

Dane nodded.

"We cannot," he said. The words echoed in the cell, full of loss.

"The verses you shared, they are part of greater sacred mysteries, teaching given to us directly over centuries. Doran the Lesser himself, spoke those words in my hearing. We've been told by the arcantor only those with pure hearts could receive them. They are not taught to common men. We are told we are ascending, that some will become like cyntae. We are chosen, sacred, elite. Those below shall be as above."

The brother raised his hands, palms up.

"Yet a dewin, after cleansing by pain, gives these words to me with his bruised hands. You refuse to break silence, no matter how I beat you. You healed the Tree. You should not have been able to remember mysteries, much less repeat them. Even our most pious struggle to retain these truths. And you speak with fae at will. You could yet become a majister yourself, if the cyntae willed it."

Dane met the cantor's gaze steadily. The cantor looked away.

Dane tapped his slate. *How does a wyrmfriend heal the Tree? I speak truth. You believe lies. No man can become a god.*

Dane saw Jax's head, peeking from the stone from the corner above the cantor.

"I do not yet understand how, but you must be pure," the cantor said, nodding.

The Storm King commanded my greatfather to guard the Lorica and wait in hiding, in peace. One from my family would receive a sign. After, we were to work. Prepare the way for his return. Dewin have been discredited, called insane. We have been captured, never to be seen again while Conclave lies spew forth unhindered.

Bren scooted over to watch as Dane wrote, impatient with waiting. Jax's head popped back into the wall.

Dane erased the words and continued.

Think on it. How do you know the things you have been taught are true? From whom did you learn?

Brother Bren's face twisted and drained of color. "Modric," he whispered. "It all came from Modric, and we trusted him. Because Modric, the Last Majister, he saved us all."

Dane shook his head. *He enslaved you all. The Storm King lives. The Song is failing with Dissonance. Lies cause Dissonance. I do not know the full meaning of the verse, but my heart says the sign my family waited for occurred the day I grounded a fae. She spoke those words to me. After, I set out on my journey and healed the Tree. She appeared again and repeated the phrase.*

Bren clambered to his feet, his lean form unfolding. He stooped to retrieve Dane's plate and spoon. "I don't want to believe you."

I know that, he wrote. Dane jerked a thumb toward his wounded back, wearily.

Brother Bren paused, hovering near the door. Several minutes later, he spoke. The words fell heavily on Dane's ears.

"I will give you three days to heal in this cell. You shall remain here, undisturbed. We shall discuss these things, and I will meditate on your answers. I wish to know more of your Lorica. In three days, I will decide my course."

Exhausted, Dane nodded.

Bren barred the door behind him.

Jax crept out of the wall, climbing down from his perch near the ceiling.

"I heard his side of your conversation. I don't trust him. It's a trap."

Dane wrote on the slate, *What choice do I have?*

Jax's face set, fierce with determination. His eyes glinted like shiny pebbles above his whiskers. "We will leave here in three days, whether the cantor believes you or not. We're leaving with Bell."

32

Jax emerged from the ground a mile to the north of the Chapterhouse compound before sunset. He doffed his cap, brushing away stray dirt, yanked it back into place, and began to explore. He needed help, needed information. He was determined to find a way. But deep down, he already knew digging their way out wasn't an option. There was too much limestone. Much of the earth here was laced with iron, impassable even for him.

This forest was not like the Heyewood. The trees were younger and much smaller. Oaks, beeches, hazel, rowan, and larches grew among pines. Some soared, stately and regal as any queen, others twisted and bent like old men among huge, moss-covered stones. The stones were massive. It looked like a giant had abandoned a game. Some stone stretched smooth, as if poured, like the floor of a cave. These dipped, with a velvet moss blanket, into hollows and crevices, bordered by patches of ivy-covered earth. Ferns punctuated the ivy.

Jax topped a ridge and gaped at a carpet of riotous bluebells below him where two badgers lounged.

Archangel vines grew over the moss, providing Jax hand and footholds to clamber down and join them.

The badgers watched him approach, their black-and-white-striped faces quizzical.

"Ho, friend badgers," Jax said, raising his hand in greeting.

The larger badger grunted in return. "Ho, stonefriend."

Jax's eyebrows shot up, and the end of his cap curled. He bowed.

"I am a traveler from the Heyegrove. My name is Jax."

The badgers nodded together. The smaller female said, "I am Ribbon and this is Fleck. Welcome to the Puzzlewood."

"I'm looking for other gnomes, other stonefriends. Do you know where the closest Burrow is?"

Fleck said, "No, we have only met occasional travelers. My mother told me of your kind when I was a cub, but it has been many years since this forest has seen your folk."

Ribbon nodded, agreeing.

Jax frowned and scratched the back of his head. "Ah, that's sad news indeed. I had hoped to gain aid. I have friends who are being held by the tall two-legs beyond the forest and need to dig them an escape."

Fleck's ears perked up as he considered this. He sat up straighter on his haunches and looked at Jax, his black eyes widening. "To dig out from their walls?" he asked.

Jax nodded. "You're an expert digger. Is it possible?"

The badger looked up at the canopy of the trees. The light was waning rapidly. Soon it would be full dusk. "It might be done, close to the wall. But the ground is riddled with stone and iron. It would make a long dig impossible for me. Dig too close and stone-eyes see. Then tall two-legs come with death."

Jax nodded. "The Watchers on the walls are a problem."

The badgers dropped to all fours and began to edge away, snuffling for food.

"It is not good to be above when the stars shine," said Ribbon, turning. "The shadows have sharp teeth. We must gather food now, before full night falls. Beware, stonefriend. And good luck."

Shadowkin. Jax shivered. He looked up into the boughs, wary of looming shadows. *Time to descend and hide.* He sank into the loam beneath his feet, discouraged, and began to make his way once more back to the Conclave.

Dane slept fitfully through two bells on his pallet bed, feverish. The speakeasy opened, and Bren greeted him, his voice muffled through the small window.

"Dane, are you awake? I've come to heal you as I can."

Dane sat up and knocked on the wall in reply. Bren entered with a handful of white tunebells and a book. Soft chimes washed over Dane, and he relaxed in the familiar scent.

Bren settled himself in front of Dane and took up an ivory bloom. "If caught with these, I would be executed," he said. "I must do two things quickly and depart." He opened his book and scanned, finding the verse he needed. "Apologies, I don't normally heal. These songs are unfamiliar."

Dane erased his slate with the edge of his sleeve and wrote. He tapped to get Bren's attention, turning it to face him.

Is that the Apokrypha?

Bren squinted at the slate, puzzled. He looked at his book and shook his head. "Not as you think of it. The Apokrypha you know, the books cantors read from in Camber services are only a portion of the full text. The dangerous portions, those are guarded well and untranslated from the old speech, the old tongue of the majisters in Anach. This is one of those."

Bren crushed a bloom and began to sing the words on the page, Canting them, sing-song. The language was unfamiliar. Dane thought he recognized the word *Brenin* but it might have been his imagination.

A buzzing started in his ears. He felt a small tickle in the base of his skull.

Storm King, have mercy.

The buzzing grew. His whole world became sound, a drone that threatened to silence even thought. He began to shake, to vibrate with it. His teeth ached.

It stopped.

The relief was palpable. He sat, dripping sweat. Then the tickle returned. The buzzing returned. It built again until he feared his head would burst.

It stopped.

Bren regarded him. His Canting had ended. He rifled through the pages in his book.

Dane shook his head and held up his hands. He picked up the slate and wrote.

You're hurting me.

Bren laid the book and flower aside and crouched, bending over Dane. "May I?" He lifted Dane's robe at the neck and inspected the wounds beneath.

"Better. They look a week healed. I'll have someone come in the morning to dress and cleanse them, and we shall do this again tomorrow night." He handed all but one of the tunebells to Dane. "Hide these in your pillow."

Dane blinked, surprised. If he broke his vow of silence, he could use the Song without them. But with these blooms, the Song was much easier to reach, and much more effective. Bren was trusting him. Dane accepted the blooms. He tore a strip from one of his sheets, wrapping them carefully and placed them just inside his pillowcase.

"You cannot speak yet, and the healing will drain you. I have but one thing more to ask."

Dane nodded, his breath catching on the word *yet*.

What happens if I speak? He shuddered.

"I occasionally see fae when I Cant with the sacred flowers. The purest of us are able. We cannot touch them, speak with them. I believe you have spoken truly and am trusting you with tunebells as a sign of good faith.

"Siles is frantic to speak with fae. He claims one will gain help for him with his project. He wishes to control certain chymaera to prove his superiority over the other high cantors. He aims to rule with Modric, to become a majister himself. Of course, to do so he must ground fae, form a harmony bond.

"Can you speak with fae in my presence? I will release you from your vow to do so."

Dane's eyes widened, shocked. Release from silence would mean he could use the Song.

Bren answered Dane's unspoken questions. "Yes, I have the authority to release you from your vow, though I advise you to remain silent and continue to use the slate except at my behest. You will need your voice to grant my request. Am I correct?"

Dane nodded and wrote on his slate. *This is for Siles?*

Bren shook his head again. "It is just for me. I believe you have spoken truly. Releasing you is a sentence of death if I am discovered. I am prepared to deny the Conclave and claim the Storm King, to help you, and accept what you say. I am just trying to understand the extent of my own foolishness and errors. I wish to hear the fae for solace and confirmation."

Release me, Dane wrote.

Bren cleared his throat. He crushed his remaining tunebell and sketched the arc over Dane's head. "I release you, Danethor Thomas Whitley, from your vow of silence in the name of Doran, without penalty."

He sang a few lines in the strange language. Canting.

"You are free."

"What would have happened if I had broken the vow?" asked Dane. His voice was rough from disuse.

"You would never have spoken again."

Dane stretched, testing his wounds. The ache was there, and the pain, but dulled to a level he could manage. He rolled to his knees and retrieved a tunebell from his pillow, tucking the others securely away. "Normally I need starlight," he said. "I'm not certain this will work, but I'll try."

He muttered a quick prayer to the Storm King and sketched the eight-sided sign in the air as he crushed his tunebell. Slowly, he sang.

The Dark One ascends,

Eight shall turn him round.

The octagon hung in the air and began to glow. It shimmered as if made of white fire. In its light, fae flashed, surrounding him. None of them lingered. Dane continued his song.

One from the heartfire

One beneath the ground,

The fae flashed in rapid succession. Dane realized he was looking for one face, Sara's face. He wondered if she would return. She had led him here. The least she could do was lead him out. He pictured her eyes and kept singing. He silently cast a prayer to the Storm King for help.

One stone rider,

One who cannot hear.

One claims the Storm King, One Names the Fear.

Sara flashed in front of him, and the octagon drifted down and settled on her brow like a burning crown. Music wafted like a fresh breeze through the cell, the melody filling it with hope and promise.

She said, "Shadows will fall across fen and glade and forest."

The sign grew brighter, blinding. It filled her form with light and raced up and down her body. She grew more solid with each pass, until finally the sign dissipated and only the fae remained. She did not flicker. He had done it. She was here in the flesh, grounded.

Sara looked around, blinking and uncertain. "This again," she said. "Where's the gnome? I thought I saw him."

"He's not here right now," said Dane. He pulled himself up to greet her, putting his hand over his heart and bowing. "Hello, Sara."

Sara focused on Dane. "Hello. You don't look so good." She walked around him, examining and jerked her head at Bren. The cantor sat, open-mouthed in wonder. "Who is your friend?"

Bren stood slowly.

"Sara, this is Brother Bren. He has a few questions to ask you," Dane said. He was just relieved the gambit had worked. He wasn't sure it would.

Bren's lined face shone in the glowlight, oily. It made the wrinkles around his eyes seem deeper. "I needed to know Dane spoke truly and meet you for myself. Thank you for speaking with me." His angular frame loomed over Sara as he bowed.

"No problem. You'll make a great addition to my dream journal. Dr. Carol will love it. The darn thing is becoming an Edda. Is this a prison cell?" She walked to the banded steel door, reaching to pull it open.

"It is, but we are safe inside this cell," said Dane. "It's a long story."

Sara stopped short. "You're not exactly convincing me. You have a black eye, a swollen lip—you're obviously hurt and in a prison cell. Wasn't this guy one of those dudes who thinks you're nuts?"

Dane stared at her, struggling to understand her strange words. *What did nuts have to do with him?*

"Bonkers. Postal. Mad?" she asked, twirling her finger near her head.

"Mad, oh, yes. Bren believes me. It's why he wanted to meet you."

"I'm your proof of sanity? That's rich. Am I mad? Because, I gotta tell you. My dreams have been just wackadoodle lately." Sara's laugh was hollow.

Dane regarded her, bemused. She scuffed her slipper against the stone floor, muttering. "Awesome, my subconscious has no sense of humor."

Sara braced her back against the wall, sliding down to sit. "Okay, Kojak, let me have it."

"Your words are strange, milady," said Bren, resuming his seat. He stretched his long legs in front of him, leaning back on his hands.

"My words are strange?" Sara tilted her head and wrinkled her nose. Her freckles stood out against her pale skin. Her laugh bounced around the tiny cell. "I suppose they would be. I apologize." She composed her expression and dropped her eyes, tracing her finger on the stone floor.

"How long do they stay?" Bren asked Dane.

Dane crossed to his pallet and sat, frowning. "This is one of the longest periods. It's usually no more than a few moments."

Sara looked up. "Relax, I'm sure I'll wake up soon." The floor where she had been doodling now held a knot pattern, as if carved in the stone. "You had questions for me?"

Bren nodded and drew his knees up under his chin. "How do you know the verses? Do you know what they mean?"

"What verses?"

"'Shadow will fall across fen and glade and forest.' You said it just now, as you entered," said Bren.

"No clue," said Sara. "I fell asleep on my couch, I'm dreaming. It's weird, but I'm used to it. Not my first rodeo. I don't remember saying anything like that."

"And you don't know what it means?"

"Nope."

Bren's brow wrinkled.

Sara sighed and clarified. "No, I do not know what they mean."

"You dream not, milady," said Bren. "You are here in the flesh." He pointed to the stone where she had carved the pattern with her finger, as if she had drawn in sand.

"That is dream weirdness. Believe me, I am off the charts when we start talking dream weirdness. Pay no attention. This is not the reality you are looking for." She held up one hand, palm out, and moved it in a circle.

Bren threw up his arms to shield himself.

Sara chuckled.

Dane stared at the floor, the pattern it held, an intricate octagon. "You are here in the flesh, Sara. This is not a dream. I'm sorry. I'm so sorry. I wouldn't have grounded you unless I had great need."

Sara looked from Dane to Bren, her eyes widening. "Look guys, you're my way of processing stress. I get it. I've had a lot of stress lately. So I'm okay with the spike in weirdness. But you're starting to freak me out. I'm doing what's called lucid dreaming. It means I know I'm dreaming. I'm just dreaming. I'm gonna buzz off now."

She shut her eyes and pressed her lips together, tightening her mouth to a thin line. A few seconds later, she opened her eyes. She clicked her heels together. "There's no place like my apartment. No place like my apartment." she said. She rolled her eyes. "I'm sorry. I don't have time for this, boys. I need my rest. See you in the funny papers." She clambered to her feet, faced the inner cell wall, and walked through it.

Jax popped out from his perch and landed on both feet in front of

Bren. "If you don't go and get her now, things will go very, very badly."

Bren didn't even look surprised to see the gnome. He scrambled to his feet and threw the door open, running after Sara. Dane poked his head out after him. He watched Bren disappear around the corner before he closed the door. "She's halfway down the hall," he said. "You might be able to explain so she will listen. She asked about you."

Jax stroked his beard, his brow furrowing. "Fae can be unpredictable, dangerous when first grounded. I'll go help. But prepare to run, to leave. We might have no choice. At least now we know how we'll escape."

Dane arched a brow.

Jax pointed to the floor, the knot pattern. "Sara can help. I've seen her kind before. She's a stone rider."

33

"A what?" asked Dane.

But Jax was already gone.

Dane paced, running his hand over his itchy scalp stubble. He waited, more fatigued by the moment. Dane strained to hear through the door, but the only sound was the soft rustle of his robes, the huffing of his own breath. He settled on his pallet to wait, upright and cross-legged, and closed his eyes. Perhaps he'd hear the Song. Stars, he had no idea what he was doing.

The cell door flew open.

"So my dreaming is your reality?" Sara said as she followed Jax inside.

Jax stomped over to Dane's pallet and plopped down with a sigh. "I don't know what your reality might be, but aye, this one is mine. It's real, lass."

Bren stepped into the doorway behind them, interrupting. "I regret I need to leave. The next bell is nearly upon us. I must ensure you were not seen. Do nothing to escape until I return. We must move carefully." With that, he was gone. The bar clanged as he locked the door.

"Do you actually trust him?" Jax said.

"I do. It's possible he is laying a trap for us, but my heart tells me otherwise. Perhaps he is merely sorrowfish."

Jax froze and peered, one bushy eyebrow arched. "Sorrowfish? Perhaps the healing affected your mind. You're speaking nonsense. Bell did that, as well."

Jax waved a hand in front of his face, Dane brushed the gnome's hand aside, laughing. "I'm fine Jax. Sorrowfish is a word from the Lorica. It's in a refrain. The Lorica always speaks to the heart of things, things too deep for words. When I was a boy, I asked Pa what it meant. He said not all people who did terrible things were evil. Most were selfish or believed lies, and some were just sorrowfish. Acting from pain. He showed me a damaged tree, how a knot formed where the wound occurred. He said people were like that. They grow but become broken when hurt. So they hurt others."

Sara's eyebrows shot up. Jax shook his head, obviously not convinced.

"He showed me a pearl. He said as a person healed, the wound could be used instead to create something beautiful. Like dust inside an oyster makes a pearl. Pa said that it depended on the person. They can choose. I have to give Bren a chance to show us his choices."

Jax snorted and scuffed the floor. "I will still plan for betrayal, best not to hope for good when you are dealing with cantors."

Sara sat and waited, silent, her head cocked like a bird. Dane wondered what she was thinking. She looked so ordinary despite her strange gray clothing, a plain shapeless hooded tunic with long sleeves and unadorned breeches of the same color.

"What's a stone rider, Jax?"

"All the fae I have ever known—and mind you, I have only met a few—had a gift. Your greatfather, Petros, he worked with a fae who fashioned stone as well as any chymaera. A stone rider, he was called. That one could walk through stone like a gnome," Jax said.

Sara blinked. "A fae?" she asked.

"Fae," said Dane. "One of the Lost Ones, though why your people are referred to as lost, I don't know. To us you are ghostly. You flicker like flames. Stories told to children say your kind play tricks on families or cause trouble, but those same stories claim you have great power."

Sara snorted. "I'm a fairy?"

Jax raised one bushy eyebrow. "I do not know this word fairy. Your words are strange. You can make amazing things. 'Tis a great gift."

"Fairy is the name for the creatures you're describing," said Sara. "But they have pointy ears and wings. They're little." She held her hands up, two inches apart, demonstrating. "I'm not a fairy."

Dane swelled with questions. Sara had seemed so knowing, but mysterious, when he had encountered her before. The Song sang to him whenever she appeared. She must have answers. "Why are all fae

I've seen your size? I've seen you many times. Do you speak with the Storm King? Can you help us to escape? Can you truly work with stone? Do you know a fae-ree? Could a fae-ree help us?"

Sara's laugh bounced off the walls like a trapped bird.

"I don't know any fairies! Why can't you escape, Mister Wizard? Aren't you strong enough to get past this door?" Sara stood, her sarcasm biting as she dusted her hands. "I don't know your Storm King, and I have no idea if I can help you. I work with clay, not stone. I sculpt, I think. It's all fuzzy. I can't remember."

Dane hesitated, thinking. He upset her. But what if she was only trying to trick him? But. The Storm King chose *her* to guide him. He must have.

"I've been taught many things but have never really tried them. My mistakes can hurt people," he said, eyes fixed on the floor at his feet. He forced himself to meet Sara's gaze. "I will do all I can; I mean that. I sought you out of all the fae to help me because I believe in you. I trust you. I'm just trying to find the right path. Truly? No. I might not be strong enough. I have no idea what will happen if I use the Song. I'm afraid. I'm afraid of killing everyone and destroying this building. I might kill the Tree and doom the world."

"Oh. Well then, I feel you." Sara slumped. "Fairies aren't real, they're only in stories. I don't have any idea what you see when you see...*fae*, no frame of reference. Everything I know about myself and home is fading away. Like a dream. I can't grasp it, can't hang on. It was all in my mind when I woke here. Now?" She shook her head. "I'm fuzzy. It's scary."

Jax stood, walked over to Sara and took her hand. He turned it over and pointed to her left index finger. "I see no fur. Your hands are the hands of one who crafts. Clean, but skin that's rough and dry. Your fingernails are too short and clay is under this one." Jax eyed Sara, his expression grave. "The Storm King Dane speaks of, His Song brought you to us. Trust. There is a reason He chose you. You can face what lies ahead. Don't be afraid."

"We'll help you get home somehow, I promise," said Dane.

"I just don't know what home even is. I remember a fireplace, writing in a notebook, statues..." she shook her head. "That's it. And I have no idea what you expect me to do or how sculpting can help us escape. Why are we in a prison cell?"

Dane's eyes drooped, and he forced them open. The healing had taken its toll. He shook himself, trying to focus. "Can you show her,

Jax? It might save time." His voice sounded weak in his own ears. "Keep inside the walls or up high, you won't be seen. I must rest."

Jax stood and nodded. "I'll be back. You rest and heal."

Sara knocked on the dressed stone wall. "This looks pretty solid."

Jax laughed. "And it wasn't solid an hour ago? You walked through the same wall as if parting a curtain. And 'tis how you must see it, lass. Gnomes look at stone but believe it has a thickness of air. We breathe and step through. You can do it as well. Fix it in your mind, hold on to me, and step through."

Sara sighed, grumbling under her breath and pushed at the wall. This time, her hand passed through. She jerked her hand out, staring at it. "It feels like pudding."

"So it does. Now if we need to climb, just think of the stone as solid under your hand, so you can push against it to climb. I'll take you to the Watchers."

Dane watched as they slipped into the thick stone wall before allowing himself to drop into an exhausted sleep.

Sara followed Jax into the thick stone walls, clutching his surcoat to reassure herself that he was there. *Sorrowfish.* The word bounced around her mind. She struggled to grasp the idea. It felt important. *People aren't always selfish, sometimes they are sorrowfish.*

Soon she forgot all but the feel of Jax's rough woolen surcoat under her fingers. She supposed the wall's interior would be dark, but as her eyes adjusted, it gradually grew translucent like vellum, with a soft white glow. Sara focused on the gnome's cap. The cone rotated, boring through the stone to the next open space. They climbed and slipped easily through several floors of the building before coming upon the roof. Jax led Sara up, emerging on a flat, narrow terrace. It overlooked a formal garden courtyard.

Sara's mind reeled as she took in the view. The building was an abbey. Or a castle. She wasn't sure. It seemed like both, huge, with steep vaulting and decorative scrollwork. The glimpses she'd had of the interior put her in mind of ancient cathedrals.

Jax pointed to the curtain walls surrounding the compound. "See the Watchers?"

"The grotesques? The statues?" Sara squinted. It was dark, but she could clearly see a silhouette with large wings. "Why do you call them Watchers?"

Slowly, the figure turned its head so its profile was outlined against the starry sky. Sara's pulse quickened. "It moves," she whispered.

"Aye, and it shares what it sees. They show the Conclave cantors. The monks. The same monks captured Dane's sweetheart, Bell, used her to bait Dane and imprison him. The Conclave Chapterhouse, that's where we are, lass. We need to escape before they hurt Bell or Dane further."

"You think I can get us out?"

"I know you can, lass. It's just a matter of telling the Watchers to fly. If you can master one, they will all obey. I knew a stone rider once, long ago, name of Odranoel. He made a Speaker dance, sing, and fly. He commanded an army of stone soldiers and rode a magnificent marble stallion. You can do amazing things, but you'll need to practice. I cannot help you there."

Sara stood watching the horizon, the forest beyond the walls. *This is crazy.*

"All right, let's go have a chat with a Watcher."

Jax turned. "Stay close."

Sara hurried to follow as the gnome made his way to the base of a vaulted arch and climbed over. In dreams, even the strangest things made sense. She was just going to keep moving. *This is an amazing dream.*

34

Sara grunted, pulling herself up and over the stone vaulting. Jax waited on the other side. He pointed to a winged lion perched on the edge of the roof, motionless. The figure crouched on top of the parapet. Its head stretched forward as if readying to dive. It spread its wings.

Sara stared. She looked out past it, gulping at the sight of the ground far below. The sky was paling over the forest, pink striations streaking the horizon. Dane needed help. She had to try. She took a deep breath. "Here goes nothing," she muttered.

Sara released Jax's hand, climbed onto the parapet and sat, dangling her legs over the edge. The ground yawned below, and she quickly looked up, focusing on the Watcher. Easily eight feet tall when standing, it towered over her, massive. Its stone head swiveled to regard her with obsidian eyes. Its wings rippled in surprise.

Sara reached out, touching one massive foreleg. The stone ruffled where her fingers trailed as if she had disturbed oil on water. She met the Watcher's gaze, looking for answers. *Who are you?*

In her mind's eye, she saw a serpentine head asking her the same question. It flashed orange, menacing, and was gone. In their stead, the obsidian eyes of the grotesque reflected the morning sunlight. She drew her hand back, startled by the vision.

"Identify yourself," the lion rumbled. Sound issued forth, but Sara saw no mouth movement. Only the head swung from side to side.

She stood, reaching for the creature's eyes, touching them quickly before it could turn away. "The eyes are the window to the soul. Live. Fly like an eagle," she half sang, half whispered, willing its eyes to fill with awareness and intelligence. She brushed them with the tips of her fingers, sketching in stone. Light sparked from her hand and rippled to its eyes, down its muscular body. The creature transformed in a flash, no longer made of stone but of lightning. One massive paw lifted, swiping to push her away.

"No!" Sara cried.

And she was sailing through the sky, screaming as she plummeted to the courtyard below.

The lion launched itself from the parapet, following, its jaws agape. It roared. Huge claws stretched forward and snagged her sweatpants. Sara gasped as her leg blazed with pain. The big cat clamped down on her foot but did not bite through. Sara was lifted, carried by her feet. She could hear shouts of dismay and running feet as monks in the courtyard below reacted to the spectacle.

They hung in the air, the lion's huge wings flapping in place. She dangled, upside down. "Put me down!" she yelled. The lion started to open its mouth, and she added, "Slow and gentle, careful, back on the roof!" She pictured in her mind what she wanted, unsure if it would help. *Dear God, help me drive this thing,* she prayed, crossing herself and shutting her eyes. If the grotesque dropped her, she didn't want to see what came next. Suddenly, she was rising. Her feet were released. She tumbled onto the flat roof. Sara opened her eyes. Jax was leaning over her, worry reddening his nose. "Are you hurt? We have to run now."

She sat up. The lion sat, perched on the roof like a house cat waiting for a meal. Its wings fluttered, its inner light fading. It stilled.

"They saw us."

"Aye, but we can hide if we go now. We can fly, that's the important thing," said Jax.

Sara scrambled to her feet, wincing. Her sweats were torn, and blood oozed from deep scratches. She pointed to the parapet. "Go back, as you were, but sleep. Speak to no one."

The lion launched itself off the roof, hovering in the air. Suddenly its eyes closed, and the lightning form reverted to stone. It fell immediately, crashing to the earth with shattering impact. Stunned, Sara rushed to look just as the creature exploded in a cloud of dust and rubble. She gasped, finding it hard to breathe.

The truth ripped the breath from her. "I'm really not dreaming," she whispered. Her heart was pounding. *I can't do this. I ruin everything.*

"You're really not dreaming," Jax said. "Sara, we have to go, now.

They're coming."

He grabbed her hand and dragged her to the outer stone wall, diving into it and pulling her down into the womblike embrace beyond. She followed, flailing, but allowed herself to be dragged under.

Bren paced through the cloisters, outwardly calm. It was time for readings from the main lectionary. No one was excused from this most important service of the day. His stomach churned as he wrestled with implications.

Siles had lied, Modric had lied, and worst of all, a cyntae had lied. He didn't know how. None of those things were possible. A dispensation could not be given to a cyntae. The cyntae worked dispensations. They were incapable of untruth. True, Modric and Siles might be granted dispensations for small lies on rare occasions. But the sheer volume and complexity of all their deceptions were staggering. Dane was proof of it, his healing of the Tree, his knowledge of sacred mysteries. Most of all, he could ground fae. He wielded the Song in purity.

There were ripples to consider. All who worked with the Song, believing lies, would add to its Dissonance. Each instance over time would make the Song more unstable, unusable, causing destruction, sickness. The truth was plain. It explained the crop failings, the illnesses, the growing effects of Dissonance he knew were occurring. Was it possible there was an explanation, some saving grace?

Bren entered the Quiet Room with his head bowed, his hands clasped. Silently, he slid into the seat reserved for him as a questioner. He stilled his breathing and waited for the Canting to begin.

White-robed acolytes joined the black-robed cantors, all spilling into the central octagonal nave. Surrounded by sacred tunebells and giant delphiniums, the devout faced the candle-filled altar.

Siles, the high cantor, took his place in front of the altar as the final bell sounded and Matins began.

The cantors sang.
Hear us, Cyntae bright,
And have mercy,
Because we have sinned against Thee.

Bren only mouthed the words, unable to sing them. He felt sick. What he had once known as familiar and true was forever tarnished.

The voices rose and fell together in unison as the simple melody was repeated. The pattern raised echoes that formed a harmony and counter-melody from the surrounding walls, the sacred flora, and the cloisters that lined the room. Antiphony rose in the vaulted, almost windowless space.

As their voices blended with the echoes and the chiming flora, the rich scent from the flowers blanketed the worshipers. Bren imagined dancing sparks flickering among the blossoms. Fragments of childhood fae stories came to mind. Longing stirred deep in his soul.

Creatures of hope
Corner stones,
Giving us the arc of salvation,
Guarding the gates of heaven,
Wash away all our
Own desires.
We beseech Thee, Cyntae bright,
In your great majesty:
Calmly forgive
Our crimes and deliver us forever.
The Wyrm rages,
Ever bound, ever chained;
Breathing Dissonance and Fire
O cyntae, keep safe those
Who remain in his sight.

The high cantor lifted his hands high as the Cant ended. A glow emanated from the candles, burning blue and wrapping his outstretched arms. The blue light intensified and drifted up. As it moved, the single arc window opened and sent morning sunlight to blend with the Canting-glow. Siles stood, limned in glory as the light intensified, before falling into the waiting arms of his acolytes, who carried him away.

Bren watched it all with new eyes, trying to understand what was happening in the light of his discoveries. The Canting accomplished something, but what? The light must have been an enchantment, a cheap show. Was the Wyrm truly chained? Did Siles mean to cause and spread Dissonance? Did he know what he is doing? He must.

Bells tolled and everyone filed out of the Quiet Room, vanishing into dark corridors beyond. Bren strode past the altar to the corridor leading to the recovery room. Siles reposed on a cherry velvet chaise longue. He stretched, feline and languorous as Bren bowed.

"Brother Bren," Siles gestured for him to sit. "The night has passed."

"Let us enjoy the new day," he answered, taking the offered seat.

"You're here to report on Dane?" Siles asked, getting right to the point.

Bren swallowed hard. "He's recovering quickly. I think he will be ready to continue by the day after tomorrow."

"Does he still resist?" Siles leaned forward, resting his chin on top of steepled fingers. His eyes gleamed, hungry and eager.

Bren's lips thinned, but he met Siles' eyes, unwavering. "I will take care of it. One thing might assist me, if you would be so kind."

Siles arched an eyebrow and gestured to a servant for wine. He accepted a cup and settled back in his cushions. "Anything you need, of course."

"'Do not give up. Do not falter. Those below shall be as above.'" Bren quoted. "This verse drives me, encouraging when my strength fails. Can you expound? What does it mean to you? It would be a great honor."

Siles put his wine cup aside and leaned forward again, his eyes narrowed. His lips, red from the wine, curved upward in satisfaction. "Fascinating passage. Also interesting in light of your task. I'm surprised we haven't discussed it more fully before. When Doran spoke this oracle, Modric did explain."

Bren's nostrils flared as he inhaled sharply. He looked at the floor. This was it. It was time to set his stones.

"Why is Doran the only cyntae we ever see? Is it truly because the others sustain us? Or is it because they must be...replaced?"

Bren met Siles' eyes, swallowing down bile.

"Are we being prepared to replace them? I've been considering your goals with the chymaera. It must be so." Bren regarded Siles intently, weighing his response.

Siles' expression did not change. He remained impassive, interested, attentive. When Bren paused, he set his goblet down, sat up and clapped slowly.

"Well done, my friend. I always knew you had it in you to deduce our true purpose. You show, once again, why your skills as a questioner are unmatched. Indeed, you may be chosen yet." Siles leaned back, stretching his legs once again on his crimson velvet, a snake uncoiling. "Do not rest. Do not falter. Those below shall be as above."

The verse dropped into the stillness of the room, chilling it. Bren's head swam. "You allow the others to believe things that are not true."

Siles brushed this away with a wave. "We keep them safe. We give them security, a solace to cling to while we care for them like children. Surely you see this."

Bren clutched the edge of his chair, somehow holding his voice steady. "But if the cyntae return?"

Siles barked a laugh, taking up his wine goblet once more. He held it up, toasting Bren and drank lustily, draining it. When he finished, he wiped the blood-red liquid from his lips with his sleeve before setting the jeweled cup aside. "You cut to the heart as always, brother. The cyntae cannot return. It's too late."

Bren's mouth dropped open. "What do you mean?"

"They are lost beyond thought. The only force that has ever hindered us from moving forward were those accursed instruments the boy Dane and his family made. Brother Aric used Trystan, the northern bard, to draw the dewin out. All our work, centuries of it, is coming to a close. If we cannot bend Dane to help us with the chymaera or use him and his fae, we will simply kill him. We know where all star-marked instruments are. We are ready to confiscate and destroy them. You heard Doran yourself. The Day draws near."

Bren shivered involuntarily and leaned forward. "What day?"

I want to hear him say it.

"The Last Day. The unmaking. The silence. The day when Dissonance destroys all creation, and we reshape the universe to our vision. It's the way forward. The only way forward. When this is done, the Song will be reshaped to *our* vision and all will kneel to us."

"And we shall be like the cyntae?"

"No, my humble friend. We shall become cyntae ourselves. So it is written, so it shall be done." Siles looked at Bren, his eyes hooded in shadow, his face a pale mask with scarlet lips. "Does this motivate you to persevere in your work?"

Bren stood and bowed, folding his hands together. His eyes shone with fervor and sincerity as he answered the man who had betrayed his faith so utterly. "I am now certain and sure in the path I must take and will apply myself fully."

Outside, there was a thunderous crash.

35

High Cantor Siles stared at the door, calculating possibilities. Causes for a crash of such magnitude were limited. Bren was hiding something, of that he had no doubt. But Bren was useful. And as long as he was useful, Siles would indulge him. Of course, now he was privy to the true endgame, so Bren would need his memory adjusted. That was plain enough. At least he didn't know the full plans for the Pryf.

Siles stood and strode out, walking quickly, but not hurrying, to the courtyard. It was never seemly to appear rushed. At his heels, Bren breathlessly yammered worries and hopes that no one was hurt. Siles ignored him.

The courtyard was chaos. Wreckage and rubble dominated its center, where a Watcher had fallen from midair to his destruction. The huge winged lion should have been perched on the edge of the south tower. Instead, it was smashed to pieces in the courtyard. Fragments lay everywhere. Large chunks nested in dust and gravel. Nearby cantors had received wounds from the debris, but no one seemed seriously injured. Siles took it all in quickly and glanced up at the south tower.

Nothing.

His voice rang out. "Leave the Watcher where he lies, disturb nothing. He will be mended. Those of you who are injured, proceed to the infirmary. You are released from duty for the next bell. That is all."

He faced Bren, issuing only one word. "Come."

Siles made for the Monitor's Wing. Bren followed, now silent. Siles could nearly hear him worrying, smell his anxiety and fear. Bren's eyes burned a hole in his back.

He knew something, or suspected it.

Siles opened the double doors to the Monitor's Hall and smiled in spite of himself. This place, of all the buildings in the vast compound, was truly sacred. Scores of cantors worked, laboring over long stone troughs fitted with suspended metal plates. The troughs ringed the room. Glowstones clustered on ledges or in tall wrought-iron holders. The cantors closely observed each metal plate. Others scribed, recording what they saw.

Acolytes poured fresh sand onto the plates to ensure they were not empty. Some sand bounced off into the trough beneath. Others moistened the sand, acolytes Canting to raise a dampening mist of water upon it at regular intervals. Small representations of each Watcher active in the Weldes perched on trough ridges. They hummed and sang. Their joined voices combined to shift the sand below them into shapes and figures, forming scenes.

White sand against black metal, the sand bunched, drawing what the Watchers saw. When several Watchers converged, each witnessing a scene, the sand gathered, sculpting a miniature representation of the event. Acolytes carefully replaced sand as it spilled into the trough, and the sands shifted quickly. Those bearing witness struggled not to blink lest they miss something.

Siles loved the music. Even with the Dissonance that had crept in over the years, the clashing of notes and the resulting tension it created. The Song was still a wondrous experience. In recent days he had come to crave Dissonance. It would eventually cause a miniature Watcher to fall silent, but each screech and crackle brought him closer, ever closer to his dream. They filled him with a black pleasure.

Runners stood ready to receive reports of important sights and relay them as needed. They bowed to Siles as he passed.

The attending monitor was Brother Sted, marked a Fennishman by the veil covering half of his face. Brown and muscular, his huge frame half filled the center of the room, where a central, wider sand table showed scenes as sculpture almost exclusively. Currently, the table was dominated by the throne room of the palace in Bestua. Two men knelt before High King Tenneth while a third waited twenty paces behind them.

Siles went to Sted's side. "I need the chymaera," he said.

He wasn't about to waste time with the records, hunting through the pages and pages of the descriptions kept daily. Not when he had his own pet Pryf at his disposal. A chymaera without talons to serve him, Doran be praised. He smiled at the thought of Zonah as a pet. She would not be amused.

Sted nodded once and gestured to a nearby acolyte, who bowed and ran to fetch her.

"Anything of particular note today?" Siles asked. "Any movement near Siarad?"

Sted nodded. "The party you were interested in entered the city last evening at sundown, Your Grace.

"The gnomes? Are you certain?"

"Five gnomes accompanied by villagers. The images were only sand sketches, but clear enough. We have only one Watcher at the guardhouse," said Sted.

"They made it into the city without incident?"

"The fugitives were escorted by armed men and two chymaera, Your Grace. We have rough sketches of one chymaera, a few of the soldiers. Events changed quickly. There was a disturbance. Of what sort, was unclear."

Siles nodded, considering. A sand sketch could not be rendered as sculpture, but Zonah could use her heartfire to access the system and commune, seeing what happened clearly. It took hours for her to do so and even longer to recover. The crash today was more important, he decided. But those gnomes should never have reached Siarad. The Shadowborn at his disposal had failed. It was really all he needed to know.

Zonah sauntered into the room, a snow-white panther in all but actual form. Her tall frame barely cleared the doorway and her hair, snow white and close cropped, framed a face that held catlike eyes of striking sapphire blue. Like all Pryf. Siles tracked her approach, savoring her beauty and grace. Rejected, but invaluable, with gems for eyes. And they sent her to him. Quite an improvement over Affra. He still could not believe his luck. True, he had not yet had the chance to exploit Zonah's resentment as he had done with Affra and his friends, but he was looking forward to the process. They were easily turned.

It was demeaning for the chymaera to work with Watchers and Speakers outside of their aerie, to work with humans at all. Pryf were sent to the Conclave when a task required chymaera lore. As the Minister of Monitors, he required their aid far more than most. It was a position he had used to full advantage over the years, turning the Pryf into a weapon only he could wield. Soon, not only Modric and Doran would know of his achievement. The world would know.

Zonah stood before Siles, her blue robes shimmering. Her skin was ivory, glowing and silken. Siles let his eyes linger, let his imagination wander, a momentary pleasure. He smiled and met her eyes, bowing deeply with his hand over his heart. Behind him, Bren did the same. "Honored Zonah, we have need of your singular talent and wisdom."

Zonah blinked and lifted her chin.

"Within the last hour a Watcher fell from the heavens rather than from a wall. It crashed here in the courtyard. I need to know what happened," said Siles.

Knowing the exact place and time made the job easier. She should be able to show them the event quickly.

Zonah placed her hand on one of the miniature watchers perched around the large central sand table, frowning in concentration. She began to sing. A perfect representation of the Chapterhouse compound rose from the sand. The onlookers gasped, collectively, as a human form fell from the roof and the Watcher dived after it, flying. It caught the human and deposited it safely on the roof. A few short minutes later, it leapt, hovered, then plunged to the courtyard below, where it shattered.

"Can you see who the human was? The form is indistinct."

"The human does not wear cantor robes, Your Grace," said Sted. "He must be an intruder."

Zonah gestured to the table and an undeniably female figure formed, her expression expectant. Curls framed a heart-shaped face. The girl wore strange garb, breeches and a tunic rather than proper skirts or robes. Siles circled the image, studying. Zonah's song faded. The Pryf's voice was a low growl as she described details the sand could not convey. "The girl's hair is blonde, her clothing, gray. She has few freckles. Her accent is strange. The images from this Watcher stop."

Siles nodded. He turned on his heel and bowed to her again. "Thank you, Zonah, as ever you have been a blessing. Please attend to the Watcher in the courtyard and do what you deem best with it."

Brother Bren cleared his throat. "That is a fae, Your Grace."
Siles whirled, astonished. "A fae? Grounded? How can this be? Your dewin is injured. Imprisoned. Bell has not the skill."

Bren nodded. "Nevertheless. The accent, the odd clothing, she disrupted the Watcher from its union with the others and made the Watcher fly. What else could it be?"

Siles felt his face heating. "There are other possibilities. Renegades and thieves have access to ancient lore. It's possible they have mounted an attack with a newly discovered enchantment, and this is but a distraction. Bring Danethor to my chambers at once and alert the guard. Have them search for this woman. If I cannot ground a fae, then that sniveling boy certainly cannot."

Brother Bren nodded and bowed. "As you wish."

Siles turned back to the form of the girl, watching it dissolve as Zonah strode away. Whoever this intruder was, one thing was certain. She would learn to regret her meddling.

Bren hurried down the steps, mind racing. He had to get them all out. Dane and the gnome had been reckless, had not trusted him and waited. Now there was no time to plan. Once the guards were roused, there would be little chance of escape. Unless...

Unless the fae actually could make Watchers fly. Her first attempt had obviously been a disaster, but it *was* possible. If he could disable the active Watchers for a short time, he could bluff his way through the building, pretending to escort the prisoners. Get them to the roof and escape.

Zonah would help me. Pryf she is, but her heartfire is strong. She has honor and kindness still, I've seen it. It's unfortunate she will never have wings of her own.

Bren headed to the courtyard to find Zonah just as the hour bells rang.

Zonah stood in front of the shattered Watcher, singing. Her wordless song filled the courtyard. Each cantor, normally unmoved by even the most reverent services, stopped to listen. Around the cloister, acolytes, servants, and guards lingered to hear the chymaera. Her song rose, echoing. It sounded like harp strings and the warbling of songbirds at dawn. It held the melody of a mountain stream and the joy of a baby's laughter. But it rang strong, with a bell-like chiming. Bren stopped and waited for her to finish, curbing his own impatience with unabashed delight at her display.

The Watcher reformed, taking shape as she sang. His smashed hindquarters, one leg broken off, shattered, were writhing into a new set of legs, using all of the stone left in the largest piece of the broken figure. Its wings seemed to melt down. They suddenly unfurled, whole. Shattered fragments merged. When she was finished, the winged lion was a born anew—no longer a huge male cat with a flowing mane. Instead, a smaller lioness with the wings of an eagle crouched, guarding the space.

Zonah turned and acknowledged Bren. "I cannot move her until my heartfire is refreshed. I shall return."

She turned as if to retire to her quarters, but Bren called after her. "Zonah, wait."

She pivoted, sapphire eyes flashing with annoyance. "You use my name freely, Brother."

Bren bowed. "I have great need, Child of the Morning."

Zonah inclined her head, a queen granting him audience. Bren gulped, stepped forward, and spoke for her ears alone. "The high cantor has lied to your people and is using them. He has captured a dewin of power and grace, one not filled with madness. He wishes to gain power over the chymaera. This dewin grounded a fae to help him escape. It was she you saw in the sands. The fae seeks his rescue even now. He and his beloved are being held against their will. I seek to free them and release you from service to one you rightly find contemptible. I need your help. What say you, Child of the Dawn?"

Warning bells began to sound, echoing through the courtyard. Zonah stiffened, hearing them. She focused her impossible blue eyes upon Bren, studying him for the space of a breath before answering.

"My heartfire is spent, Brother," she said. "But I shall aid you as I can."

Bren's jaw dropped. She had not even truly hesitated. Seeing his confusion, Zonah added, "I heard the dewin. Both of them. It is as you say. I understood this. The high cantor is dead in my sight. I shall not serve him further. I was making ready to leave before you spoke to me. I merely needed to reshape this little one." Zonah gestured to the newly mended grotesque.

"Can you disable the Watchers?" he asked.

Zonah nodded, her answering smile feral.

Bren licked his lips and muttered a prayer of thanks to the Storm King. "This way," he said. "We don't have much time."

36

Bell sat in her windowless cell, waiting for Jax. The past weeks would have been unbearable without him. Curled up on her cot, she watched the Watchers. They were unmoving as usual. If she stood and paced, they turned their heads. One was a small imp, thin and mischievous. He stood in one corner. One was a monkey with wings, perched at the ceiling. The other was above the cell door, a donkey's head. She had named them in her first days after being moved here from the comfortable room. Sam was the imp, Tempi was the monkey, and Dane was the donkey.

Dane hadn't come for her yet. She tried to be furious, but all she could do was worry. The truth was, she was furious with herself. She felt absolutely useless, powerless.

She had met chymaera, but not at an aerie. She had been blindfolded and taken to a grove. A blue-eyed male chymaera had sneered, pronouncing her unfit, never speaking directly to her at all. The grove was near the World Tree. She had seen the Tree, lights flowing up and down its length. The fog and mists normally shrouding it burned away. The cantors had rushed her to the Chapterhouse and locked her in her room. The same day, she was given these, her new quarters.

Her prison cell.

The first night, Jax crept in, poking his head through the corner to survey the room. He'd motioned her to silence, bidding her cover the glowstone. He had whispered promises of escape, encouragement. He said Dane had partially healed the Tree. Jax was gone as quickly as he had come, before the Watchers could report her for covering her glowstone. Since then, he came every night for a few minutes to tell her not to give up, always poking the tip of his cap through the stone. She would cover the glowstone, crawl into her cot, and he would push through the wall and report.

She kept the glowstone covered each night until guards came to uncover it, a small rebellion. After the third night, they began to slap her. The beatings became worse each night she disobeyed them, but she persisted.

The day he found Dane, Jax whispered they could escape. Last night, he'd said they would leave soon. Today, she waited. She would be ready.

Bell amused herself by walking around the room to keep her muscles from stiffening, telling herself stories of home. She slept. She drew pictures in the dust on the floor. Once every two days they brought her fresh wash water. She was fed once a day. Her guard, Cosette, had been replaced by a stern battle-axe of a woman named Gerta. Gerta was a cantor with no sense of humor. She tended to Bell, but made it clear, Bell was less than human. She was refuse.

"I'm not refuse," she said to donkey-Dane. "She is. What kind of person allows another to be treated like this, for no crime? A crime of birth? I'm dewin but cannot hurt anyone. The chymaera said so. He said I was beyond mending. I'm useless." She sniffed and reached for her wash bowl. She washed the blood from her face where it had been cut, a gift from last night's beating.

"What do you think Tempi? Am I beyond mending? Sam?"

The monkey regarded her, his stone eyes unresponsive. The imp smiled. It always smiled. It was carved that way. Bell's eyes widened as she saw Jax's cap poke out above its head. He was here well before his usual time. When he emerged from the wall fully without giving her time to put out her glow, she gasped. Behind him, a girl emerged from the wall as well. She sputtered and blinked, obviously disoriented. Jax nodded at Bell.

"It's time to go. This is Sara, she's fae," he said. "Sara, we need to stop the Watchers from seeing."

Quickly, Sara thrust her hand into the imp's face and twisted, removing its eyes. She smoothed the stone face flat. She climbed up the wall, doing the same to donkey-Dane. She scanned the room. Bell pointed to the winged monkey. Sara dropped from the lintel and ran up the wall, pushing her arm and hand into it to hold her. She wiped away the monkey's eyes and mouth.

Sara dropped to the floor and grinned. "This fae gig is fun."

Jax hopped up on the bed so he could look in her eyes. "Are you all right?"

"I'll mend," she said. Bell squeezed his hand. "You came for me. Thank you."

Sara cleared her throat. "What now?"

"Now we leave. Dane waits one floor below. We join him, get to the roof, and command a Watcher or two to fly us to safety," said Jax.

"Jax, Watchers cannot fly," said Bell.

Sara said, "They're a bit complicated, sensitive, and seriously, way too literal. But...they fly for me."

"We'll run into guards and acolytes in the corridors. I know the way, but if they attack us, we'll need to fight. Remember what I told you, Sara," said Jax.

Sara's jaw set in a grim line. "Put their heads into the stone. I heard you. I'd rather not."

Jax grunted. "I'd rather not as well, lass. Let's hope it doesn't come to that. We'll just run away if we can. Off you go."

Sara slipped through the wall next to the door. A few moments later, it was unbarred. They crept into the hall where Gerta lay, unconscious. Bell arched an eyebrow.

Sara shrugged. "I had aikido classes in high school."

Jax hopped over the large woman and took the lead, marching toward the stairwell. Another Watcher perched above the door, a gargoyle. His short wings jutted over a face so ugly it was endearing. Sara touched it and sang. "Live. *Fly Like an Eagle.*"

Nothing happened. Sara's brow wrinkled. She bit her lip.

"It worked last time."

"Leave it," said Jax

"I need the practice."

He sighed heavily and scratched the back of his head. "Did you do it the same way?"

"Oh," said Sara. She looked into the gargoyle's stone eyes and sang *"Fly Like an Eagle."*

The gargoyle shimmered and glowed as if made of blue lightning. He flapped his wings and detached from the wall, hovering near Sara. Sara fixed the ugly imp with a stern expression. "Those are the only words I know to that song. Follow and defend us if anyone tries to hurt or stop us. Got it? I don't want to be forced to stick people's heads into walls."

The gargoyle rumbled at her in response. "I shall defend you."

"You're amazing," Bell said.

Sara blushed.

Bell had heard fae stories, but this was not what she had expected. Fae were ethereal, capricious, otherworldly. Sara was decidedly odd and powerful, but not wise or mysterious. She looked like a normal girl in spite of her strange garb. She moved through stone like a gnome, commanded Watchers like chymaera, and used the Song like dewin. Yet Bell couldn't imagine her commanding Jax to find a golden apple or kiss a toad.

Bell swallowed the envy that rose within. As a dewin, she should be able to assist, not wait helplessly for others to rescue her. *Stop it. You are what you are,* she told herself. And there was no time for self-pity. "Amazing," she repeated, resolving to choose thankfulness. She hurried after Jax, Sara, and the gargoyle.

The next two Watchers got their eyes wiped flat. Sara dispatched them with efficiency. A bell tolled, ominous. Jax turned down a short stairwell into a long hallway and unbarred a third door. All of them piled inside.

Dane was awake, struggling to get to his feet. Bell barely recognized him. His thick black hair was gone, shaved. His face had been beaten to a pulp, and he moved slowly, grimacing, obviously in terrible pain. She could see dressings for wounds peeping out of his robe's neckline. His eyes were haunted, sunken. Even as they lighted on her, she saw terrible uncertainty and exhaustion. He was a thinner, paler shell of the confident, sweet man she knew. He had aged and lost something vital. It scared her more than any cantor ever could.

Bell pushed past Jax and Sara, and threw her arms around his neck, hugging him fiercely. "I've missed you so much. We're going to get out of this. We'll be out soon."

Dane tensed, and his breath caught. Bell pulled away.

He winced. "Sorry, I'm a bit tender yet. Acolyte discipline, you see."

Bell covered her mouth, horrified. "I'm so sorry."

As Dane started reassuring her, Jax interrupted. "We must leave. Now. Save your moony-eyes for later."

"What's the plan?" asked Dane. "Shouldn't we wait for Bren?"

The single glowstone cast shadows of them on the cell walls. The small gargoyle hovered behind Sara. Its wings flapped a breeze in the little cell, moving the stale air. Sara stepped back to lean against the wall and whispered to the gargoyle, "Sit. Wait."

Jax shook his head. "We had an accident. They'll be coming for you and Bell, it's time to get out. The brother can follow if he truly wishes. My priority is you. We'll go to the roof and fly away."

"You know where to go?" Dane asked.

"I've a good idea. I've been watching for weeks. The bell that just tolled means they're on their way to their next assignment. We need to wait a few minutes," said Jax. He knelt and drew in the dust at their feet. "We're here." He pointed to the middle of the rectangle. "Two stories below ground level. We need to get here." He pointed to the southernmost edge of the rectangle. "On the roof. This section is unused. We can take a stairwell here. Once we're on the roof, we fly away from the Tree, north into the forest. If we're lucky, we can make it to Bridgeton or Sahxe by tomorrow."

"Do you think it's safe yet?"

The bells chimed again. This time they rang with urgency and did not stop. Bell shook her head. "That doesn't sound like safe. We need to move," she said.

Dane's mouth tightened into a grim line. "We will wait for Brother Bren."

Jax stared at him and sputtered. "That cantor will truss you up like a Firstday goose. Look at what he has done to you already! You've been whipped within an inch of your life. We need to go."

Dane shook his head, wincing. "No, he won't betray us. He healed me as well."

"A ploy to gain your trust," said Jax. He snorted. "He likely wanted to use Sara here for some nefarious task, and he tricked you into grounding her." The gnome's cap quivered with indignation.

"The rest of you can go. I will wait for Bren," said Dane. "I'll meet you on the roof."

"Wait a second. This guy whipped you? And you trust him?" Sara asked. "He made Bell lose her sanity and imprisoned her. She's been beaten as well. Look at her. Not to mention, he nearly killed you. But you believe him."

"I choose to trust him," Dane said. "I would rather trust him and be wrong than not give him a chance to prove he has grown. Everyone deserves a chance, even cantors. Some are not truly evil, they've just believed lies. It takes rare courage to accept that you've been deceived, and to move forward. I've seen that courage in Bren. I forgive him."

Sara frowned and wrinkled her nose, her eyes thoughtful.

Bell searched Dane's face. She knew that look. He was not going to change his mind. It didn't matter what Jax or anyone else thought. She sighed. Turning to Jax, she said, "You need to listen to him, deema."

Before Jax could answer, the door flew open. A bearded cantor stood there, filling the doorway. Two other cantors stood behind him. The cantors held censers and were canting together. Thick Essence rose, wafting into the little cell. The cantor's voice rang out before anyone could move. "Stop. You will come with me immediately, all of you. If any of you attempts to escape, Bell will be purified. The effects will be permanent."

Bell didn't wait. She was nearest the door. Her head swam as she rushed at the cantor, furious. "No, I am finished with this. You will not use me again!" Putting all of her weight behind it, she backhanded the cantor in the jaw and pushed past him, kicking, scratching, and elbowing the other two. She held her breath, grabbing the censer chains and jerked, smashing them against the walls. They bounced off of the stone with a ringing sound and flew open, spilling their contents.

Sara and Jax were right behind her. Jax began hopping on the burning incense to put it out. Sara pushed the first cantor with all of her strength. His head sunk into the wall. She kept pushing. His body shook and twitched and went utterly still. The other two cantors stared at her, horrified, and began to back away, still Canting. A bright light appeared, pulsing between them. Sara turned and yelled at her gargoyle. "Defend us!"

The gargoyle whizzed overhead and flew straight for the cantors, claws outstretched. They turned and ran. The light vanished.

Bell's vision blurred. She blinked to clear it, but her head was swimming. She coughed and gasped. "I need air," she said, stumbling backward. Jax was at her side instantly. He took her hand and dragged her down the corridor, speaking softly as if to a child.

"You'll be all right, my Bell. Just breathe the fresh air. That's it. You'll be fine."

Behind him, another tall, bald cantor turned the corner, trailed by a chymaera. His eyes flicked over the scene, taking in the censers, Bell, and the others. "I've come to get you out." He pushed past them into Dane's cell and grabbed the thin blanket from Dane's pallet, emerging a moment later. "There will be more of them. Do not inhale the Essence," he said. He began ripping the blanket into strips, handing one to each of them. "Tie these around your nose and mouth and follow me. Zonah has disabled the Watchers, for now."

He sidestepped the cantor's body, brushing past Jax and Bell to rejoin the chymaera, who stood watching in the main corridor. Dane followed him, tying the fabric as he walked, Sara close behind him. Bell clutched the strip of fabric in her hand, staring at it, then tied it around her face. It was hard to think, to focus. She stood there, unsure, until Jax took her hand again and led her after the others.

Sara stood between two Watchers, their wings flapping gently. They rippled with energy formed from blue lightning. The others were climbing on their backs. Dane and Bell gripped the lightning-laced ridges on the mane of a winged lion. Jax was clambering up the other grotesque, a winged dragon that held Brother Bren and the chymaera, Zonah. She didn't know if they would fall if something happened to her. It was more responsibility than she cared to think about.

She was so intent, thinking about how to drive two Watchers, she almost didn't hear them coming. A scraping noise caught her attention. Cantors in black robes poured out of the hatch, some with censers. They all chanted like Benedictine monks. Some carried metal staves shaped like large tuning forks. Others carried handbells. She saw white lights forming in the surrounding air. She froze.

Sara couldn't breathe. There wasn't time. She was going to crash and kill them all. She could just go home. She could just...fade.

Lightning crackled. Sara couldn't move. She looked at the others, wide-eyed. They were depending on her. Bell's face was expectant. Confident. *She thinks I'm amazing.* Dane's eyes met hers, full of compassion and understanding. Sara wanted to scream. *What if I'm not good enough? What if we fall?*

Dane's voice rang out over the roar of thunder, "Sara, you can do this. We'll fly. Trust the Song. You've been chosen to help us."

Time stood still.

Trust the Song.

She wasn't sure about the Song. But she trusted Dane. He was right about Brother Bren. He was very...wise? Kind? Something.

Sara took a deep breath and pointed at the dragon. "Obey the gnome as you would me," she said. She ran to the lion and mounted in front of Bell. "Obey Dane, as you would me!"

Lightning flashed toward them. It hit the wall and dissipated. *Whoa.*

They were throwing lightning bolts!

Sara smelled ozone.

"Fly!" Sara yelled. "Get us out of here, fly as fast as you can!"

The air crackled as they rose. Silvered arrows whizzed past, volleys sent in desperation. One narrowly missed Sara. Then they were soaring through mists.

37

"Where are we stopping again? Bridgeton?" said Trystan as they drove their cart out of the forest. The sun was setting. The trees cast elongated shadows, gnarled fingers reaching for them.

"No, Sahxe. It's an actual town, so we won't have to camp. A logging town, lots of burly woodmen itching to gamble here, much better than Bridgeton," Tabor said. "One word of warning, however. Do not get into a tavern brawl. They tend to become destructive, very quickly."

Gint, sitting in the seat behind Trystan, leaned forward and nodded knowingly. The boy had grown several inches since Trystan had first made his acquaintance, but still looked younger than his age. "Tha's the voice o' experience talkin'. The miller's daughter woddint it?"

Tabor drew himself up to his full seated height and flicked the reins. "I don't recall."

The trio had opted for commoner's garb for the journey, rather than bringing a group of soldiers to guard them. There was no curing Gint's accent, so it inspired their disguises. Tabor insisting the boy would be invaluable once they arrived in Bestua. Trystan was mystified as to how the scamp could help them, but agreed. He enjoyed Gint's company.

As they topped a low rise, the village spread before them. A stone bridge crossed a stream. Huge old trees half-hid a sawmill, but the water wheel was unmistakable. Beyond the mill, cobbled streets lined a central village green. Trystan glimpsed a Conclave Chapterhouse, an inn, a smithy and several shops as they crossed the bridge.

Gint saw to their horse and cart while Tabor arranged for rooms. The inn was crowded, with a large common room and polished wood floors. Trystan saw no Watchers and breathed a sigh of relief. He had only seen one in the town thus far, next to the Chapterhouse. Six square tables set up for stones games lined one wall. These folk loved their wagers.

The innkeeper, round cheeked and portly, nodded at Trystan's lute case. "Give us songs, and I'll give you free ale and dinner."

Trystan hesitated. He hadn't seen a cantor, but the presence of a Chapterhouse made playing here a risk. Tabor, dressed as an elderly bespectacled manservant, decided for him. "Of course he will play," he said, gesturing grandly to the stage. "And I'll wager it will be the most amazing tunes you've ever heard."

The innkeeper eyed Tabor, taking in his measure. "How much will you wager?"

"Dinner, ale, and the price of rooms, or I pay you double," Tabor said.

"Done."

"You do realize my lute can get us both in trouble, don't you?" Trystan said. Tabor waved his worries away, dismissing them. "It takes a well-trained ear or a chymaera to hear the difference between your lute and an ordinary instrument. Just don't crush a blossom. Play ordinary tunes."

Trystan picked a scale to check his tuning and launched into a rollicking ditty, "The Bawdy Barmaid." The crowd joined in, singing the chorus. It must've been the lute. When he began the next song, a folk dance, tables were pushed back. Couples began to whirl. Five songs later, the applause was thunderous, and the innkeeper was forced to admit his loss. Trystan spied him shaking Tabor's hand. He chuckled, surveying the crowd.

His eyes fell on a tall blonde woman, sitting alone. She wore a crooked smile. The sight of her stabbed him, tearing an old wound. *Esseylt.* Trystan bent his head to watch his strings, blinking away sudden tears.

He pushed Esseylt from his mind. She had married Marcus. She was his sister now.

He was nearing the end of his set when a couple took a table near the back of the common room.

The young man moved carefully. His face was bruised, and dark stubble clouded his head, as if shaved recently, but growing in. His clothing marked him a farmer. His companion attended him with barely concealed concern, watching him closely. Long brown hair hid her features as she leaned forward to speak to him. Trystan might have taken them for normal villagers, but the man was staring openly at his lute. He pointed and said something to the woman, who winced as she turned to study him. She was hurt too.

Trystan thought about ending the set immediately, but decided to play a ballad. "This last song is dedicated to the good innkeeper," he said, smiling. "May his cups overflow."

He began to play, and the young man paled, reacting visibly to the music, the lute. The woman patted his arm, soothing. He didn't look like a cantor, even an acolyte. But if he was, he'd know soon. Trystan pushed his worry away and concentrated on the song. It was an old tune, a song from home. The lute carried the melody.

As the notes rippled through the hushed room, the story unfolded. He sang the words, unable to restrain himself, completing the images the music formed. A young wife, left alone. Her husband serving the king in the war against the shadow. An arrow flying true. The lute played the wind on the husband's face as he fell. It played the tears that lay on the wife's pillow as she waited every night in vain.

When Trystan's song ended, no one stirred. A silence hung in the air. The applause started quietly in the back and became a wave. It thundered, threatening to bowl Trystan over. He blinked and took a step back, his eyes blurring with unexpected tears. He bowed quickly to cover his emotions.

The brown-haired girl waited for him next to the stage. Trystan knelt to place the lute in its case.

"Pardon me, but is your name Trystan?" she asked.

He fastened his lute case and slung it over his shoulder pointedly. "You've heard of me, I see. I normally play in Bridgeton on my circuit but decided to vary my route this time. May I help you?"

She smiled at him and curtsied. "Indeed milord. My friend would very much like to meet you. It seems he planned to make your acquaintance in Baehnt some time ago but was unwillingly detained. His friends delivered a package to you in his stead. He is very anxious for news of them."

Trystan peered over at the table again. Stars above. It was the luthier. He was here. Trystan struggled to keep his composure. "Yes, I very much appreciate the package she delivered, though I confess I did not meet her myself. My associate might have some word, however. I will speak with your friend ..."

"Dee," said the girl, winking broadly. "And you can call me Penny."

You can call me? With a wink. The luthier and his friend must be concealing their true names. Trystan threaded his way back to her table. Danethor struggled to get to his feet as he saw them approach.

"Don't get up," Trystan said, offering his hand. "I'm glad to meet you."

Danethor took his hand, shaking it firmly, and settled back in his seat. "We just stopped for some supplies, but I heard music and thought I recognized it." He gestured toward the lute. "You do know who I am?"

Trystan slid into a chair and cocked his head toward *Penny*. "She says you're called Dee. I believe I owe you a great debt of thanks. Your craftsmanship? It was perfect."

Danethor nodded. "Glad you received it. I wasn't sure... My friends who delivered it, they are well?"

Trystan frowned. "Mod delivered it, though I did not meet her. My associate retrieved it for me. He might be able to tell you more."

Danethor's brow wrinkled. "Two Northmen and a dwarf promised delivery as I was...delayed. Storm King be thanked, they must have found Mod at the ship. But I worry for them all the same."

Trystan pursed his lips, thinking. "My friend might be able to shed more light."

Danethor shifted in his seat and leaned forward, pitching his voice so Trystan had to strain to catch his words.

"Our party is on the other side of the village green waiting. 'Twould be better to discuss in private. You need to meet them, regardless. We have much to say regarding your package...and those who sought to intercept it."

Tabor chose that moment to interrupt. "Our free meal is at our table, Trystan. You played so well that the innkeep wasn't even angry. Are these new admirers?"

Trystan's laugh sounded hollow in his own ears. He stifled his unease as it rose in his chest. Danethor had undoubtedly been held against his will and injured.

"In a way. This is...*Dee*. He sent me a very special package through your service. They're amusing a bawler and need to dance the shadows. We should discuss it."

Tabor's eyes widened as he translated the Spinner's Cant. They were dodging cantors and needed to disappear.

"I might be able to assist," he said, bowing. "Call me Burtyn. I am at your humble service. We'll rendezvous after our meal?"

Danethor nodded as a barmaid appeared with a covered basket. He started to reach for his purse, but before he could, Trystan was on his feet. He whipped out coins and paid her. The lad had fallen into torment and 'twas his fault.

"Please, the least I can do. Bring them a bottle of wine, as well," he said, adding an extra coin. Waving away their thanks, he followed Tabor back to their table.

Dane struggled to keep up with Bell as they strolled down the narrow street. The smells emanating from the basket made his mouth water. His wounds ached. He was dizzy, though he wasn't sure if from exhaustion or from the shock of hearing his lute. The bard was playing in public. He shook his head, marveling. So dangerous.

Bell cut a path straight toward the empty shop they had "borrowed" for the night. A party with a gnome and chymaera couldn't rent rooms at one of the inns. They would be remembered, when they most needed to stay out of sight. Dane grunted, out of breath. Bell cast a glance back and stopped. When he caught up, she walked more slowly, her expression thoughtful.

"So you really crafted that lute?"

Dane's breath caught. "I did."

They reached the storefront, but Bell hesitated. She put her small hand on his arm. "And you've always known you were..."

"Dewin?" Dane said, facing her. "My whole family has the gift, going back generations. I've known what I am for as long as I can remember."

Bell looked into his eyes as if searching for something. She dropped her gaze and shook her head. "It explains a lot."

"It feels strange to speak of it openly. You're gifted as well."

Bell shook her head. "The chymaera said I was broken, and Jax said I've never displayed the signs. Not that I would know what they are." She scuffed a stray pebble with her shoe. "I'm not sure whether I should be relieved or not. On the one hand, I likely won't go mad. But I felt so useless when we were imprisoned. Especially after Jax showed up with fae to rescue us all. How did you do that? Do you always work with fae? Will you go mad?"

Dane held up his hands, laughing. "Whoa. All right. Let me think how best to explain." He looked up at the star-filled sky. "When I was a boy I saw fae. I thought everyone could. They appear as spectres... not dark, not angry. They just look like...normal folk. Pezzik and my Pa saw them, but Ma could not. Pa said the Storm King had given me a special grace to hear the Song...to use it and serve others, always to help them. He said many fear us, and we must keep it secret. Sometimes fae would speak to us, but it was rare. It was *always* a message from the Storm King. We took great care to heed their warnings, though they rarely shared anything but riddles. That part of the old stories is true enough. I grew older, learned more..." He looked into Bell's eyes and took both her hands. "Pa explained how the gnomes protected us from dewin madness, their cadence. My ancestor discovered their ability. It strengthens knacks, and it guards us. If Jax said you never showed any signs, he likely meant you didn't see fae. Be thankful. As a small child, they scared me powerfully."

Bell pressed him. "And you really hear the Song?"

"I hear it all the time...in the north wind, the horse's stride, the bees' hum, the birds' chorus. The Song rolls through my mind but the world sings, too, and I hear it. Sometimes it's overwhelming. Sometimes 'tis barely a whisper. Always there." He shrugged.

"How can I be dewin and not hear? Is it possible the cantors were mistaken? Perhaps the purification affected me, but I'm not truly dewin?"

Dane shook his head. "No. We have been shielded from Dissonance by the gnomes. All deemling families have potential for the talent, 'tis why we have deema. They guarded us even before the War of the Wyrm. It was part of a majister experiment to stir up the gift. If the purification affected you, you are dewin."

"So why can't I hear the Song?"

"We could ask Sara. She might know."

Bell gulped. "Do you know many fae?"

Dane laughed and shook his head. "Honestly, most only appear once. Sara is the first to appear time and again. I can't believe I grounded her. 'Twas an accident the first time. I didn't know I could do it again."

Bell placed one hand on her hip, inspecting Dane. "Does this grounding make you a full majister?"

"No. A harmony bond between a faisant and a majister begins in the world of the fae and can be sealed only at the Majisterium, with a special rite."

"But you could become a majister? If a fae message is from the Storm King, wouldn't it be another kind of message if you were able to ground one? Wouldn't that mean something even more important? All of the majisters disappeared. Perhaps the Storm King is working to make new ones."

Dane stared at his feet. When he answered, he looked up and spoke slowly. "I haven't really thought about it. I guess it's possible. There's much I don't know."

"Could you bond with Sara? See what happens?"

Dane sighed. "I know the rite but could hardly do it myself. I don't know how to get to her world. I have to guess. The rite could hurt us. It isn't like I actually used the Song before Pa died. Oh, I did at first, when I was a boy. I nearly killed Poll. After that, I was very careful indeed. Then Ma got sick..."

He stole a glance at Bell, watching for her reaction.

Her eyes filled with tears, understanding. "You tried to save them."

Dane nodded. "I couldn't."

He swallowed back the bitterness at the memory. "I quit trying to do much, after that. But lute orders must be filled. The Conclave tracked the last one. That's why I need to speak with Trystan. He isn't safe."

Two figures emerged from the darkness, walking toward them.

"It looks like you'll get your chance."

38

Sara peeked through the shutter. It was too dark to see anything but the village green, stretching across the center of town like a blanket. This herbalist's shop was closed for the night, the owner gone home. With any luck, they would be gone before he returned in the morning.

Sahxe was charming, with narrow winding streets and tall storybook buildings. She hummed a few bars of "Bibbidi-Bobbidi-Boo," half expecting to see a pumpkin turn into a coach.

Bren and Zonah busied themselves in the back, looking through the wares for useful salves and ointments. Jax had vanished as soon as they arrived, returning with fresh clothes for Sara and Dane. Now they waited for Dane and Bell to return with food.

Sara found a chair in a corner and closed her eyes. She didn't know if she'd get home. Where was home? When she reached for her memories, she found nothing but snatches of a very different life. She clearly remembered television, movies, electricity, banks. She knew her world. She just couldn't glimpse her life. Those details were blank, like trying to remember a dream. Sara fidgeted in frustration. But she was in a dream? This whole thing was ridiculous, and she couldn't make any sense of it.

Jax popped through the wall. "The owner of this shop will be back very early," he said. "The streets are clear, but I sense Shadowkin nearby. We need to move on as soon as we're supplied. Can't risk exposing the village."

Shadowkin? What are Shadowkin?

Zonah's sapphire eyes regarded Sara, her inner lids blinking. "You are very loud, more than Dane. Pryf will track us easily if they get close to you."

"What do you mean, I'm loud?" asked Sara.

"I hear your thoughts. Your heartfire is small and cold, yet your thoughts shout."

My heartfire? What is a heartfire?

Zonah pointed to her chest, answering the unspoken question. "The heartfire gives and receives love, beauty, hope. It fuels our desires and our makings. It begins like a rough block of stone. We shape it with our choices. When we feed it through trust, love, right thinking, it will burn bright and true. Or we may lie to ourselves. We may act a coward or live for pleasure. It will grow cold, and we live as Pryf. Unfit. Rejected."

Sara stared at Zonah, shocked and insulted. "Rejected from what? I'm fae, not chymaera. And that's not a heartfire, that's a spirit you speak of."

"Faisant are creators," Zonah said matter-of-factly. "Chosen by the Storm King to bond with a majister and feed the heartfires of others, much as our Profi. This is known. The heartfire is but one thread of a spirit. It strays, wayward like a child. You must master it, stonerider, to be faisant, not merely fae."

Bren nudged the conversation back toward immediate concerns before Sara could ask more questions. "Can we fly above the Shadowkin? We could be in Siarad tonight."

Jax shook his head. "Too dangerous to try, we could all fall if even one attaches itself."

Sara went to the window and cracked the shutter again. Across the street, Bell and Dane lingered, deep in private conversation. Embarrassed, she closed the shutter.

"Let's ask Dane what he thinks," said Sara. "They're outside. I vote to move on tonight."

Ten minutes later, Bell and Dane slipped in the back door. They weren't alone. A young man with close-cropped blonde hair and a short, scruffy beard had joined them, followed by a gray-haired, bespectacled gentleman. The old man nodded and murmured to himself when he saw Zonah and Jax. Dane carried a basket of food and a bottle of wine. Bell held a folded blanket. She spread it on the floor of the shop and took the basket from Dane, setting out bread, cheese, sausages, and apples while Dane made introductions.

"This is Trystan dan Tenkor, a bard from the Bindery. I made a lute for him and was on my way to deliver it when I was captured. His friend there is his manservant, Burtyn."

Bren started, hearing Trystan's name. "Trystan?"

Trystan squinted at the cantor and gaped in open-mouthed astonishment. "Brother Bren? You left the Bindery?"

Bren grimaced. "Forgive me, I am a brother no more. I have only just deserted the service of the Conclave. I was sent to serve at the Bindery partly to observe you. I must share now, you are to be captured and held at the next opportunity. The orders were sent to the king for his seal weeks ago."

Burtyn leaned on a chair in the corner, resting his aged frame. "He will not approve it," he said, sniffing. "Lord Trystan is a prince."

Bren knelt next to the blanket, choosing an apple. "Actually, he likely will. The high king has been at the mercy of the Arcantor for some time. They planned to send a force to Pelegor. The Conclave would wrest control in the name of aid. Shadowborn will soon mass to attack Pelegor. Trystan was to be used as leverage to force acquiescence. It's been planned for years. A long game." He took a bite of his apple and chewed.

Sara grabbed a seat next to Bren and began cutting off pieces of the bread and cheese. She listened closely, trying to sort out what it all meant. This dude was in danger. That much was clear.

Zonah said, "It's true. Cantor Siles plots to bring the Wyn under his control as well."

Sara studied Trystan. The young bard stood like an eagle ready to fly. Tense. Eyes hard, jaw set.

"I left home not just to deliver the lute but to warn you before the Conclave intervened. I knew you were likely in danger," said Dane. "We are on our way to Siarad. Come with us."

Dane's voice unleashed Sara's memories, sending her headlong into reverie. In her mind's eye, she saw a clear image of a young man in jeans, stooping with one hand out as he approached a growling dog. He had a crooked smile. *Peter...*

The image faded before her eyes as suddenly as it had come. Sara shifted on her chair, unsettled, and filed the image away to think on later. *Who is Peter? I know him, I do.*

"In Siarad, the Conclave cannot reach you easily. They cannot use you if they cannot reach you," said Dane.

Burtyn tilted his head, birdlike. "Will the Dread not cause you much distress? Could you be trapped, unable to leave?"

"I will risk it. I must seek answers. I believe the Caprices have them. My deema, Pezzik, waits there." Dane shrugged. "If the Curse disables me, I'll come up with something else. But it seems a wise place to lie low, provided we can leave again, unhindered."

"Why wouldn't they just send in the guard to capture us?" asked Bell.

"The Caprices control and protect the city," said Trystan. "They suffer the guard's presence at the waypoints along the road in and out, but that is all. Any guard force sent into the city proper has simply vanished, like the cantors. They don't return. The guard won't enter. Not unless forced."

Jax retrieved the wine from Bell, uncorked it and took a swig before passing it to Sara. Wiping his mouth, he said, "Begging your pardon, sirs, but you also need to know there are Shadowkin massing right now. I sensed them and confirmed. Dark clouds, deadly. If we are leaving tonight, it must be soon. It might already be too late."

Dane turned back to Trystan. "Come with us, please," he said.

Trystan arched a brow at Burtyn. "What do you think?"

In answer, Burtyn straightened and removed his spectacles and wig, revealing a much younger man.

Gasps rose around the room. The deception had been complete.

Burtyn blinked, satisfaction spreading over his face. He bowed with a winning smile. "My real name is Baron Tabor Demitri. I'm very pleased to meet you. Apologies. I disguise myself most regularly, especially when meeting new acquaintances. I believe you may know my colleague, Mod."

Dane chuckled and bowed in return. "I know her well, milord."

Tabor settled back in his chair, tapping his foot. "This Conclave plan for Pelegor changes our course. We need to reach Bestua, but we should rendezvous with our agents in Siarad, send messages, prepare. Learn what we may. Shadowborn complicate matters, of course. Can you hold them off with the Song?"

"I can try. I've never done it," Dane said.

"You will have both of us to assist you. One has a magnificent lute," Tabor said, pointing at Trystan.

Jax tugged his beard. "But we have no songsteel. The Shadowkin mass in a black cloud that surrounds a person and strips flesh from bone. I've seen it. Just one speck from the cloud can burrow into a man like an insect and kill him. You won't have time to learn to hold them off. Songsteel sets them afire and destroys them. The Song itself might do the same, but it's a risk."

"How so?" asked Trystan.

"You have never faced them. One mote, if it attaches to a person, is deadly. They delve into your body, your eyes, and mouth. Are you willing to risk it?"

"You know little of my people, if you think I have never faced Shadowkin," said Trystan, quietly. "A man can feel their presence before they rise. I know the fear. I know its true name. *Dissonance.* It's much like the Dread of Siarad, forged by evil. Dissonance given shape. But aye, I will risk it."

"Do we have a choice?" asked Tabor. "We are not completely bereft of songsteel, though our weapons are few. The Song itself may prove a more effective defense, if we are careful."

"We'll find another Watcher," said Sara, surprising herself. All eyes rested on her. "The two we have won't hold everyone. If we ride them, we can travel more quickly."

The back door flew open, and a scruffy young boy burst in, panting. Trystan's lute case was slung over the boy's shoulder, nearly dwarfing him. He shut the door and leaned against it, catching his breath. "Lord Trystan, cantors're askin' fer you. Th' town guard with 'em."

Trystan took the lute case from the boy.

Tabor rose, replacing his wig and spectacles. "That's our cue me lads and lasses. It's time to dance the shadows. Gint, show this young lady"—he gestured to Sara—"where a Watcher sits. I'll be back in a few minutes."

"Where are you going?" asked Trystan, alarmed.

"I am going to delay our friends from the Conclave," said Tabor. He flashed a grin at Trystan. "Stars. I love my work."

With that, he was gone.

Gint led Sara across the green. The moon was full. Its light fell on them like a blessing and for the first time since she had woken in this dream, Sara felt grateful instead of afraid.

The boy, Gint, looked at her with a sidelong assessment. "Yer be needin' the Watcher fer what?" he asked, all blue eyes and freckles.

"I'm going to ride it. Or you will," said Sara. She grinned at the boy's doubtful expression.

"Ride it? Are you a dewin then? If'n you are you'll go mad," said the boy.

Sara laughed. "No, that's not me, I'm fae. That's what they've told me, anyhow."

Gint stepped back, impressed but suspicious. He poked her shoulder gently. "Yer not fae if I can touch you."

Sara tried not to laugh. "I'm a girl from another place. My name is Sara. Don't think too much about it. I'm really trying not to. I'm not sure what else I am, but maybe, through all of this, I'll find out."

Gint scratched his nose, smudging some dirt there in response.

Two town guardsmen passed. They ignored Sara and Gint. They weren't looking for a woman and child. Sara watched as they trudged across the common. They reached the corner and crossed the street, disappearing behind the row of shops.

"Let's go steal a Watcher," Sara said. Gint brightened, and they strode across the green. The Chapterhouse loomed ahead. Its distinctive arc window reflected fragile moonlight, falling upon a horse. Sara's heart stirred.

Unbidden, Marilla's face flashed before her. She was laughing as she cantered next to Sara. *I have a sister. A twin sister. Marilla.*

The horse had no wings. It would need them.

Sara reached out and touched the stone horse. "I can ride. I know horses," she murmured. She ran a hand through her hair and inhaled deeply. The horse's head moved, observing her. She smiled and placed both hands on its head, singing, "Fly Like an Eagle."

Nothing happened. Gint watched her, eyes rounded. The Watcher chuffed.

She tried it again. "Fly Like an Eagle."

Again, nothing happened. Gint wiped his arm across his nose and sniffed.

"What are you tryin' to do?" he whispered.

"Shh," said Sara. "I need to concentrate, that's all." She laid her head on the stone horse's neck and stroked it. She closed her eyes and emptied her mind, listening. She saw wings, the ways she would sculpt them. A song popped into her mind. "Fly Me to the Moon," she sang. She imagined the statue taking flight and pictured the flaming wings. A web of light jumped from her hand, and the stone rippled. The horse stamped its feet. It pulled away from her, whinnying. Blue lightning crackled through the creature. Its wings unfurled, formed from bright flame.

Gint choked and sputtered, backing away. "Doran's arse!"

"Wait, hold still," she commanded the horse. She offered her cupped hands to Gint. "Here, I'll give you a boost."

He looked from her to her hands and shook his head.

"Tell them to meet me where we landed the others," she said, sighing.

"Meet yer there," Gint said, flashing an impish grin. The boy turned and dashed back toward their hideout.

Sara climbed onto the horse's back. "Let's see what you can do, baby," she said. "Fly."

The horse rose into the air, flying in a slow spiral. The wind blew Sara's hair back as she directed him to the far side of the bridge. The town twinkled below. They rushed toward a meadow. A huge glowing green moth appeared, flying straight at Sara's head. She ducked to avoid it. When they neared the tree line, Sara squeezed the horse with her knees. It glided smoothly down, landing near two other stone figures. She dismounted.

"Stay here." Sara inspected the other Watchers. Both completely inert, their stone eyes stared into the night. Suddenly, Sara felt exhausted. The flight had drained her of all energy and will.

Sara sat down on a log heavily, her breathing loud in her ears. A cloud rolled over the moon, obscuring it. Crickets chirped. An owl hooted. Water burbled in the brook. A branch snapped. Prickles brushed the back of Sara's neck, as if a cold wind had kissed her. The sensation spread down her spine. She felt exposed.

"Who's there?" she called. The only answer was the rustling of the wind in the trees. Sara hunched on her seat, making herself smaller. Scarier than this forest at night, memory haunted her. Marilla. She felt a horrible sense of guilt, fear, and shame, as she called up the image of her sister's eyes. Eyes like her own, accusing her. The memory of her life, her family, her school, all of it came flooding back in full. She gasped under the weight of it. Worst of all, she remembered Marilla, silent in her coma.

It's my fault. All my fault.

Cold licked Sara's ears, slowly. She shivered and looked around. The moon was obscured as a cloud drifted by. The owl sounded more distant. Despite her chill, the air pressed in, heavy. Her breathing became irregular. She stood and walked a few paces from the log, trying to breathe normally. The moonlight dimmed.

Two men came striding over the bridge road. They slipped into sparse brush at the roadside, coming out on the grassy knoll where Sara waited. The moon shook off its cover, unveiling them.

Dane and Trystan. A jackdaw cried. Sara held up her hand to wave and gasped. It was transparent. She was fading, but a thin veneer of darkness surrounded her arm. She looked down. Darkness flowed over her fading body like a skin.

Shadowkin.

"No," she whispered.

Sara looked up. Dane was charging toward her, singing. She wanted to scream a warning, to tell him to stop. Tell him she wasn't worth it, to save the others. No sound would come. The black cloud swallowed Dane, obscuring him from view. He screamed, and Trystan waved a sword made from fire. A jackdaw cried again.

Sara blinked.

A moment later, she was in her own bed, safe. Moonlight streamed through the window.

39

Tabor crossed Sahxe's village green, pausing only to adjust his cravat, wig, and spectacles. His disguise was not ideal, but it would have to do. He would rather be demeaned than recognized as himself, the Baron Tabor Demitri. Cantors and the town guard were seeking his companion, Trystan. They weren't looking for his manservant, Burtyn.

Fools underestimate those they consider beneath them.

He set off again, this time at the pace of an aged gentleman, unhurried and diffident in mien.

The inn sprawled along the narrow edge of the green. The moon's arc glowed just above the roofline. It was an hour before midnight, the hour when most of the townsfolk should amble home from the pub. Yet, the streets were empty. Tabor pushed through the door to find the innkeeper protesting while two acolytes prepared censers. Five guards stood by, their faces impassive, ready to quell protests. The room was filled with patrons, yet hushed. It was devoid of laughter and music.

The villagers were being detained for purification.

Tabor licked his lips in thinly veiled disgust. The cantor in charge was a pompous coward, eager to not only protect himself from perceived danger posed by the broken Song, but to bully the village. Cantors knew the difference between a dewin and someone who played an enchanted instrument. Purification would not affect a mere player. The incense and Essences would, however, send a message to the townspeople. "We can wipe your mind if we choose."

It was the true reason to prepare this rite.

Unless they were seeking Dane and his companions, as well.

Tabor paused, considering. It was possible, if the Conclave knew Dane was here. If they knew Dane was dewin? If they knew Dane had recently escaped from High Cantor Siles' tender care? Then this rite was a precaution. Perhaps the cantor was not a fool. Perhaps he was *informed*. There was no further time to consider. At that moment, the innkeeper's eyes fell on him. The innkeeper pointed, babbling. "There's no need for such trouble, there's the bard's man now. He can lead you."

Tabor tilted his head and shuffled forward, squinting. "What's all this?"

A narrow-faced cantor in full regalia rounded on him, brandishing a staff. "We have questions for your master. Lead us to him." The cantor gestured, and two of the town guard flanked Tabor.

Tabor blinked, bemused, and looked askance at the guard. He rubbed his nose, assuming his most benign expression. "Of course, of course. But might I know what your interest is in my Lord Trystan?"

The cantor's face purpled. "Your prince has exposed these good people to the broken Song!" The statement was loud enough to broadcast to the entire common room. "We are ensuring their safety. I have orders from High Cantor Siles himself to detain your master."

Tabor kept his voice and expression mild, feigning offended shock and disbelief. "The Song, you say? My master is a bard-in-training. I'm certain there is some misunderstanding. Trystan performed for these good souls, 'tis true. But the only effect was a desire to dance." He coughed, and glanced across the room, seeing several villagers nod in agreement.

"We shall make sure there was no harm done," said the cantor, his tone ominous. He nodded to the acolytes who had paused, listening to the exchange. They hurriedly returned to their task.

"That you will, I'm sure, Your Grace." Tabor shuffled to the acolytes, peering over their shoulders at their mixture of dried herbs. "I've always wondered what you put in those. The stink is abominable," he said, wheezing as if already affected. As he turned back to the cantor, Tabor's hand slipped into his waistcoat pocket. He produced a tiny snuffbox. He opened it gently and offered it to the nearest guard. "Care for a pinch?"

The guard smiled and nodded, taking a generous pinch. As he inhaled, he started sneezing uncontrollably. He stumbled forward and knocked into one of the acolytes, sending the censer and its contents tumbling to the floor. The acolytes stooped to retrieve it at the same time, scrabbling to scoop up scattered herbs. Tabor shut the box with a snap and put it back in his pocket, clucking. "Oh dear. Deepest apologies."

The guard choked and gasped, his eyes streaming tears. He stumbled toward a table with empty chairs and sat heavily. The cantor's eyes blazed. "Leave it," he ordered the acolytes. "You come with me."

He turned to face the common room. "All shall remain here until my assistants attend you. No one leaves." He glowered at the remaining guards. They nodded, two of them falling in to escort Tabor forcibly. Tabor sighed and bowed his head in submission. He allowed himself to be led outside, trailing the acolytes and the imperious cantor. The town Chapterhouse loomed, its distinctive steep-pitched roof visible just beyond the inn proper.

"My master was in the stable..." he began. A glowing horse with wings formed from flame rose into the air just in front of the Chapterhouse.

Sara, she did it, she found another Watcher.

He stopped and pointed.

The cantor's eyes rounded in horror as the horse swooped over the village. He made the sign of the arc and rushed out of the courtyard, trying to keep the horse in sight. The acolytes and one of Tabor's guards followed.

Tabor lost no time. Stamping on the remaining guard's foot and twisting hard, he punched the guard in the chin, precisely below his jaw. The guard's head snapped back, and he crumpled instantly. Tabor dragged him into the shadows.

"Sorry dear fellow. Nothing personal," he whispered.

Tabor loped toward the outer courtyard wall. He removed his wig and spectacles, jamming them into his belt, and began to climb, scaling quickly. He crouched low and scrambled over, dropping to the other side, silent as a cat. The Chapterhouse stable, a plain stone building with large arched entrances and a thatched roof lay before him. A pavilion stood in front of it, roofed with planks. Under this, an elaborate gilt coach gleamed in the moonlight.

"Hello beautiful," Tabor said to the carriage. "You're perfect. The cantor *does* love his comfort. I approve." He slipped inside and checked the interior. The coach was cleverly built and large enough to hold his entire party. It had a strongbox hidden in the seat, under the cushions. Tabor inspected this, finding a sizable amount of gold, a bottle of wine and an extra set of rich robes. He quickly donned these, retrieved a cantor's pin and ring from his waistcoat and assumed a pious expression, making the sign of the arc. "Thank the Cyntae for their blessings," he said, uncorking the wine. He sniffed it and took a swig. Nodding to himself, he placed the wine and his discarded effects in the strongbox. He descended carefully from the coach. An acolyte crossing the yard froze, staring at him. Tabor straightened.

"I need this coach readied immediately," he said, waving one hand like a scepter. "I've come from the Rift Chapterhouse on important business, and my horse *died* from exhaustion. There is no time to waste."

The acolyte stared at him, uncertain.

"Now, boy!" Tabor roared.

The acolyte bowed and hurried into the stable. He returned post-haste, leading two horses.

It would take time for the coach to be readied. Tabor eyed the chapterhouse and allowed himself a small smile.

The rear entrance was unlocked, and he stepped into the cool darkness beyond. Tabor blinked as his eyes adjusted. The landing opened into a large corridor. To his right, the hall turned. To his left, a stairway led down to living quarters. Tabor turned right, following the hallway.

Most chapterhouses were built in the same manner throughout the Weldenlands. This hall contained offices, Tabor knew. It would open into the Quiet Hall. Tabor went to the high cantor's office to wait.

The man is a pig, Tabor decided. A mahogany desk strewn with papers and ashes from a filthy pipe sat in the midst of chaos. Books lay haphazard, sideways and upside down on shelves and tables. The fire had burned out. A lone glowstone flickered in a corner sconce. Dust lay thick on every surface. Tabor sniffed and set to work. Two missives from Siles lay on top of a pile, their seals broken. He scanned them and sighed in relief. *No mention of Dane.* Messengers hadn't reached this village yet. Trystan was to be detained if seen. The wording suggested a general warning. *They don't know precisely where he is. Good.*

The office door flew open, and the high cantor swept into the room. Behind him, Bren followed, with Zonah, the chymaera. Tabor drew himself up with his most regal expression, eyes narrowed, and addressed Bren, his tone made of ice.

"Where have you been?"

Bren blinked.

Play along man, Tabor implored, silently.

The cantor looked from Bren to Tabor, uncertain.

Bren folded his hands and bowed his head in submission. "We tracked the bard, Your Grace. I apologize for riding ahead."

Tabor nodded, briefly. His eyes flicked to the priest. "You must be the local cantor...I see you have received our message. Have you seen the blackguard?" He held out his hand, presenting his ring to be kissed. The cantor stepped forward and kissed it, perfunctorily.

"I...we...have one of his companions being questioned, your eminence," said the cantor, covering his confusion.

Zonah strode forward, presenting herself to Tabor. Her catlike grace made each movement a dance. Her sapphire eyes glittered. "The trees whisper of the bards passing. They move north, milord," she said.

"Find them." His terse reply cracked the air, whiplike.

Zonah half bowed from the waist and loped from the room without looking back.

"I require your carriage. My horse is dead," said Tabor. "I have ordered it to be made ready. You will take all resources available. Search the northern road and forest. Spare no one."

"The village...it must be purified, Your Grace."

"All available. Immediately. *He must be found.* Am I understood?"

The cantor choked, purple creeping up his neck to suffuse his narrow face. His eyes were defiant as he answered. "Yes, Your Grace."

Tabor returned the man's gaze steadily. He said nothing. His silence chilled the air between them.

The cantor lowered his eyes.

"Now!" said Tabor. The cantor jumped and turned, hurrying to obey. Tabor heard him shouting orders as he rushed out the door.

"You saw Sara?" Tabor asked Bren, breaking into a grin.

Bren nodded, "We shall rendezvous with her and the others, beyond the meadow to the south."

"While the good cantor searches north. Not my finest work, but it will do. Come, let's dance the shadows, my friend."

The coach was waiting for them. Tabor shook his head at the acolyte perched in the driver's seat. "No. Brother Bren will drive." The boy frowned but clambered down, handing over the reins. Tabor winked at Bren before climbing into the coach. He lifted the seat cushion and opened the strongbox, retrieving the wine.

The carriage jolted, moving toward the road. Tabor settled back in the deep cushions and sighed. "Not my finest work, but not bad." He took a swig of wine. "Not bad at all."

40

Sara stared up at the ceiling, cursing silently. Tears streamed down her face. "Really? Really?" She felt like screaming.

She replayed the scene in her mind, over and over. Dane running toward her. The black cloud reaching to envelop him. *They strip flesh from bone.* She shuddered. They didn't get her because she faded away somehow. *Dane couldn't do that. Could he?*

Jane tapped on the door and opened it, poking her head in. "You okay?"

"Come in," said Sara, wiping her eyes with her red flannel pillowcase. She sat up and tapped her bedside lamp, waving Jane forward. "What time is it?"

"A little past midnight, I just got home," Jane said. She made a face. "I'm glad you're here. I checked a couple minutes ago and didn't see you. I thought you were still at your studio."

Sara shook her head. "I've been home all night," she said.

Jane's brow wrinkled. "Your sketchbook is on the couch, but you weren't here when I got in. I promise."

"Hm," said Sara. "Maybe I was sleepwalking?" She had proof! Finally! She could hardly contain the feeling exploding inside her. A mixture of wonder, overwhelm, anxiety and joy, followed by panic. *They strip flesh from bone. Dane. I have to go back. I have to help him somehow.*

"I was in the living room. You didn't walk past me." Jane settled on the edge of the bed, her eyes narrowing. "You've been crying. What's going on, Sara?"

Sara blinked, taken aback at the sudden intensity of the question. Jane was her upbeat, cheerful friend. The one who balanced her sarcasm and anxiety. Her serious tone was unnerving. No way she would believe her if she explained. She couldn't blame her. But she couldn't explain. There wasn't time. She had to go back. She had to help Dane if she could. He couldn't die.

But Jane was just getting started. She took a deep breath, as if getting ready to jump into deep water, and continued.

"I mean we've barely talked these past few weeks. You're doing a lot of things I've seen you do since we were kids, and it's killing me to watch. I'm done ignoring it all. Back in high school, you weren't hurting my brother. Blowing off Pete...kissing a guy you barely know? That's not who you want to be, I know that. But it's what you've done before, when anyone tries to get close. Remember the way you pined over Corey Simpson in high school? And Michael, who was a really great guy, you just froze him out. There's a pattern here." She held up one hand as Sara sputtered.

"Hear me out. I could go on, and you know it. The stakes are a lot higher now. It's not like you're just dodging homework anymore. You haven't been able to finish your final project for *your graduation*. When you do make headway, you destroy it. And instead of facing this stuff? You're drinking? You sorta pulled together for a while, but it's like Marilla went into a coma, and you went into a tailspin. I can't just sit by and do nothing. Now you're *disappearing*? Losing time? Seriously. What's really going on?"

"I don't really know," said Sara. Her heart pounded. She couldn't breathe, couldn't think. Her head felt full of white noise. She fought the urge to get up and run away. Far away. "I'm trying to figure it out."

Behind Jane, a shadow formed.

A tall shadow.

Sara felt all the blood drain from her face. She gasped but kept herself from screaming.

Jane's expression softened. "I'm not coming down on you. I'm just worried, that's all."

"Yeah, I know. Hey...Jane?"

"Yes?"

Sara struggled to keep her voice natural. "Do you see anything weird over there?"

Jane stood and moved toward the door. She walked right through the shadow. "Uh...no, all normal. Okay, you're half asleep, and I just totally unloaded. I'm sorry. Really. I love you. It's late. Just think about it, okay? We can talk in the morning. But if you want to talk things through, I'm here. I want to help."

"Thanks, Jane," Sara said, mechanically. She tracked the shadow as Jane shut the door behind her. It flickered and coalesced, hanging in the air, a ghost. Transparent. A tall young man who had recently shaved his head shimmered, grinning. He looked like the loser in a bar fight, with half-healed bruises and nasty scars. He approached her bedside table, silently, palms out.

Dane. Oh my god he's dead, and he's gonna haunt me.

Dane reached for the lamp. But instead of turning off, it only flickered. His hands passed right through it.

"Can you hear me?" whispered Sara.

He looked at her and nodded.

Sara eyed the door. The last thing she needed was for Jane to catch her talking to herself. She rolled over and reached for her clock radio, sliding the toggle to "on." Violin music blared. She winced and turned the volume down. She drew her knees up under her chin and studied Dane. *Was he a ghost?* He had to be a ghost.

His lips were moving, but no sound issued forth. Sara would have sworn he was trying to lip sync, if the music hadn't been completely instrumental.

The song ended and a new one began. A concerto by Paganini filled the room. It swelled, surrounding her and filling her with peace. Abruptly, she could hear Dane. It was as if someone had toggled a mute button.

"...your world?"

Sara blinked. "Come again? I couldn't hear you."

"I said, are we in your world?"

"Yes, this is my bedroom. We need to be quiet or we will disturb my roommate." Sara bobbed her head toward the door.

"The other girl? I saw her. She walked through me." Dane waved his hands, staring at them.

Sara cleared her throat. There was no good way to ask this. "Are you dead?"

"I don't think so," said Dane, smiling. "I have become fae to you."

"But the Shadowkin covered you. I saw. You didn't even hesitate, just charged them, knowing the risks." She shook her head. "I can't believe you did that. I'm so not worth it."

"I had to save you. And I did. I sent you home," said Dane,

gesturing around the room. "You are worth it, Sara. You're special... even if you don't see it."

"The Shadowkin blanketed you." Sara's eyes filled with tears. "They strip flesh from bone. Are you sure you're still alive? Is this normal? To come here?"

"Trystan. He had a songsteel blade. When they swarmed me, he was a madman, shouting, '*Ealltæw blōd sylfum Pelegor.*' Wherever his blade touched them, the shadows burst into flame. I blinked, and..."

"And you woke up here?"

Dane nodded.

"So you really don't know what happened. Do you think you'll go back?"

"I must. I..."

The radio song ended, and the station cut to a commercial. Dane's lips kept moving, but Sara couldn't hear him at all. Her forehead puckered.

"I can't hear you. Gimme a sec."

Sara tuned the radio to a new station. John Lennon sang "Imagine." Sara motioned for Dane to continue speaking. "Try again."

"That box is marvelous. Is there someone within?" He bent to examine it, peering expectantly. "A fair-ee? And your glowlight!" He twisted to look under the red lampshade.

"No fairies. Focus." Sara gulped. "So, is this normal? For you to be here?"

Dane shook his head. "It has never happened to me. I have heard of it happening, but only..."

He cleared his throat and began again.

"Trystan has his lute. He may use it and heal me. I just have to wait. If I die instead, when I pass, I shall pass from here. Either way, I will fade." He paused for a moment, his features contorting with emotion, and added, "I may have used the Song in the wrong way, somehow. I don't really know."

"No, you didn't, and you cannot die! Not like this. Is there anything we can do? Think," said Sara.

Dane's eyes glowed, too large in his pale face. "We can try to bond," he said. "It would change...strengthen me. Strengthen both of us."

"What kind of bond? Like blood brothers?" Sara asked, her eyes narrowing.

"The bond forms between fae and dewin with an ancient rite. The rite calls for travel to your world, when mentioned. A harmony bond.

It changes both of us forever."

"Changes us how?"

"I would become a majister, not just dewin. You would be faisant, not just fae. Bound to me. We would share our strengths. Other than this, the scroll was vague. This bond was common in ages past, before the war."

Sara frowned. "Sounds like marriage. What does bond mean?"

"Greater ability with the Song, beyond that I cannot say. I only know the rite because it was passed down, along with the Lorica's refrain. It is not a marriage," he said. His face reddened. "Such things are Dissonance. Forbidden, like wedding a sister. In fact, I do not know of any bond occurring with a woman. But the Storm King has brought us here."

He talked faster, changing the subject.

"There is a golden flower, prized for love and healing. It is like the tunebell, but grows only in your world. Its Virtue is strong. We bring one to a House of the Sign with a thunderstone. We use the stone to burn the flower. When the smoke rises, we call upon the Storm King to bind us together in the Song."

Dane looked triumphant, like what he had just said was a simple recipe. Sara swallowed her frustration.

"How will this get you home?" asked Sara.

"The binding ritual itself should transport us both to the tower of Anach, in Siarad. The rite is completed there. Parts of it must occur in each world."

Sara leaned forward and crossed her arms. "*Should* transport us? I don't like the sound of that."

"Yes. When the Storm King answers our call, we finish the rite in the tower of Anach. Otherwise, I will just fade." He fell silent. The pause lasted a long moment. Sara could see he was wrestling with something. "You asked if there was anything we could do. You don't have to try this. We can wait. Trystan may be able to heal me."

"Has Trystan healed before? Do you know?" Sara asked. Dane's bleak expression spoke volumes. *It's a long shot. If the Shadowkin destroyed Dane's flesh...*

She took a deep breath. "Are you sure you want to bond with me? You don't know me."

Dane smiled. "I know enough, trust me."

Trust me.

She thought about Brother Bren, the way Dane had defended him.

She did trust him. "Okay, so a house of the Sign? Any idea what that is?"

"The Sign is an eight-sided figure." Dane bent to pick up the pencil and notebook on Sara's desk. His hands passed right through them. The music on the radio faded, and Neil Diamond began to sing. Dane's voice cut off again, silenced. Sara leapt to turn the channel. She paused on a country station and gestured for Dane to speak. He obliged, but Sara heard nothing. She moved the dial, muttering about fussy-choosy-persnickety magic. The next station was playing Jars of Clay's "Liquid." Dane's voice came blasting through as if he had been shouting.

"...you draw one?"

Sara picked up the notebook, opened it to a blank page, and drew an octagon. "Like that?"

Dane nodded.

"Okay, got it. An eight-sided house? A gazebo works, that's simple enough. There's one at a park in the Highlands. Heck, there's one at my parents' place."

Sara walked over to the clamshell iBook on her desk. She opened it and checked to make sure it was connected to the 'net, sat down and signed into AOL. She typed into the search box—*thunderstone*. Sara clicked on the first result and read aloud.

"Flint arrowheads and axes turned up by farmer's plows were considered to have fallen from the sky from lightning strikes, caused when gods fought in heaven. They were often thought to be heavenly arrows and are called thunderstones.

"I know I saw the word somewhere...Joe's!" Sara said, triumphant. She grinned and held up her hand for a high-five.

Dane tracked her hand with his eyes, expectant.

He had no idea what she was doing.

Sara dropped her hand. "They're arrowheads. Flint. Flint sparks and makes fire, I get it now. I don't have any arrowheads myself, but I know someone who does. Now...a golden flower?"

She typed the term into the search box and read the results. "A Chinese herb...But it isn't known for love and healing."

She cleared the search and entered yellow flower, scanning the results.

"Daisy, dandelion, rose, goldenrod..." Sara smacked her forehead. "Of course. *Goldenrod*. The state flower. I even saw background on it at work this week. It totally fits. It must be the one. It's perfect. I know where we can find some, too."

Dane did not respond. She looked up and found him staring at her laptop quizzically, his mouth moving as he asked questions she could not hear. Annie Lenox was playing on the radio. Sara sighed and got up to change the station back to classical, Beethoven.

"Why does it do that? Only let me hear you when certain music is playing? Do you know?"

"The Song weaves around us at all times, yet not all music is filled with the Song."

"We don't have magic here."

Dane pointed at the radio. "This is not magical?"

"No, invisible waves go through the air from one place to another carrying the music..."

Sara stopped.

"Fine. It's magic. But not the way you think of magic. Magic isn't made from music or even connected to music. There's no Storm King here."

"The Storm King exists in all places," said Dane, patiently, as if he were explaining something to a child.

Sara opened her mouth to object, but thought better of it. Yesterday, if someone had told her there were other worlds, she would have argued. There was a lot she thought she knew that simply wasn't so.

She checked the time. Almost one a.m.

One a.m. and Pete was mad at her.

One a.m., Pete was mad at her, and she needed to ask him for an arrowhead so she could perform a ritual.

Tricky.

She grabbed her phone and typed out a text.

Hey, you awake? I need to see you. Really bad.

41

The reply came quickly. Sara exhaled a sigh of relief. Pete was still awake. If he had been asleep, there would have been no chance of finding an arrowhead tonight.

Okay. You coming over now?

She tapped out her answer. *If it's okay, that would be great.*

Sara glanced at Dane. He was standing over an art magazine she'd left open, his eyes wide with wonder. The page was open to a print of *The Kiss* by Gustav Klimt.

"It's a magazine. Like a book, but we throw them away when we are finished reading them. They tell us news, stories. They teach us. The pictures and text are produced by a machine instead of being drawn by hand. Same with the books," she said, pointing to the bookshelf next to her desk. "It isn't magic."

Dane shot her a doubtful expression and walked over to the bookshelf. His hand drifted up and traced a few of the spines.

Sara's phone vibrated. *I guess so. See ya in a few.*

"Okay, if we're going to do this, we gotta go. I guess I won't be able to hear you once we can't hear music. Just make signs with your hands. I'll figure them out."

Dane nodded. Sara hurried to her bathroom, splashed water on her face, and finger-combed her hair. She looked pale, exhausted. With a shrug, she pulled on her Chucks. When she emerged, Dane was hovering over her laptop. "Come on, wizboy."

Sara grabbed her jacket and purse, opened her bedroom door, and crept down the hall.

Dane followed, silently. Sara slipped outside, shivering as the cold air hit her face. The snow had mostly melted, but the wind still had an icy bite.

The street was quiet. Huge old trees with bony branches overhung the boulevard. The occasional sound of light traffic droned a block or two away. Sara walked quickly to her car, parked on the street in front of the stately Victorians. Her breath clouded as she slid into the driver's seat. She opened the passenger door from the inside, waving Dane in. He eyed the car uncertainly but climbed inside.

Sara held her breath, half afraid Dane would fall through the seat. He couldn't touch anything, how can he ride with her? But he sat on the leather seats as naturally as if he were fully solid, inspecting the dashboard with a curious expression. He looked more solid too. Sara sighed, relieved, and started the engine.

"This is a carriage?" asked Dane.

"Yeah and why can I hear you? What's changed?"

"It is like the music. The Song pulses through this carriage. You cannot feel it?"

Sara revved the engine, considering her car. The Karmann Ghia was vintage and very hard to find. She loved driving it...but magical? "I don't get it, sorry."

"A fae created this carriage."

"So wait, I thought faisant make things. Art."

"This carriage is art." He paused and settled back in his seat. "Fae make things as well. They may be moved by the Song, or they would not flash into my world." He peered out the window. "Those are also carriages."

"We call them cars, but yes. We're going to visit my friend Peter. He has an arrowhead."

Dane's brow wrinkled.

"A thunderstone. We can get one from him. They aren't just lying around the city."

"What is the name of this city?"

"Louisville. It's named for a foreign king."

Dane nodded and waved at the houses and street lamps as they passed. "So many lights."

"Electric. They've only been common for about a hundred years or so. Before that we mostly used gas flames." Sara was babbling. She was anxious and unsure how to face Peter. He was really hurt. She needed to make things right, not just show up and demand an arrowhead in the middle of the night. The problem was, she really had no idea how she felt. She had to figure it out in the next five minutes. It was hard to sort through with a wizard looming in the seat next to her.

"Gas? Your words are strange. Where are we going?"

Sara decided not to try to explain electricity. Discussing the scientific laws of the universe with her wizard friend from an alternate reality somehow just didn't seem appropriate.

"Just down the street. Peter's a boy scout, literally. Was an Eagle Scout. He'll have an arrowhead we can borrow. The problem is, we were supposed to go out Friday, and I blew him off, and now he thinks I have friend-zoned him."

Dane's brow furrowed. "This...Peter is a woodsman? He wishes to court you?"

Sara slowed for the stoplight, glancing at Dane, surprised. She didn't answer. He was grasping her world much better than she had dealt with his. Of course, he was a wizard. But still.

"Yes, court me. But I couldn't go with him when he wanted to go courting. He was hurt and believes I do not care for him as more than a friend."

"I understand."

The light changed, and she continued down the street, past the university and the fraternity houses. Pete's tiny duplex apartment was on the other side of the underpass. Not a great part of town. She pulled up in front of the cottage and turned off the engine, leaving the radio on.

"I don't know how long this will take. You'd better stay here," she said.

"If you do not return before I fade, may the Storm King guide you all your days, Sara."

Crap. Sara hesitated. She didn't think of that. He was probably dying right now. "Ugh. I can't stand it. If you fade, and I'm not here..." She couldn't even finish the sentence. "Come on, you're going with me. But no funny business. Just be quiet, and act like you're not there. Because to him, you aren't."

She reached across and opened the passenger door for him. "I'll try to make this quick."

Sara mentally prepped for the conversation as they crossed the yard. *Hi Pete. Allow me to introduce my buddy, the Invisible Man.*

God help me.

Pete answered the door with tousled hair and a sleepy expression.

He was wearing blue flannel plaid pajama pants and a gray Slashdot tee shirt. He stood back, waving Sara in.

"Thanks for letting me come over, Pete. I know it's really late. It couldn't wait."

Pete's apartment was on the first floor of the cottage, decorated in early American garage sale. He had plenty of plants and several pieces of art scattered around. Mostly gifts from her. A large painting from her impressionist phase hung in a place of honor over the mantel. The fireplace was bricked up, but still held a certain charm. Sara ducked her head and made a beeline for his overstuffed sectional couch. She sat, tucking her feet up under her, took a deep breath, and met his gaze. Dane stood in a corner, behind Peter. Sara did her best to ignore him. This was going to be hard enough as it was.

"No big deal," he said. "What's up?" His voice was controlled. Unnatural. He was really upset.

Sara shifted her weight and bit her lip. "I need an arrowhead. Do you have one?"

Coward. Avoiding the real problem. She was *such* a coward. But she didn't have to be, did she?

Peter frowned and crossed his arms. He didn't answer for a long moment. The silence stretched.

"And I needed to tell you that you're not friend-zoned, and I'm sorry." She finally looked into his eyes. "I'm just going...."

A short girl Sara didn't know, clad only in an oversized white button-up shirt, slipped out of Peter's bedroom. Long honey-blonde hair fell nearly to her waist, swaying as she walked down the hallway and into Peter's kitchen. The girl ignored them. She emerged a minute later with a glass of water and walked back to Peter's room, closing the door behind her.

Sara couldn't breathe. Couldn't think. Tears welled, threatening to spill. She swallowed, stood, and edged toward the door. She had to get out of there. "You're not alone. I'm sorry, I didn't mean...this was a mistake."

Peter shrugged. "It's no big deal, Sara. Really. You need the arrowhead for your piece?"

Sara focused on Dane to steady herself. She could see through him, see the door. Was Dane more transparent? Was he fading?

"Sort of."

"Okay, any particular kind?"

"Bigger the better. Size matters," said Sara, smiling weakly.

Peter didn't even take the obvious bait to make a stupid joke. He just went back to his room, returning with a four-inch greenish-black flint arrowhead. His fingers brushed hers as he handed it over. The small touch sent a shock up her arm. Sara looked into his eyes, searching. "I don't need it back," he said.

I have really screwed up.

"You saved my life, you have no idea. Thanks." She cleared her throat and backed toward the door. "I'll get outta your hair."

"Yeah, okay, see ya later."

"Later."

Her tears didn't start till she was halfway to the car. The handkerchief she found in her jacket pocket only made her cry more.

Dane followed Sara to the horseless carriage, musing. So many things in this world were strange. The fae world. Their unfamiliar music, odd words, and marvelous tools, all these captivated him. Yet he recognized troubling things as well. Peter, Sara's friend, had been angry with Sara. Sara had been shocked to see Peter's doxie. Doxie the girl must have been, to show herself in such a state of undress, wearing only a tunic. But perhaps such was their custom? Dane had much to learn. Yet there was no mistaking Sara's upset. She wiped her eyes when they were safely in the car. She had been crying. She turned the key to the carriage and music played once more.

"You are upset," he said.

Sara fastened a harness over herself and looked up. She nodded, her lower lip trembled. "Peter is my best friend, and he wanted to be more..."

"But he has a doxie," Dane said.

Sara tilted her head, puzzled.

"A woman of low repute. She did not speak. Her dress was most improper."

Sara laughed. "A bimbo? No, no, no. He is free to be with anyone. She wasn't a bimbo. Pete hasn't done anything wrong. I blew him off. I was supposed to go out on a date with him. Go to dinner and a movie. Courting. But I stood him up. I didn't go when I was supposed to and...I also kissed someone else, and I told him about it. He's really hurt. He found someone else to...to court. It's okay. I want him to be happy."

Dane shook his head slowly, not understanding. "You wish to be courted by this other man? The one you kissed? So why are you crying?"

Sara shrugged and fixed her eyes on the road. She adjusted a mirror. The carriage began to move. "It's complicated."

"Where are we going?"

"We're going to find goldenrod. I work in a garden. There will be goldenrod. We can get some to use. It's very late, but I have a key to get in the greenhouse. The other guy, the one I kissed? Scott? He works there, too. But he is a selfish jerk. Not a good person."

"Peter is a good person?"

"One of the best."

"So why did you want to kiss the jerk? A jerk...is like a cantor?"

Sara laughed again. "Definitely. Jerks are people who have no honor. That's the general idea, someone who lies, someone you cannot trust."

A red light flashed ahead, and the carriage slowed.

"Peter is too good for me," Sara said softly. "He deserves someone perfect. I want a jerk...I don't know why."

"You are not a jerk," said Dane.

Sara's eyes widened as she glanced at him. Her breath caught. She looked back at the road. "I'm glad you think so. But you don't know me very well."

"A jerk would not try to save me," said Dane. "You are not a jerk. I trust you."

Sara didn't answer. Dane noticed her lower lip trembling again and resolved to be silent. He looked out the window and watched the city roll by as chamber music washed over him. He had upset her even more. He'd never understand women.

42

Trystan held his lute at the ready, his sword sheathed on his back. The swarm of darkness had retreated into the forest, but it could emerge again at any time. He set the lute at his feet carefully and drew his sword in one motion, inspecting it. Pitted where he had struck the Shadowkin, it still held true. Forge blades dissolved as they were used against such enemies, but this one promised to bring him through at least one more battle.

He never thought he'd face the Shadowborn here. Not like this. Not as a bard. Trystan was trained in battle, swordplay. Most of his life had centered around weapons, songsteel, and the Forge. Music and history were for him a refuge, not a blade to be wielded.

With this lute, all that had changed. He'd known it before, but in this moment a prescience fell upon him, and he glimpsed all the battles to come. This war, his own personal war against the Shadowborn and the Wyrm began here. Now.

He named the fear and let it wash over him.

Trystan pictured a similar black cloud streaming into the mountains of his homeland, descending on its villages and cities. His brother Marcus. Essie. Disintegrating. He pushed the image away and sheathed his sword.

Bell held Dane's head, cradling it in her arms. She sang wordlessly, rocking back and forth. Dane looked for all the world as if he were sleeping. They had bandaged his arms, hands, and chest crudely, with strips of fabric ripped from Bell's underskirts. The swarm had eaten into Dane's skin and muscle. Trystan still had no idea how it all had happened.

One minute Dane was singing, charging forward to defend Sara. The next she was gone. Dane was covered with crawling black death, no longer singing, but screaming. Trystan had sliced through the swarm, watching as they burst into flame where his Forge blade touched them. Light had flared into that impossible darkness, consuming it. Where the Forge flames covered Dane, they also cauterized his exposed wounds, the raw flesh. He didn't so much bleed now as *ooze*.

Dane should have been dead within seconds. Perhaps his Song shielded him? Probably shielded them both. Trystan should have been flayed. Now they had to find shelter. On this ridge, they were exposed. The Shadowkin could return at any time. They had planned to leave town in small groups of two or three. When Bell, Jax, and Gint had appeared, Trystan had sent Gint back to find Tabor, Zonah, and Bren and explain the situation. But they shouldn't stay this close to the trees.

"We need to leave," said Jax, echoing Trystan's thoughts.

"Let's get him closer to the road," said Trystan. "If the swarm comes back, we will at least have a few more minutes to prepare a defense."

He carefully put his lute back in its case. "Milady, if you will?"

Bell rose and took up his lute case while Trystan attended to Dane. He managed to wrestle the tall man to his feet, then hoisted him onto his shoulder. Sweat dripped into his eyes, but he gritted his teeth and pointed himself toward the small bridge, just down the hill. He prayed the deathly shadows would not follow.

A large carriage rumbled over the bridge, its silhouette menacing in the moonlight. It slowed and halted. A robed and hooded figure swung down from the driver's seat and stood next to the road, waiting. Trystan squinted. "That had better be Tabor," he said under his breath. He headed for the caroche. The driver hurried down the slope to help Trystan. As he came closer, Trystan could see the angular features of Brother Bren. Trystan set Dane on his feet with a grunt, coming up under his shoulder to support him while Bren hooked Dane's other arm around his neck. Together they half dragged, half carried the luthier to the carriage and wrestled him inside, where Tabor waited. Trystan caught sight of Gint, dressed as a footman. The boy winked at Trystan and disappeared behind the carriage. Trystan shook his head, climbed in, and helped Tabor settle Dane.

The door swung again. Bell and Jax clambered inside. Bren leaned in at the door. "I'm going to take the main route to Siarad," he said, briefly. He closed the door as Bell fussed with Dane. Soon the carriage was moving.

"Conclave carriage?" asked Trystan, raising an eyebrow.

"They were most generous," said Tabor, with a broad grin. "Especially for Cantor Bren and Cantor Burtyn." He gestured to his own rich robes and chuckled. "We've given them strict orders to look in the wrong direction for their convicts. Zonah had a frank discussion with the trees. Did you know the chymaera talk to trees? They do."

Tabor's droll expression sobered as he studied Dane, his brow knitting in worry. "What happened?"

"Shadowkin. They swarmed Sara. Dane rushed to save her, singing. She disappeared, but he..." Trystan gestured to the bandages. "I did what I could, but my blade is nearly gone. If we meet another swarm, we shall not stand."

"They won't attack this carriage," said Tabor absently as he inspected the bandages. "We'll have safe passage."

Dane's breathing was shallow, his face pale. A light sheen covered his brow. Trystan touched the back of his hand to Dane's forehead. Clammy.

"Is there anything you can do?" asked Bell.

"Keep him comfortable and take him to the Caprices, milady," said Tabor. "They have craft beyond our ken. We can use the Song, but our supply of tunebells is running low. We will only have a few minutes to play."

"Do it," said Bell. "Whatever we can do, we must." She nudged Trystan's lute toward him.

Tabor nodded and drew forth a small flute from his surcoat. Trystan wrestled his lute from its case. Trystan closed his eyes and slowed his breath, listening to his inner man. He inhaled the Essence of tunebell. The pungent odor filled the carriage when Tabor crushed it, and suddenly, the Song roared in Trystan's mind. His fingers responded, playing a melody Trystan did not know, but heard clearly in his heart.

Trystan played and the music swelled, Tabor's flute playing descant. It was the Song. A Song of peace, of joy, of light. It covered all of them like a blanket, renewing their strength and loosening the tight knot of worry that clenched Trystan's heart. He breathed easier, leaning into the music, and closed his eyes. He saw a figure, made of light. The figure gestured as if bestowing a blessing. It faded in a sparkling cascade.

Trystan opened his eyes. Dane's skin had knit together. Where before there had been bone or exposed sinew, there was now a thin layer of skin, bright pink and fresh. He was breathing easier and color had returned to his face. Trystan looked at Tabor, who nodded. The Song faded, and they let the melody end as one.

"Will he wake?" Bell whispered. Trystan smiled and nodded with more confidence than he felt.

"I saw...something. A person made of light. I think he will wake, milady."

Bell's eyes widened. She nodded and stared out the window. Trystan fervently hoped he was right. He, too, stared out the window. The darkness beyond held no answers.

"Storm King, keep us safe. Keep Dane safe," she whispered.

Sara fumbled with her key and flashlight. Her hands shook. Only the side entrance to the Tank was accessible after hours. The plants all needed at least six hours of darkness. Late night work was generally discouraged. The overhead fluorescents would draw unwanted questions if she turned them on. Her breath steamed in the cold. She tucked the flashlight under her arm and managed to insert the door key, holding her breath as it turned.

"Sorry, I never come here this late," she said. Dane shimmered next to her, his face painted with concern.

"It will be fine. We should have the place to ourselves. But I need to keep the lights off. Let's go."

Dane nodded and motioned for her to proceed.

Sara hefted the heavy door open and slipped inside, holding it for Dane. Earthy scents reached out and covered her like a blanket as soon as they entered, mixing with the perfume of the blooms. The vast greenhouse yawned, pitch black but for diffused starlight that trickled through the panels above. Light-blocking shades covered the walls. A utility light on the far side of the chamber cast a feeble glow above the flowers. Sara flipped on her flashlight. She pulled out her phone, checking the time. Three a.m. The early crew would come in at six. Hopefully none of them would notice a few missing goldenrod.

Quickly, she skirted the edge of the chamber, getting her bearings. This pod held flowers, but the goldenrod were in an isolation compartment in one of the adjacent greenhouses. She gestured to the connecting door with her flashlight, outlining it with the beam. "This way."

"Lead on," said Dane.

Sara stopped, staring at him. "I heard you! You almost look solid."

He grinned at her, childlike with delight. "The flowers," he said. "They have Virtue."

"Heck yeah, they do. Well, this makes things easier."

"There are many golden flowers here?"

Sara nodded. "Tons, trust me. It's okay."

Dane looked at her, mystified.

Sara chuckled. "That means everything will be well. Okay means good."

"Okay," said Dane, with a solemn expression.

Sara laughed again. She punched his arm. "You know what? You're all right. Okay. Let's go, wizboy, before I decide to keep you."

They made their way through the next building and were halfway through the third pod when the next connecting door burst open, and Chantal Goddard spilled into the pod, laughing. Scott Black followed, mock-chasing her. Sara stopped, frozen in place. She hated herself for reacting, even as the sight of him made her pulse race.

Maybe if she just stood still enough, they wouldn't notice her.

She crossed her arms, scowling. Chantal looked up and spotted Sara. Her smile morphed into a look of pure malicious satisfaction. A smirk. Sara itched to wipe it off her face.

Chantal turned suddenly and fell into Scott's arms, pulling him close. "I thought you said we'd be alone, baby," she cooed. Her words slurred enough for Sara to get the picture. She was drunk. Scott looked from Chantal to Sara, to Dane, who was dressed like someone from a Renaissance Faire. His homespun linen shirt, breeches, and leather boots were definitely not frat boy garb. *Huzzah.*

Scott's smile faded, and his eyes darkened. He drew himself up to his full height and squared his shoulders, setting Chantal aside as if discarding her. He took a few steps toward them, glowering and ignoring Chantal's protests.

Sara almost felt sorry for Chantal. Humiliation flashed across the girl's face before it settled into an icy mask.

"That's the jerk," hissed Sara, drawing closer to Dane as if to protect him. "He can see you. I'll handle this."

"You're here late, ace," said Scott. He kept his eyes on Dane, measuring him. Sara forced a cool smile. She was suddenly acutely aware of Dane's scars and shaved head. But he looked much better. The bruises might have even faded.

"My, but you have an impressive, foolish air," Sara said, in a Southern drawl that dripped like molasses. She loved her movie quotes. "Actually, I'm up really early. Hans here doesn't speak English well. Exchange student. I was giving him a Tank tour."

She was babbling again.

Scott's eyes narrowed. Chantal drew up next to him and slid an arm around his waist. "At three a.m.?"

"Well it was this...or bring him in during work hours. This is more fun." Sara smiled and went on the offensive. "What's your excuse?"

As if it isn't obvious, you pathetic sickening man-whore. "None of yooour business," slurred Chantal. "Let's gooo, Scott. Let the losers play with flowers. We got the we..." Scott cut Chantal off, turning her toward him roughly with a sharp look.

He probably gets all the girls drinking before he...wait. Not drinking. We...weed? Had he hidden marijuana here, with the hemp? No one would be that much of an idiot. Sara almost felt sorry for Chantal.

Dane ignored them. He bowed gallantly, offering his arm to Sara like a blessing. "Milady, I am most anxious to view the golden blooms you spoke of."

Sara smiled up into Dane's eyes and curled her arm under his. It was not really solid, but she could feel something there. Enough to fool Scott and Chantal. At that moment, she was just fervently grateful, however it had happened, the tall wizard was with her. And he didn't want more than friendship. She could trust him. Somehow, he made *her* feel more solid. Sara grinned at the irony. This must be what it was like to have a big brother.

Together, they left the greenhouse. The sounds of Chantal's shrill fury with Scott faded as they passed through the door.

Sara's flashlight beam bounced merrily through aisles of plantings. The goldenrod compartment was at one end of the cavernous space. She yanked open the glass door. Behind her, Dane made a strangled sound. The edges of his form shimmered.

"I feel...I feel strange," he said.

"Let's get what we came for and get out of here," said Sara. She pressed her lips together, worried. Hopefully they weren't too late. She went to the first row of goldenrod and carefully plucked three blooms and waved them under Dane's nose.

One moment they were hurtling through the darkness, the carriage rumbling under their feet. Bell sang softly under her breath, a wordless tune, stroking Dane's forehead. The next moment, Dane was gone. Bell gasped and sat up.

"Trystan!"

She yanked at Trystan's sleeve, pointing at the empty seat.

Trystan jumped, startled awake.

"Dane vanished. He was here...I...I..." Bell's eyes filled with tears. "What happened?"

Trystan shook his head and leaned over, shaking Tabor's knee. The baron slept, head back, snoring lustily. "Tabor. Wake up."

"Hmm?" Tabor's eyes opened, and he sat up, instantly alert. He took in Bell and the seat where Dane should have been. "Where is Dane?"

"He just disappeared," said Bell.

Tabor's eyes narrowed. "The man is dewin. He was attacked by Shadowkin, but...he was also trying to save one of the fae. Sara. She vanished. He became unconscious. Those are the facts in hand. Now he has vanished?" He tapped his nose. "What does that tell you? Think."

Jax cleared his throat. The little gnome perched next to Tabor. He gingerly climbed down to sit beside Bell, holding her hand in his. "He's not dead, love."

"How can you be sure?" Bell asked. Her breath caught. "Where is he?"

Jax shook his fist. "If Dane were dead, his body would be here, not vanished. No, this is fae business, mark my words. Sara must have done something. She's trying to help. Trystan saw a figure made of light. Hold on to that."

Bell nodded. She pulled her cloak and hood tight about her, burrowing into them like a child hiding under the covers.

The carriage rumbled on.

Golden light slipped from the flowers. It enveloped Dane, emanating from the blooms and encompassing his form. He shimmered as he had when she had first seen him in her bedroom. As the light surrounded him, he solidified. This time, he was truly solid. No wavy gaseous edges. No transparency at all. Bandages wrapped him, rough strips of linen that looked relatively clean. Sara reached out and touched his shoulder. Her fingers met the cloth of his tunic, rough homespun.

"I've been grounded here," Dane said.

He thrust his arms out, examining the bandages with a grimace.

"Are you well enough to go on?" Sara asked. Now that he was fully here, she could see the extent of his injuries. His arms and hands had taken most of the damage. She glimpsed raw pink flesh as he partially unwrapped one. The places that received healing. She was sure of it. It must have been much, much worse at one point.

Dane smiled. "Trystan must have healed me. I will still need to have care, but it is enough, for now."

"Okay, because the next stop is the last one."

"The House of the Sign," said Dane. "You said there is one in a park?"

"Gazebo, yep. The park gazebo is too public, though. It's close to a busy street. I'd rather not risk being stopped by the authorities. So we'll have to find one that is more private." She paused, trying to think of a third option. Any other option. Finally, she exhaled noisily in resignation. Best just do this. Get it over with.

"You, sir, are in for a real treat. We're going to my parent's house. With any luck, we shall avoid my mother," said Sara.

Siles cursed, facing the pool. The scenes playing on the surface of these waters told a dangerous tale. The luthier and the bard, together. The Song destroying his servants. Worst of all, the fae and the sacrifice Danethor had made to save her. The few Shadowkin left to him would not be enough.

This was the beginning of a Harmony Bond, something no cantor could ever hope to achieve. He knew where it would end. With a new majister, and it wasn't him. He must stop this, or all his work would be set back centuries. The curse would be broken. The Majisterium would return. He couldn't enter the city until the lightning struck. But when it did...

Siles stalked inside and rang a bell. An acolyte appeared in the doorway. "Bring me children. Ten should do."

Siles found a tunebell, cut his finger and allowed his blood to drip onto it. He lifted the blossom, sang a line, and watched as it burst into flame. He Canted softly, insistently, letting his words rise into the darkness. Acolytes led ten small children into the courtyard. Each was chained, silent. Siles waved the acolytes away.

He passed up and down the row of children, waving his tunebell over them. They did not respond. Each stared sightlessly, their stupor complete. Street urchins, some village waifs, taken during purification rites, these were fed, clothed, and cared for. But their minds had been overwhelmed long ago, all reason and will destroyed.

Cattle. They did not even cry out as they died, one by one. As their innocent little souls poured from them, Siles kissed them on the mouth, inhaling their last breaths. They fueled his black song. The spell drifted over their blood, making it bubble on the tiles. Siles waved the tunebell and danced, feeding on their anguish.

The blood transformed, becoming shadows. The shadows rose from the ground and pooled. The small bodies lay discarded as the shadows multiplied. Siles sang, his face streaked with blood. As the last child fell, he cut another finger and allowed his blood to fall on another blossom. He set it aflame, speaking the last black word. "Feed."

He gestured to the corpses. Some still breathed. They screamed as the newly formed shadowkin descended.

Hours later, a clattering of jackdaws filled the sky. They flew swiftly toward Siarad.

43

Dane swayed, but steadied himself. "Your mother...she..."

"She's nine kinds of meddlesome, and...she's a doctor. A healer. If I show up in her backyard with a man who needs to be in the hospital in the wee hours of the morning to perform an arcane ritual? Let's just say both of us will be in trouble. A lot of trouble. But she should still be with my sister, both of them out of town. I just don't know when she'll be back."

They retraced their steps, walking slowly. "A healer might be welcome," Dane said.

Sara looked him up and down, assessing. Her brow furrowed. "Lean on me," she said. "We'll get you home."

Dane accepted her offer, draping one arm about her shoulders. "Sorry."

Sara shook her head. "Not a problem. You'll be back where you belong soon."

"You'll go with me," said Dane. "The rite begins here, but ends there. You must be prepared."

Sara grunted as his full weight settled on her for a moment. Dane recovered, but Sara chewed her lip, worrying. How would she return home? She said nothing. One problem at a time. If she could get there, she could get back.

They made their way through the other greenhouses, not seeing further sign of Scott and Chantal. As they lumbered together to her car, Sara was acutely aware of Dane's shallow breathing. Sara glanced at him. His genial face held a placid expression, but Sara noticed a tightness around his eyes. He needed a doctor. She was of half a mind to take him to the emergency room.

"We can go to a hospital," Sara said. She opened the passenger door. "You could get your wounds looked at."

Dane frowned and shook his head. "The rite will send us to the Caprices. They will help me. We should continue. All will be well."

Sara pressed her lips together, silently disagreeing as she walked around the car. She knew better than to argue. Dane wasn't going to cooperate with any delay. Honestly, she couldn't blame him. Being in a strange world was unnerving, even if you just thought you were dreaming. *He knows he isn't.*

She dropped the goldenrod in the backseat, slid behind the wheel, and changed the subject. "When we get to my hou...my parents' house, we'll go around back. The gazebo...the House of the Sign...is in the backyard. We've got the arrowhead, but we'll need a striker. A piece of steel. I've got a pocketknife in the glove box. It should work. So what's the rest? We burn the goldenrod, then what?"

Dane paused for a long moment. "Sara, I must petition the Storm King himself. He alone can form our bond."

"Cool. I think meeting him will be awesome," Sara said.

"No, you don't understand. We'll only see lightning if he answers."

Sara tilted her head. She could feel her eyes narrowing. "Lightning?"

"Yes, if the Storm King hears our petition, lightning will answer us. It will transport us to Siarad."

"We'll be struck by lightning?" Sara's voice rose. "You sorta forgot to mention that part!"

"I am explaining now," said Dane. "You do not have to go on. We can try this...hospital. But without the Song, I will not last."

"What do you mean?"

"I am dewin. I need the Song to live like a fish needs water. The longer I am here, away from the Song, the more weak I will become."

"But the flowers strengthen you?"

"They do."

"Hm." Sara couldn't very well drag him into the Tank and just leave him there. He couldn't stay on earth. There was no getting around it. *But lightning? It was going to hit her? Them. Would she die here? Go to Dane's world for good? It wasn't exactly heaven.* She slowed the car and pulled into a parking lot, letting the engine idle. The radio filled the silence with soft piano music.

"I need a minute," she said. Sara looked out the window. A light rain began, tapping on the car roof. Sara focused on her breathing, looking out at the empty streets.

Sara imagined lightning. She'd been shocked before. It might not be that bad. Over quickly.

She breathed.

She looked at Dane, his arms and hands covered in bandages.

My fault. My fault. If he hadn't rushed in to save me from that swarm, would I have woken? Here? Would I have faded or just been consumed? Did it matter?

She thought about Marilla. Peter. Her work. She could just go home. Take Dane to a hospital and go home. She closed her eyes. She couldn't be a coward. The chymaera, Zonah. What was it she'd said? 'We may act a coward or live only for pleasure.' Nope. Not this time. She didn't understand why all of this was happening, but she was in it. She was going to see it through.

Sara opened her eyes and gave Dane a level look. "Okay, I'm scared to death. I don't want to be hit by lightning. It's really big on my list of bad ideas. But you risked your life for me. I know it. I'm gonna do this, and I'm gonna do it afraid. All I ask is that if I die, you gotta find a way to tell Peter the truth of what happened. I need to know he'll know."

Dane nodded, his eyes shining. "I will find a way. But you will not die, Sara. You will live. You will find your way back to Peter."

"You can't be sure. But all of this defies science, so why not?" Her lips quirked in a grin, despite herself. She leaned over and opened the glove box, pulling out a pocketknife. She handed it to Dane. "You've got the arrowhead, right? The thunderstone."

Dane held it up for her to see.

"Okay, so open the knife and use it as a striker. You know how?"

He peered at the knife then unfolded it, laying the edge against the arrowhead. "Simple enough. We do make fire at home. We also cook and bathe." Dane's tone was dry, though his face remained impassive.

Sara laughed. "Okay, wizboy. I just wanted to make sure. And what do we do if we perform this rite and nothing happens? You'll go to a hospital? Get some help?"

Dane said, "The Storm King will answer us."

"I don't mean to be a skeptic. Dane, but magic isn't exactly a thing here. I'm just covering my bases."

He looked at her blankly, waiting for her to explain.

He had no idea what bases were. "I'm trying to plan for failure."

Dane's eyes narrowed. "There is no planning for failure. The only way to fail is to quit. We will not." He leaned back in his seat, eyes ahead, as if that settled the matter. Sara turned the key in the ignition and pulled back out into traffic. She muttered under her breath.

"I guess we won't fail then."

Dane laid a hand on her arm. Sara glanced over, her eyebrows raised. Dane's expression was somber.

"Sara, you must stop trampling your blooms."

Maybe the swarm affected Dane's sanity? There was that whole dewin-can-go-bonkers issue. She rolled her eyes and said, "Dane. The plants at the tank are on platforms. I don't step on them."

Dane laughed, a good-natured chuckle. "I'm not speaking of real plants. It's an expression."

"Okay, explain."

"When you plant a garden, do you expect blooms the next day?"

Sara sniffed. "No."

"When sprouts shoot up, do you become angry? Do you complain there is no rose?"

Sara shook her head. She changed lanes, keeping her eyes on the road, but listened.

"Yet you do this with your life. You love Peter, it's plain to see. Love takes time to flower. You have made mistakes? So has he. If you forgive, you can start again. Don't give up. Give it time and light. Talk to him. The jerk? He was a worm-faced dissonant lackwit with a harpy companion. But you saw your mistake. You want to right it. You are growing. The final fruit, the outcome, will be good.

"The Storm King may not answer us in the way we wish. But he is no liar. Do not step on the blooms in your life or despair if you do not have what you wish. Leave room for sprouts to grow. Leave room for the Storm King's aid.

"I am afraid I will not be enough. I have never been very good with the Song. I could not save my parents. But I have been growing, getting better. I cast a glamour. I grounded you. I have to trust Him, trust I will grow and *try*."

Sara didn't respond right away. She mulled it over. "The problem is, my head and my heart don't match. I know Peter is good for me, he's everything I want, really. I want to love him. Part of me does love him. But the person who makes my blood sing is the dissonant lackwit. I run away from Peter and am drawn to Scott. Like a magnet. Why? I hate myself for it."

Dane shook his head. "To the starving, what is bitter tastes sweet. You mistake sparks for seeds. Sparks consume. Seeds stir, grow, and live."

Sara sighed. "Maybe. Anyhow, thanks. I'm glad you're here."

"I'm glad too. The proverb isn't mine, though."

"No?"

Dane shook his head. "Pezzik. my deema. It's a gnome proverb. a good one."

"You miss her?"

"More every day."

Sara pulled into the daycare down the street. Its parking lot was empty. As she leaned into the back seat to pick up the discarded goldenrod, she said, "The house is just up the road. I don't want to wake my mother. She shouldn't be home, but I'm not taking any chances. We walk from here."

Together they headed for the road, walking on the narrow shoulder until they reached the driveway. "Okay, the gazebo is around back. Just stay quiet."

Sara checked her phone. 4:32 flashed from the display. "Here goes nothing," she muttered. Sara squared her shoulders and turned down the driveway. It wound up the hill, making a circle in front of the two-story brick home. She slipped around the side of the house to the gate, opening it silently. She held a finger to her lips and waited for Dane to pass through before stepping into the manicured backyard. The walkway was fieldstone and led to the patio, but beyond, near the back of the lot, a white gazebo stood, dripping gingerbread details. Flower beds surrounded it, bare now but for dark periwinkle and rosebush skeletons. Sara smiled when she saw the fairy lights dangling from the cupola. They lined the inside of the gazebo. *Our playhouse.* Her eyes misted suddenly, remembering happy childhood days with Marilla. She blinked them back.

Focus. It's time to call down lightning and return to an alternate universe.

The portable firepit in the center of the structure was clean. Sara rifled through the deck box and found plastic baggies full of dryer lint, like gray cotton candy. "Dad's favorite kindling," she said, holding it up. She knelt and made a nest in the firepit, laying the goldenrod on top.

Dane watched, eyes twinkling. "You remind me of a bird."

"Ha ha, tweet, tweet," she said with a grin. "You ready to do this?"

Dane's smile faded, and his eyes shadowed. "I'm not sure I'll ever be ready."

"You're going to be great. What's the worst that can happen?"

"Uh…" said Dane. He shrugged. "You're right. Stand opposite me. Once I start, just follow my lead. Can you do that?"

Sara nodded, gulping. Her hands felt dry. Itchy. She fidgeted.

Dane laid the knife on the edge of the firepit. He held the arrowhead up over his head with both hands and tilted his head back.

Dane focused on the rite, the melody he heard underneath. Dread weighed heavily in the pit of his stomach. One false move, one wrong note, this could go badly. Very badly.

He looked at Sara, her face lit by the fire. She was so brave. Doing it afraid. If she could, he could. He rejected the dread.

The words poured forth.

Lord of All, we ask for rescue.
As you were stricken for us, I strike this stone.
Lord of All, we ask for solace.
As you were stricken for us, I strike this stone.
Lord of All, we ask for harmony.
As you were stricken for us, I strike this stone.
Lord of All, we ask for your bond.
As you were stricken for us, I strike this stone.
Lord of All, we seek transformation.
As you were stricken for us, I strike this stone.
We trust in you. Hear us now.

Dane looked at Sara. He pleaded with her in his heart, unable to stop and instruct her. *Join me.*

"Hear us now," she repeated.

He knelt and struck the flint with the knife. Small sparks scattered to the kindling below. Thoughts rose, unbidden. *Maybe I'm not strong enough to do this? Only a handful have done it, and they were…* Dane stopped and closed his eyes. He breathed. No. It was not his strength he trusted. He trusted the Song.

"Knit us together. Bind us in love. Forge us in mercy. Shape us in truth. Make of us tools for your hands. Wield us for your purpose!"

Nothing happened. Dane blinked.

The Essences Pezzik sent. *Of course.* Dane pulled the small bottle from the pouch at his belt and unstoppered it. A delicious aroma wafted over the flowers. He struck the stone again. Sparks dropped onto the kindling, this time catching. Small flames licked the tinder.

"Use us for your purpose," Sara repeated.

"Make us One for your glory!"

Sara burned. Blue flames licked the flowers, sending tendrils of smoke into the dawn light. But it was Sara's arms, hands, her face, absorbing heat. In the firepit, smoke gathered, forming shapes. Butterflies? A bird warbled. The sky lightened, chasing long shadows.

Through the rails of the gazebo, Sara saw her father's tall form open the back door. He stood on the deck, watching. Sara gasped.

Dane stuck the flint another blow. A bright light, the brightest she had ever known seared her. Roaring. Bells chiming. Dane. Ozone. Her fingers curled around Dane's arm automatically.

She tumbled with him, in space, surrounded by stars.

The stars were singing, a song without words. Sara's heart leapt in her throat. She choked.

The stars went black.

44

Dane tumbled with Sara, floating in the impossible deep, before coming to rest on a wide platform. It hung, unmoving, overlooking the galaxy. Sara crumpled to the floor of the platform, lifeless. Dane checked her, choking down panic. She wasn't breathing. *Was he breathing? Did he miss something, fail somehow? Would she live?*

The platform shifted. One moment they were in a fairly open region, and the next, they were hanging in front of a star. It filled Dane's vision, huge and too bright. He threw up his arm to protect his eyes, wondering why felt no heat. They shifted again before a cry could escape his lips. This time, they stopped in front of a moon. The platform began to descend gently.

The platform came to rest on the surface of the moon. Unlike the earth's moon, which Dane had glimpsed the night before, this moon sparkled. No, it dazzled. Huge crystals jutted into the air, rising from a sparkling blanket. They covered the landscape like a sea of diamonds. This was his moon. The Storm King's eye.

The platform moved, skimming over the surface. It maneuvered around a set of large crystals and dropped into a fissure, diving deep. The descent continued, deep into the core of the moon. Dane held Sara and huddled, crouching. He covered his face with one hand, willing himself not to throw up. "Storm King, help me," he whispered, desperate. Lightning struck her. Perhaps she was not strong enough. She was so afraid and so brave. He should never have tried this.

Dane risked opening his eyes as the platform slowed and shuddered to a stop. Starlight penetrated into the fissure high above them, revealing sheer cliff walls. A cavern stretched before them, illuminated by a soft glow. Strange moss covered the stones and walls. It emitted a greenish glow. A stream burbled on one side of the cave.

In the center of the stream, on a small island, a tall being made of lightning waited.

Come.

Dane gently laid Sara on the platform. Her face was pale in the unearthly glow. He stood and slowly faced the Storm King. His heart thumped in his chest. His voice was small in his own ears. "She breathes not, Master. Is she dead?"

The Storm King's expression softened with compassion. "What is the true question of your heart, Dane?"

Dane gulped. *He knows me.* The question came out in a rush. "Did I kill her?"

"Can you decide who lives and dies, Danethor Thomas Whitley? Have you the power of unmaking? Or even the power of death? You have not failed Me. When you fall, I am not so small I cannot lift you or even carry you. She lives. You, too, shall live. Let go of your fear."

You have not failed Me. The words shimmered, hanging in the air, borne by their own light. He wasn't just speaking of Sara. In that instant the weight lifted. Tears pricked his eyes and streamed down his face.

The Storm King approached the platform and held his hand over Sara, making a fist. Light emanated from him, flowing over her still form. A few drops of glowing liquid fell from his hand and slid down her temple. It left behind a trail of red, staining her cheek before it faded, like water seeping into sand. His blood.

The Storm King pointed at Sara. "Rise, beloved."

Sara's eyes opened. She gasped and sat upright.

Sara blinked and looked around in wonder. "I'm alive. It worked!"

They were in the bottom of a tall, round tower on a marble floor, alone. The edges of a silvered octagon inlay and delicate patterns of silver and copper reflected sunlight, drifting down from above. A spiral staircase wound up the sides of the round chamber, enclosed by a wall with a carved handrail. Stone arches topped the railing. No roof enclosed the structure. Just a disc of blue sky hung above them.

A floating figure drifted into the chamber.

Dane's breath caught. "It's a Caprice," he said. "We are in Siarad."

Sara noticed Dane's bandages were gone, his skin looked fresh, uncut, unscarred, unbruised.

It had worked. Dane was healed. *Holy cow. Was it over?*

Evidently not.

The hood of the Caprice's robe fell back, and Sara could see the form had no head. It was as if an invisible man were wearing robes. The Caprice herded them toward the staircase. Before they could obey, the chamber darkened. A cloud of darkness, a swarm, blotted out the sky, dropping toward them. The Caprice lifted his hand in a warding gesture. The shadow parted like water, flowing to the sides of the octagon. It roiled and pooled again, coalescing into a tall black pillar. The pillar writhed and gathered into the form of a huge black dragon. The dragon opened its mouth and spoke with a human voice, using words Sara did not understand.

The dragon's voice was as gentle as a lamb being led to slaughter. It was as patient as the grave. The dragon began advancing on them, Canting. Its eyes glowed red with an eerie whirling light.

"Get behind me," said Dane.

Sara watched the dragon. It was covered in gleaming black scales. Its sharp claws scraped the marble floor with an excruciating screech. She took a step back, not quite behind Dane, considering her options. This was no dream. She could not wake up safe in her bed.

But other things were also true. She was a stone rider. Dane stood next to her. *I am not alone.*

The dragon inhaled sharply, and a stream of fire blasted the Caprice. His robes flamed instantly, flaring, and fell to the floor in ashes. Dane paled, but held his ground. There was nowhere to run. Sara saw him close his eyes for the space of three breaths. He was listening. Dane opened his eyes and squared his shoulders, facing the dragon. His face set in a grim mask as he began a song of his own. A bright tune, it silvered the air and drowned the dragon's Cant.

Three swords appeared. They whirled, wielded by invisible hands. They danced, thrusting and slicing from different directions. The swords moved quickly, flashing. The dragon drew himself up and began Canting again. His song felt dark, a wailing minor. It sent a shiver up Sara's spine.

The swords shattered.

But the dragon was bleeding. Black ooze shimmered on its underbelly.

"Dane, don't back off. You've got this. You can do it," shouted Sara. She looked at the walls of the tower, at the stone. She knelt and examined the marble, and the dragon, focusing on the floor where the dragon stood, just outside the octagon. She pictured the stone becoming soft mud and softly sang a tune now playing in her mind. It was some crazy mix-tape track Jane had made her listen to months ago. It had to be the Song. She'd only heard this once, and she knew the words?

Somehow it didn't matter. She changed the words to make them apply to the dragon.

"Sink into the Underground," she sang.

The dragon began to sink. Marble covered its feet quickly. He roared, thrashed, and dissolved once more into a cloud of darkness, reforming on the other side of the chamber.

Why didn't he attack them as a swarm?

As soon as the question occurred to her, she knew. As if a voice had answered, she knew. The octagon. The swarm couldn't pass the silvered pattern. The dragon could, but the swarm could not. If she could trap it inside the octagon, he would not be able to dissolve and reform.

"Stay inside the Sign!" yelled Sara. She took a deep breath and ran toward the dragon. It stepped forward to meet her, to blast her into oblivion with fire.

It stepped into the octagon.

She sang again, picturing the marble below the dragon's feet covered and bound. "Sink into the Underground."

Once again the dragon's feet sank. This time, it sank inside the Sign. Sara saw the dragon's eyes widen as it kept sinking. In a panic, it spouted flame, scorching the stone walls before turning on her.

But Dane was there, singing. His voice lifted above the roaring flame, a tuneless song of peace and hope and life and joy. Sara nearly wept to hear it. The music enveloped them both and gave her peace. It was the Song. The true Song.

The dragon's flame dissipated harmlessly as if it had struck a wall.

Dane advanced, still singing.

The dragon sang a counter-melody, full of screeches and popping. Dane kept singing. As he drew closer to the dragon, it burst into flame. The dragon howled. Held as it was by the Sign, it could do nothing to save itself. It flapped enormous wings, sending gusts throughout the chamber. Dane knelt, buffeted, but kept singing. Sara watched, uncertain. The dragon inhaled again ready to scorch Dane.

NO!

Sara's heart nearly stopped. She was shaking, angry and impotent.

A melody began to play in Sara's heart. Sara opened her mouth and joined Dane, singing the tune in her mind. She didn't comprehend the words, but she sang them with all her strength. Her voice complemented Dane's baritone, soaring above it. Their song wove together in perfect harmony.

Flames shot up from the dragon's hide and swept through his form in a rush, consuming him.

When only ashes hung in the air, Dane stopped. He turned around, a huge smile on his face. "That was amazing. Unbelievable. We did it."

"You were awesome," said Sara. "Really, I think you saved my life."

From the stairwell, another Caprice emerged, hovering toward them. It gestured urgently, motioning toward the stairs.

"Let's do this," said Dane.

Sara followed him, her heart still racing from the excitement of the battle. As Dane climbed the steps and disappeared around the spiral, the Caprice floated in front of Sara, blocking her path forward. One empty sleeve of its robe raised in front of her. Its silent message was clear.

Sara's mouth twisted, and she pushed at the sleeve to move it out of her way. If this was the end of their bonding rite, she should be with Dane.

The Caprice shook its headless head.

"So I stay here?"

The Caprice shook its head again. It drew back, allowing her to climb the steps. She couldn't see Dane.

Sara took the stairs two at a time. In the distance, a bell chimed.

45

The moment Dane stepped on the stairs, he could hear a joyous melody surging in his heart. He stopped on the step to listen to it. The Song dwindled. It surged again as he took another step upward.

"I guess they want me to get up these stairs," he muttered. He glanced back, to see if Sara had followed. The Caprice was blocking her path forward. The music grew louder, more strident.

He had to go on alone.

He continued and came upon a landing. The carved figure of a huge man sat on a golden throne, swathed in carved ermine, a circlet upon his brow. All unnecessary. His expression alone shone with nobility. His left side was made from white marble, the other side, obsidian. A book lay open on a small table at his right hand.

Dane picked it up and began to read aloud.
"It was given to the Elders, the cyntae, first of the Creator's children, to join him in His work. Eight sang. The greatest was Domini the Wise."

The words disappeared as Dane spoke, leaving the page blank. Dane inspected the figure. "Domini?"

A chime answered him. The statue of Domini shimmered. It spoke to him in a voice as cold and terrible as a blizzard.

"Danethor Thomas Whitley. Dewin, you have laid down your life for another. You have asked for an eternal bond. You have spoken with the Storm King and yielded. You have stood against darkness. You have chosen to become a majister in these, the Last Days. Do you accept the call?"

Dane went to one knee before the cyntae. "I accept, milord."

"Arise. You will meet six more before you take up the staff."

Dane stood. The statue fell silent, once more lifeless.

Dane continued up the stairs.

Sara was breathing heavily by the time she came upon a landing.

A small table stood in the middle of the landing. A book lay open upon it. She picked it up and read aloud.

William and Catherine Moore are proud to announce the birth of twin girls, Sara Elizabeth and Marilla Jette...

As she read the words on the page, images surrounded her, replaying her past. She was in the vision, but an unseen observer. A witness. Her father held her in his arms and whispered in her ear how much he loved her. She blinked back tears. He never told her he loved her growing up. He always was too busy.

Everything shifted, blurring. Her father practiced a song, a composition of his own, scribbled on staff paper. Sara stood behind him, watching. At the top of the page, in his bold script, the title was "For My Girls." The music soared through his study, liquid joy.

She'd never heard that song before.

Shift.

Sara saw her mother holding her, her father holding Marilla, rocking gently together in matching rocking chairs. "Trade!" said Dad, rising. Carefully they exchanged babies and settled back down in the chairs.

Shift.

She saw her mother and father waking up, feeding twin babies. Up every four hours. The images flashed by rapidly.

Diapers, late nights, chaos. Toddlers, potty training. Toys, books, laughter.

Bills piling up. Her mother's face, ashen as she returned to work. Her mother's face drawn with fatigue, coming home late. Her father, home with them. His cello rested on its stand, unused.

Shift.

Dad argued with Mom, their bedroom door closed while she and Marilla slept in toddler beds. He wanted to spend time with Mom, and she had to work.

Shift.

Her father's face, forlorn, as he put them on a yellow bus for the first day of school. Sara watched him retreat to his study. He began to play his cello, this time, a dirge.

She'd thought those were happy days, though...
She had never considered her parents just as people. They were her parents.

A tear rolled down her father's cheek. It broke her heart.

So young. Dad was happy taking care of them. But he had less and less time to play his own music. Mom supported them on her salary as a doctor, but was never home. The music echoed. So lonely. She thought he was happy to have time to play again. He wasn't.

He missed us.

He missed Mom.

It was the root of his betrayal. His leaving them. His yelling? *Was Dad...only selfish? Or was he hurting, too?*

The room faded. Only the pages of the open book lay before her, now empty. Rain fell, christening her. Sara looked up. The sky was cloudy. It was sprinkling, water dripping onto her forehead through the open roof. Sara set the book on the table and climbed the steps.

A bell chimed as she ascended.

Dane arrived on the next platform to find a large, round fountain. On a table next to the fountain lay a book. He picked it up, eager to read it.

Renato, Second of the Cyntae, reigned over many waters. Her heart ever pure, she sensed Doran's anger, and sought to bring him peace.

The words disappeared from the page as he read.

He set the book on the table and a bell chimed. The note this time was D. Was the last one a C? Might have been. Would the ritual contain a scale? Did that matter?

The thought vanished as waters rose from the fountain, spraying around him until he was surrounded by a perfect sphere of liquid, turning and flowing. Enclosed in this ball of water entirely, he floated above the ground. It flowed under his feet. He watched, mesmerized, as the sphere separated and another, much smaller, sphere circled before him, floating like a bubble. A face made of water shimmered within. The voice that spoke to him had something in it of a rushing stream

"Danethor Thomas Whitley, you must seek the truth of the Lorica, find its refrains hidden beyond sight. You will need a pure heart. Will you be cleansed?"

Fear gripped Dane. It fell on him, as heavy as a curse, a black layer of despair and shame. It rose up, threatening to strangle him. He choked. He saw in his mind's eye long, cold nights sleeping on the ground. He saw himself, in the grip of Dissonance. Towns burning, people dead, their bodies splayed, disjointed.

If I'm not cleansed now, I cause this.

Dane bowed to Renato, fighting his rising tide of fear. "I accept," he gasped.

The waters crashed over him as the sphere collapsed, leaving him wet and sputtering.

All of his fatigue, his fears, and his worries washed away in that instant.

He felt stronger. Lighter.

He shook his head in wonder and turned, running to the next step.

Sara reached the second platform and found another book on top of a podium. She stood behind it and read aloud slowly, feeling the weight of the words.

Name your sorrow.

Her sorrow.

In her mind, she saw Marilla, that night.

Marilla's face, a mask of pain, tears streaming down her cheeks.

Marilla ran at Rick, beating his chest.

Marilla turned and spat on the girl Rick had been kissing. The girl Marilla trusted above all others. Someone she loved.

The girl who had broken Marilla's heart.

Marilla spit on Sara, grabbed her keys, and ran out the door, into the darkness.

She didn't return.

Tears flowed like rain down Sara's face. She never even let herself think of this memory; it was too painful. She had spoken of it to no one, not even Dr. Carol. She felt her shame wash over her, unsuppressed, and could not meet it. Sara blinked through tears as family and friends coalesced before her. Marilla, her parents, Peter, Jane, Dr. Carol, Professor Polly. All of her classmates stood behind them, a huge jury. They crowded the landing, now a stage. She stood behind the podium, and they waited for her to speak.

Sara looked at the book again. The words on the page remained, adamant. *Name your sorrow.*

Paralysis gripped her. Sara's thoughts moved sluggishly, her face growing numb.

They all waited, silent. Looking at her.

I can't do this.

Unbidden, Dane filled her vision. He was running to save her, blue eyes blazing as he sang at a flesh-eating swarm.

Sara thought of her father, playing a dirge, lonely. *Sorrowfish.* She saw herself. Her fear she was too much. Her fear Marilla was better, and she didn't count. Her *envy.* She saw herself wondering what it would be like to *be* Marilla, to have everyone love you. Rick's mouth on hers.

Sorrowfish. Not just selfish.

Sara held onto the idea, gulped, and let it all out in a rush.

"I betrayed my twin sister, Marilla. I kissed Rick. I was full of envy. I was stupid. Jealous. Afraid. I broke her heart. Sorrowfish. I hurt you, pushed you away. All of you. I sabotaged my work. It's my fault Marilla is in a coma. It's all my fault," she said.

Tears streamed down her face. "I don't deserve you, any of you. Please, forgive me."

The people in front of her looked shocked, sad, hurt. Sympathetic.

None of them looked hateful. They shimmered, fading one by one.

Only Marilla remained.

Marilla walked over to Sara, took her hands, and drew her out from behind the podium. Sara looked into Marilla's eyes, mirrors of her own, pleading. She found compassion there.

"I understand…I do. I was always jealous of *you.*

"I've had a long time to think. Every day, lying in that bed. And I've had to forgive myself. You. Rick.

"It was terrible and a betrayal on your part. But I was afraid of you, too, Sara. Like you were of me. I was a total mess.

"I'm the one who chose to swerve in front of that truck. I'm the one who made a choice to die. It's not your fault.

"I heard when you came and talked to me. Every time. I saw you weeping. You stood by me. I know, Sara. I know you love me.

"I forgive you."

Sara dropped to the floor and curled up in a ball, overwhelmed as the weight lifted, the horrible weight of shame and grief. She shuddered, sobbing. Marilla leaned down and embraced her. "I'm here," she said. "But...I have to go now. Just remember, I forgive you. I love you, Sara."

Sara lifted her head, calling after her sister. "Love you, Rill!"

A bell chimed.

With a radiant smile, Marilla ascended the stairs. Sara rose to follow, still shaking.

Dane took the steps quickly, coming upon the third platform. This one was brightly lit, though Dane could not see the source. A garden filled the platform. Dane searched for a book and found it nesting in the crook of a sapling, pages open. Dane breathed in the scents of tunebells and delphiniums.

He retrieved the book and read.

Miah was beloved and tended the flowers. Her song gave strength and Virtue. It was she who bound Doran beneath the ground.

A melody burst forth, the Song erupting and filling the room. The sapling flowered. A face appeared above it, strong as an oak tree. Miah's voice held the sound of boughs sighing in the wind.

"Danethor Thomas Whitley. Dewin. The refrains have been hidden within the earth, sky, air, and water. One you carry. Seek seven more. This food I give you for knowledge."

The flowers on the tree turned to fruit. Dane lay the book in her boughs and plucked the fruit. As he ate, the garden disappeared, replaced by a new scene.

A wiry man with a big nose and long dark hair crafted boxes in the shapes of octagons. He placed scrolls inside. A teenaged boy assisted the crafter.

Images flashed before Dane so quickly, he could hardly retain them.

The boy and the man spoke to a large dragon. A lakeside palace. A Fellishman spoke earnestly, his dark features sharp against the sunset. Pink light bathed the high moors and a mirrorlike lake. Walking together into a dwarvish mountain. On a ship at sea, diving to meet tiny merfolk. Slogging through a swamp, surrounded by fluted columns, hanging moss, and olive-colored men wearing gossamer veils. Kneeling before a winged lion made of fire.

The old man wept before a winged unicorn, alone.

As the images faded, the garden vanished, leaving only a bare stone room and the moonlight filtering down from above.

"Remember," said Miah, her voice resonating throughout the chamber.

A bell chimed.

Sara climbed, half blinded. She couldn't stop crying. Marilla had forgiven her, but she felt weak and drained. Shaky. Raw. She stumbled onto the next platform and saw a book sitting on a normal dining room table and chairs. The table was a perfect replica of one she'd eaten at as a child. She sat down at the table and pulled the book to her, reading only one phrase.

In remembrance.

A plate appeared before her, filled with her favorite meal. It smelled wonderful. Her father used to make it. Beef Bourguignon, pronounced with a horrific French accent in imitation of Julia Childs. Dad would serve a warm red merlot and make flatbread. Everyone would take turns saying silly things in equally terrible accents. Then Dad would play the cello for them, "La Vie en Rose."

Sara smiled at the vivid memories and picked up a wine glass. Sara toasted her family and dug into the meal. It was as good as she remembered. She sopped up the sauce with the bread and sipped the wine. Church bells sounded in the distance, from St. Francis down the street. Warmth spread through her.

A wave of strength enveloped Sara, like an embrace. When she was finished, she felt much better. More solid, at peace. As if broken pieces within her were knitting. She stood and looked at the book. Its words were gone.

A bell chimed.

46

On the fourth platform, Dane found the book resting on a table shaped like an arc.

He picked it up, apprehensive. He'd had quite enough of the Conclave.

Faron chronicled the days and nights, the years and the ages. He was tasked to prepare for the Last Day.

As Dane read the words, he saw worlds and stars, all their light woven together. He saw an old man, robed with a scythe, the blade shaped like an arc. The man poked a hole in the sky like tearing a tent. Suddenly, the moon appeared, its arc shining with a soft light. Dane saw a Wyrm wrapped around the World Tree, climbing.

The old man stepped forward to look at Dane, his eyes shimmering, filled with unshed tears.

"Doran wanted to usurp Domini's place. He fell. He was bound into the form you know. In his hatred for all beloved, he cursed each one, vowing their destruction. And so he became the Wyrm, unable to hear the Song.

"Speak your hatred, my son. Release it, lest you fall."

Dane nodded. He was angry with the Conclave. The anger lay simmering, under the surface, waiting for the opportunity to flare. He had not given it attention.

Snakes wrapped around his legs, climbing. Dane's emotions surged. He felt the hatred, luring him. It beckoned for him to give in, to accept it. He saw in his mind's eye Siles. The man cast a spell to kill his parents. Siles stood next to a pool and sang and Dane's parents sickened. Dane held them in his arms, watched them die. He saw Bell, drooling, unable to speak or think. She scraped the earth with broken fingernails, her eyes dull and lifeless. Dane saw himself, covered in a swarm of blackness so thick it choked him, his skin disintegrating. Agony swept through his body, a fire that could not be contained. He screamed.

He was so angry. He wanted them dead. Dane stood his ground, shaking. He grit his teeth, filled with cold fury.

The snakes coiled, undulating higher up his legs.

Storm King, help me.

Wasn't it the Storm King who had allowed all this? Didn't He have ultimate control?

The thought skewered Dane.

The snakes stopped climbing. They waited. The pain fled as suddenly as it had arrived.

The Storm King was the Creator of all things. In control. And He let it all happen. Dane closed his eyes and remembered the Storm King, his form, glowing. Made of lightning, though it was only one side of His true form.

He let it all happen.

He thought about Sara, suddenly. He saw her.

She wanted so desperately to love Peter. But she was afraid, and instead of loving Peter, she chased the lackwit. But the truth was, she did love Peter. She was just running out of fear to things she thought she could control. Someone who didn't want her was safe. Much safer than a man who would love her, ask things of her.

And if she made the lackwit love her, wouldn't it prove she was worth something?

You couldn't *force* someone to love you.

The Storm King couldn't force love either. Wouldn't.

Nadir hurt Bell. Siles killed Dane's family. Because the Storm King wouldn't force love. Nadir and Siles didn't love the Storm King or the cyntae. They loved themselves. They loved power and control, sought it.

But the Storm King was there, in all of it, fighting…through *him*. Through Dane. What had they really done but set Dane off on a quest to heal the Tree and become a majister?

The Storm King had moved to help Dane. The story was far from over. The Storm King was even now, turning events for good. Even the most horrible events.

Anger seeped from him. Dane spoke aloud. "I forgive them."

He would not seek revenge or the Conclave's harm. He would trust the Storm King.

"I choose to release this hatred."

The snakes disappeared along with Faron and the Tree.

Only the table and the book remained.

A bell chimed the next note in the scale.

Dane sat down, heavily, breathing. It was several minutes before he forced himself to rise and continue.

Sara reached the fourth platform wondering if it would be her last. The book stood on a tall pedestal along with a crystal vial filled with amber liquid.

Chesed's alabaster likeness filled the space. Sara blinked, remembering his death. She saw it again in her mind's eye. This statue had moved, beseeching. It kneeled in that position still, one hand over its heart, the other reaching out.

It was like him...and not like him.

Somehow it seemed more noble, more beautiful than she remembered. Sara reached up to nudge the book off the tall pedestal. She caught it and read, *Find your heart's inner fire.*

She stamped her foot in frustration. "I've tried to find my heart's inner fire. I have no idea what it means!"

The air next to the column rippled, and the statue of Chesed turned and spoke.

"Do you know what I am?"

Sara shook her head, surprised.

"The signet of Chesed. Daily he came to sing to the Storm King. He sang his hopes and dreams, his anger and disappointment. He Canted each of his failings without fear, with honesty, seeking to grow. He fought his own darkness daily. He never ran or neglected the work.

"His Song formed me, his signet. At the appointed time of Quickening, Chesed would have merged with me to receive his wings. He could transform and put on his true shape as a Derbyn, a gryphon. He could fly."

Sara stared at the signet. Slowly, she answered.

"I can choose. I'm like a chymaera in some way. I don't understand how, but I am. Zonah...she said...my heart's inner fire, it isn't what I think, is it? It's something I have to keep on seeking. Like Chesed, every day. I create."

Sara thought about going to work on one piece, every day, for centuries. She thought about the love and care Chesed had taken with his signet. How for so long he had worked, knowing that he possibly would never be able to quicken. But still he worked. The chymaera sang to the Storm King all his thoughts and hopes and dreams, and as he did, his signet changed.

Could she do that? For centuries?

Would she be willing to open herself fully in her studio? Not running from what was inside her, but channeling it through her to her art?

No matter what was there.

No matter what ugliness she found.

No singing would change the clay she sculpted with. She had to dig her hands in and work. She had to bring truth from clay.

But wasn't it still the same as what Chesed did? Didn't she wrestle with herself?

Could she be honest, for as long as it took to get the work right? Even when it possibly didn't matter to anyone else? Show her biggest fears? Her faults. Her hopes and dreams? Could she do it?

Not alone. She couldn't do it alone.

But what if I wasn't alone? What if the work wasn't a monologue, but a conversation? A conversation could mold her heart, much like Chesed's song molded his signet. What if the Storm King were there to help me? What if I heard Him?

Sara bowed her head. The Song roared up, engulfing her. It swelled in her mind and heart, approving. She heard it and understood. She wasn't alone. She had never been alone.

"When I work, I won't be alone," she said slowly. "The Storm King will help me. I can do this with Him."

She wouldn't ruin everything again. But if she did mess up, it wasn't a final verdict. She wouldn't be alone. The truth was, she never had been.

The signet stood and smiled as a bell chimed. He took the vial from the column where it waited and uncorked it. He poured it over her head.

"You have done well, Sara Elizabeth Moore. You shall yield your heart's inner fire to the One able to shape it, every day, and you shall fly."

Sara smelled lavender as the oil covered her. She inhaled the scent and rubbed it into her skin, but it was already gone, as if evaporated. Her body no longer ached. She felt full of energy and light. Where she had been raw and wounded, she felt completely restored and healed. At peace. She looked at Chesed's signet, incredulous. It had resumed its former posture, beseeching. In its outstretched hand was a golden horn.

Sara took the horn. A bell chimed.

Slowly, she walked around the figure, stood on tiptoe, and kissed his cheek.

Dane laughed as he reached the next platform. It held a pond filled with goldfish. A deer grazed. A pair of bluebirds sang. A bright red toad sat on a lily pad in the midst of the pond, croaking.

When Dane reached the top of the stairs, a bell chimed.

A princess sat at the edge of the pond, playing with a golden ball. She reached for the toad and kissed it. It transformed into a tall and handsome price. The prince embraced her. They stood, holding hands, staring into one another's eyes, smiling. Then they broke apart and approached Dane, together. As they did, the woodland pool disappeared, leaving only the stone room.

These were the lovers, Solimon and Lalo, fifth and sixth of the cyntae.

They bowed deeply. Lalo presented him with a book.
He took it and read aloud, "Solimon and Lalo love all living things, the fish of the sea, the beasts and birds. They speak for those with no voice."

The pair bowed again. Lalo came to stand beside him. Solimon stood on his other side. They joined hands so that he was within the circle of their arms. Their faces blurred, transforming. Instead of Solimon and Lalo, he saw his parents. Sanders and Maggie. They looked older than he remembered. Dane fell into his father's arms.

"I tried, tried so hard to save you. You shouldn't have died." Sanders spoke to him, his rich voice comforting Dane. "We know you did, son. The illness was unnatural, an enchantment. You weren't strong enough. There was nothing you could have done."

"We are proud of you. We're watching over you each day," Maggie said. "I approve of Bell. Keep her safe."

Sanders pulled back and laid one hand on Dane's shoulder. "May the blessings of the Storm King ever be with you. May the Song lead you home. Speak your refrain when the time comes, my son. Do not be afraid. You never need fear again."

They faded, leaving the room empty.

A bell chimed.

On the fifth platform, a piece of neon pink paper lay, folded, on a small side table in the center of the room. Sara tucked the horn under her arm, opened it, and read.

Do you wish to help? To stay?

The page was decorated with clipart butterflies. It looked like Miranda Vine's flyer. Sara's lips crooked in a wry grin. *Nice touch.*

In her heart, she saw her parents, her sister, her home as a child. She saw Peter, strong and kind. She saw Dane and Bell, Trystan, Tabor. She saw little Jax and the boy Gint.

She was a stone rider. She could help. Dane could use her help, too. The shadow dragon was proof.

She wanted to stay. She blinked at the pink flyer in wonder. *I really have changed.*

She looked up, blinking back tears.

"Yes, I need to stay. I need to help. It would be easier to be home. Sort of. I could go back home and deal with all that waits for me. But I'm ready to join Dane's fight. I can deal with my own stuff when it's over. I'm needed. I'm not running."

A bell chimed.

Dane reached the last platform, his breath coming hard. The stairs wound higher this time. He could see the sky above and realized full night had fallen. Stars were shining. He saw the moon. One more set of stairs remained, leading to the surface.

In the center of the room was a bird, a peacock. Next to it stood a table shaped like an open hand. A shepherd's crook leaned against it, propped up by the table's fingers. In the center of the hand was a book.

He crossed to the table and read aloud.

Tieson gives the gift of transformation. Speak to begin.

Dane took the shepherd's crook and leaned on it. He remembered his father's instructions. He felt a familiar hesitancy rising in him. He pushed it back down.

Dane sang the words he'd been taught by his father in their entirety. He sang the entire refrain of the Lorica.

The Dark One ascends,
Eight shall turn him round.
One from the heartfire
One beneath the ground,
One stone rider,
One who cannot hear.
One claims the Storm King, One Names the Fear.
As the Last begins to sing
One may be reborn
Speak the words of wisdom
Sound the golden Horn.

As Dane Canted, the peacock's colors drained from it. It blazed, glowing white, then ruby red. Finally it flamed, golden. A shower of sparks shot up into the night. His eyes widened, watching. The refrain was about them. About him, Bell, Sara, the others. *What did the next verses mean?*

Heedless heartless helpless
Blast, blast away
Lone fire lighted
Truth cannot stay
When the heartfire kindles
All that is writ
The king will spend the knight's blood
Bone fells Spirit

The bird burned, brighter, incandescent. Flames washed over Dane. The flames felt cold. They passed over him with no effect.

A horn sounded. He turned and saw Sara, sounding a golden horn.

He kept Canting.

As the Last ends refrain
To die fade away
Duty binds the heartfire

Dullard shine, play
Fire sears the Melody
Sorrow, Sorrowfish
The Storm King returns
Wyrm to vanquish
A bell chimed.
Silence fell like a cloak.

The flames receded, and in place of the peacock stood a florid man. He was large, with dark hair, dressed in white robes. Sara stood next to him, a golden horn in her hand. She set the horn at the man's feet. Her form was shimmering, translucent. She was fading.

The man turned to her, shouting, "Finish the work, do not give up, do not falter. Fulfill your purpose. Create. You are now faisant."

Then she was gone.

The man's brown beard, neatly trimmed, ringed his face. In one hand he held an obsidian staff, carved into a twisted rope. He struck the ground with it once and boomed with laughter. Then he approached and circled Dane in a massive embrace, twirling him like a child.

"Stars above, you did it."

47

Dane coughed and pushed himself away from the huge man with as much dignity as he could muster. The majister was openly weeping and laughing at the same time. He set Dane down and looked at him as a parent looks at a child from whom they have long been parted.

"Who-who are you? I'm Dane." He shifted from foot to foot, nervous.

The man's eyebrows shot up. He laughed again, a great belly laugh that filled the room and echoed down the tower. He bowed, flourishing with one meaty hand.

"I am Theophrastus Bombast, but you may call me Theo. I am a majister, First Order, trapped five centuries, waiting for you to come and fulfill the refrain. You did it. And if I'm not mistaken, your fae shall soon finish her work. Your Harmony Bond will break our curse completely and set the rest of us right."

Sara's eyes flew open. She sat up in her bed. Her clothes were piled in the corner chair. Sara dressed quickly, donning a black tee shirt emblazoned with the words *Art Matters* and her favorite pair of jeans.

The sun was rising. The sky was golden. She breathed deep, inhaling the scent of lavender. She remembered.

She had reached the last platform, saw Dane with the peacock. Dane was singing. A book was on the table. The Song filled her heart. It was hope distilled into sound. Without fully understanding why, she had put the horn to her lips, and she blew with all her strength. Caprices, more than twenty of them, descended as the horn blew. They took on flesh, men once more. Their robes flashed, empty. The peacock flamed. One of the Caprices stepped forward, running down the steps and into the burning peacock's flames.

The fire died. In its place, a man, fully fleshed stood, smiling. The other Caprices still floated, their empty robes fluttering in the breeze.

"Finish the work, do not give up, do not falter. Fulfill your purpose. Create. You are faisant."

Sara had something to do, something important. This work would manifest her Harmony Bond with Dane and somehow, release the caprices from their curse. She had to create, to sculpt a piece. But not just any piece.

She had to use the Song.

But first, she had something to make right. She grabbed her phone and tapped out a text to Peter.

I wasn't friend-zoning you. I was pushing you away because you are real and you matter. I was scared. I'm not anymore. I'm ready. I hope it's not too late. But I'll fight for you. You're worth it. I'll call you later. I have to finish my piece. And Pete? I'm really sorry. Really. I love you.

She stopped for a moment, hearing the sound of her own breath. She sent another text.

Dad, I'm okay. I love you. I'm sorry I've been so angry.

That done, she grabbed her keys and ran down the stairs. She had to get to the studio. It was freezing. She jumped into her car, grabbing her hoodie from the backseat. It wasn't warm, but was better than nothing. She revved the engine, willing the car to warm up quickly.

Jane stepped outside, wrapped in a robe and wearing fuzzy slippers. She ran down the steps to Sara's car and tapped on the window.

"Where are you going?" she asked.

"I have to go, right now. What day is it?" asked Sara.

Jane looked at Sara as if she had three heads. "It's Sunday. It's six in the morning on Sunday, and you're awake, dressed, and rushing off. With no coffee." Her tone was accusing.

"I found Jesus, gotta go to church," Sara said. She laughed at the look on Jane's face. "I have an idea and have to go to the studio and make it happen before I lose it. I'm okay."

Jane looked at her, still concerned, but she raised her hands, acquiescing. "Okay, I get it. Artist weirdness. Call me when you're on your way back."

Sara nodded. "I will." She rolled her window up and turned the heater on, full blast. She slowly pulled away from the curb.

Theo pointed to the staff in Dane's hand. "You're nearly a majister now, my boy. A faisant is a maker, foremost. Their work manifests the Song. Sara's first piece created through the Song will seal your Bond."

"How does the Bond make me a Majister?"

"Oho, through love, my boy. A love willing to sacrifice all for a brother. Or in this case, a sister. You've been cleansed, healed, equipped, and called. Love echoes from her to you, from you to her, into your work. You're bound forever through the Storm King and His love. The Song is not a tool for power, but a path to follow. The Song guides us.

"Sara's piece will be part of the Song. Think of it as a manifestation of life, a miracle. Much like a child. There are many kinds of faisant. All have different works with different fruit. Their work brings forth life in others. Have you never been given healing, hope, or aid through a bard's tale or a ballad? Now come."

He led Dane up the stairs. The other Caprices waited. The top of the tower was level with the ground, like the mouth of a well. Dane had risen from its depths. The Caprices surrounded Dane and Theo as the Dread fell upon them, full force. Theo cursed roundly, feeling its weight for the first time.

"God's blood, that's a blackness!" he shouted. "They are singing. Let them crowd in close as a shield. When you are bonded 'twill unmake the curse for all. It won't be long now."

Sara froze when she got to her studio. The familiar feeling of overwhelm struck as she entered the space. Paralysis, doubt, and fear washed over her. Sara took a deep breath.

I'm not alone. I can do this.

She listened, and an image formed in her mind.

The fear vanished. She knew what to do.

Sara worked feverishly. She wasn't certain how rough the work could be and still be successful. She dragged the waste bin full of all the broken pieces from her previous sculpts to the center of the room and inspected the remnants to make sure they would work.

She ran to the metalworking lab to get a few pieces of steel, welding the shape she needed as a base. She worked chicken wire around it. She hefted the base onto a cart and rolled it back to her studio. Finally she took up the pieces from the waste basket and began to fasten them to the chicken wire form.

She stopped only to turn on her cd player and set her Beethoven cd on eternal repeat. Beethoven's music was filled with the Song. She could feel it. She leaned into the melody and sent all her questions and anxieties toward the Storm King as they welled up. He was with her.

Hours later, she paused and rooted for a small candle in the drawer of her side table. She lit it and placed it carefully under the sculpture. The hole in the bottom of the form fit over the candle. She stood back, evaluating.

The candle flickered inside it, lighting the interior.

It was finished, just as she had envisioned.
She had sculpted her own signet.

It was large, double her size. The sculpted-Sara was sitting cross-legged, with hands raised, face uplifted, and eyes closed. She was singing with all her heart, mouth open in response to the world she faced. Her face and head had been sculpted from fresh clay, but the body and the rest of the figure was formed from broken pieces of her previous work, fitted carefully back together. The arms and torso formed with alternating snakelike textures and the cloudy, tornadic ripples from her *Storm King* piece. Jagged cracks where the pieces did not fit together lay exposed.

Through the cracks shone a single flame. It blazed up, making the figure glow.

The candle lit the falling darkness.

"It's called Sorrowfish," she said aloud. As if from a great distance, a bell chimed.

Epilogue

Sara was happy not to be driving. She hated parking garages. Peter pulled the Karmann Ghia expertly into the parking garage behind the museum. The car's engine purred. He turned to Sara without killing the engine, searching her eyes. "You ready for this? Just imagine I'm naked. You'll be fine. Or you can call on your imaginary friend."

"My imaginary friend? Like you have any right to talk, with what you've put me through." Sara crossed her arms, trying not to pout.

"Hey now, Tasha is my cousin. I was letting her crash at my place and sleep in my room. If you jumped to other conclusions, it's not my fault. You're the one with your mind in the gutter." Peter laughed and leered at Sara.

"Your cousin needs to wear more clothes," Sara said, her voice a low growl. "This is Kentucky. Kissing cousins are a *thing*."

"Well. I might have cried on her shoulder. And she might have decided you needed a good kick in the pants," Peter said. He shrugged. His tone sobered as they pulled into the parking lot. Peter found an empty space and turned off the engine. He faced Sara, his eyes suddenly serious.

"I know you're nervous. But you have nothing to worry about. Not with Tasha. Not with anything. Stop trying to pick a fight with me." He put his hand under her chin and planted a soft kiss on her lips. "I love you."

Tears pricked at Sara's eyes. Her lower lip trembled. She took a deep breath. "Ok."

She plucked at his tuxedo lapel, brushing off an imagined speck. Her hand crept up to his cheek, and she smiled through sudden tears.

"I couldn't have done this without you. Happy Valentine's Day."

He leaned in to kiss her. "Happy Valentine's Day. You ready?"

Sara nodded. Happiness fizzed within her like champagne. The Song burbled within her heart. She fidgeted with the sequined gauze that floated over the form-fitting silk of her gown, unused to bare shoulders. She stumbled, tottering as Peter helped her out of the car. "I never should have borrowed these from Rilla," she complained, bending to inspect the Manolo Blahnicks her twin had insisted she wear. "I'm used to Chucks."

Peter held his hand up. "I thought you might feel that way. Just a sec." He opened the trunk, returning with a black shoebox. The box was adorned with a huge pink bow. "Size seven, right?"

Sara gasped and grabbed the box. A pair of high-top sequined Chucks nested within. She squealed, hurriedly stepping out of the four-inch heels. Peter knelt on one knee and held out a sneaker. "Better than Cinderella," said Sara. "I can't believe you did this."

Peter bowed over her hand, kissing it. "As you wish." He laced her shoe as she stepped into the other sneaker.

"How do I look?" Sara twirled.

"Breathtaking," said Peter, seriously.

He claimed the box and discarded shoes, stowing them away, and returned to offer his arm. "Shall we?"

"So gallant."

"I've been practicing for this most of my life," Peter said, grinning. "All those dragon flicks are great training for knighthood."

Sara rolled her eyes. "Nerd."

Peter clutched at his heart. "You wound me, madam."

She pulled him toward the skywalk that led to the reception. "I think you'll live." Sara rolled her eyes as Peter muttered under his breath.

"... flesh wound."

The atrium glowed with candlelight, reflected by the far wall, which was entirely glass. Moonlight filtered through onto the stage set before it. The stage held three shrouded sculptures.

Sara tried to ignore them. One was hers, to be unveiled when the winner was announced. The finalist's table was set before the stage, so they could be on display.

The room was cavernous, forty feet tall with a floating stairway along one wall. Beneath it, a sea of round tables set with linen and crystal accommodated guests. The floral arrangements were sculptures in their own right, calla lilies and greenery. Tree branches had been wrapped in fairy lights, leading the way to the adjacent gallery where the other entries stood. Sara glimpsed them through the hall, people swirling about them like birds, chattering and dispersing. She gulped and edged toward the tables. Her heart tap danced before settling into a hard gallop. She stopped, took a breath.

Peter squeezed her hand. In front of her, a face came into focus. A sneering face. Chantal Goddard. Her hair was upswept, makeup perfectly applied. She wore a simple black gown with oversized pearl jewelry. Sara felt gaudy, overdressed in her gold, by comparison. She lifted her chin, forced a smile, and waved. Chantal rolled her eyes and looked away. Peter followed Sara's gaze and huffed when he saw her rival. He leaned in to Sara's ear so she alone could hear him.

"She looks like she's going to a funeral. Ignore her. Come on."

Peter led her to the finalist's table, seating her as far from Chantal as he could. Miranda Vine's smile was genuine as Sara slid into the seat beside her.

"Good luck tonight," Sara said.

"You too. I'm so nervous. Can't stop fidgeting." The tall redhead grinned conspiratorially. Her dress, a green chiffon A-line, made her skin glow like cream.

"You look fantastic," said Sara. She scooted her chair and displayed her sneakers. "Pete saved me from tripping all night."

Miranda laughed. "I'm jealous." She turned to her own date, an extremely tall black man and pointed to Sara's shoes. "Aren't they great?"

"Love it. I had to be me as well," he said with a slow, wide grin. He pulled up his trouser leg to reveal royal blue socks and winked. Sara laughed.

Peter nudged her and whispered, "Your friend is a rebel. That's Tae King. Basketball player for our rival team. All-American. He'll go early in the draft."

Waiters placed salads before them as a quintet in the corner began to play. Sara settled in, focusing on the food, the music. She looked up, blinking, once or twice, only to find Peter there with a quip or comment to relax her. In the deepest recesses of her mind, the Song thrummed, a whiff of Dane's happiness echoing her own. She had almost forgotten her nerves by the time Bastien Crowe approached the podium with Polly.

A hush fell over the room as Polly gave the opening remarks. She introduced Bastien to polite, but sincere, applause.

His crooked grin enveloped everyone as he waited for silence. Bastien cleared his throat and leaned forward.

"Last month, my production company, the Wryneck Workshop, issued a challenge in the hopes of finding a special person to work with us on our new venture here in the Commonwealth…."

Sara's eyes drifted to Chantal, seated next to Scott. She hadn't even registered he was there until now. Chantal whispered something to him, her head huddled close. *Rude.*

"The lucky winner receives a paid internship with my company for a period of one year, after which they are welcome to remain with us and negotiate a pay raise." He winked. The audience laughed.

Sara's eyes wandered to the sculptures, Bastien's speech not truly registering. Black-clad figures removed shrouds while he spoke. Someone lit a flame. Her sculpture blazed to life.

"The winner will work with directors as great as Spielberg to tell stories that will change the world."

Chantal's weeping woman sculpture elicited sympathy, and Miranda's horse sculpture stood guard, impatient to gallop away. Made from wire and found objects, it evoked a joyful spirit of freedom.

But Sara's signet pulsed with an energy that dominated the room.

"The winner, Sara Moore."

The crowd erupted suddenly into enthusiastic applause.

Peter squeezed her hand. "You've won, Sara. He said your name. It's you."

The room rose with her, granting Sara a standing ovation as she approached the podium. Sara blinked rapidly, fighting tears. She saw her parents, with Marilla and Jane, on the other side of the room. Bastien smiled down at her. "Well done." He handed her a glass plaque engraved with her name and shook her hand before offering her the podium. Sara stepped up to it and stood on tiptoe to thank everyone, now wishing furiously for the discarded four-inch heels. She mentally counted back from ten and threw up a silent request for help as the applause died back.

But the Song rose and wrapped her with joy, a calming embrace. It rang in her mind.

Not alone. Beloved.

And she was free.

Sara smiled and began her acceptance speech.

Bastien extricated himself from the crowd of local and state dignitaries who descended after Sara finished her remarks. He found a quiet corner, grateful for a respite, but his eyes remained on his new protege, considering.

"Has she crossed over yet?" The elderly gentleman who appeared at Bastien's side nodded toward Sara.

"Almost certainly, sir," said Bastien. "I feel the Song from her piece. Very strong, as you can see. Its nexus alone is compelling."

He gestured to the signet that still shone on the stage.
"She's still new to this. Raw and untried. It will be fascinating to see how the master bends her. The effect she will have, when he is finished."

"Odd for the enemy to have chosen a young woman, don't you think?"

Bastien shrugged. "Despite what they say about Him, He has done it before."

"Bring her to Los Angeles soon."
Bastien opened his mouth to reply, but the elderly man was already gone.

Lexicon

aerie: pronounced [AIR-ee], villages of the chymaera, forbidden to other races to enter; usually on top of mountains or trees, named by its sigil

Anach: pronounced [Ay-nack], the ancient citadel of the Majesterium

Apokrypha: the sacred writings of the Conclave

arc: the Moon, it didn't exist before the War of the Wyrm. The Wyrm is said to be imprisoned within it. For this reason it is sometimes called "The Wyrm's Eye" or "The Storm King's Eye." The moon waxes and wanes like Earth's, but it always contains an arc shape within it, as well

Arcanum: the teaching of the Conclave regarding the Song

Canard: a world within an alternate universe that all Earthlings visit when they dream. Those attuned to the Song on Canard can see these dreamers, and refer to them as *fae*.

canting: usually a singsong chant that imparts some effect on the person enchanted. Also used in the Camber services to strengthen the Song and support the Cyntae.

Camber: Conclave worship services. The general population attends once a week on Moonday. There are services twice a day, every day.

cantors: the priests of the Conclave

Caprice: pronounced [Kah-prees], mysterious oracles in Siarad

chymaera: pronounced [ky-MEER-ah], elusive race of shape-changing humanoids bound to the Song

Communion: speaking heart to heart, directly sharing thoughts and emotional states psychically. This is considered insulting if forced, as you are questioning the honesty of the one you demand to commune with. It is very intimate and an honor shared with those you deeply trust or consider family otherwise.

Conclave: ruling religious order founded by the Arcantor, Modric. He was the last majister. The only majister remaining after the War of the Wyrm

Cyntae: pronounced [Seen-tay], the First Ones, immortal protectors. First beings to be made by the Creator, their voices joined with His to begin the Song. The Conclave teaches that when the Storm King sacrificed himself, the Cyntae took over sustaining the Song. They need support in this, which the Conclave provides with their endless Canting.

Cyntaf: pronounced [SEEN-tov], one of the four sigils of the Chymaera. Also the huge statue that dominates the songpitch in an Aerie. The Cyntae can manifest to a sigil by animating the Cyntaf, much like the Song animates a Speaker

deema: pronounced [deem-ah], term of endearment, title for a gnomic guardian

deemae: pronounced [dee-may], - generic term for a human whose family is protected by a gnome

deemling: those under a gnomes protection, a term of relationship. Bell is Jax's deemling; also plural, more than one deemling is deemling

Derbyn: [dar-bun] Accepted, a Chymaera that can transform. The Wyn transform into gryphons. There are other aeries that transform into other forms, but all have wings. You will sometimes hear the Derbyn referred to as "winged." when they have transformed and "unwinged" in their humanoid state.

dewin: pronounced [day -oo-in], wizard. It sounds like *divine*

Dissonance: Dissonance is a destructive or harmful force, directly opposing the Song. Its presence twisted and inverted creatures, making them Shadowkin or Shadowborn. Dissonance could ultimately destroy the World Tree, the Song and all of creation. Lies feed it and give it power, as does any evil action.

Domini: first of the Cyntae, the greater.

Doran: Eighth of the Cyntae, the lesser in the octave. Doran is identical to Domini in power and strength, though not in tone. The only Cyntae to appear at a sigil since the War.

Draig: pronounced [DRAY-g], one of the four sigils of the Chymaera (transform into winged drakes)

Equis: pronounced [EK-wiss] one of the four sigils of the Chymaera, also known as March (transform into winged horses)

fae: the Lost Ones, ghostlike beings in Canard, known for their mischief and magic

faisant: pronounced [fay- SOHN] a fae who has been Grounded by and harmony bonded to a dewin. This bond elevates a dewin's powers and makes him a Majister

Faron: Fourth of the Cyntae, sometimes called Father Time.

flashing: the state of a *fae* who is not physically present in Canard

gargoyle: In architecture on Earth, a chimera or grotesque is a fantastic or mythical figure used for decorative purposes. Chimerae are often described as gargoyles, although the term gargoyle technically refers to figures carved specifically as terminations to spouts which convey water away.

gnomes: smaller than dwarves, this race of small humanoids is rarely seen outside Dohnavur. Some believe they no longer exist. They are known for their crafting, their ability to walk through stone or earth and their friendship with animals. They move in a cadence and rhythm which is very obvious when two or more are together. Usually very talented musically, they are sought after to play or sing by human musicians. If they adopt a human family they are known as deema. They are very strong and can lift many times their own weight. They are fun-loving pranksters.

grotesque: pronounced [GROW-tesk], an animated stone figure made by the Chymaera. There are three types of grotesques in Canard; Watchers, Speakers and Takers. Takers and Watchers are fixed, Speakers can move from place to place. Speakers only function in the Sundered Cities and in the Aeries. Takers have no power to speak, they serve as refuse removal with limited observational power.

grounding: the act of bringing a fae physically into Canard.

Harmony Bond : bond between a majister and a fae that transforms a fae into a faisant and a dewin into a majister

heartfire: the central essence of the chymaera

Lalo: Sixth of the Cyntae, always seen with Solimon

Lorica: The sacred book of the majisters, written in refrains. Lost after the War of the Wyrm and replaced by the Apokrypha

March: one of the four sigils of the chymaera, also known as Equis. (transform into winged horses)

Matins: pronounced [MAH-tun], morning song service

Miah: Third of the Cyntae

pitch: octagonal space where a Chymaera works

Profi: [PRO-vi] Unproven, Chymaera that cannot transform yet

Pryf: pronounced [pruf], outcast from the Chymaera, unable to transform, vermin

Renato: second of the Cyntae

Shadowkin: swarm of miniscule black particles that can bond together to form other creatures or simply appear as a shadow. They strip flesh from bone if they attack and can burrow into flesh and devour from within. Destroyed by songsteel. Shadowkin are controlled by powerful Cantors

Shadowborn: general term for creatures that were twisted or jnverted by Dissonance. Also refers to creatures that embrace Dissonance like the giants.

Siarad: pronounced [SHA-rod], the former headquarters of the Majesterium, the Tower of Anach was here

sigil: pronounced [sih-gel] loosely translated, a tribe. A representation and servant of particular cyntae

signet: the stone vessel of a chymaera

sign of the arc: gesturing to form a crescent over your head from your right shoulder to your left. It represents the arc of the moon and protection.

Solimon: Fifth of the Cyntae

Solfeggio: Do re me fa sol la ti do

Speakers: animated stone creatures (grotesques) made by the Chymaera. They function as guards and guides in the Sundered Cities and can walk about, unlike Watchers. The only grotesques with the power of speech, they are not found in human communities outside of Cimaehne and Ciclaehne. There are many of them in the aeries.

Storm King: A form of the Creator. Called the Storm King because He has been seen in clouds, lightning or fire. The Conclave teaches that He is dead, sacrificed on the World Tree to save Canard and the Song from the Wyrm. He exists in all worlds, though his name changes.

Takers: animated stone creatures made by the Chymaera. They function as a plumbing system in human cities. These are what you might think of as gargoyles, though they actually feed on waste and refuse. There are many of them in the aeries. These do not move from their base where they are set. They can also act as monitors.

Tieson: Seventh of the Cyntae, the diminished.

tunebell: sacred flower that enhances the Song.

Vespers: evening songs

Watchers: animated stone creatures (grotesques) made by the Chymaera. They function only as monitors for the Conclave. Watchers generally only move their heads in order to observe. What one watcher can view, all watchers can view as well. They can transmit images to sandtables or directly to a Chymaera.

Wyn: pronounced [oo-win], one of the four sigils of the Chymaera They transform into gryphons.

About the Author

Anne C. Miles was born in Chicago Heights, Illinois in 1971. She studied modern languages (Spanish, French, and German) at Kentucky Wesleyan College and Murray State University. In 2001 she founded a web design studio in her kitchen. She earned a degree in Visual Communications and married Rodney Miles in 2003. Anne and Rodney work together full time at their company to this day. Anne was confirmed in the Anglican Church (ACNA, High Anglican) in

2016. She takes communion once a week. When Anne isn't working or writing, she plays violin badly and spoils her grandchildren.

She is currently hard at work on Book 2 of the *Call of the Lorica.*

You may visit her blog at https://www.annecmiles.com.

For games, pictures and more, visit https://www.sorrowfish.com

CPSIA information can be obtained
at www.ICGtesting.com
Printed in the USA
LVHW051603120820
662995LV00002B/641